Degree of Difficulty

This is a work of fiction. Any resemblance to actual persons, places or events is coincidental or inspired.

www.tomogrady.com

ISBN: 1-4636-3186-3
ISBN-13: 9781463631864

Degree of Difficulty

Tom O'Grady, Jr.

2011

Evan House International

Thank you
to Susan Iwanisziw, Ph.D. and
Denis Mercier, Ph.D.
for your help and support.

Thank you to my readers.

"Got the company car and the credit cards
Covered 200 miles a day
Driving roads going nowhere
Looking good every inch of the way.
I never lived too long on the Avenue of Kings"

-Tom O'Grady, Jr.

chapter 1

July, 1977

"WHO THE HELL handled this?"

The voice was loud and snarling.

"Who? I want his ass in here fast! I don't care where he is!"

Rain, blown hard by a muggy summer wind, slapped at the window of a modern, tenth floor office in the PSFS Building in downtown Philadelphia. Bill Golden's blood pressure had reached its high-water mark.

"Who is it?" he snarled again.

Several formerly calm office people scurried in different directions outside Golden's office. The investment firm crackerjack at Doner, Elson and Simons had just lost his investment firm cool. Bill Golden was still standing between his thick black leather chair and glass trestle desk poised to strike. Computer printouts spilled from the glass to the floor along with a previously upright cup of coffee. When he bolted up from his seat, Golden didn't see the cup fly. If he had he wouldn't have cared. Words came out of his mouth like buckshot and they were aimed at every poor, incompetent fool on the planet.

"How does this bullshit happen?!" Golden continued. "That's what I really want to know. How does it even start? Ten million dollars and nobody knows how or where. Unbelievable!"

Warren Ebbetts was calm, although something inside him was tingling. He looked at the twisted face of his partner and felt something like pity. There stood before him a fifty year old man, balding and grey with stress on his skin so taut it pulled his neck down to his chest. Bill Golden hadn't stood upright in ten years.

And for what, Ebbetts thought? To make a few measly thousand more a year? To be able to eat dinner at expensive restaurants with the other assholes in this company? To take vacations where you spend a lot of money to be ripped off like the dumb tourist you are?

Warren Ebbetts knew it wasn't pity he felt at all. Pity was not an emotion he was familiar with. No. What he felt was the same thing he felt for all the obsessed scroungers he'd met in the money peddler business and all the fools they sold to. Contempt.

"Take it easy, Bill, we'll track it." Ebbetts' tone was soothing, almost jocular. "You know this stuff occurs once in a while and we always find it. Some poor paperwork or processing on someone's part. Just relax."

Ebbetts hid his contempt well. It sat beneath the calm, friendly moon face and feathery reddish hair of a man later into his forties than he wanted to be. It was in the thick ridges around his eyes and the fleshy jowls below his mouth. It tucked itself into the numerous folds and layers of pig-pink skin that jounced around him when he walked. Contempt lay inside the great bulk of his body like a layer of insulation that kept the coldness of his soul equal to the temperature of his heart. Warren Ebbetts was three hundred pounds of quiet, frozen rage.

"Come on, Warren!" Golden barked back. "Take it easy? This is Cook International we're talking here. Ten million dollars worth! I busted…, we busted our asses to get in the door with those people for three years. We busted another two to put this deal together. We sign up four thousand employees and a year later I can't find their money?!" Bill Golden's veins were beginning to swell. His face was already scarlet from screaming as he swung his crazed stare at Ebbetts. "I can't find their freakin' money!"

Something about the intensity of Golden's fury seemed almost theatrical to Ebbetts, like a bad actor in a bad play. It wasn't that Golden wasn't sincere or convincing, it just felt too explosive, too dramatic. These screw-ups did happen once in a while. Bill knew that. And they were always figured out eventually. Someone was embarrassed, someone got their hand slapped and, at worst, someone had a few accounts transferred. But something about this situation had Bill Golden at the edge, something Ebbetts had not expected.

The secretary, normally a confident woman, tiptoed to the door of the office and waited for Golden to get quiet.

"Bill?"

"Whaaat?"

Golden flung the word at her causing her head to snap upward. She gulped air.

"Kim Melon did the processing. She's on her way up."

Golden just stared at her as if to say, well, what are you standing there for? Get the hell out of the way.

She understood his message and moved quickly back to her desk.

"Terrrrrific." His voice dropped. "I'm ready to tear the balls off somebody for this bullshit and I get some woman who's gonna piss and moan about sexual harassment the minute I tear into her. And she'll get all upset and won't...," his voice began to rise again, "...be able to give me a goddam intelligent answer."

He spun on Ebbetts.

"Warren, you stay right there because after I rip her friggin' tits off I want a witness to say I didn't."

Golden turned to stare out the window as if the answer might be there. Two minutes of silence laced with heavy breathing passed slowly while they waited for the arrival of the soon-to-be breastless Kim Melon. Warren was glad for the quiet time, hoping it would give his partner a chance to simmer down. Bill's anger was really beginning to make him nervous.

Kim Melon, a dressed-to-succeed, petite woman in her mid-twenties walked into the office, completely unaware of the topic since no one on the way in had had the guts to stop her and warn her. She addressed his back.

"You wanted to see me, Mr. Golden?"

Golden turned like a vampire, his fangs bared.

"Where the hell is ten million dollars from Cook International?"

Warren Ebbetts thought he saw blood for a minute on Golden's teeth but realized it was spittle. All of a sudden, a burst of laughter went off in his head as he tried to decide where this poor girl's breasts would land and whether he should try to catch them. Would that constitute feeling her up? Would his fingerprints be on the evidence the same as Bill's? Do you save them like a finger and then have them reattached later? He quickly put his hand over his mouth and forced a grimace hoping the whole gesture looked like consternation. Then, much to his surprise, the young woman answered without a trace of fear.

"Processed through the system just like always."

The young lady was ready. Somehow when the vampire turned, she had assessed the whole scene and decided the only shot she had at surviving was to stand her ground. If she was going down she was going down fighting.

"What do you mean through the system just like always?" Golden said, mockingly. "It ain't in the system, missy."

Golden's anger had eased just a hair, the woman's confident answer backing him up a step.

"I mean I process the monies every two weeks just like always," she answered. "As a matter of fact, I took extra care with the Cook package because most of us downstairs were aware of how much work had been put into setting it up. So I triple-checked where I usually double-check."

Her tone had adjusted slightly to something bordering on reassurance but she didn't soften the edge on her attitude one bit. She took a deep, imperceptible breath and stepped to the desk, taking the pad of printouts from Golden's waving hand.

"Cook wires the money to the STIF account at First Pennsylvania every two weeks and I get a notice from Cook as well as a receipt copy from the bank."

She flipped through the papers, finding what she wanted then turned slightly to let Golden look at them as she led him through the process.

"You get my confirmations each time and all the transactions are put into the computer. You guys," she continued, swinging her head sideways to pull in Ebbetts, "call them up on screen, make the investment allocations, and I produce the paperwork which you sign. The custodial doesn't move without you. I can take you through every step of my part of the process and show you every cent. If you want, I'll pull out all the records so far and back-track them to see if there were any corrections at our end or at First Pennsy's. But I'm certain there weren't any from here."

And there it was. Instead of witnessing a debreasting, Warren saw a defanging. Bill Golden was staring with his lips sealed, not a tooth in sight, wearing the realization that he was not going to get his pint of blood from Ms. Melon. She was by the book.

"All right, fine, I'll take you up on that offer," Golden snapped. "Give me everything mapped out so I can follow it, and when you go as far as you can go, bring it to me. Don't overlook anything and don't let anybody tell you that you can't do this or that. If they do, you send them to see me and keep on moving, understand? I want to know where that money is."

She nodded her head confidently.

"Good.. It's a priority."

Golden turned away enough so the woman knew she'd been excused. She turned and walked quickly from the office. Warren could tell Golden still wanted to tear somebody's balls or breasts off but it wasn't going to be Ms. Melon's.

"See," Warren said. "Relax. You've got a tough number on the case."

And when she finishes looking, he thought to himself, you still won't know a shit more than you know now. And I won't have to be around to listen to any more of your pissin' and moanin'.

"Yeah, right," Golden said to no one. Then, looking at Ebbetts so quickly it almost startled him, he said, "Look, we have to find this shit and find it fast, Warren. Something isn't right." He looked down and paused, then back at Ebbetts. "You gonna be around this weekend?"

"Sorry, partner, I can't," Warren said. "Got guaranteed plans for sailing down Chesapeake this weekend. I won't even be around too much later today. I plan to get a jump on the traffic."

The thought of the weekend plans gave him a pleasant chill. My time has come, he thought smugly. He went back to his calm, soothing tone.

"Bill, you just put Miss Marple on the case there. This is Friday. She's not going to produce anything for you to work on till Monday at the earliest. Take the weekend and forget about it. Then we'll both come back Monday with a fresh attitude and maybe see something we didn't see before. You and I ought to be able to find what we need. No one else really touches the account. Right?" He pulled his elbows in towards his soft body, turning both doughy hands palms up.

Golden looked at him, unsure whether Ebbetts' words were reassuring or disturbing.

"We'll see," Golden said.

Warren Ebbetts rose slowly and turned, then stepped out of Bill Golden's office. He waved his hand over his shoulder and disappeared from view.

chapter 2

Detective John Glancey sat at his cluttered desk in a small office of the Easton Police Department sipping coffee. It was quiet and he had been able to clean up paperwork despite the fact that a Saturday on Eastern Shore was full of activity. Boaters, tourists, fishermen, all were active and moving around the town and the Bay. A transplant from Philadelphia, Glancey liked the town and its pace.

The phone rang and he put his coffee down.

"Easton PD, Detective Glancey. Hey, Paul,. . .yeah, my turn to cover Saturdays. What's up? Uh, huh,. . .all right. I'm walking down. Be there in a few minutes."

Glancy stood up and stuffed a pen and pad into his pocket as he spoke to a uniformed officer at another desk.

"DNR just called. Said they've got two missing persons from a boat went out of Crabbie's. I'm gonna walk down. Shouldn't be too long. Want anything?"

"How about a lemonade?"

"Sold."

Glancey strolled down the street towards the water, a brilliant sunset bursting over the Bay in front of him. He reached the marina in three minutes and was met by a Department of Natural Resources officer who shook his hand.

"John, how are you? How's the family?"

"Good, Paul, thanks," Glancey said, motioning his head toward the gorgeous sunset. "Another day in Paradise, eh?"

"Well, for some of us," the officer answered with a crooked smile.

He led Glancey to a man sitting on a bench on the dock with a large towel wrapped around him. The only thing more prominent than the man's Hispanic features was a large bruise that had swollen up big on his forehead.

"This is Mr. Alvarez," the Lieutenant said. "He went out sailing earlier today with a friend and a boathand."

"Mr. Alvarez, I'm Detective Glancey, Easton Police Department. That's a nasty bruise you have there. Are you all right?"

"No, I'm not all right. Nothing is right."

The man rocked back and forth without looking at Glancey, his voice thick with pain as he struggled to hold back his emotions.

"We'll get you to the hospital right away, sir," Glancey said calmly, "but can you tell me briefly what happened?"

"The storm, it came out of nowhere. It just threw the boat around like a toy."

"What happened to your friend and the mate?"

Alvarez' expression turned more painful as he continued to rock and stare at nothing.

"They went overboard. The last thing I saw was the mate trying to secure the mainsail. It was swinging wildly across the deck. Warren was just holding onto the railing. I got up to try and help with the sail and the boat heaved. I fell and hit my head.

When I woke up they were both gone and so was the storm. O, Dios mio!"

The man put his head gingerly in his hands. Glancey looked sadly at the officer then turned back to Alvarez.

"I'm very sorry, Mr. Alvarez. What was your friend's name? Is there someone we can contact on his behalf?"

"Warren Ebbetts. We met as businessmen and became personal friends. I know he has a wife, Marilyn, but I've never met her and I don't know her phone number."

"All right, Mr. Alvarez. Let's get you to the hospital."

Glancey looked up and saw an EMT approaching. He waved her over and waited till she had placed Alvarez in the ambulance, then turned to the officer as they walked toward the street.

"What's your take on this, Paul? Anything out of the ordinary?"

"Not really. The storm was legit. They've been popping up all over the Bay for the last few days and they're not done yet. That's the problem. The forecasters tell people and we put out the craft warnings, but people go out anyway. The old, 'it won't happen to me' syndrome."

"Any chance of finding the bodies? Could these people be out there holding onto something?"

"We've got S & R out there already, but it's a big bay and we're a couple of hours behind the occurrence. The area he gave us is deep water too, with lots of current and tide. Plus, we've still got storm activity coming and going. And he said that his friend Ebbetts is a big guy, heavy guy. Not in great physical shape. I'm not optimistic."

"How about the mate?"

"Unfortunately, the mate was Ricky Spencer, a local kid home from college for the summer hiring out for charters. Nice young man, too. Working his way through school. I knew him. Been on the water all his life."

"Is there family to talk to?"

The officer put his head down and shook it. "That's a tough one. His dad's gone and his mom was hospitalized for years and passed away last year. I think he has a girlfriend but I'm not sure. That's about it. Like I said, nice young man. Good sailor."

The officer lifted his head back up and turned toward the sinking orange sun over the bay as he spoke. Glancey followed his gaze.

"Guess it doesn't matter how good you are sometimes. Gotta respect the water, John. It's always at home and you're always a guest."

chapter 3

Two Years Later

"MIKE AND THE Old Man want to see you."

Ian Connors froze long enough for Betty, the receptionist, to feel sorry for him. The cold tile of the pale green lobby felt even colder before he could gather his thoughts.

"Help me out here, Betty."

Ian was begging. He always counted on her for the inside track. She handled all the calls, saw everybody come and go. She had to know something. But her face said it before she did.

"Sorry, fella. No clue."

Ian headed upstairs, his long, muscular legs covering the two flights of stairs more quickly than he realized. At the top of the steps he turned toward the two-story wall of glass that was the facade of Cook International and saw his reflection, a face he remembered staring at when he came for the job five years earlier. He had been struck that day by the austerity of the place. Not a downtown-Philadelphia, gleaming skyscraper but a two story brick box clinging to the edge of the city limits. No rugs, battleship gray metal desks and painted sheetrock walls disrupted only by a color map indicating the locations of Cook plants all over the world. The whole place said, Look, we're not interested in impressing anybody. We come here to work.

Betty was the first person Ian met. Not unattractive, pleasant and obviously efficient; an older woman by Ian's standards, in her early fifties. That first day she had handled five calls in three breaths and him with one finger. She held it up as signal for him to wait, and he did.

"No, I'm, sorry. He's not. You're welcome. Thank you for waiting," she'd said to him in a continuous flow. "Can I help you?" Her eyes twinkled as she smiled.

"My name is Ian Connors," he had said with a smile to match hers. "I have an appointment with Mike Mahon."

"Okay, Mr. Connors. I'll let him know."

He had wanted an edge that day for the interview and so he leaned forward, almost secretly and asked, "Is he a nice guy?"

Betty answered without missing a beat, a sly smile appearing on her face.

"Oh, I think he'll like you."

And she'd been his inside help ever since.

But now, five years later, staring at the glass with no idea what Mike and the Old Man wanted, Ian was on his own. He smoothed his navy blue pants, set his soft briefcase down against his legs and pulled on the suit coat he'd carried in. Despite long legs, Ian just broke six feet, the upper part of his body well developed but not elongated. Years of swimming and diving through high school and college had molded his body into solid proportions, the shoulder and waist of his suit coat forming a noticeable V from the back. His dark black hair, kept trim for the corporate style and crisp shirt collar gave his soft-featured face the look of someone younger than his twenty-nine years. But there was more to this young man than his appearance and as a sales rep that was a plus and a minus. Sometimes Ian's face sold; sometimes it gave away. For now, the face in the glass had to get moving.

Ian moved through the double doors at the end of the hall and walked past the corporate executive offices, half wood, half glass-walled boxes that lined the perimeter of a giant room cluttered in the middle by secretaries and clerks at desks. The layout kept everybody visible and everybody busy. Ian nodded and smiled to the execs as he passed by. John Chambers, VP for Engineering; Al Bock, VP for Manufacturing; Frank Gellig, VP for Finance. All nodded back, Chambers and Gellig smiling. Bock had nothing to smile about. The man spent three weeks a year near his home and the rest of the year in any one or all of thirty plants spread across the country. Occasionally, one or two out of the country.

Working for Cook International had been rougher than Ian expected. The company was tough: tough on its competition and tough on its employees. The corporate attitude was no frills, all work and no play. If you wanted accolades you had to relive your high school championship because there weren't any here. The president of the company was a tough, street-wise businessman who looked at two things; daily production and inventory. If the production numbers were high and the inventory numbers were low he was as close to happy as he could get, which was just shy of not being angry.

On Saturday mornings the VPs and the sales force were there, fanned out around him at the big conference table like apostles at the Last Supper. No one booked tee times at Cook.

Sitting at that table they all knew what they brought individually was mediocre. What they brought became powerful when the Old Man used it as part of his vision of things. For that reason he had their respect and loyalty. Everyone, from the executive vice-presidents to the plant managers to the engineers, had a packed travel bag in the trunk of his company car. If the Old Man said be in Texas tonight or Ireland tomorrow, they went. And they stayed until they could explain why they came back or he told them to.

Oddly enough the managers weren't highly paid. The Old Man rewarded them with stock options, a stock that paid no dividend but never lost money, soared and split occasionally, was directly tied to the performance of the corporation and whose shares were controlled by him. It guaranteed them employment, the education of their children, and eventually their retirement. Now was never the time to bathe in the financial successes of the company. They all worked for the future. The Old Man not only had the respect and loyalty of his managers, he owned them. Jacob Aloysius Cook, President and Chief Executive Officer of Cook International, liked it that way.

Ian hadn't quite signed up for the idol worship package yet. He was naturally too independent to jump in quickly. But, from what he had observed in the company over the last five years, he could see why these men had. He still wasn't sure where he belonged at Cook, if at all. Right now he knew where he didn't want to be. The Old Man was standing inside the glass door of his office, watching.

Ian's mental checklist broadened. Hair, suit, shoes; was the expense report too fat this month? It amazed Ian the effect the man had on him, like meeting an attractive woman. He was completely intimidated.

Cook was a square built man, shoulders like the cut of an old fashioned suit. Everything about him spoke of sixty years ago; his gray hair, flat and short, the part almost cut into his scalp; his suit, a style Brooks Brothers made their name selling;

his shoes, a thick-welt Brogan guaranteed to last a lifetime. He couldn't have been more than five foot seven, but the few times Ian had spoken to him, or more accurately, been spoken to, Jacob Cook seemed to be eye to eye.

Ian slowed halfway across the big room, deaf to the ringing and rustling monotone around him and unsure what to do next. The Old Man hadn't moved. A long minute buzzed in his forehead and then Ian saw Mike Mahon appear outside Cook's door. He waved Ian towards him and the door opened. Cook took one step out and waited.

"You remember Ian Connors, Jacob?"

Mahon, Executive Vice President of Sales and Ian's boss, was one of a handful of people that called the Old Man by his first name. Jacob Cook leveled his eyes at Ian.

"How are you, Mr. Cook? It's good to see you," Ian said in his best sales voice, not giving the man a chance to answer Mahon's question.

"Fine, thank you." Cook answered in a quiet voice, his tone neither sharp nor patronizing. "How are we doing out there?"

Ian felt the gears lock in his brain. Oh, jeez. Does he want sales numbers? Projections? Actuals? Account names?

Mahon covered smoothly.

"Ian's having one of the best sales years in our division, Jacob. Might set a record. If everybody pays, that is."

Mahon kept it believable.

"Well, that's excellent, young man. I'm glad to hear that." Something resembling a smile broke across his face.

If this were any other executive in the company, Ian would have felt invincible. But standing here now, Ian wanted the Old Man to forget him the minute he walked away. His knowing who you were was scary.

In thirty seconds it was all over. Cook nodded to Mahon and Ian without explanation and moved back inside, someplace deep in the President's office. Ian could still feel tension in his body while he sat in Mahon's office.

"He make you nervous?" Mike said, a slight glint in his eye that told Ian it was all right.

"Absolutely," Ian said, letting his relief show. "But I have no idea why."

Mike Mahon, in Ian's mind, was a great balance of tough, no-nonsense management, and human being. Sometimes the two seemed contradictory in this trim, ruddy-faced man of forty-five, but he managed to make them both work. Mike had brought Ian into the company and was one reason Ian was still there. He was the one person at Cook that made Ian believe it was possible to buy into the corporate world, be successful and still maintain a personal sense of identity. The lure of success was great for Ian but his soul always got in the way. Mike seemed to have a soul.

Mahon could make the shit hit the fan some days in a way that made you run for cover. But on most days he made his people, at least the ones that worked hard, feel like he cared about them. He told stories the way salesmen tell stories, embellishing the laughs and tearing down the pretensions of wealthy and prestigious people. Mike had worked the territories his salespeople now handled, and he never forgot it was work.

"Well, he still makes me nervous," Mahon said. "But not too many other people seem to make you nervous. I've been hearing good things about you, and seeing them too, in the year-to-date figures."

"You've been there, Mike," Ian sad. "Sometimes it just goes your way. Some things have fallen in place, Bishop coming through with that big contract, uh, Aircon gets screwed by Precision Press and we're at the door. You know."

"But that's what I'm talking about," Mike said, smiling. "You were there, at the door and ready. I was told quite plainly at the last show that they wanted an excuse to give you the business. They really like you."

Ian was confused. This all sounded great but Mahon was still business first. He didn't call Ian up here to pat him on the back. Mike always let you know if you were doing well but this wasn't his style.

"How would you feel about covering the country?"

Whoa! There it is. Ian felt the same excited, scary feeling he had when he'd gotten the job at Cook.

"Ohhhkay," Ian said, slowly, a nervous smile breaking out. "Can you elaborate?"

"Sure," Mahon said, obviously enjoying Ian's embarrassment. "A lot more of our smaller accounts, like Aircon, for example, are being bought up by larger operations, national outfits that are eliminating unprofitable plants and centralizing their purchasing. I'm talking machinery parts orders that cover seven or eight plants. Phenomenal numbers. Some are still purchasing locally, but more aren't. I think it's the long term trend and I want someone developing a strong relationship with the headquarters, the parent companies. Someone who knows the small and local operations but has the balls to handle the big boys. I think that's you."

Ian's head was spinning. It was happening. The kind of thing he thought could happen when he started here. His heart was pumping, random thoughts jumping in and out of his mind. Like a good salesman, he knew he had to step out and regroup, give himself time to ask the right questions and get the right answers. Plus, a clump of something unidentifiable had mixed itself in with the exciting things. Ian had to know what it was.

"Wow."

It was the safest thing Ian could think of to say and still give Mahon some sort of positive response. He followed it with a nervous laugh and a stretch of silence.

"You know I have to think this out a little," Ian finally said. "I mean, my first reaction is that I'm flattered, which is probably the worst condition to be in to make big decisions."

Mahon smiled and nodded.

"That's why you're a good salesman, kid. Look, you have a vacation coming up, right?"

"Yeah, a week."

Mahon rose as he spoke to signal a close to their meeting.

"Good. Soak it up. I'll be away for a couple of weeks, plant visits and whatever. Call me when you get back and we'll talk then. If you're interested we'll get into some details. Fair enough?"

Still hasn't lost his sell, Ian thought, feeling the pull of the question at the end of Mike's sentence.

"Thanks, Mike. I really appreciate it."

Shaking Ian's hand Mahon said, "Don't let the Old Man spook you into anything. Call your own shot and stick with it."

Ian saw the flash of an unfamiliar look on Mahon's face that quickly disappeared. It confused him momentarily. It was the final zap on a charged thirty minutes that left Ian tingling as he walked back past the walled-in row of managers. He reached the landing on the lobby steps without feeling any of them and u-turned blindly, almost crashing into a startled Ed Bernardi.

"Whoa, knock me on my ass, why don't ya," Ed said, grinning.

"Oh, man!"

Ian stopped quickly, ending up on his toes.

"I told you to stay off the drugs, didn't I?"

Ed Bernardi's face was a welcome sight. In his mid-forties, he was one of those men who went silver, not gray, early. And with the smooth, tanned skin of someone much younger he always looked like money. Mixed with a six-foot-three frame and a Peter Lawford charm it was no wonder he was a sales manager. But it was the real person behind the charm that had drawn Ian to the friendship they enjoyed.

"I'm sorry," Ian said. "I am buzzed." Ian was about to explain about the meeting with Mike when he realized it might not be news to Ed. "Did you know anything about this?"

Ed looked genuinely confused.

"About what?"

"Oh, great," Ian said, feeling awkward at the fact that Mahon hadn't gone to Ed first. "Where you headed?"

Ed straightfaced him.

"Going up to look at Patty Resnor's legs, but it can wait. What's up?"

"Let's take a walk through the plant," Ian said, pointing back down the steps. "The noise will do me good."

chapter 4

THE BIG CORPORATE move, sliding upstairs with the bigwigs. Life in a car, on a plane. Ian's mind bobbed in the pressurized cabin. The claustrophobic feel of the airplane traded places every so often with his thoughts.

Management. With it came recognition, more opportunity, slightly more money and a few more perks. Hey, there was even a plant in Mexico. Maybe he could make his next trip on the company. But along with that came more responsibility, living out of a suitcase and being at the mercy of the Old Man's whim. It meant time to sign on for the Cook package, time to get in line with the others and worship at the altar, time to make a conscious decision about the future. It meant commitment.

"Hey? You with me?"

Spook was staring at him. Ian stared back at the big, hollow brown eyes of his best friend. Spook's face was all sharp features; a nose you could cut bread on and cheekbones so far out in front of his face his eyes disappeared at night. When he talked he was all arms and legs. He was five feet ten but stood five feet eight, his shoulders permanently hunched from leaning over car engines. With his dark longish hair washed and brushed, Eddie

Pergola wasn't a bad looking guy, but catch him in his auto shop and the name Spook was appropriate.

"Yeah," Ian answered, clearing his head and looking away.

"Whoa!" Spook teased, "what I tell you about that deep thought shit? What's up, that corporate invitation?"

Ian looked at Spook then back towards the seat in front of him.

"My head is still spinning."

"So hey, you must be feelin' pretty good about yourself."

"Yeah, I guess so," Ian said, not cutting off his thoughts. "I don't know. I like the money, and sometimes I really like the action, you know, mixing it up with people. But in between is a lot of bullshit."

"Hey, I understand the bullshit end of it," Spook said, "but that's everywhere. What are you lookin' for? If it's money, man, get used to it."

At times like this Ian couldn't decide if he really appreciated Spook or if Spook just irritated the hell out of him. They had been friends since they were kids, and Spook knew him better than anyone.

"Somewhere in between there's something," Ian said, looking at the floor.

He knew that money was at the heart of the matter. Before Cook, back when he earned a meaningful and pathetic music teacher's salary, there were no trips to Acapulco. No dinners in nice restaurants. No new company car. No money in the bank. Just the constant frustration of an empty pocket and an uncertain future. But that something in between was out there. Ian wasn't sure if he'd been too short-sighted to find it or too lazy to look for it. But he sensed it was there, like the pea at the bottom of the mattresses.

"Just don't know what it is yet, aye Kimosabe?" Spook asked, breaking Ian's thought. "So when do you start?"

"I've got this week to decide whether to take it."

The pilot's voice coughed its way through the plane.

"Señores a Señoritas. The weather is warm and sunny today with the temperature at eighty-eight degrees."

Spook had his nose pressed flat to the window.

"Oh, man, will you look at that!" he shrieked. "I can see the bottom of the ocean. Ain't no pollution on this beach, baby."

Ian was jealous. They hadn't even landed in Acapulco yet, and if the plane turned around right now Spook would've had a great trip. They were on their way to Paradise and the decision to commit to Cook nagged Ian like a late autumn fly. So maybe this trip was perfect timing, he thought. Take some time to get loose.

But deep down Ian knew the real reason for this trip. A childhood fantasy that had never gone away and now was a real possibility.

The Dive.

All those years he'd thought about it, played it in his head, watched it on TV. The Cliff Divers, the Clavadistas of Acapulco! The thought swept everything else away. Cook and work was replaced by the camera zooming in on a diver high above the canyon, floating out into the air, hanging over the blue water.

I'm going to Acapulco and doing the cliffs, he said to himself. Here I am. And I'm gonna do it. And it has nothing to do with money or a job.

Ian looked to his right and saw the wing disappear as the plane dipped, coloring the porthole with aqua-blue water.

chapter 5

"I NEED THIS thing taken care of, and that's all you need to know."

The white hankie was limp as the Fat Man pushed it up under his hat to wipe the sweat from his head. His tone was firm to the point of intolerance, and he gave his squat companion the added insult of no eye contact. Dust blew in little tornados around them as they stood by the roadside phone booth. The cantina behind them seemed to float in the heat.

"You don't make your money asking me questions, just doing what I say. Isn't that right, amigo?"

Warren Ebbetts, Wilson to his nosy accomplice, turned abruptly and glared as he said "amigo." There was nothing friendly in the use of the word in either of their languages. The short, stocky Mexican listened, his pug-face bunched and unchanged.

"Yeah, das right," he answered, inoffensively. "I take care of eet. I see you later in da week."

He turned and walked to his car without waiting for acknowledgement.

Ebbetts turned back to the phone booth, muttering as he dialed the multiple digits.

"Cops in Mexico are as bad as cops back home."

He wiped his face again, listening to the endless clicks and tones coming through the earpiece, then hearing the voice he wanted to hear.

"Hello."

"I'm finishing the last detail," Ebbetts responded. "Should be completed by tomorrow."

"Fine."

Ebbetts could hear the resistance in his partner's voice, as if knowing the information made him part of it.

"Are you still on schedule for this week?"

"Yes. Nothing's changed," the voice answered.

"Good," Ebbetts said.

No changes in plans meant pay-out time again. But Ebbetts could hear something else still hanging back in the voice, waiting to come out. Before Ebbetts said so, the something came out.

"He's going to jail, you know."

So that's what it's all about, Ebbetts thought. Guilt. No stomach. Just like everybody he had to deal with to get where he wanted to be. Spineless asses who wanted it all but didn't want to do the dirty work to get it.

Ebbetts felt the bile in his throat. He'd had enough of the beggars. The beggars like Bill Golden who begged the big-wigs for a bigger share. The pitiful investors who begged him to take their money so they could dream about their retirement home in Florida. Well, he'd obliged them all and taken their money. Ten million dollars of it.

"Look," Ebbetts said, trying to keep the disgust out of his voice, "I don't give a fuck about Bill Golden and his problems. I'm doing all the work here and I'm finally getting paid properly for it. And so are you. That's all you should be concerned with."

Ebbetts resented this big shot. The guy was in a position to come up with a scheme and had set it up, but he needed someone as ruthless as the Fat Man to make it work. Someone to help embezzle the money from Cook, disappear and start a new life. Washing the money in Mexico and cleaning up all the assholes that might screw the thing up came easy to Ebbetts. But it was still the dirty work, and he knew his partner saw it that way and thought less of Warren Ebbetts because of it. Get off the phone, he said to himself. You're getting too pissed.

"See you when you arrive?" he said succinctly. It was almost an order.

"Yes," the voice said, shakier than it started.

The sweaty Fat Man trudged back to his big American car and flopped down sideways on the seat to wipe his face again before sliding behind the wheel. The icy air blowing from the dashboard vents struck the side of his head as the cool of the interior collided with the heat of the Acapulco sun. The car roared out of the roadside clearing headed back to the city, spitting rocks over the steep slope on the ocean side of the highway.

Almost two years of living in Mexico as a wealthy man had made Warren Ebbetts feel invincible. He'd definitely done the dirty work to get there, planning his "death" just before Bill Golden had discovered something wrong with the Cook account. Shame about that Chesapeake kid, he thought, feeling the rush of bashing the young mate's head with a fish club before dumping him overboard. It was a small price to pay for being reborn. He would've liked to do the same thing to that idiot Alvarez, but he had needed him to tell the sad story of their tragedy on the Bay. He had also needed the worthless shit to get him into Mexico and help set up his new identity; retired Canadian businessman, Andrew Wilson.

The system they constructed had worked, and the embezzled money, sent into Mexico as working capital in the shell company his American partner had established, was regularly washed into Mexican and other currencies through the Fat Man's network. Ebbetts had the Comisione Nacional Bancario fooled as well as the U.S. Treasury Department.

Alvarez was a loose end that, fortunately, someone else had tied up. He'd been found in his car with his throat cut a while back, no thanks to Ebbetts, who considered it a well-deserved stroke of luck.

"Fuck them all," the Fat Man said to no one, enunciating each word. As he said it he gunned the big eight cylinder Chevy, roaring up on an old bus just ahead.

⁂ ⁂ ⁂

"But what if I meet a nice girl," Spook was saying, a false seriousness to his face. "She'll notice I keep wearing the same thing."

"First of all, you ain't gonna meet no nice girls in Acapulco," Ian said, using his Philly-palooka accent. "Not that there aren't any nice girls in Acapulco. Just you ain't gonna meet any. Second, if you do, it'll take you till the end of the week to find her so she won't get a chance to see you wear anything twice anyway. Third, if you handle it right you'll be taking clothes off not puttin' 'em on and fourth, don't be boggin' us down with Mexican romances. You want the one night stands. In and out. Understand? Comprendes?

"I hear ya," Spook said laughing and giving Ian an ironic face.

Ian knew why. If there was ever a romantic it was Ian and he would be the first one to get caught up in some half-assed romance and blow the whole point of the vacation.

The transfer to the hotel from the airport was a big old bus. Ian had expected a nice air-conditioned limo or taxi, but no. The air in this bus was conditioned by fans, bolted to the ceiling, one every three seats. They did an excellent job of pushing all the hot air collected at the top of the oven-on-wheels down onto the passengers. Ian couldn't help reminding Spook that Spook's sales pitch for the trip had been, "everything at one low, low price." But Ian didn't mind. The realization that he was in another country, one he had always imagined coming to, was starting to sink in.

I like this funky old bus, he thought. All I need is some flies buzzin' around my face and bandits pullin' us over. Yeah, Mexican bandits with ugly teeth and whiskers and belts of bullets across their chests. Bahjes? We don' need no stinkin bahjes, gringo!

He laughed at his thought and took in the scenery. To his right he could see green, gradually rising towards sand colored mountains in the far background. To his left, the same colors, only flat, running to what he could figure from the compass in his head was the ocean. He had tracked the location of the water from the time they left the airport and unless they made another turn along the way, the water would stay to his left. He could see the top of a modern hotel rising from the flat plain of green, designed to imitate an Aztec temple, a pyramid with a flat top. As they drew closer he could see gaps in the plain formed by palm trees on a carpet-smooth golf course.

They passed the main entrance and he could see all the way up the driveway, which split the golf course in two. It looked like an ad for Beverly Hills. Later that week they would get a firsthand view of the Royal Prince Hotel, but for now it was a roadside postcard.

Ian looked to the right side again and what he saw made the skin around his eyes bunch up. Dotting the roadside were three-walled huts. Most of them were made from pieces of corrugated metal. There were no floors or fronts to the huts and from what Ian could tell nothing much inside them. People were standing or sitting around on crates and chairs, and as the bus passed they glanced up. Ian could see the obvious disinterest in their eyes. It looked like a neighborhood of sorts: children playing, people sitting out in front of their houses. The donkey was a little out of place, Ian noted, but regardless, the contrast with the lavish hotel to his left was stark.

❊ ❊ ❊

The bus waddled slowly along the mountain road, carefully navigating the curves. Ebbetts realized it was a bus full of tourists fresh from the airport and with the fuel of contempt bubbling inside him he swung wide to the mountain's-edge side of the road and stomped the gas pedal.

"Tourist bastards," he yelled into the cool of the car and raced up alongside the bus just as an oncoming pick-up truck appeared in the lane. His invincibility certain, Ebbetts held his ground. The pick-up swung to the right and skidded, stopping two feet from a drop it would never survive. Ebbetts cut hard across the bus's lane in one continuous move, flicking his eyes to the rear view mirror to see the bus jerk to the right. His scalp tingling, the Fat Man rolled toward the city, the thought of the tourists sprawled across each other at the front of the bus causing his cheeks to rise.

"Welcome to Acapulco," he cackled.

⁂ ⁂ ⁂

Ian could still see the water far to his left. Spook was hopping around from one side of the bus to the other, not wanting to miss anything. Neither of them saw the big American car at first, they just heard it, the boowah of the wide-open carburetor sucking gas flat out. Ian turned immediately to his left and caught view of a Chevy flying up along the side of the bus, his vision picking up another vehicle headed the other way.

"What's this guy nuts?"

Before the entire sentence left his mouth Ian lurched forward then to his left as the brakes of the bus squealed. He smacked into Spook, who was almost in the aisle, as a collective shriek came from the inside of the bus.

"I don't believe that guy just did that," Ian said.

He pulled himself upright, helping a woman and her daughter who were momentarily wedged in the space between the seats. He looked at Spook and smirked.

"I guess that's our welcome to Acapulco committee."

"All for one low, low price," Spook said with a smile.

chapter 6

"LOOK AT THIS FRIGGIN' VIEW."

Spook was standing on the balcony with his arms spread like the Pope preaching to Vatican Square.

"You can see the beach, the pool, out over the bay. Man, this must be the deluxe view."

El Casa Grande was a reasonably priced hotel used by the vacation package agencies. Like most of the other hotels it was located on the Strip, the main drag that followed the curve of horseshoe-shaped Acapulco Bay. The room was comfortable, with the same view as many of the more expensive hotels. It differed from them in ways that meant little to Ian and Spook, like extra towels at poolside.

"And it's all yours, Ian," Spook said, as Ian joined him on the balcony. "A world of pleasure at your feet."

"Come on, man," Ian said walking back into the room. "Let's go check out the food and beverage department of our deluxe accommodations. I'm starving."

"I am there," Spook said, bouncing in from the balcony.

In five minutes they were downstairs. They entered the main restaurant through double glass doors, a huge room with two glass walls facing the Bay. By separating the restaurant from the open lobby, there was no wasted air conditioning, and from what Ian could tell, they needed it. He could spot the tourists easily. They were the ones with the giant dark rings under their arms. The Mexicans didn't seem to notice the heat but they had enough experience to know tourists didn't like dripping into their dinner.

A huge buffet was spread out along one side of the restaurant. Within a few short minutes Ian and Spook were sitting at a table covered with plates of shrimp, chicken and salad along with several icy bottles of Dos Equis beer.

"I see they have the good sense to keep the beer cold," Spook said. "Man, does that taste good." He looked up from the food for a second. "You still serious about that cliff diving thing?"

Ian took a long swig of beer and tried to look unmoved.

"Absolutely."

"Isn't it pretty dangerous, I mean isn't there something about the tide and the cliffs and all?"

Something about the way Spook asked the question made Ian feel like Spook wanted to understand, unlike a brief conversation they had had back home before they left.

"Well, it isn't the same as diving into a pool, that's for sure. The height is something to consider, somewhere around eighty-five feet. I've done about sixty." Ian could feel the tingle on his arms and legs just thinking about it. "Increasing the height takes some adjusting. But you're right about the tide and the cliff. You have to get out away from the cliff when you dive. The bottom of the cliff is obviously…," Ian was using his right hand as the top of the cliff and his left as the bottom, "…further out than the top, so when you dive you push off hard to get out over the water."

His right hand sailed out in an arc over the table stopping shy of the food.

"The tide's in and out so you want the tide high, but more important is to wait for the canyon to fill. The waves surge in and out and if you wait for a wave to come into the canyon and fill it up and you dive before it recedes, you're talking another three, four feet of water when you hit. And you want all you can get."

Ian was pleased with his explanation and Spooked looked satisfied. Ian was sure the huge shrimp headed towards Spook's mouth followed by beer had something to do with the look.

"Well, it sounds pretty exciting. Anybody ever get hurt doing it?"

There it is, Ian thought. The heart of the matter and, once again, Spook hit it. It was the one thing that made Ian get that unidentifiable feeling low in his stomach, the feeling that after all his dreaming and all his talking that one day he'd step to the edge, look out at a view he'd seen in his mind all his life, and not dive.

"Well," he said, "there's a story I read one time about a cliff diver here in Mexico who died."

"Really?"

Spook sat up, pushing his half empty plate forward. Ian suddenly felt like a kid at a campfire about to tell the ghost story.

"Did you ever see the movie Tarzan and the Mermaids?" Ian said.

"I think I've seen 'em all but I don't know which is which, except for the one when he goes to New York."

"Well, in Tarzan and the Mermaids there's this story about a phony guy who rules this tribe by putting on a costume and acting like a god. Tarzan is hanging out with these people and they have this big party, you know, fire twirlers and beach party cookout and the whole bit. Well, they have this big challenge because the tribe is full of cliff divers, something spiritual about it I think, and they have a bunch of guys going off different levels into the water. Then the big kahuna of the divers gets up and they all get real excited 'cause they know where he's going. To do the Big Dive. Seems there's this real high spot where only the big kahuna has the balls to dive from and he challenges Tarzan to do it. So Tarzan's the real deal, plus it's in his movie contract, I guess, and he has to do it. Off he goes to make the dive, only they don't tell him that the real nut buster is getting to the spot where you dive from. He had a good chance of dying just climbing the cliff."

A waiter approached the table and Spook shook him off.

"Anyway, it's part of the plot because the whole time Tarz is climbing, which is probably almost the last fifteen minutes of the film, the tribe gets called to the temple by the phony god."

Ian flicked a glance at Spook who was now listening intently.

"So ole Tarzan's bustin' his hump to get up to the Big Dive, and in the meantime I think the phony god's got Jane or Boy or Cheetah, I forget, one of the family, and he wants to sacrifice them to prove to the tribe that he's still in charge and still a god. Tarzan finally gets to the top and somehow manages to hear all this going on. He's way up on the side of a cliff above the ocean and he knows all this shit's going on. Whatta guy."

Ian grabbed a beer and took a swig.

"Soooo...?" Spook said, impatience in his voice.

Ian swallowed slowly on purpose, put the bottle down and wiped his mouth. Spook was hooked.

"So the fastest way down is to dive but now nobody cares because they're all at the sacrifice. Can you imagine? All that climbing and a death-defying dive and no audience, and they were the ones that got him up there in the first place. Well, Tarzan makes the dive, saves the day and shows the phony god is a phony. The phony gets fed to the whooped up tribe because now they're pissed. I mean they've been tossing perfectly good virgins into the volcano for years on his say so, and this doesn't sit well with them. I don't know whether they missed the virgins or they were worried they wouldn't get credit for them with some real god, but either way they use the phony god to make soup."

Ian paused and took another swig of beer, partially for effect and partially because he was thirsty as hell.

"That's it?" Spook looked really disappointed. "A happy ending? Shit!"

"Well, not exactly," Ian said, putting his beer on the table and looking Spook hard in the eye. "The diver I mentioned who died, the guy's name was Angel Garcia. He was a Mexican diver and stunt man. When they shot this film they hired him to double for Tarzan and do the big dive scene from this special cliff spot."

Spook leaned toward him again.

"The guy had made the dive several times before. This time he climbs to the spot to make the dive and the cameras are rolling for the big scene. The guy goes off, beautiful, out over the water, fabulous dive, hits the water clean."

Ian paused for effect, and the split second of silence was suddenly shattered by breaking plates. They both snapped their heads sideways to see an overdressed woman glaring at the splattered terracotta tile beneath her feet as if the plates had overloaded themselves then leapt from her hands in disgust. Within seconds four white-shirted waiters removed the offensive collage from the floor and ushered her back to the buffet as the woman huffed at them, reconfirming whatever status she had awarded herself. Ian turned back to the table, refocusing on Spook.

"All right," Spook said looking nervous, "now that I've had the shit scared out of me, he hits the water clean and?"

Ian looked down, then up at Spook.

"And a big wave comes in and crushes him against the rocks. Kills him. Dead. Washed away."

"Whoooaa," Spook said, intensely, his eyes popping.

"But the dive was so nice," Ian continued, "they kept the film and used it. As a tribute to the diver. So the next time that movie's on TV, watch it, because the scene where Tarzan makes the big dive is actually the last few seconds of Angel Garcia's life, captured on film."

Ian had told the story before but for some reason sitting here today, he felt a chill when he finished. There was noise all around in the restaurant, but at his table the silence was deafening.

chapter 7

"WELL, I FIGURE maybe today we do a tourist day," Ian said, leaning on the balcony railing, a wide angle view of the bay tickling his nerve endings. "You know, see the sights, hit the shopping places. There's a couple of spots near where the cliff divers perform. Maybe pop in there and get the lay of the land."

"You're not wastin' any time, are ya?" Spook responded.

They had spent the remainder of their arrival day and night checking out the hotel beach and pool and absorbing the local beer. Now, with a fresh day ahead, Ian itched to get to the cliffs to see whether or not he'd be allowed to dive. Until he knew, and then did it, he wouldn't relax. At ten o'clock he was at the car rental desk signing his life away for a roofless, tasteless, yellow excuse for an automobile called appropriately, "The Thing." It had been conceived by someone at Volkswagen, as far as Ian could figure, as punishment for Germany having lost the war.

"Twenty bucks a day," he said, shaking his head in the parking garage.

"At least it doesn't use much gas," Spook added, skimming through the literature from the rental desk.

Thank God we didn't defeat the Arabs, Ian thought.

After some basic directions from the agent, Ian felt confident finding the cliffs. The duo headed out of the hotel garage and onto the main boulevard. As they headed down the Strip, the road rose slightly, presenting them with a breathtaking view of the bay. Several large cruise ships sat motionless in the water, their bleached white skins a stark contrast against the unnatural blue of the water. On the right, mountains shot severely upward towards another shade of blue more ethereal than the first one. Small hotels and palatial villas dripping with flowers sat precariously on natural levels of rock, like people on a wall dangling their legs. Ian sucked it all in and felt small. Small and small time, as though he'd never been out of his neighborhood before. He felt excited by the adventure before him and frustrated that there were so many more adventures like this all over the world he'd never even know about, much less see.

"We should be getting close," he said to Spook after fifteen minutes of driving.

As they came down a hill to a five-way intersection he slowed, then stopped to be sure he made the correct turn. A small Mexican boy with eyes the size of walnuts was standing on the medial strip in the middle of the intersection. As Ian pulled the car to the edge of the strip the boy spoke in a very pleasant tone.

"Hola, Señores. Would you like a guide?"

The boy's smile was wide and friendly and his English clean.

"No, thanks there, buddy," Ian said, noticing the warmth of the boy's face and ignoring it at the same time. He would have asked the boy to confirm his directions but figured the kid would assume they needed a guide. Ian turned left and the road rose and banked right.

Yeah, headed up, that would be right, he thought.

"How about that little guy ha?" Ian said, out loud. "What a hustler. Why isn't he in school?"

The road turned left again and right and then headed downward.

Crazy mountain roads.

The road straightened out, continued to decline and, there, a hundred yards away, was the intersection they had just turned at, complete with the boy. Spook said nothing. Of the five choices at the intersection, Ian had now eliminated two.

No big deal, I picked the wrong turn.

The intersection was empty except for the boy. Ian kept going, making a soft left. He watched the road move uphill and bank right, just like the last road; a different road but the resemblance was amazing. Five minutes of twisting, turning, rising and sinking, and there sat the same intersection. Ian stopped the car. He was seething, using every ounce of self-control to keep from exploding.

"You sure you don't want to hire this kid, Ian?" Spook asked through tight lips, a huge smile leaking through.

The boy stood there, smiling innocently, not a trace of satisfaction in his face.

Little shit. He's not even gloating.

"I tried every turn but one," Ian said, trying to project as much even-temperedness as he could. "It's got to be that one."

He turned the car right and headed up the last of the five choices, hard-eyeing the kid as he went by.

Yeah, you'd love to get paid to tell me to go this way when it's the only way left.

The final road inclined immediately and began twisting right and left at an even pace. For every right bend there was an equal left bend that gave Ian the sense of going straight. When the road curved sharply left, it ended at another T intersection that forced him to turn again. Ian recognized it. Either way would put him face to face with the kid and his intersection of the damned. If he was serious about loosening up for the vacation this was a moment of truth. He turned his head far enough to see Spook biting his lip and looking everywhere but at Ian.

"All right," Ian said, "I think we're renting a guide for the day."

Ian turned left and a minute later pulled up to the boy, still holding the same expression from the last four passes–a big smile.

"All right you, ya got this intersection rigged?" Ian said, laughing. "What's the deal?"

He'd found his sense of humor as much from the boy's smile as from trying.

"I can be your guide, Señores. Wherever you wahnt to go, I tell you thee best way. Eef you shop I tell you what to pay so you don't get cheated."

The boy couldn't have been more than twelve or thirteen, the silky brown hair trimmed neatly and lying flat against his head. He was average size, not particularly thin or heavy and dressed neatly in a pair of khaki shorts, Acapulco tee shirt and brown leather sandals. Ian wanted to assume he was something of a Third World street urchin but the lad's appearance and demeanor refused the stereotype.

"How much?" Spook asked.

"Oh, cheap. It is how long I spend, but cheap."

The boy was not selling. There was no attempt to try and convince the tourist gringos that this was the deal of a lifetime. It was all very matter of fact. Ian tried to imagine a twelve year old boy back home getting in a car with American strangers, much less foreigners, and suddenly felt protective of the young entrepreneur.

"What's your name there, buddy?" Ian asked.

"Manuel."

"Well, Manuel, you've got yourself a job. Manny's what we'll call ya, okay?"

"Okay," Manny said, still smiling.

"Hop in."

The boy climbed up the side of the "Thing" and stepped carefully onto the seat behind Spook and sat down.

"Yo, ManEE," Spook said, and held out his palm.

The boy slapped Spook five and his smile broke into a wide grin. Now Ian loved this kid. He turned around further and said, "Manny, this is Spook."

"Hello, Señor Spook."

The way he pronounced it, it rhymed with book.

"And I'm Ian."

"Hello, Señor Een."

"Now how do we get to the cliff divers?"

"Turn left," Manny said, still no trace of gloating.

Ian shook his head and hit the gas. Within five minutes he saw a hotel sticking up above the horizon. Cars and several buses were parked about a hundred feet away, and Manny said to pass them. The road bent to the left and Manny pointed to a small lot next to El Salto, a large, old-fashioned hotel, its style right out of a Bogart movie.

"Everyone sees thee cars back there and pulls een right away. Then they have to walk een hot sun. In Meheeco, we are very aware of thee heat of thee sun."

"Check it out," Spook said, "VIP parking and all. Way ta go ManEE!"

Manny's smile got bigger.

"If you want to watch thee divers, they dive at twelve-thirty. Thee best place to watch eez down there at thee wall."

"Well, it's eleven-thirty," Ian said. "Good. That gives us time to grab some lunch and a beer. Maybe I can find out from someone in the hotel about diving."

"I wait here to watch the car," Manny said.

"No, Manny," Ian said, gently, noting how seriously the boy took his job. "You don't have to watch the car. Come on in and have some lunch. You'll get a chance to earn your keep."

"No, Señor Een," Manny said, politely explaining. "You don't know. I should watch the car. Eet ees part of my job, and thee tourists sometimes get their cars taken. I know thee people who take them. If they see me they leave eet alone."

Ian was still not comfortable with the idea but realized the boy was not going to change his program for some dumb, well-meaning American tourist.

"All right. If you say so but if you need anything you come find us. Spook, why don't you grab us a table. I just want to check out the cliffs before the crowd starts to gather, okay?"

"You got it," Spook said, and walked toward the hotel.

Ian walked a few feet to the end of the parking lot where the ground began sloping downward to a large stone patio. A three foot wall of the same stone had been built across the front of the patio facing the water, a gold, rough-faced rock that seemed to glow from the sun's light. The patio was positioned at the back end of the canyon, across from and about three hundred feet right of the diving area, offering a panoramic view of the water and cliffs. In the middle of the patio was a metal sculpture atop a long thin pedestal. The sculpture, tarnished from exposure to the outdoors, was the graceful form of a diver in a classic arched-back swan dive, the trademark style of the Mexican divers. Ian stopped and took it all in at once, working hard at ordering it in his mind. There before him stood the source of a childhood's worth of wonder and awe, like and nothing like the TV image beamed thousands of miles to a boy in Philadelphia–an image that had haunted his thoughts for many years.

This was the place. La Quebrada.

Ian moved to the far end of the patio. From there he could look in a straight line at the cliff and the spot where he would have to stand.

There, his mind said, simultaneously realizing the ineffectiveness of the word. He could feel the rush of current up and down his spine. The diving area was nothing more than a flat spot at the top of a skinny, upside down V of rock on the other side of the canyon. It looked as if walking along the top of the cliff was impossible. The only way to get to there was to climb the face of the cliff from the water.

There was no doubt about it. Whatever he had imagined over the years, watching it on TV and recreating the image in his mind as he leapt from diving platforms, it was not what he saw here. What he saw here produced an immediate and clearly identifiable reaction in his gut.

Fear.

The sheerness of the cliff face, the height, the wide openness and vulnerability of that wind-blown perch made his stomach flutter while a steady stream of thoughts zipped through his mind.

Oh shit. Oh God. So here you are, boy. You didn't even get up there yet and your nuts are in your throat. What's the matter? You afraid? Good, you should be. If you're not you have no business going up there. All right, what do we have here? Do we have some excitement? Oh yeah. Yeah, we're excited, man, we're here. This is it, Acapulco. The real thing. All right, do we know how to dive? Yeah, just gotta go a little higher and put a few more calculations in. Okay, what else? Oh yeah, we got fear. You betch yer sweet ass we got fear. So what do we do? We give it up? We quit? We back out and run? Yeah, we know how to do that don't we? That'd be easy, too easy wouldn't it?

Ian could already feel what it would be like to get back in the car and drive away. How he'd have that feeling, the thick ooze, lying in his gut. How he'd drink it away for about a month and then let it drive him nuts forever after. How he'd add it to his list of back-outs and no-commitments that he kept posted high up on the inside of his forehead, the list he checked whenever he needed an excuse. A relationship, teaching, music, corporate success.

No no. NO! His fists clenched.

"NO!"

It came out of his mouth and flew across the canyon, smashing into the side of the cliff and circulating back around the stone wall. In his peripheral vision he saw a group of people turn sharply in his direction, startled by the outburst. He didn't care. He stood up and pointed to the spot where he now knew for sure, he'd make a stand. The words spewed from his mouth, a breath in between each of the last three, his arm and finger stabbing the air.

"I'm gonna KICK!...YOUR!...ASS!...," he put his arm down, paused long enough to slow his breathing and then lowered his voice to a near whisper, "or you're gonna kick mine."

He turned and walked across the patio, ignoring the group of buzzing witnesses, and headed up the incline to the hotel.

chapter 8

"DO WE KEEP making money or don't we?"

The Fat Man's perspiration was doing considerable damage to the shirt he was wearing as well as the air around him in the tiny office. The office, despite its darkness, was filled with the heat of the day, the only air a small draft blowing from the doorway leading to the store.

"Ees slow."

Long and thin and a third of the weight of his antagonist, the storeowner answered quickly, less intimidated than irritated at the sweaty man's tone.

"Ees hot. Word ees tighten up, you know? People nosin ahroun."

"Who's nosing around? You mean cops? Federales? Who?"

The idea seemed to annoy Ebbetts rather than scare him.

"Cain't tell. Probably local. Whachu wan from me?"

Ebbetts could tell the skinny man was annoyed now. Didn't like being pressed on his own turf.

"I gotta check my store," the man said, walking through the door.

"Arrogant bastard," Ebbetts said under his breath as he watched the storeowner leave. The Fat Man reached awkwardly for his handkerchief and wiped the sweat from his face and head. "All of em, arrogant bastards. Wouldn't make a fucking dime without me." He shook his head, then rose with great effort to follow the man into the store.

⁂ ⁂ ⁂

"Hey, Tarzan, so how's it look?"

Ian could tell Spook was on his second Corona. His eyes were glassy which was usually what happened when Spook drank during the day. He could hold his own at night, but the minute he had a beer for lunch he was half-shot.

"Pretty good as a matter of fact," Ian answered.

He pulled out a chair and sat down. The dining room of the hotel was packed with tourists, identifiable by their hats and cameras. That was about all Ian noticed, his mind spinning with the thoughts of his dive.

"I talked to the hotel manager," he continued, "who wasn't very excited about the whole idea but he let me talk to the guy who manages the divers. That guy asked me some questions. I gave him my school references, who I trained with, where I did my diving, you know, like a résume. I guess he got enough right answers to figure I wasn't some kook on dope that wants to fly."

"So when you gonna do it?" Spook said, looking excited.

"Well, this coach is pretty thorough, which is good. He wants me to do some lower height checkout dives so he can see for sure that I know what I'm doing. And get a feel for the adjustments I'll have to make once I get up top. He said I'm only getting one shot at it."

A look of concern spread across Spook's face and it took a second for Ian to realize why.

"Meaning," Ian reassured him, "that after the one dive he's not going to let me do any more from the top,...not like I'm gonna die or anything. But one shot's all I want. Anyway, to answer your question, tomorrow." Ian looked at Spook and grinned.

"Really?" Spook asked. "Are you ready?"

"Well, I look at it this way. I've been waiting all my life to come here and do this. Why put it off? I might not get another chance. Besides I don't want to be sitting around this whole vacation with it in my head, you know, too much time to think about it and all that. Just get up there, do it, get my ultimate orgasm and then party. How'zat?"

Back me up, Spook, Ian thought.

"Man, in all the years I known ya I ain't never seen you with a more clear picture of what you want to do and how you're gonna do it." Spook was looking at him with awe. "Tomorrow it's gonna be. And I'm gonna be here to witness it. And then we're goin' out afterwards and kick Acapulco's ass. ALL RIGHT?"

Spook pulled his clenched fist to his chest then presented it palm-out to Ian.

"ALL RIGHT!" Ian hollered back and smacked Spook's hand solidly.

Spook threw his head back to his left and hollered, "Dos cervezas and dos Cuervos, Señorita."

"Ladies and gentleman, may I have your attention."

The voice crackled into the restaurant and reverberated outside through a bad PA system.

"For your pleasure and excitement El Hotel Salto offers to you an opportunity to see members of the internationally famous Mexican National Diving team who will perform from the cliffs of La Quebrada. The Clavadistas are preparing themselves now and will be starting their dives in about five minutes. Thank you for coming."

Ian jumped up at the announcement.

"Come on. I want to get a good view," he said, and hurried out of the restaurant.

Spook quickly chugged the end of his beer and sprang after him, trying to close the distance between them. He didn't catch up till they reached the patio.

La Quebrada was the name in the travel brochures for the area where the cliffs were, as well as the cliffs. Ian had asked the diving coach for a translation but found, as was the case with most translations from Spanish, the words did not match up in English as cleanly as Ian would have liked.

"It is a word that means more about the place," the coach said, swinging both his arms outward to engulf the scene before them, "than the thing."

The closest literal translation Ian could get was something to do with the way the rocks and cliffs jutted out into the ocean. But having seen the cliffs he understood the coach's problem. It was like standing before the awesome power of Niagara Falls and labeling it a waterfall.

There was a crowd of about fifty people now. Ian squirmed his way to the far end of the wall where he had stood earlier and saw five divers scaling the side of the cliff, clad only in bathing suits. Their dark brown skin, darker than the golden-yellow stone, formed a natural contrast against the cliffside. He could feel the sensation of their bare feet against the rough stone as they carefully placed their steps, a foot hold, then a hand hold, then another foot, like spiders in slow motion. Two of the divers reached a ledge area about twenty five feet above the water and stood up straight. They faced the crowd and began waving. The crowd applauded and waved back. The other three divers continued to climb, one finally reaching a ledge about forty five feet high and the fourth stopping at about sixty feet. The last diver, who had started up the cliff first, continued to the top. Now they were all facing the crowd and waving, the audience response having increased as each diver reached a higher level.

Ian stood mesmerized. For a moment he felt like a young boy again, thinking this was something done by trained professionals, not kids from Philadelphia. Ordinary people like him didn't ever become movie stars, or major league pitchers, or Acapulco cliff divers.

The divers stopped waving and one of them on the lower ledge put his hands out and stared forward, indicating his concentration on the dive. The crowd went quiet instantly. He paused about ten seconds, more for effect, Ian thought, and then sprang from the ledge into a perfect, one and a half open pike somersault, cutting the water cleanly as he entered. He popped to the surface almost instantly and waved to the crowd. The crowd cheered and whooped and applauded as he swam back to the base of the cliff. The second lower level diver began his concentration. The crowd quieted and he leapt, completing the same dive as smoothly as the first diver.

Ian wanted to study some technical details but found himself overcome by the spectacle. He was just one more cheering, excited spectator, clapping and yelling as if he had no idea how this magic thing was done.

It is magic! he thought. It's flying. It's leaving the earth. It's sailing through the sky and landing in soft blue water. Real magic!

The third diver was now set to go. Ian saw that he was not a young man, possibly in his late forties. He was soft around the middle, his stomach not big but extending a bit further forward than his chest. He wasted little time. Obviously, he'd made this dive hundreds of times and his instincts were all programmed. He pushed off firmly from his perch and dropped a perfect swan dive into the swelled canyon. He surfaced, gave a quick wave and swam towards the rocks.

The fourth diver was a young boy, not more than fifteen or sixteen. He was thin but there was musculature in his arms and legs as he tensed on the small ledge that was his platform. Ian could see something in the boy's face that bothered him. There was no trace of fear, not a hint of any concern about what he was about to do. Here he stood, sixty feet above the earth, about to hurl himself out into space with the possibility of bouncing down the side of the canyon or breaking his back on the water and his expression said, piece a cake.

The boy shot from the cliff like a spring, pulled his arms way back like a gull and floated to the water. He barely disturbed the surface as he disappeared. When he surfaced he milked the crowd, waving and splashing and clenching his fists in triumph. The tourists loved it and gave him more noise and applause than they had given the other divers.

Ian looked up at the last diver and a chill went up his spine. The difference in height between his perch and the young boy's was maybe twenty feet or so, but standing at the very top of the jagged ridge with only the cloudless, metallic blue sky above, nothing to lean on or grab hold of, gave the diver the appearance of standing on the edge of the earth.

God, he looks lonely, Ian thought.

The diver seemed about Ian's age, probably twenty nine, thirty. He was muscular but not bulky, with longer legs than the others, his hair, jet black and shiny from being wet. He was paying no attention to the crowd or its reaction to the last diver. He was in a tense state of concentration looking at the water. Out towards the ocean. Back to the canyon. Back to the ocean. Then he stepped back from the edge. Ian couldn't tell if there was something wrong or if it was part of a personal routine, like a batter at the plate tapping his spikes before the pitch. Either way, Ian thought, it's not entertainment for this guy. He's taking it seriously.

Then the diver turned away from the water and the crowd and faced what appeared to be a small shrine tucked into the other side of the top of the cliff. He put his head down and blessed himself and then stepped back to the edge of the diving ledge. He looked towards the ocean, then set himself, wiped his hands on the back of his bathing suit, and stretched both arms out in front of him, palms down.

Ian was positive that no one else standing on the patio was breathing either. The only sound was the water sloshing around inside the canyon and that seemed somehow muffled. The diver looked to his right again without changing position, and then put his arms down and stepped back. Fifty people pushed the same patch of air out of their lungs at the same time, creating a collective uunnggh that disappeared as quickly as it came.

Ian hadn't realized it but Spook was just to his right.

"What's the matter, Ian?" he whispered. "Something wrong?"

"He doesn't like the water level," Ian said, without taking his eyes off of the diver. "Wants another wave."

Ian realized the only thing at that moment separating the inside of his head from the inside of the diver's head was space. He had never been up there before but right now he could see exactly what the diver was seeing from the top of the cliff; the water, the rocks, the crowd, hell, he could see himself standing there watching with his arms folded across his chest. He could feel the air moving up there and the vacuum being created by the simultaneous intake of breath by the crowd.

The diver stepped to the edge again, and Ian's toes curled to grip the stone. The diver looked to his right once more. Ian's stomach muscles sucked inward and knotted. The diver extended his arms forward again and Ian's body tightened all over, his legs hard as a rock. The diver dropped his arms smoothly in a semi-circle and flung his body forward away from the cliff. Ian felt a rush of air, heat and chill, that lasted forever and only three seconds, enough that it made him shudder noticeably. The diver floated in mid-air, turned vertical, then disappeared like a javelin into the water. Ian stared at the spot, unable to move, watching the water foam around the spot where he and the diver had entered the blue vortex.

Too much time passed by. Ian's lungs were beginning a slow scream for air. CLAW! KICK! CAN'T BREATHE!

The diver's head and shoulders broke the surface of the water and Ian's body came unloose all at one time. The crowd was yelling and screaming and applauding, completely hooked on the whole experience. The diver was smiling but it was a weak smile, as if to say I'm glad that's over with. He swam slowly to the base of the cliff and climbed out. He stood up and turned, putting his back flat against the cliffside, and waved weakly at the crowd. The crowd responded loudly, needing badly to pay more tribute in order to exorcise the tension they felt.

Spook turned to Ian, his eyes blazing, completely caught up in the drama.

"Wow, that was unbelievable man! What a ride! You're really gonna do that?"

There was no response to the question. There was only Ian's pasty white face, locked in a frozen stare across the canyon at the blood trickling from the side of the diver's head.

chapter 9

SPOOK HANDED THE wrapped cheeseburger to Manny who stood by the Thing with the fixed look of a Secret Serviceman guarding the President.

"Thank you," Manny said. "Eet was not necessary."

Spook shook his head and jumped into the passenger seat. "You work, you gotta eat. So eat."

"Do you wish to shop, Señores?"

Ian slid into the driver's seat and asked for direction, noting the irony of the moment, then pulled out of the lot. Manny assured them of some excellent bargains, then set about demolishing the cheeseburger as they rode. It went quickly along with two bottles of Coke.

About ten minutes up the road Manny led them to an unpaved stretch of gravel and dirt. Ian thought it odd that a place catering to tourists would be so out of the way and unadvertised when Manny said, "Thees place I take you is not a place where as many toureests go. Only people who know Acapulco know to come here. You get better merchandise here than in toureest shops and you don't pay as much. And I make sure."

There it was again, Ian noted, the giant Manny smile. It was not bragging. It was pure pride beaming from the boy's face. Manny took this work as seriously as a surgeon. Maybe, Ian thought, it's about survival for this kid. Maybe it was about food for him and his family. Maybe it was a new blanket or scarf for his mother. But that big fat smile, that wasn't survival. That was pride. That was an attitude.

They parked and exited the car, standing in front of a white stucco building with a wood sign that said, The Silver Mine.

"Eef you want to buy something, you ask thee price," Manny said. "Look at me when they tell you thee price and I weel shake my head yes if it is okay or no if it is a high price. They weel lower thee price if you say it is too high. Okay?"

Manny was looking up at them and squinting.

"Sounds like a fine plan to me," Spook said. "Won't these guys get mad at you for cuttin' into their profits?"

"No, Señor Spook. They know I bring them good beesness. I don't bring everyone here. Just when I meet people who are good guys. You are good guys. I think you weel be fair."

"Well, you're right, Manny. Thanks for sayin' so. Let's check it out."

Spook turned and walked towards the ranch style building. Ian waited till Spook was two steps ahead and then put his hand on Manny's shoulder and stopped him, turning the boy towards him.

"Manny, I'm glad you think we're good guys," Ian said, warmly.

"Eet is true, Señor Een, I can tell."

"Well, I think you're one too. And thank you."

Manny looked slightly confused.

"You are welcome, Señor Een, but thank you for what?"

Ian looked closely at the boy's face, trying to think of an answer that made sense.

"For pointing me in the right direction today."

Manny, ever the smiling professional said, "That is my job, Señor Een."

"That it is," said Ian, walking towards the building. "That it is."

The shop was draped from ceiling to floor with merchandise and smelled strongly of leather and wood. Garments, saddles, ponchos, all hung from the ceiling and posts of the building which appeared to have been a house at one time. At the far end of the room was a stairway leading to a loft, also packed with merchandise. The stairway had jugs on the steps and blankets hung over the railing. Rough cut tables held the bulk of the selection of carvings, jewelry, cut glass and pottery. The only resemblance to a modern store was the line of glass display cases on one side of the room where they kept the real jewelry, the silver and gold. Spook was already trying on leather vests and sombreros.

As Ian took stock of the room he noticed two men behind the glass cases, one at either end. They were both dressed in long white shirts, worn outside the pants, with an open collar. The fronts of the shirts were decorated with embroidery, although Ian had seen others less decorative on other men. Manny explained to him later that the shirt, called a guayabera, was a traditional style of dress comparable to a dress shirt and tie. Ian chuckled to himself, wondering how wearing one into the office on a hot day in July would go over with the Old Man.

The air of the two men suggested business rather than catering to tourists. The Bandito Brothers, Ian thought to himself, and smirked. A woman and another man, both noticeably more friendly than the Bandito brothers, were walking the floor and offering assistance to customers, smiling all the while. One of the Brothers was talking to a customer near Ian's end of the case. The other, standing at the far end, was obviously the boss. He was watching the transaction at Ian's end of the case while simultaneously sweeping back and forth across the whole shop.

"Man, I gotta get me one a these. Talk about your party hat."

Spook walked up with a big sombrero on his head.

"Now where are you going to wear that?" Ian said, laughing.

"Are you kidding? Man, weddings and cookouts, stuff like that." Spook looked at him with a mock serious face. "Na, I really want it to hang on the wall. See the way they look? I think it's neat."

Spook pointed to where seven or eight hats, all different sizes, were hanging on the wall. Spook was right. They did look neat.

"I want to get this big one and then a little one too. Manny? Let's get hagglin'."

Ian browsed some more, amazed at the prices. Leather coats for forty dollars if his calculation from peso to dollar was right. A bargain's only a bargain if you need it, he thought, resisting the urge to buy. He was interested mostly in souvenirs he could take home for his family. Cool stuff for his brother, something cute for his sister, anything for Dad because Dad never wanted anything. And always something special for Mom.

He turned back toward the glass cases and noticed that the Boss Bandito was now talking to someone who appeared to have come through an open door in the wall just beyond the end of the cases. Ian's curiosity was tweaked by the fact that the new arrival was dressed in a tropical suit rather than the traditional Mexican shirt. That the man was quite large probably helped draw Ian's attention as well. The man's back was to him and from what Ian could see, he was sure he was not Mexican, his skin being very light, almost pink around his neck. The two men were doing serious business, although Ian couldn't see the heavy man's face. But the Boss Bandito's expression made it clear that the face looking back at him was not smiling.

Ian zig-zagged his way through the tables casually, gazing at the items piled on each of them until he was at the glass cases, full with sparkling gold and silver jewelry. Some of the pieces at first glance were dazzling, with intricate layering and sculpting across the surface. Ian almost forgot why he'd gone to the cases when the other Bandito Brother asked him in English if he needed any help.

"No. No thank you, just looking," Ian said, slightly startled.

He realized he had been paying more attention to the two men talking than to himself. The lesser Bandito moved towards another customer. Ian moved again and glanced over at the Boss Bandito and the large man, whose face he could see now. What he saw surprised him.

He knew the man. Not knew him, but knew his face. Ian had a memory for detail, especially faces. He could pick actors out of old films, when they had bit parts and weren't stars or celebrities. Small part actors, faces in a crowd scene. Ian could spot them. But it was both a blessing and a curse. In his sales position, it was a valuable tool. People were always amazed that he remembered them and took it as a compliment. On the downside, people's faces stuck with Ian so much that when he saw someone he didn't know instantly, he was never sure if he had met the person or that he had just absorbed their face for some reason. Like the face of the Boss Bandito. If Ian saw him walking in an airport two years from now, he'd know his face. But he didn't really know him.

Ian knew this heavy man's face. He just couldn't place it. He had no immediate mental connection, no sense of place or time. Only the feeling that the face he saw now, which seemed extremely serious, bordering on angry, had been first viewed in pleasant circumstances. He'd seen that fat face smiling and friendly, not tight and menacing.

Where, where? Come on, Ian. Pick it out, man, go through the files.

Ian was concentrating on the man's face so much he didn't realize that the Boss Bandito was looking at him. When he finally focused on the two men together the Bandito looked back towards his companion, who now turned and looked at Ian.

Oh, boy, do I feel stupid, Ian thought. Well, either this guy's going to recognize me or he's going to think I'm some jackass minding his business.

"How ya doin?" Ian said with a smile, raising his right hand in a weak wave and trying not to look too sheepish.

He saw the Fat Man's eyes narrow as if he'd suddenly realized Ian was looking at him. Ian thought for a second he saw fear flick across the man's face but then decided it was more shock at Ian's sudden greeting. The man struggled but managed to squeeze a painful smile out of the folds of his face.

"Pretty good. How about you?"

Ian could sense some recognition on the man's part, but unless the man offered more information, Ian was going to have to slide out of this one politely.

"Can't complain. A little vacation always helps, right?"

"Right. You enjoy it. Okay?"

The man turned towards the door in the wall, touching Boss Bandito on the arm as a signal to go with him.

"Yeah, I'll try."

Good, Ian thought. That was uncomfortable, weird even.

"Hey, Ian. You with it or what?"

Spook and Manny were standing to his left watching him. He hadn't even noticed them.

"Yeah, yeah. I was just concentrating on something."

"You know that guy?" Spook said.

"Well, that's what I was thinking about. One of those 'I know his face but not from where' deals. You know me with faces."

"Oh God," Spook said, turning to Manny, "he'll be drivin' us crazy now till he remembers. The man can't let go of a face till he nails it down."

"If I met that guy in a bar," Ian said, feeling a need to explain, "I'd just tell him I know his face but can't remember from where. But he was a little weird, maybe doing heavy business or something. Did he look familiar to you?"

Spook shook his head and gave him a 'yeah, right' face.

"Ian, the guy probably sold you a hot dog at a ballgame one time. Forget it, man, you and that memory. Hey, you want to remember something, remember my man Manny here at the end of the day. Guess what I paid for all three hats?"

Ian's focus shifted from the image of the stranger to Spook, who was standing there with three hats on his head, all different sizes stacked from big to small.

"I have no idea, Spook," Ian said, a smile breaking across his face.

"This big one alone the guy wanted thirty bucks for. Manny gets into the action with me and I walk away with all three hats for thirty five. This boy's somethin' else." Spook was in his glory.

Ian looked at Manny. If his smile got any bigger, Ian thought, they'd have to start moving tables and merchandise out of the store to make room. The kid was beaming up at him, quite proud of his accomplishments.

"What would you like, Señor Een?"

"As a matter of fact I did see something that interested me, Señor Manuel. This way, por favor."

Manny hopped forward, pleased to once more prove his value.

When Ian stepped into the sunlight outside the shop, a small, solid silver cross, formed by the joining of three crudely forged nails, hung from a leather string around his neck. The only thing shining brighter in the afternoon sun was the face of a Mexican boy they'd just nick-named Manny the Hustler.

chapter 10

THE ODD TRIO sat in the Thing surrounded by bags and sombreros. Manny had taken them to the bargain shops in the section known as Old Acapulco. He had been the perfect professional, telling them what to pay and what not to pay. When they went into a shop to explore, he carried everything or waited in the Thing to mind the previous purchases. And every time they returned with a bag of merchandise his smile got bigger. When it was all over, the Thing was full, Manny was ecstatic, and Ian and Spook were laughing and shaking their heads because the whole spree had only set each of them back about a hundred dollars. Putting everything into the trunk at the front of the vehicle, they walked a few feet away then sat in the cool, shaded plaza, the Zòcalo as Manny called it, sipping fresh fruit drinks and plotting the rest of the day with Manny's help. The plan included a stop at their hotel to shower and change and temporarily escape the hot afternoon sun.

"Are you staying on thee Costera, Señores?"

Manny asked the question as they walked back to the Thing.

"The where?" Spook asked.

"Thee Costera Miguel Alemàn?" he said. "Thee Strip."

"Oh, yeah," Spook said, understanding. "The main boulevard, yeah."

With Manny directing, they were back at the hotel in fifteen minutes. Ian ran to the bar and bought sodas while Spook and Manny hauled the booty up to the room. When he got upstairs Spook was already in the shower and Manny sat on the balcony. Ian sat down in the chair next to him.

"Is that the church up there on the right that we're going to?"

"Yes," Manny said

"And how about that big white place there near the water?"

"That is thee home of a very reech man from South America."

"Now how about up in the mountains there? At night we can see all kinds of lights strung out across those hills."

"Many of thee houses are private veeyas. Sometimes the owners leeve in them and sometimes people pay to stay een them. There are some restaurants up there also because the view of thee bay ees beautiful, but as you get too far into the mountains you have to be very careful."

"Why's that?" Ian yelled over his shoulder. He moved inside the room, quickly coming back to the balcony with two bottles of Coke. He handed one to Manny.

"There are bahd men in thee hills, Señor Een. It ees where the women and the marheewana ees and so there are many banditos."

Spook was walking towards the balcony toweling his hair as Manny finished explaining.

"Women and marheewana. Sounds like the place to go," Spook said, laughing.

Manny looked at him very seriously.

"I don't think you want to go there, Señor Spook. Eef you want thee pot you can buy it cheap on thee beach, right there." He pointed out over the railing. "For thee women, eef you ride down the Costera tonight in your car the men weel drive up and give you a card. Or you can go to La Huerta, but eet ees not nice. But do not go to the ones far into the mountains."

Ian was watching the boy's face as he issued the warning. Manny had not only offered them advice for their safety and welfare, but made it very clear there were services he did not provide. They'd been approached by four or five kids his age on the beach already, selling pot and Chiclets. But not this boy. He drew the line. He'd provide them with the best and most professional services available in Mexico, but he wouldn't compromise his own standards. Prostitution and selling drugs were not in his catalogue.

"Ah, don't worry, amigo," Spook said. "I ain't up for chasin' around no mountains to get a woman or a buzz. There's plenty of women runnin' around this hotel, and I ain't had any trouble gettin' buzzed so far this week."

"That's for sure," Ian said, smirking. "Manny, you want a shower?"

"No, thank you, Señor Een. I don't get so hot like you do."

It's true, Ian thought. There wasn't a bead of sweat on the boy all day.

They were on their way by five-thirty. Manny led them to the upscale casitas at Las Brisas, a style of living Spook felt strongly he could get used to, and on to the church of San Antonio, high above Acapulco Bay. The mountain climb to the top put the Thing's transmission to the test. Some of the hills were so steep the strain on the vehicle made Ian consider getting out and walking to reduce the weight. The car slowed to a near crawl at several points but never stopped.

The church, more of a chapel, was fairly modern, not at all the quaint Mexican mission Ian had expected. He walked in, took a picture, and quickly whispered a prayer for courage on his upcoming dive, then moved outside to enjoy the view.

The view at the top had made the whole excursion worthwhile. In back of Ian, jagged peaks of the Sierra rose like brittle fingers into the deepening blue sky. In front of him the entire Bay was visible, spread out like a fisheye lens. Ian had a sense of the curvature of the earth, the horizon arcing left to right with the sun beginning its slow but steady drop into the Pacific. Being an East Coaster meant bay sunsets, which were beautiful, but land was always visible in the picture. It was a nice flip-flop experience to watch a deep, horizoned body of water drinking in the molten red liquid of a setting sun. He almost expected to hear a hiss.

Spook jumped behind the wheel as they headed from the church down the mountain to their next stop, the Royal Prince, the hotel they'd passed on their way in from the airport. It had taken them a good fifteen minutes to get from the main road to the parking lot of the church on the way up, but going back down Spook was closing in on the six minute mark as they neared the end of the twisting chute. It was only Ian's prior experience with Spook's driving back home that restrained him from sliding over and stomping his foot on the brake. Spook did take his driving seriously. He drove a little quicker and a little less patiently than most people, but he drove that way all the time, not just when he'd had a bad day. Sort of like controlled mayhem.

The road banked hard left and right with little consistency except that there were more lefts. Spook held the wheel and the car tight to the road, braking and gassing at a regular pace and not appearing particularly bothered by the roller-coaster effect of it all.

Ian felt some relief as they neared the bottom of the mountain. He knew the highway sat just beyond an outcropping of rock on the left. The best method was simply to slow down and prepare to stop. Spook was pumping his brakes on the downgrade, anticipating the quick hook turn where he would back off the brakes momentarily and then brake hard at the main road. When Spook made the blind turn, Ian's foot instinctively went to the floor as a small white car appeared on the right side, parked on the almost non-existent shoulder, narrowing the margin of error. If Spook went to the brakes now he would fishtail and definitely smack the other car. Spook held back on the brakes a second longer to clear the other car, holding the wheel hard to not lose the edge on the turn. The tires screamed to let go and then, clearing the white car, Spook slammed on the brakes to avoid shooting out onto the highway full of speeding traffic, the tires in full protest again.

Ian had seen Spook's reactions and had braced himself, but Manny went flying over the front seat, stopping fortunately at Ian's left arm which was anchored and locked in place at the top of the windshield.

"Oh, man," Spook yelled, as the car skidded to a stop. "Is everybody all right?"

He sounded scared and angry at the same time. Ian could feel the spot on his forearm where Manny's head had hit.

"Manny, you all right"? Ian said.

"Si, yes, I think so," Manny said, a little dazed.

"That dumb shit! What a stupid place to park!" Spook hollered.

They all turned around towards the parked car. The driver was sitting there looking at them as if nothing had happened. Ian had seen the man's dark face when they passed by and his expression now was unchanged. It was clear, in a chilling sort of way, that this man could not care less that he had almost caused them serious injury. The man returned Ian's stare for a minute and then looked the other way to demonstrate his indifference.

Spook was heating up.

"Man, I oughtta tell that fool how stupid he is. What kind a…?"

"Spook, Spook, take it easy, man. Calm down. Vacation, remember?"

Ian was a little surprised at himself to be taking it all so calmly, but something in that guy's face told him there would be no satisfaction there.

"Look, the guy probably doesn't speak English, you don't speak Spanish, and from the look on his face he either has no idea what he did or couldn't care less, so let's just shake it off. Everybody's okay. Let's have some more fun. Besides, I'm starving."

"Yeah, but…."

"You had it under control the whole time," Ian said, looking right at Spook and smiling.

"Hey, you know, you don't think about it," Spook said, modestly. "But thanks. When did we eat last? I'm starvin' too."

He pulled the car up to the highway, picked a slot and shot out into the steady traffic. Ian sat back and felt his arm throb and his neck tighten.

And I'm worried about jumping off a cliff, he thought.

They pulled into the driveway of the Royal Prince about seven-thirty, a few golf carts still cruising the fairways on either side of them as the hard-core duffers got their money's worth.

Spook drove the Thing around the circle that passed in front of the hotel and into a parking area.

"Just look like you own the place when you walk by the front desk," Ian said, as they got out of the car and headed for the lobby. He took four steps, then stopped and turned back, folding his arms across his chest. "Wait a minute."

He looked at Spook and then toward the car. Manny was still sitting in it.

"And what are you doing?"

"I wait here with the car," Manny said, his usual, 'I'm just doing my job' smile on his face.

"No one is going to steal our car from a hotel parking lot, Manny. We don't have any packages for you to protect. And you haven't had any more to eat today than we have, so don't tell me you're not hungry."

Ian stared at him making it clear he was not accepting any more excuses for not coming with them. For only the second time that day, Manny's smile disappeared.

"Señor Een," he said looking at Ian, obviously struggling with the explanation, "some 'otels, they do not like for me to come in."

If Ian could have found a large rock, he would have bashed his own head on it. He was stumped, entangled by the understanding of why things were the way they were, and frustrated by the injustice they inevitably produced. Manny knew his place, as distasteful a concept as that was to Ian, but Ian had no right to come to this boy's country and tell him it wasn't acceptable.

And what was he, Ian, anyway? Some great white hope who came to save the third world from class discrimination? Wasn't he there for fun, with money to piss away on liquor and food and souvenirs, as he drove past the three-walled shacks and tripped over the dirty children selling matches?

"Are you sure?" Ian said, sadly. "I mean, you better not be just saying that. You know that you're with us."

The magic smile came back to Manny's face.

"You speak to me with respect, Señor Een. That is enough."

"You deserve it," Ian said. "Is there anything we can get you? Anything special?"

"No. Thank you."

"All right."

Ian turned and walked back towards Spook.

"He's some kinda kid, isn't he?" Spook said, as they walked toward the hotel.

Ian looked at the ground and shook his head.

"Wise before his time, my friend."

chapter 11

THE ROYAL PRINCE Hotel appeared to be some architect's wistful attempt at imitating the Aztec Temples of Mexico. Although not entirely successful from an archaeological standpoint, the hotel did offer an interesting and luxurious blend of twentieth-century comfort. The building, a good twenty five stories high, was hollow in the center. Four interior walls, fronted by shops on the lower floors and guestroom balconies on the upper floors, met to form a quadrangle which, when viewed from a seat in the middle of the lobby, was capped by the sky. The balconies were full with flowers and plants, creating the effect of cascading gardens.

Walking through the lobby to the ocean side of the structure brought guests to a tropical forest complete with marked trails leading to the beach, shower facilities, several restaurants, a nightclub and a few romantic hideaways suitable for late night fondling. Interwoven amid the entire maze-like layout were canals that reached like the tentacles of an octopus in all directions, some disappearing into the flora. Their source was the biggest pool Ian and Spook had ever seen.

The pool had no particular shape. It seemed to flow with the natural landscape, curving around trees, becoming shallow near clear patches in the brush, and deepening towards the center. Sitting in the middle was a small mountain about twenty feet high connected to land by a two-person footbridge. Water fell from the top in several directions, one path being a sliding board that dumped its occupants into the pool. In two other areas, the water splashed over irregularly shaped rocks to create a steady, therapeutic wash of sound. The place reminded Ian of a giant miniature golf course for people with money.

As the two moved around to the other side of the pool, the final dazzler in the fantasy lagoon came into view. One whole side of the mountain had been hollowed out at the bottom creating a large cave both under and above the water. The flow of the mountain water had been diverted to create a waterfall over half of the cave opening, the other half was dry. Inside the cave, Ian could see a busboy, dressed in a white shirt and black pants, busily stocking a bar. The bar itself formed the pool wall with the top of the bar a good foot above the water level.

"Look. Stools under the water," he said, pointing.

"Izat crazy or what?" Spook hollered. "Man, I could handle that on a hot day. Jump in the pool to cool off, then swim through the waterfall and plop my ass on a barstool without gettin' out of the pool. They'd find me floatin' in the lagoon all the time." He started laughing and leaned back waving his arms and rolling his eyes.

Ian spotted a white-jacketed young man with a tub of dirty dishes.

"Excuse me, is there anything special going on tonight for dinner, you know, Mexican Night or anything?"

The guy looked at Ian with a 'don't worry, I've heard dumber questions from guests' expression and said, "Buffet. At the Beach Grill, Señor. But you need a reservation. Do you have one?"

Despite the expression on his face, his tone came off respectful, even helpful.

"No, we don't," Ian said, trying to sound disappointed. "What's that buffet like?"

"Oh, it's fantastic. Everything you can thing of: fish, shrimp, steak, chicken, ribs, all cooked on open flame grills. Beer and wine is included," he added.

Ian turned and looked at Spook knowing his eyes and mouth were probably wide open. They were, and Ian tried hard not to laugh out loud.

"Hey, yo, Spook! You wanna stop slobbering around the pool. Somebody's liable to walk in that."

"Ian, man, we gotta do something."

Ian turned back to the man who seemed to be anticipating Ian's next move. Ian reached into his left pocket and left it there.

"Listen, with all the stuff going on around here we didn't know about the buffet and reservations thing. But I bet you probably have enough clout to put in some last minute reservations. In fact, I'd bet ten bucks on it."

"You'd probably win," the man said, smiling. "One minute, Señores."

He disappeared with the tub of dishes and reappeared without them in about thirty seconds. In that time, Ian managed to pull a ten out of his American money. Manny had told him earlier that day that American money had more weight than Mexican currency.

"Would you like to place that bet now, Señor?" the busboy said.

Ian laughed and said, "You'll handle the wager for me, I trust?"

Ian discreetly handed the boy the ten.

"That is true, Señor. Come this way."

He turned and headed through the jungle. As they twisted and turned their way along the softly lit trail, Ian's senses were peaking. He could hear ocean waves somewhere in the direction they were headed, and traditional Mexican music produced by several guitars. Overlaid on the sounds was the maddening and ever increasing smell of food.

Grilled, open flame, seared grease, spitting like a charcoal broiled pigfest, he thought, definitely nearby.

Something about this wandering through the jungle was having a disorienting, drug-like effect on him. For some reason the faces of the Boss Bandito and the Fat Man flashed through Ian's mind, mixing with the leafy greens around him. He had no idea why but he had a panicky feeling, like driving at night in a strange part of town. He couldn't get his bearings. Finally he forced himself to stop abruptly in the middle of the trail. Spook plowed into the back of him like a Three Stooges gag. Ian sensed the strange stupor was not limited to him.

"What, are you on drugs or something?" Ian said, feigning serious.

"Well, whatcha stop so fast for?"

Spook rubbed his head like a sleepwalking child.

"Señors, right this way."

The man was standing about ten feet in front of them pointing beyond the turn in the trail, a smile suppressed beneath his professional politeness.

"Does this mean we're here, finally?" Spook said.

The music and the waves were much louder now. As they stepped even with their guide a huge porch appeared. A railing ran all the way around its wide rectangular girth, with a huge thatched roof covering the entire structure. They could see a large bar and the flames from the grills over to the right. The whole thing sat on the beach, about three feet above the sand, with the ocean only fifty yards away. Ian guessed sixty or so people were already on the porch, some obviously returning from their first assault on the buffet, their plates overflowing. The man waved to a woman standing by the front of the porch. She nodded and smiled.

"The hostess will take care of you. Enjoy yourselves."

He gave a quick, head bow and disappeared into the jungle.

"Wow, things do happen rather strangely here in Oz, don't they?" Spook said.

Ian was still trying to shake off the drugged feeling of the jungle. The woman motioned them forward, smiling and nodding the whole time. They stepped onto the porch and followed her across its complete depth to a large table in the corner of the structure.

The penalty for having no reservation was to be placed at the absolute farthest point from the bar and the buffet, but the consolation was the view. The ocean waves rolled softly in front of them with nothing in between but beach. If Ian reached to either his left or right he could drop his food on the sand.

"Man, is this fabulous or what?" Spook said. "Look at that view."

Ian turned to see about a dozen people on the beach, several of whom were females wearing the latest in minimalist beach wear.

"Ah, the beach, ey lad?" Ian said, with an exaggerated sigh.

⁂ ⁂ ⁂

The white car pulled quickly onto the highway despite the steady traffic. The dark-faced man behind the wheel gave the other cars no more consideration than he had given Ian and Spook when they had turned back to look at the cause of their near collision. The man drove purposefully at moderate speed, never losing pace with the Thing just a few cars ahead. When his target turned at the entrance to the Prince he slid his car to the side of the road and stopped. An hour later it moved slowly up the driveway.

chapter 12

WAITING FOR THE waiter's permission to attack the buffet, Spook and Ian had already finished a pitcher of wine. Ian leaned back in his seat, feeling the wine roll across him like the waves across the beach. He looked out across the wide scape of the ocean, saturated by all that he could take in at a glance, then noticed without effort several shapes moving in the foreground of his postcard. Three women, having drained the sun of its usefulness for the day, stood up and began shaking out their towels and beach bags. One of them was shorter than the other two, her bathing suit much more modest than those Ian had witnessed as acceptable beach wear in Acapulco. The other two, although not overly tall, were longer and leaner, one of them strikingly more noticeable because she seemed to be fulfilling the original intent of her bikini. With what little light was left behind the group, making out their faces was difficult, but each turn they made left or right provided Ian with an outstanding array of silhouettes against the darkening backdrop of sky.

This is all just vacation fantasy, he thought, dreamily, and that girl was shaped by the gods. Reality's gonna kick in any minute. When they walk by here they'll have warts and missing teeth, two heads, boils on their necks.

The female trio starting walking towards the porch. Ian could now see their faces and they were friendly, attractive faces. The wine had him on a roll.

"Tropical breezes, ocean sunsets, wine, and a bikinied love goddess." Ian caught Spook's attention and led him to the approaching ladies, then narrated while Spook grinned. "I mean that's what all this scenery is here for, Spook. Scene 3. Sunset, crashing waves. Cut to poolside. She lays there, her tropical tan glistening in the sun. I wave from the high dive. 'Oh,' she gasps, 'my hero.' Big dive. Crowd applauds. I swim underwater and surface at poolside in front of her. She leans down exposing incredible cleavage and kisses me passionately. Cut to the balcony. I'm bare-chested in loose, white cotton pants. She's behind me, her arms tight around my waist, thoroughly sated, and wanting more. Cut. Print. That's a wrap. Get on the plane and go back to reality." He looked at Spook again and announced, "Well, I'm having fun."

Spook looked at him to reply just as Ian made his move. The three ladies had reached the deck, continuing on a path that ran alongside it.

"Excuse me," Ian said, standing up and leaning over the rail. His head spun momentarily. "Are you staying at this hotel?"

The women all stopped and looked up. They appeared about the same age, maybe younger, Ian thought, maybe the same. One of the taller ones, a brown haired girl with big round eyes, answered with a smile.

"Yes, we are."

She seemed unsure of why a stranger was asking her this question but not concerned by it.

"Do you know if you have to be a guest to do things here like eat or swim?"

Now she looked at the other two quickly, then turned back and said, "I'm not really sure. Why?"

The other two were beginning to look distrustful. Ian lowered his voice and leaned further over the rail.

"You see we're not staying here. But we came to check it out because we'd heard so much about it and we got here and were starving." They were still listening and it made Ian even more bold. "And we managed to get into this buffet, which by the way looks like heaven. Anyway, do you think they'll ask us for a room key or number or something? Like do you pay cash for your meals or just sign for everything?"

As he explained, the expressions on the women's faces relaxed and turned to grins. This was like some college prank and they were amused.

The brown hair girl said, "Well, we've been signing for everything, but that doesn't mean you can't pay cash. We're really not sure."

Her eyes looked nice to Ian and full of genuine sorrow that she couldn't help; or maybe the wine did it. He wasn't sure and it didn't matter.

"Are you all planning to eat?"

"We were going to eat here," the shorter one said, folding her arms and raising her eyes at the third person in the party, a black haired girl with amazingly white teeth, "but somebody forgot to make the reservations."

"Well, look, that's perfect," Ian answered, quickly, sensing opportunity like a salesmen. "We managed to get in with some help from one of the waiters. There's plenty of room. We'll just say you're with us. And then if they need a room number or key, you've got it covered. And look," Ian put on a good little boy face, "we have money and we don't eat with our fingers or anything like that. Whatta ya think?"

The three all turned and looked at one another simultaneously and the shorter one said, "It sounds good to me. This is where we wanted to eat anyway, remember? Beer and wine included?"

The white toothed girl said, "Sounds good to me."

"All right," the big eyes girl said. "It's a deal."

"Great. Now look, we're starved to the point of danger. If you don't want us to sit and watch you eat, you'd better hurry. No fancy clothes or make-up. Y'all look great just the way you are."

He put a big 'now don't that sound great' smile at the end of the sentence.

"See ya in fifteen," Brown Hair said, with a friendly look and the three of them headed into the jungle.

Ian turned around and sat back down. Spook had a smile on his face.

"You are amazing sometimes," Spook said. "You never lose your sales smooth, do ya?"

"What smooth?" Ian said, laughing. "I wasn't using any smooth. It was an honest invitation for a lot of practical reasons. They're a nice bunch of young ladies and they seemed like they'd be a lot of fun. And now we don't have to worry about being guests or not. What? Bad idea?"

"No, no, great idea," Spook answered. "I just figured you'd be busy right now. Mentally, I mean."

"You're right, which is another reason I stopped them. You want to talk about my dive for the rest of the trip?"

"Hell, I get it," Spook said. "I'd much rather look at them than you."

Their new acquaintances arrived in the promised time looking fresh and still friendly. The hostess led them back to the table and said, not in an unfriendly way, "I thought there were just two in the party?"

"Well, we didn't know if they were going to be ready on time or not. Out shopping all day, you know."

Ian was having fun now, the wine softening any rough edges left in his mind. He looked at Brown Hair with a silly smile.

"Hi honey, I'm glad you got back in time. I missed you. We're just getting ready to go up for food. Grab some wine and we'll all go together."

It worked. The hostess looked uncomfortable and walked back to her post at the front of the porch.

There were two chairs on the restaurant side of the table. Spook was in one and moved to the bench on Ian's side. Brown Hair sat down in the chair Spook vacated, Shorty grabbed the other and White Teeth, being the last to make a move, sat down on the bench next to Spook.

"Are you as crazy as this one?" Brown Hair said to Spook.

Spook wagged his head and Ian answered for him.

"I'm really impressed. I really didn't think you all could get back here this fast."

"Neither did I," Shorty said, sounding a little flustered. "But the Sarge here," she tossed her head towards Brown Hair, "kept whipping us to keep moving."

"I didn't whip anybody, I just didn't let you stop moving." She looked at Ian. "I didn't realize till I got out of the shower how hungry I am. I'm starving."

"Then let's eat," Ian said, and motioned for Spook to move. "Oh wait," he said, just as everyone began moving, "in case we get separated or lost at the food table, this is Spook and I'm Ian."

"And I'm Robyn," Brown Hair said, then gestured toward White Teeth. "That's Donna," the teeth flashed, "and Kim." Shorty smiled.

"And we're the hungry family folks," Spook mocked. "Let's eat."

chapter 13

IAN FELT GOOD. And it seemed everybody else did. The wine and beer were coming in pitchers and going just as quickly as they came. He could still feel the sore spot on his arm from the near-accident coming down from the shrine but it was faint, nothing more than a reminder that something had happened.

The food was outstanding, all of it having a fresh, open-grill flavor. There had been little talk during the first ten minutes after the group returned to the table with their first rations. Everyone seemed comfortable enough, or hungry enough, to forgo the usual small talk until after the first round. Then Brown Hair, Robyn, put down her fork and sat back in her chair, snatching a glass of wine from the table as she did.

"So where are you guys from?"

Spook looked up to see if Ian would answer and saw he had a mouth full of food.

"Philadelphia," Spook said.

"No kidding," Robyn said. "Well, we shouldn't like you guys. We're from Pittsburgh. The Steelers and the Eagles never did get along. Or the Pirates and Phillies."

Ian swallowed quickly.

"Where at in Pittsburgh do you live? I go up there on business almost every month."

Ian wasn't surprised when she said Pittsburgh. In the little conversation they had, he could pick up a slight accent, but not enough to nail down.

"Do you know where Bellvue is?" she asked.

"Yes, ma'm. Where the money is. I used to drive through and practice my envy."

"Oh, right," she said, ignoring the jab.

"So what do you do up there in Pittsburgh?" Spook said, looking at his plate as he said it and then at Kim.

"We go to school at Pitt University," Kim answered, as if she'd been asked her social security number. "But we'll all be finished in May."

"Hey, that's great," Spook said. "You must feel good bein' that close to gettin' your degree."

Kim's face noticeably softened.

"It does feel kind of nice to think about graduating and getting out of school. I feel like I've been going forever. Graduate school has really worn me out," she added.

"You're finishing your Master's?" Ian said, impressed. "In what?"

"Mine is in clinical psychology," Kim said, modestly. "So is Donna's. Robyn's is in organizational psychology. They overlap in a lot of areas so we've all been together in school for a while."

"Organizational psychology, huh?" Ian said with a smirk. "Remind me to discuss my company with you later." He nodded at Robyn. "Some great material for a thesis there."

"Oh really?" Robyn said. "What company?" She seemed politely interested.

"Cook International," Ian said. He realized it came out almost proud, but why, he had no idea.

Both Robyn's and Donna's eyes opened wide.

"Oh, I know about Cook International," Robyn said, reverently. "Jacob Aloysius Cook. The man's a legend."

Ian was momentarily stunned at the reaction, but tried to downplay it. He was just trying to make conversation and the last thing he wanted was to end up sitting in Acapulco talking about work.

"Is that so?" he said, glibly.

"He was a case study in one of my courses," Robyn continued, now looking excited.

"He's definitely worth studying," Ian said, his tone sarcastic.

"Actually this vacation is a combination early celebration and back-off-the-pressure week," Kim said. "A great idea by Donna." Donna immediately put her head down as a bashful smile showed. "She's been here before and convinced us we would love it. Boy, was she right."

"That's for sure," Robyn seconded. "The beach and this wine are doing the job." She closed her eyes and shook her head.

"Yes ma'm," Ian sighed, work already gone from his mind. "I've definitely been backing some pressure off this week. Which reminds me. I see an empty beer and wine pitcher. Let me outta here, Spook, before they run out."

Ian hooked the two pitchers with one hand and started weaving his way through the tables to the bar at the far end of the room.

"Ian's not taking any prisoners at that bar tonight, is he?" Robyn said to Spook.

"Well, for all the pressure he tried to leave back home, he's added on some new stuff here," Spook answered, sounding slightly cryptic.

"Does he have trouble relaxing or are you guys just having a lousy time?"

Spook hesitated imperceptibly then said, "Have you been to the cliffs yet, to see the divers?"

The conversation did not interrupt his movements as food continued to disappear into his face.

"No," Robyn answered, not sure if he was changing the subject, "not yet. We were thinking about going."

"Well, Ian's planning to dive those cliffs tomorrow."

"Wow," Kim said, her face widening. "I'll bet it's on his mind. Why does he want to do that?"

"Do me a favor, okay?" Spook answered, grimacing. "Don't mention it unless he brings it up."

"Don't worry, we won't say anything," Robyn said, turning to Kim. "Will we, Kim?"

"I won't say anything."

Ian worked his way back to the table and set the two pitchers down without sitting.

"Yo, Donna," Ian said, in his South Philly voice. "Keep it down will ya. All you do is tauwk."

Donna's white teeth appeared followed by as visible a blush as was possible on her sunburned face.

"I'll be right back," he said and headed for the food. He was back in three minutes.

"Another plate of food?" Kim said, with a look of amazement on her face.

"Well, actually this one's not for me."

The plate was piled high, too high, with just about every main dish from the buffet.

"I have to figure a way to smuggle this out of here to the parking lot," he said, dropping his voice to a whisper. "You see, we have this young fella with us, he's our guide."

Ian was having trouble holding on to too many ideas at once. He was trying to think of an uncomplicated way to explain why Manny wasn't with them. One came to him.

"But he's real professional and refuses to come in with us. Wants to guard the car, you know, professional ethics and all." Boy that sounded shabby. "So I want to take him out some food."

"Why don't you just hop the railing and follow the trail back?" Robyn said.

Ian looked at the rail, then the front of the porch. Probably no one would see him hop the rail.

"But I'd still have to get past the front of the restaurant to get on the trail, which at this point I'd probably get lost and fall in one of the canals."

"No, not here," Robyn said. "There's another trail about fifty feet that way." She pointed up the beach. "It goes straight through to the main pool. Just hop over, walk up the beach where it's dark, and then turn left when you get to the trail."

"All right, that could work. Here." He put the plate in front of Spook. "Hand this to me after I get over."

Ian backed up to the rail at the end of the bench where Donna was sitting and sat on it. He looked up towards the front of the porch where the hostess was standing. She seemed very far away. Ian quickly swung his legs to the left, clearing the rail and dismounting all in one movement, landing feet first in the sand with his right hand still on the rail. He stood motionless for about five seconds, waiting for his head to catch up to his body.

He wobbled a bit, then heard Spook say, "Here you go," and the plate of food came over the railing.

"Be back in five minutes," Ian said looking up, a silly grin on his face. "Save me some wine."

He heard Spook laugh as he headed into the darkness.

chapter 14

IAN HUSTLED UP the beach trying to walk as quickly as he could in the soft sand without dumping the food. Robyn had laid a cloth napkin over the top so Ian could hold everything, but it still took some doing to keep it on the plate. The wine didn't help with his balance, but he was having fun.

"Don't drop it ya dumbshit," Ian muttered. "Hey, Manny, how'd ya like a nice piece a gritty chicken, ha? Like them sandy hot dogs I used to eat at the beach. Oh, Mom, please buy me a hot dog. Okay, but don't drop it. Boom right in the sand. I told ya not to drop it, now pick it up and wipe it off. Yeah, right Mom. Wipe it off. Ya never get it all off. Gritty friggin' pumice dogs. Take the enamel right off your teeth."

He giggled and looked up the beach. The trail appeared and Ian turned left, pleased to find that he could see a good fifty yards ahead in a straight line. He quick-stepped the distance, still balancing the small feast, and came to a bend. He veered right and then left, exiting the jungle at the pool and heading to the base of the hotel knowing it would bring him to the parking lot. If anyone had taken note of this slightly sloppy American with a plate of God knows what, Ian hadn't noticed. The outer edge of his vision was a wash. He had enough presence of mind to avoid the lobby and instead walked around the right side of the hotel, keeping outdoors. When he got to the front of the building he was at the parking lot, but at the other end, considerably above where he had parked the car.

Ian walked out past the first row of cars, turned left and headed for where he figured the car to be, straining to see in the dimly lit lot. At first he thought he could see someone standing along the row further down, but his eyeballs were bouncing in and out of focus.

Then he saw the figure again. It was the back of a man standing between two parked cars. The man was moving around so that more of him was becoming visible.

He looks like he's trying to get a dog or something out of a car, Ian thought, like it's being too frisky for him. He could hear the man talking, no, growling in Spanish.

Then it hit him all at once, like walking into a low ceiling. That's the Thing! He's in our car. HE'S GOT A HOLD OF MANNY!

"HEY! WHAT'RE YOU DOING? LEAVE HIM ALONE!"

Ian dropped the plate and broke into a run all in one movement. The adrenaline pumped through his system in one big shot, like an injection from a hypodermic, and the fog around his brain vanished. It all came together in his mind. By the time he reached the car he'd be in a dead, high speed run.

Arms up, chest high, put the head down and ring his fuckin' bell. I'm gonna hit that son of a bitch full square and snap his friggin' neck. The hospital will swear this guy was hit by a truck.

But the second Ian yelled and broke into the run the man turned and saw him coming. He hadn't planned on a confrontation and ran immediately to the front of the car and down the lot. Ian knew he'd have no chance of catching him if he didn't move over to the next row, but he'd never make the turn at this speed. He picked his spot, about four more cars down, slowed just a hair at the last second, then planted his left foot like a running back feinting left to cut right. He made the cut, but the momentum was too great and he slammed thigh-first, then shoulder, into the side of a car. He tried to bounce off and keep his footing but hit the other car on his right. When he cleared the two cars and turned left again a white car pulled wildly out of the lot and roared up the driveway. Ian kept running till he reached the Thing.

"Manny, you okay, y'all right?"

The words puffed out with what little wind Ian had left in his lungs, then he started breathing hard to get his air supply back. Manny was crouched on the back seat with his back to Ian, rubbing his head and neck at the same time. He didn't answer at first.

"Are ya okay buddy? What happened?"

Manny still didn't turn around but answered this time in a whispery attempt to sound composed.

"I'm okay, Señor Een. Eet's all right. Just a bahd mahn."

Something in his voice was untrue. Ian reached down slowly and put his hand gently on Manny's back. When he did, the boy turned and looked up at him, and Ian saw for the first time that day the face of a little boy; a frightened and defenseless little boy, with none of the street savvy that had amazed and impressed all day long. Manny's eyes began to fill, a visible struggle taking place between his fear and his discomfort. This was not Manny the Hustler. This was little Manuel Arroyo, twelve years old, who should have been home and asleep in his jammies under his NFL comforter, with his night light on. Ian put his arms out to pull the boy towards him, and Manny reached around his waist with both arms, burying his head in Ian's stomach.

"Hey, it's okay, buddy," Ian said, fighting the emotion in his own throat. "You're all right."

Ian stroked his head as the boy sobbed and shook. Spanish words were coming from the sobs, but Ian couldn't understand them.

"Manny, English," Ian whispered. "Tell me in English."

"He he he he was try try trying to kiiiiiihhhillll me."

The word kill poured out of him in a way that demonstrated incomprehension at such a thing happening to him.

"He he choke me and pull my hair."

"Sshhhhh, it's okay. Just take it easy. We'll talk later. You just calm down for now. You're all right, I gotcha buddy."

As upset for Manny as he was, Ian was amazed at the rage churning inside him. He couldn't understand, holding this boy and remembering the look on his face, how a human being could do this to a child. Nowhere in the black box of anger that Ian kept locked up inside could he find the ingredients to do something like this. But he also knew that right now, this very moment, he could empty the box with insane pleasure on that son of a bitch that got away.

Ian pushed hard and forced the box shut. He took Manny's head between his hands and pulled him back from his stomach.

"Lemme see now, he didn't hit you or anything, did he?"

Ian scanned the boy's face. Other than tears, his face seemed clear. But he could see finger marks on Manny's neck as he raised his head.

"No. He grab me from behind by my hair and then he put hees other hand around my neck."

"What did he want? What'd he say?" Ian asked slowly.

"He ask me your names and what you are doing here. He ask me what you say about Señor Wheelson."

"Who?" Ian said.

"Señor Wheelson."

"Wheelson?" Ian said, wanting to be sure with Manny's accent.

"Yes, Wheelson."

"Wilson," Ian said, getting it. Then, "Wilson," again, out loud, rolling the name around in his mind. He shook his head. "I don't know any Wilson. Was this guy who grabbed you some kind of policeman or hotel security guard do you think?"

"No, Señor Een. He was a bahd mahn. Very bahd." Fear shot across Manny's face again.

"Okay, come on. Let's go and get the others and get you something to eat. I think most of your dinner's all over the parking lot."

Ian lifted Manny out of the car and set him down, then put his arm around his shoulder. As soon as he stepped toward the hotel, Ian thought of Manny's reluctance to enter the hotel when they first arrived. He didn't want to upset the boy more.

"Look, let's go the way I came out so I can pick up the plate I dropped. Somebody might run over it, you know."

They headed back to the far end of the lot. Ian could see where the plate and food had landed, all in one place. The plate had broken but most of the food had stayed on top, keeping the broken plate pieces from flying away. The rest of the food had toppled to one side with the cloth handkerchief still laying on it. Ian picked out the broken plate pieces and piled them on the handkerchief.

"We'll leave the food for the birds, all right?" he said smiling softly to Manny.

Manny nodded.

When they got to the pool, Spook and the three women were sitting on benches looking at the waterfall.

"It's about time," Spook said, then seemed to notice something in Ian's and Manny's faces.

"What's up? Everything all right?"

"No," Ian said tersely. "Some creep grabbed a hold of Manny out in the car and started asking him questions about us and choking him. Shook him up pretty bad."

They all looked at Manny, who by now had composed himself pretty well. But he still wasn't Manny the Hustler. He seemed shy. Spook looked confused.

"Hey, Manny, y'all right, man?"

"Yes, Señor Spook, I'm okay. Señor Een scared thee man away."

"Manny, these are some friends we met tonight," Ian said, gesturing to the others. "This is Robyn, Kim, and Donna. This is Manny."

"Hi, Manny," Robyn said. "It's nice to meet you. Gee, I hope you're okay. God, he's cute."

"Yo Mannee," Spook said with a big smile. "Cute, huh?"

"How come you guys are here?" Ian asked.

"We thought you'd be back sooner, so since we were all full, we figured we'd walk it off a little and meet you here," Kim explained.

"Well, we gotta get this boy something to eat. I had to drop his food when I took off after the creep."

"Wait here a minute," Robyn said. "I'll be right back."

She turned and shot off into the jungle before Ian had a chance to say anything. Donna and Kim fussed around Manny, obviously as taken with him as he and Spook were. They sat on a bench talking to him and Ian could see some calmness return to his face. Ten minutes later Robyn appeared with a covered plate.

"That hostess is such a nice lady," she said, with a wide smile. "Gave me a cover and silverware too. Come on. We'll take it up to our room and Manny can sit down and eat it comfortably."

Ian hadn't expected that.

"Are you sure?"

"Sure I'm sure," Robyn answered cheerfully. "This little guy's gotta take it easy for a while and try and enjoy his dinner." She looked at Manny and smiled.

Kim stood up, grabbed the boy's hand and said, "Come on, Manny. You like TV?"

"Ah,…yes, Señorita."

He looked up at Ian, totally confused at this point. It made sense to Ian.

"Well that's nice. Thank you," Ian said. He looked back at Manny and nodded encouragingly.

The room was on the fifth floor, and when Ian entered, the first thing he saw was the view through the sliding glass doors. The ocean sat calmly out beyond the balcony railing, glowing eerily from the light of an unseen moon. As he reached the doors and stepped out onto the balcony, the top of the jungle came into view, blanketing the ground from where Ian stood to the ocean. Closer to the building, the lagoons from the pool were visible, snaking their way through the jungle like powder-blue arteries. Lights dotted the entire layout, sparkling through the dark green.

"It's like looking down on a fantasy world, like it isn't real," Ian said to Robyn, who had stepped out onto the balcony after him.

"Yes, it's beautiful isn't it? It's gorgeous during the day too, and at sunset. The first night we were here we just sat on the balcony from about six o'clock to nine-thirty. We were hypnotized. This view is worth the price of the room."

"Manny's all right," Spook said, coming out the glass door. "He just about wiped out that plate of food already. Man, that boy can chow. Look at this view," he added, without taking a breath.

"That's good," Ian said. He lowered his voice. "He was really upset, just like a scared little boy, not like the Hustler, you know. I wish I would've caught that guy."

The padlock on the box rattled.

"What'd you say the guy wanted?" Spook said.

"Manny said the guy was asking him who we were and about some guy Wilson. You know a Wilson, Spook?"

"Nope," Spook said.

"This bothers me," Ian said, shaking his head. "I mean, it's one thing if Manny's the victim of some random mugging. But it sounds like he gets grabbed because he's with us."

"Maybe the guy thought there was stuff in the car and just wanted to get it," Robyn offered.

"That's possible, but still he should have seen the car was empty as soon as he got to it. I mean it's wide open, no roof, no locks. I don't know." Ian paused, disgusted. "I'd like to ask Manny more about what happened but I don't want to get him upset."

"I guess you really need this tonight, huh?" Robyn said, and then immediately realized her mistake and looked away.

Ian looked at her, not sure he had understood, and then understood. He looked at Spook, who already had his head down and his shoulders hunched.

"It just sorta came up in conversation," Spook said, wincing. "I'm gonna check on Manny."

He slipped through the sliding door quickly.

"No, we bugged it out of him," Robyn said.

"Ah, it's all right. Actually, all this has taken my mind off it for a while so what the hell."

"Well, I think it's pretty neat," Robyn said.

When she said it, Ian saw her face a little more sharply. Considering the wine, dinner and the incident in the parking lot, it was actually the first time he'd really looked at her with clear eyes. It was a very nice face; sharp lines at her chin and cheeks but roundness near the eyes. Her nose was thin but slightly crooked, perhaps the result of a break when she was young. It wasn't noticeable at first but something that emerged as Ian studied her. He liked it. Her brown hair, though straight, was very full and cut short and pushed to one side revealing a slender neck.

"Yeah? Not nuts?"

"Well, maybe for some people. Definitely for me. But I get the feeling you know what you're doing."

"I'll take that as a compliment. Thank you very much."

Ian held the thought for another few seconds then dropped it.

"Anyway, it's getting late and I'm concerned about what we're going to do with Manny. He never said anything about what time he goes home, or if he has a home." He leaned in toward the glass door. "Hey, Spook."

Spook appeared at the glass.

"Do you think anybody's waiting for Manny to show up?"

"He said something earlier about dropping him off somewhere near our hotel, like on the Costera," Spook said, "but we can't leave him out there now. It's late."

Ian nodded his head in agreement.

"No way, especially after what happened. Unless he gives us someplace to take him like a house or relative, we'll take him with us in the hotel."

"Sounds good," Spook said.

"That's some neat kid," Kim whispered as she and Donna stepped out onto the balcony.

"Yeah, he is," Ian said. "How's he doing?"

"Just fine," Kim said. "He put that food away in no time. Then we were just talking. You know he does this guide thing all the time? I said, 'Don't you go to school?' He said he does but there's no school now and even when there is his work is important."

"Did he say anything about his family expecting him home or anything?"

"Yeah, well that's what I said," Kim continued. "I said, 'Won't they be worried about you not being home this late,' and he says no, that if he has work sometimes he won't go home till very late. Can you imagine a twelve year old boy being away from home at night to earn a living? He's something, and he's so polite and...and...."

"Professional," Spook finished.

"Is that what it is?" Kim said.

"Yep," Ian answered. "He has his own set of rules and standards and he takes them very seriously. The only reason he's in this hotel right now is because he was real shook up by that guy. Otherwise he feels that it's not his place to be here."

"That's amazing," Robyn said.

"Anyway, we should get going; big day tomorrow, right Spook?" Ian gave Spook a big-eyed look. "Get a good look at this view for a minute. I'll talk to Manny."

Ian went inside and crossed the room to the two queen size beds. Manny was on the far bed, curled up in a fetal position. The only light in the room was from the TV in the corner which washed the beds in flickering gray.

"Hey buddy, how ya feeling now, a little better?"

Ian walked around the bed, past the TV, and up the side of the bed before he realized that the boy was sound asleep. Ian crouched down next to the bed.

"Manny," he whispered, to see if he'd just dozed off. "You asleep?"

The boy didn't flinch. He was in a deep sleep. All that excitement, plus it's been a long day, Ian thought. He looked up and saw Robyn at the bottom of the bed.

"He's sound asleep, wiped out."

Ian stood up and walked back towards the balcony following Robyn.

"Hey, he's out you guys, tapped. I'll carry him to the car."

"Why don't you leave him here?" Robyn said, right away. "He's so beat, and he's comfortable in the bed. Don't wake him."

"Yeah," Kim said. "He doesn't take up any room. He'll be fine here."

Ian hadn't expected these strangers to be so generous, and yet it didn't surprise him. Something about them, their faces when he'd stopped them back at the beach.

"But he's going with us tomorrow to the cliffs," Ian said.

"We can work that out," Robyn said. "We were planning to go see the divers this week anyway. Tomorrow's as good a day as any, plus," she smiled, "we'll know one of the divers. We can take pictures and show our grandchildren someday." It was a pleasant tease. "What time should we be there?"

Ian looked around at everyone and saw agreement on their faces. He double checked Spook who gave him a makes-sense shrug.

"You're sure?"

"Absolutely," Robyn said.

"All right, but I'll tell you what. Why don't you meet us at our hotel for coffee about nine-thirty? El Casa Grande. Manny knows the hotel, and it's on the way to the cliffs. This way I get a chance to make sure he's all right. By the time I get to the cliffs I'll have other things on my mind."

"Okay, that sounds good," Robyn said. "Coffee at nine-thirty, your place."

"Let me just check on him."

Ian went back to the bed. Manny was definitely out. More importantly, he looked peaceful, unafraid. Ian felt like he should cover him but the room was warm. Instead he just touched his head lightly then moved towards the door.

"We really appreciate this, I mean the whole night was a lot of fun. You're very nice people. You're probably sorry you met us."

"Don't be silly," Robyn said. "You're nice guys and we had fun tonight too. And we're glad we could help. Now tomorrow, you'll make your dive and we'll get to see it and we'll all have some more fun. Go get some sleep and don't worry about Manny. Okay?"

She smiled a nice, reassuring smile.

"Okay," he said. "See you tomorrow. Listen, Donna? Don't be up talkin' all night now, ya hear?"

Ian couldn't see her blush in the dim light but the white teeth were clearly visible. A minute later, in the elevator, Ian felt the weakness in his legs as the car dropped.

"Man, I'm beat," he said.

"Hear hear," Spook added. "They're really nice, aren't they?"

"Yes, they are," Ian said, his mind wandering.

The elevator doors opened and they stepped out into the lobby.

"You got the keys?" Ian asked, struggling to remember their arrival a few long hours ago.

"I do," Spook said, pulling the keys from his pocket.

"Good," Ian said, flopping into the front seat of the Thing. "Get us home without any more excitement. Please."

chapter 15

HEAT COMING THROUGH the glass doors of the balcony woke Ian. Despite the air-conditioning and closed drapes, the intensity of the morning sun cooked the air in the room. Ian's first sensation was perspiration on his forehead, then light, a bright flash striking his eye as his head moved. He turned his head away and opened one eye. A gap in the overlapped drapes formed the laser beam that angled straight down at his pillow like the sight on a rifle. The next thought in his mind was the cliffs, and then slowly, like liquid wax hardening into some shape, a collage of scenes, all vivid and all meaningless except for the effect each had on him; the blood on the side of the diver's head; the cold stare of the man at the bottom of the hill; the man running from him in the parking lot; Manny's scared face looking up at him.

A chill shot up his spine and he shuddered. Then just as quickly he told himself to shake it off, to forget it. No dreams, no omens, nothing was going to stop him. There was no room today for unfinished thoughts, second guesses or doubt. He had to bury it!

Besides, he felt good, well rested. Despite the blurry, shapeless thing in the back of his mind that was the dive, he felt strong and sharp. Spook was still asleep. Ian looked at his watch and was surprised to see it was only seven-thirty. He slid open the glass door and stepped onto the balcony. Even with the heat of the sun, the air was still cool. Cool by Mexican standards, he thought. Deadly quiet. And then his mind started questioning.

What am I doing today? Why am I doing it? Look out there. It's beautiful, peaceful. You're here enjoying it. What if you really get hurt today, permanent damage, paralyzed or something? Or die? For what? To prove a point, or something to yourself? Lose weight or quit drinking or never eat red meat for God's sake, like normal people. Why do I need to face death to get myself together?

But he knew the downhill roll had started. There was no turning back, at least not till he reached the cliffs. He could get up there and call it off, and that wouldn't surprise him. Maybe no one else. But he couldn't call it here. He'd have nowhere to hide.

⁂

The girls and Manny were in the coffee shop when Ian and Spook walked in.

"Good morning," Robyn said, cheerfully. "You guys look like you had a good night's sleep."

"I feel good," Spook said.

"Good morning," Ian said.

He looked at Robyn and the others quickly. They looked nice, nice in the sense that they weren't shockingly different from the night before. Ian did not see them last night as clearly as he saw them now but there wasn't much difference today. They had sharper lines in their faces and clearer colors on their skin and clothes but they looked…well, nice. Real. They hadn't lost any of their friendly look or their...authenticity? Manny looked a little embarrassed.

"How you doing there, Manny? Taking care of our friends?"

"Señor Een, may I speak to you a moment?" Manny said, looking oh-so-serious.

Ian could tell what was coming.

"Certainly, young Manuel," he said, affecting a formal tone. "Excuse us, please," he said to the women and Spook, then looked back at Manny. "Step over to my office."

Ian motioned to another table, then followed Manny to it and sat down.

"Señor Een, I must apologize."

Manny looked so serious Ian didn't know how long he'd be able to let him go on.

"You hired me to stay weeth you, and I fell asleep and did not complete my job. I should not have gone to...."

"Manny, Manny, wait.....listen to me." Ian couldn't let him go any more. "First of all, you don't owe anybody an apology. If anybody should apologize it should be us. That guy last night grabbed you because of us. Why, I don't know, but either way, it wasn't your fault. Second of all, you fell asleep because you were upset and exhausted. We all were. Third, and most importantly, you're not just our guide, you're our friend, our buddy. We look out for each other. We wouldn't let anybody hurt you. Besides, we know you're the best darn guide in Mexico. So don't you worry about last night. Worry about helping me make my dive today. Okay?"

Manny looked hesitant, trying to be sure this didn't alter his standards any. Ian saw the struggle.

"Gimme that Manny the Hustler smile."

That did it. Manny's face went wide as could be, and Ian felt a wave of warmth pass over him.

"Okay," Manny said.

Ian reached over and rubbed his head.

"How do you like those ladies? They take good care of ya?"

"Oh, they are very nice," Manny said, turning professional again. "They take very good care of me."

"Good. Let's get some breakfast."

The two cars arrived at the cliffs at ten-thirty. Unlike yesterday, the hotel and surrounding grounds were pretty empty, the lunch and diving crowd not having arrived. Ian went right to the hotel to find the diving coach, who, as promised, was waiting for him in the restaurant.

The coach was a bearish sort of man, the word *thick* in every attempt Ian made at a description; thick hands and arms bulged from his oversized teeshirt, a thick head of wiry hair on top and a thick mustache that went from one side of his face to the other, like a Mexican Gene Shalit.

He asked Ian if he was ready to do some work and Ian nodded yes. He led him to a door at the back of the hotel, near the cliffs, and directed him to a locker room where he could change. Not knowing the setup at the hotel, Ian had worn his swim suit under his shorts. He threw the shorts and his tee-shirt and sneaks in a locker and went back outside. As they walked towards the cliffs, the ground level dropped off to the right, out of sight of the spectator patio on the left side. Stone steps led them to the water at the back of the canyon and about halfway down, the cliffside became visible to Ian, the long canyon wall running out to the ocean and horizon. The coach explained that he would walk along a ledge that ran to the diving area and Ian would continue down the steps to the water. There he would enter the water and swim along the base of the cliff, meeting the coach at the diving area.

As Ian descended closer to the bottom of the canyon, the air got cooler. Looking down at the water he could see sand and rocks at various levels under the surface. Here at the back of the canyon, the water was surprisingly deep. Ian hoped the same was true of the diving area, at least when it was time to dive. He reached an area of flat rock about three feet from the water's surface and lunged head first, feeling that tingly, dry-body anticipation of the water's temperature just before he hit. The morning sun was just reaching the water, but the water was warm.

He swam hard, feeling the movement of the water push towards him as it headed for the back wall and then ease a little as it swelled and pushed back towards the ocean again, lifting him up and forward. He looked to his right and saw the coach about forty feet ahead, pointing to a spot at the base of the cliff. Ian swam towards it and saw a natural stepping-stone exit from the water. He climbed out and headed towards the coach.

"You ho-k?" the coach said, as Ian reached him.

"Yeah, fine," Ian said, realizing he hadn't actually thought about it.

"Good. Now you make two dives hhere," he said, pointing to a ledge about twenty feet above where they stood.

The coach's accent was also thick, his h's coming from the back of the roof of his mouth.

"Nice, hheeasy. Most im-por-tantay! Poosh!" The coach crouched and shot his hands and arms forward. "Hhere!" He slapped his thighs several times.

Ian nodded his head and moved past him. He climbed easily to the ledge, then turned to put himself in position. As he did he heard a whistle; Spook's. He looked up to the wall across the canyon and saw Spook and the three girls waving. He waved back quickly, then looked down. Except for the surroundings and the fact that some cliffside was visible below him, it didn't seem different from platform diving he'd done into pools. This was about a ten meter dive with no competition and no Degree of Difficulty. Just a straight dive. He set himself, remembered to push, and took off.

He sailed out over the water, the quick rush of air feeling good. He looked down for the cliff base and the water and immediately knew he'd screwed up. He pulled his head back to try and counter the movement but it was too late. He hit the water way past vertical, slapping the backs of his legs as he flipped into the water.

Stupid ass! You want a good look at the scenery? Take it before the dive!

He popped to the surface and slapped the water with his hand. When he climbed back up to the ledge the coach was laughing. He slapped the back of Ian's legs.

"Hhyou get nervous to take a look."

Ian smiled sheepishly, glad to know the coach understood what he did.

"That eez hwy you poosh. To make chure you get out." He flattened his hand, palm down, and shot it out towards the water. "Thain you must hhold eet out long."

He put his arms out on either side to demonstrate the swan position, pulling his arms and head back as far as they would go.

"Baitter you be chort from hheere," he pointed to where Ian was standing, "thain be long from thayre." He pointed to the top of the cliff.

Ian understood clearly. Being short from the low height meant going in shy of vertical, something that, although it might not look pretty, wouldn't do much except make his legs hurt. Going in long from the top meant going past vertical before he reached the water, forcing an unwanted, last second decision; hope you had enough time to tuck, flip over and get in feet first or hold it and hope your back didn't break when you hit.

The point is, STUPID, you can screw it up at thirty feet and walk away. Not at eighty five.

He positioned himself on the ledge again, cleared his mind, and went. This time he stretched the dive, watching the other side of the canyon and holding position till the water appeared. He cut the water a little short, deciding he wanted that little extra when he got to the top. Survival, not perfect scores.

"Looks good," the coach said when he got back to the ledge. "Leetle extra, si, yes?"

"Si, yes," Ian said, smiling.

"Ho k. You look good. Hwone from there," he pointed to a spot a good thirty feet higher, "and then hwee talk. POOSH!" He threw his hands forward.

Ian started climbing. A well-worn and recognizable route was carved out of the cliffside and Ian reached the spot the coach had pointed to in about two minutes. He stood up and turned towards the water.

When he did, he realized that till now it had all been sort of mechanical. But the view here was definitely different. The height at this perch was the beginning of a psychological factor for him. He turned back toward the cliff wall, placing his hand against it and looked up. The top was still a good twenty five feet away but it looked like five times that. If he let his concentration slip, like a tightrope walker looking down instead of straight ahead, he would have a problem. And if he didn't deal with it here, he'd never get to the top. He turned back towards the water and looked down at the coach who was holding his hand up towards Ian, signaling him to wait.

"Thee tide eez good," he hollered. "Juss hwait a moment for thee hwave."

Ian saw the water swell.

"Ho k." the coach said, flapping his hand forward.

Ian looked straight ahead, knowing if he hesitated he might not go, then pushed off. The rush of air was tremendous. He could feel the weight of his body hurtling towards the water. Right when he figured he'd hit the water, he didn't. Then he saw it, and a second later he did.

I must be vertical, he thought, not feeling any smack on the front of his legs. He could feel himself knifing deeper into the water, more than usual. Then he slowed and let his legs drop to begin kicking to the surface. He kicked hard and felt two sharp pains, one immediately after the other. The first was from his foot as it scraped across a rock, shredding the skin on the front of his toes. The second was in his chest as he realized how close his head had just been to that same rock.

chapter 16

IAN PUT HIS foot up on the locker room bench. The coach pulled a can of spray antiseptic out of a first aid kit and began spraying the watery, bloody mess that was Ian's toes. It was a seepy wound, more messy looking than serious. Ian was surprised he still bled from that area having developed scar tissue there from years of tearing his feet up on duraflex diving boards. It was stinging like hell now, and would sting like hell whenever he got it wet for the rest of the day. Tomorrow it would be nothing.

"Hhwen you dive today the tide weel be good. But you mus remaimber thee hheight. Eef you get varteecal," he flattened his hand again and pointed the fingers downward, "you mus fleep when you heet thee water," he curled his fingers toward his palm and made a scooping motion, "to not go so deep. Si?"

"Si."

Ian knew to flip under the water on vertical entry, but the height and the new experience had overloaded him at entry. Once again he reminded himself that his only shot at making the dive was to concentrate on the technical. Analyze it, calculate it, and execute it. Think about the how and you make it. Think about the why and you don't.

"About forty meenutes. You dive hweeth the team at twelve-thirty. You're not afraid of an audience, no?"

"Ah,....ah....no," Ian stammered.

"Good." The coach smiled. "Theese is a pairformance for the toureests. We hweel announce you as a diver from Amereeca veesiting Team Mehheeco. You ho k?"

Ian nodded his head and managed a weak smile as he pulled on his shorts and tee shirt.

"See you in a leetle hwhile," the coach said, and left.

"Yeah, maybe," Ian said to the locker room and hobbled up to the restaurant.

The ladies and Spook were sitting at a table looking at him wide-eyed.

"That was incredible," Robyn said. "I never saw anything like that before."

"Fantastic," Spook said, and slapped his back as he sat down. "Want a beer?"

"No way," said Ian, a little surprised that Spook had offered.

"I thought you'd be ready to celebrate," Kim said.

Suddenly Ian realized what was up. They thought that was it. They thought he was done.

"I still have a dive to make," he said.

Their expressions all went dumb at the same time.

"Gotta go to the top. That's what it's all about."

"But why?" Robyn said, sincerely.

Ian looked at her and took a deep breath. Spook folded his arms across his chest and sat back in his chair.

"Not a good question right now," Spook offered quietly.

Ian looked quickly around the room not really seeing anything.

"Where's Manny, guarding the car again?"

"We don't know where he went," Kim said. "He was with us when you made your dives and then he said he had to check something here at the restaurant. We thought we'd find him in here when we came in but I guess not."

Ian felt concern run across his forehead.

"We should find him. After last night, you never know."

"Yeah, that creep could show up still looking for the wrong people," Spook said.

Ian felt a flash of anger at the white car roaring up the driveway, out of reach.

"Are you guys going to eat?" Ian asked.

"Are you kidding?" Robyn said. "I was, but not now. How high's the top?"

"Around eighty five feet."

She looked stunned.

"Am I gonna eat? Right. I need another beer."

"Let's take a look for Manny," Ian said, looking at Spook.

Spook nodded and they excused themselves from the table.

"You all right?" Spook said, when they got outside.

"Yeah. Scraped my foot a little but it woke me up, you know?" Ian wanted to say more but held it. "Let's look around the patio down there and near the lot."

Spook shot off to the left towards the parking area and Ian walked to the other side of the patio. They moved through the now-growing crowd and met at the other side near the wall. They split again, moving into the parking areas. Ian could see Spook way on the other side of the lot appearing and disappearing behind buses and cars. About five minutes later they met at the Thing.

"Nothing, man," Spook said, exasperated. "Where the hell could he be? Yesterday I'da figured he was just out hustlin'. But after last night...."

Spook didn't finish the sentence. He strained his eyes over the area, turning first his head and then his entire body.

"Let's try around the hotel and restaurant. Maybe he's got connections," Spook said, trying to lighten the air a little.

"Okay," Ian said. "I have to get back there anyway. It's almost time."

They headed back up the hill and into the restaurant, not noticing the small white car moving quickly across the far end of the parking lot.

"No luck?" Robyn said.

"Na, nothin'," Spook said, throwing his hands up.

"Look," Ian said, "I have to get ready. Just sweep through the hotel, like the lobby and whatever, and see if you can't stick your head in the kitchen maybe. If you don't come up with him, go back to the patio for the dives and maybe he'll meet you back there."

Manny's disappearance was starting to bother him. In a way it helped kill the time before his dive, but now that dive time was here he didn't have room for both of these things. He headed out the back door and down to the locker room.

Ian stepped into the locker room, which now was occupied by several of the Mexican divers. There in the corner stood Manny, talking to one of the divers.

"Manny! Where have you been?"

It came out a little angrier than Ian wanted. Manny and the diver both looked up at him in surprise. Ian recognized the diver as the top diver from yesterday. He was older than Ian had thought, mid-thirties or more but in such excellent shape Ian couldn't be sure. He seemed as tall as Ian but was actually an inch or two shorter. Ian sensed a confidence and strength in the man's manner.

"Manny, we've been looking all over for you." Ian softened his voice. "We were worried about that creep being around again."

"I am okay, Señor Een. Señor Een, thees ees my cousin, Carmelo Arroyo, a great diver for Meheeco." The pride was thick in the boy's voice.

"A pleasure to meet you, Señor," the diver said.

He took Ian's outstretched hand and grasped it with both of his.

"Manuel has told me about you and your friends. I am very grateful to you for your concern and for the way you have taken care of him, especially last night."

There was sincerity in the voice but the man's sharp blue eyes looked carefully at Ian, as if checking for something that wasn't visible on Ian's face. Ian felt the probe but quickly ignored it, choosing to note the similar characteristics the man shared with Manny–dark, fine hair, although combed back stylishly, soft brown skin and a wide, handsome smile. The only difference was that the man spoke perfect English. There seems something almost American about him, Ian thought, not knowing what he meant by it.

"Well, last night was just wrong," Ian responded. "We don't know what it was about but it had nothing to do with Mann..eh...Manuel. But aside from that, he's something special and we've all kind of really taken to him, you know?"

"Yes, I can understand. He is a boy of very strong mind and will. And because he is of fine character he is a very good judge of the same. I was told an American would possibly be diving with us today and I am greatly pleased to see that it is someone strong of heart."

Ian felt embarrassed.

"Manuel, we must get ready now," Carmelo said, placing his hand on the boy's head. "Would you wait outside, please?"

Manny nodded and headed towards the door. As he passed Ian he looked up and smiled, and Ian grabbed the back of his neck and pinched it.

"Manuel came to me because he knows the dangers of the cliffs, and he is very concerned for your welfare," Carmelo said. "He asked me if I would look out for you." He smiled when he said, 'look out for you'. "Do you wish any sort of assistance?"

"How about if you make the dive and I pop up out of the water and take the credit," Ian said, letting a lung full of air blow out of his mouth.

"You are nervous?"

"Oh, you bet."

"That is good. So am I. Every time I dive. Let me introduce you to the other divers and then we must get to the cliffs."

Carmelo took him to each of the other four divers, introducing him to three of them in Spanish and one, the young, cocky one from yesterday, in English. He didn't seem quite as cocky today.

"When we swim out to the cliff, you and I will exit first. Follow me up the cliffside. When we get to the top, we will have time to go over a few things. Okay?"

Ian shook his head nervously and took a deep breath.

"Good. Let's go."

As they stepped out of the locker room, Manny, who was standing outside the door, walked up to Ian. Ian squatted down.

"Señor Een," his Hustler smile gone again, "please listen to Carmelo. He ees a very good diver. He knows the cleefs."

The concern on Manny's face both comforted Ian and upset him.

"You must be very strong here," Manny continued, putting his finger on Ian's forehead. "I know that you are strong enough here," he pulled his finger back and replaced it on Ian's chest, "el corazón."

"Thanks, buddy. Here." Ian took off his silver cross. "Wear this for me till I get back, okay?" He put the leather cord over Manny's head and kissed the cross. "Now do me a favor will ya? Get up to the patio. Everyone's been looking for you and they think you're still missing. And tell them you talked to me, okay?"

Ian watched him disappear, then turned and headed for the water.

The divers were standing at the water's edge when Ian caught up. Carmelo gave him a quick wave and dove in. Ian took three quick steps past the other divers and dove in after him. The water felt even warmer now. Ian noticed as he swam that the cliffside was wet a good foot higher than the water level as the waves swelled in and out of the canyon.

Tide's going out, he thought, nervously. Just what I need.

The water seemed rougher now as well. He could feel himself being pushed in different directions, most noticeably towards the back wall of the canyon. He swam hard against the wave then felt it ease. He hurried to get to the cliff base not wanting to face the next wave.

Carmelo climbed out of the water and began scaling the canyon wall. Ian climbed out and waited a minute before following. He could hear sound bouncing around the canyon now. It was coming in the same way he'd heard it years ago in diving competitions. You heard it but didn't hear it. You could pick out distinct sounds, someone's laugh, a child crying, a boat engine; but it was one continuous fabric that wrapped around you, out there somewhere. Then a voice struck Ian's ears sharply.

"Ladies and gentleman, thank you for coming today to see the incredible, internationally renowned Team Meheeco Cliff Divers. As you see our Clavadistas are now………"

Ian's foot slipped and the voice disappeared. All he could hear was his heart attempting to leave his chest by way of his ears. He looked up and saw Carmelo standing about twenty feet above him, nothing but blue sky framing his body.

"You okay?" Carmelo said, his voice sounding thin in the air.

"Yeah," Ian answered, putting his head back down and staring at the rock in front of him. He looked at his feet, marked the trail ahead with his eyes and continued. In a minute he was reaching his hands up onto the flat surface where Carmelo stood. When he did he felt a strong breeze strike his face. He stood up and surveyed a flattened area about four feet by six. Across from him was the small shrine he had seen from the patio. To his right and left were a few jagged upshoots of rock continuing another three of four feet above his head. Despite these physical objects around him, Ian had a very clear sense of standing on top of a mountain, as though nothing else surrounded him. He was also conscious of his own reluctance to turn around and face the water. Carmelo stood to his left.

"Do you feel fear?" Carmelo's question seemed to be a challenge.

"Yes, I think that's an excellent description," Ian said, breathing deeply.

"That is good," Carmelo said. "You have no business being up here if you do not. But remember, your fear is born of respect, respect for the cliff and the water. You know how to dive. Let your instincts guide you. There are only two things you must do consciously today. The first is to push off. You need to move outward not upward. Do not leap from the cliff, lunge forward. The second is to hold your position to the last second. The surface of the water will deceive you. It will appear to be there but will actually be lower, so hold out when you think it's time to enter, then lock your hands. Okay?"

He locked his own hands to demonstrate then looked at Ian's eyes for confirmation.

Ian made an exaggerated nod and popped a "yeah" out along with his breath. He was breathing hard, not sure if it was the altitude, the climb, the dive or all three making simple respiration a difficult task.

"You will dive before me," Carmelo said. "I will tell you when to set yourself, and when to go. If you are not ready, step back and we will wait for the next wave. Don't be embarrassed. I never am. And besides, the crowd thinks it is very dramatic." He gave a quick smile which Ian appreciated. "Also, try to swim to the others and get out of the water before the next wave enters the canyon. You do not want to fight the water."

Ian pictured himself completing a successful dive then being smashed against the canyon wall. Shades of Angel Garcia.

By the time Ian managed to tune in what was going on below him, the young boy at the level below was preparing to dive. Ian stood to one side and leaned forward to watch. He purposely avoided going near the spot where he would set himself. Years of diving had conditioned him to step to the edge only when he was ready to go. In all the years he'd been diving, he'd never stepped back.

The boy spread his arms, wings almost, Ian thought, from his view above him, and sailed out over the water, a long, flat object becoming shorter and thinner till he hit the water as nothing more than a brown button on a blue panel. The crowd cheered and hollered and the PA system reverberated again through the canyon.

"Paco Reyes, ladies and gentlemen. Give him a big hand. And now ladies and gentlemen, we have a special treat today. We have a guest from Amereeca, an excellent diver who has come to enjoy himself in our beautiful home of Acapulco. He has decided to perform with our divers today and make the great dive from the top. Ladies and gentlemen, will you please give a warm welcome to our American guest, Ian Connors."

The crowd, obviously more Americans than Mexicans, cheered and hollered loudly.

Well if I'm gonna die, Ian thought, at least I'm going out with an audience.

"Wave to the crowd, amigo," Carmelo said. "You are a celebrity today."

Ian looked at him with a silly look on his face and then stood up straight and waved his hand and arm high above his head. The crowd noise surged loudly again. Ian smiled and waved as he spoke to Carmelo.

"They all think I'm nuts, Carmelo, but hey, you know Americans. They love nuts."

"Okay. Get yourself set," Carmelo said.

"How about...," Ian glanced towards the shrine.

"Certainly."

Ian stepped towards the small white plaster grotto. He blessed himself and whispered a prayer, then turned and walked to the front of the diving area.

"Let me know when you are ready," Carmelo said. "Watch the wave fill the canyon from right to left."

Ian stepped to the edge.

chapter 17

MANNY HEADED UP to the hotel and scurried quickly through the kitchen to an exit on the other side, avoiding the restaurant. He hurried around the building and ran to the top of the slope, spotted Spook and the others on the patio, then moved toward them. He took three steps down the slope when a man stepped into his path. The man's stare met Manny's eyes and the boy froze. The stare came from deep, cold eyes, the eyes of a bandito, the eyes of a man who would hurt a child.

Manny recovered enough to move to his right and continue walking, moving immediately into the thickness of the crowd. As he did the man turned quickly and walked towards the parking area.

"MannEEE," Spook hollered. "All right man. Hey, where you been? We've been lookin' all over for ya."

Robyn, Kim, and Donna all huddled around him.

"It ees okay, Señor Spook. I had to speak to my couzen. He is one of the divers and he is going to take care of Señor Een. I spoke to both of them a few moments ago."

"Oh, okay. Good. Ian was worried. Your cousin's a diver, really? Which one?"

"He weel be at the top with Señor Een."

"How about that," Spook said, amazed. "Talk about your small world. Well, that's good. Ian needs somebody up there talkin' to him. C'mon. Move up here to the wall so you can see."

Manny slid in front of Spook. The girls moved up behind him and Robyn put her hand on Manny's shoulder. As soon as she did her expression changed. Robyn could feel the tension in the small boy's body. She leaned down and spoke quietly.

"Hey, are you okay?"

"Yes, thank you, Señorita Rowbin," he answered, a strained smile on his face.

"Are you sure?"

"Yes. I am worried for Señor Een."

"You're such a sweet guy, Manny. Don't worry. I think with your cousin helping, Ian will be fine."

Robyn stood up straight again, not sure she believed what she said, and rubbed Manny's shoulder as both their heads tilted up to the sky.

⁂

Pleasure boats blanketed the water's surface just beyond the mouth of the canyon, each displaying their own form of pretension. Well-shaped and well-exposed young women led the list of deck adornments followed by darkly tanned out-of-shape men twice their age. From the size of the boats it was clear that the cost of bobbing in the free waters of the Pacific Ocean was considerable.

"What's the matter?" Warren Ebbetts said, his face filmy with sweat and annoyance.

"Hwen thee hwaves comb from they cahnyon they boat rise up an down too mawch."

The thickly accented Garo spoke without moving, holding his position on the flying deck, his eye never drifting from its focal point. His face, naturally bunched, was even more pug-like from squinting. The lone figure in his crosshairs stood motionless, a tiny sketch of rippled lines atop the sharply drawn crags of the cliff. To the naked eye in the bright midday sun of Acapulco, the figure was nothing more than a change in the color of the rocks. Through a high powered rifle scope, it was a pick-your-spot target. Despite the distance between the boat and the figure on the cliff, the Pug had a clean picture of the vein on the right side of the diver's forehead.

"I didn't come out here for excuses," the Fat Man answered with a bite. "And I sure didn't come out here to rub elbows with any of these phony bastards." He threw his head violently to the left as if the sweat on his face were acid to spray across the water at them.

"Ssssshhhh," came hissing quietly back across the cabin. He saw the Pug drop his right arm a hair and his body swell and tighten. The boat rose smoothly into the air like an elevator moving to the next floor. When the movement stopped Garo's body jerked back slightly at the shoulder.

As the sound of Salsa music slid itself across the well-lubricated bodies of the powerfully unaware, no one heard the high-whining *thewp* that flashed from the top of the boat. All they heard was the sound of their collective "oohs" and "ahs" as they peered through binoculars at the graceful arc of a diver.

***

Standing on the edge, eighty five feet from an answer to his commitment question, Ian looked out at the world before him and took several deep breaths. He decided to take the time to inhale what was around him before locking his mind on the dive. He looked out toward the ocean and could see boats dotting the surface near the mouth of the canyon, bobbing in a soft cadence with the tide. He looked to the left, across the canyon where the crowd now filled the patio to the maximum. Cameras were mounted on the wall in front of them, their lenses flashing from time to time. He could pick out Spook in the front of the crowd, in front of him, the dark haired Manny, and next to them, the girls.

The air was warm. It felt good on his body. The sun, the air, the ocean, the....

He could feel his mind starting to race, to panic. There was too much going on now. He could see the sensory overload signs inside his head starting to flash.

"Watch the water," he said out loud.

He looked down into the canyon. The water seemed a mile away, as if he'd dive and never hit it. This was not anything like the other dives he'd made. This height was incredible. He couldn't believe he was looking at it, about to try it.

What try it, he thought. You don't try it, you either do it or you don't.

He looked hard, feeling the desire to step away, knowing he was thinking about it too much.

Don't. Don't back out. Don't give it up. No more backing out, no more quitting. Okay? Okay. The sky is beautiful, the water is incredible, you're finally here, you're on the cliff, everybody's waiting, they all think you're crazy. Fine. Maybe you are. Now get it all out of the way because you're going damn it. Go ahead, do it. No, not yet.

He felt his mind relax slightly. Watch the water, he said to himself one more time.

He was afraid if he tried to speak at this point, nothing would come out. He flipped his right hand at his side to signal his readiness to Carmelo.

"You can go now," Carmelo said.

He felt a rush of current shoot up his spine, the hair on the back of his neck stood up, and then instinct and reflex took over.

He bent deep, compressing his body downward and tightening every muscle in his body. At that instant he heard and felt something whiz overhead. Later, he would imagine it to have been a fast flying bug, one of those freaky creatures that showed up in his hotel room. He thought he heard it splat into the rock to his left. But right now it was one sensory detail among thousands being factored at amazing speed inside his head. Instead of leaping upward, he let gravity pull his body forward as he pushed against the mountain, his rock hard thighs propelling him out over the cliffside, the water, and into space.

Incredible, untouchable space. For a split second he was free. Free of everything; earth, people, pain. Nothing held him in any way. He was suspended above the world and all its puny problems. He could not be touched. He owned his soul. In those incredibly fast fragments of seconds he knew it was a sensation he would never forget and probably never repeat.

And then the earth reclaimed him.

Dead silence and stillness quickly changed to a screaming whistle in his ears as he rushed to meet the water. He arched his back sharply trying to keep his head high and body level for as long as possible. Carmelo had told him the water was deceiving and that he had to hold position till the finish, the thought beginning to flatten and warp inside his head. The whistle in his ears became the mental scream that came with plummeting head first towards the earth. His chest and stomach tightened, a strained "errrrrrhhhh" escaping from his clenched teeth. He could see the water now, crystal blue and undulating as he approached, his mind still fighting the blur and knowing the only thing he couldn't tell was how close to the base of the cliff he was at that moment. If he looked to be sure, it would pull his torso vertical and start flipping him as he entered the water. Besides, if he was getting ready to kiss the mountainside there wasn't much he could do at this point.

And there it was. The water.

It came up at him like a frozen lake, flat and solid, only ten feet from his face. He pulled his hands together instinctively, locking his arms at the elbows to cut the water's surface, and tucked his head anticipating the impact, noticing a good ten feet between him and the base of the cliff. He could actually hear the *choot* as he ripped through the water and somersaulted under the surface, praying all the way he didn't hit anything else. He turned vertical, kicked his feet and felt nothing. Plenty of water he thought, already feeling the cockiness of having survived. Two more kicks and he burst into the world, gulping the first breath he'd taken in what seemed like an hour. He shot his fist into the air and let out an unearthly sound that came from his groin.

"YEEEEAAAAAAAHHH!"

⁂ ⁂ ⁂

Manny reached up and blessed himself then smiled his Hustler smile.

"OH BABY!!" Spook hollered. "YEEEEHAAAA!!! OH BABY BABY! Didja see that? Didja see it?"

Robyn was clicking off pictures as fast as she could, aiming at the jubilant figure thrashing around in the water as the crowd around her whooped and cheered.

"MAN O MAN! OOOOOOEEEEEEE!" Spook continued to yell. "He did it! The son of a bitch did it! And it was beautiful too! Manny, did you see it?"

"Yes, Señor Spook."

"See Manny, he's fine," Robyn said breathlessly, hugging him from behind. "He made a beautiful dive."

"Yes, Señorita Rowbeen, eet was a beeuteefull dive," Manny said, having forgotten the man with the cold stare.

"Come on," Spook said, turning to the others, "let's get up to the restaurant and get a table before this crowd fills the place up. We gotsta staht pahtyin." He scrunched up his face when he said it.

"Wait," Manny said. "My couzen is going to dive."

"Damn," Spook said, smacking his head. "Sorry Manny, I forgot about that." He moved back into position and looked across the canyon.

***

By now Ian had swum to the base of the cliff where the Mexican divers were standing. He looked up at Carmelo who seemed hesitant to step to the edge. He was standing back from the diving area, near the shrine. Every few seconds he would peek his head forward and look to his right. Finally he stepped forward quickly, set himself on the edge, and shot into the air. It was one continuous movement, with no hesitation. The dive was clean and smooth, but direct, with little crowd pleasing flair. Carmelo popped to the surface, gave a quick wave to the crowd which seemed to have been caught off guard as well, and swam to the cliff to join the others. When he climbed out of the water Ian shook his hand then raised both their clasped hands in the air.

"Ladies and gentleman," the PA voice boomed, "a big round of applause for our divers today. And special thanks to our American guest Clavadista for a beautiful dive here from the cliffs in Acapulco." The divers were now all facing the crowd and waving. "On behalf of El Hotel Salto, thank you for visiting us. Do take the opportunity to enjoy our fine restaurant and please enjoy your stay in beautiful Acapulco. Buenas tardes. Señoras a Señores...."

The announcement continued in Spanish as Manny hurried off toward the side of the hotel.

chapter 18

IAN TOWELED DOWN in the small locker room, trying to hold on to the rumbling emotion working its way through his charged body.

"Listen, thanks a lot for your help, Carmelo. I mean, whoa! It was just, I mean. I was really shaky there at the last minute."

Ian was looking at Carmelo while he spoke, knowing that nothing coming out of his mouth made sense. He took a deep breath and tried one more time.

"I'm very grateful is what I mean. Standing up there alone would have been very different."

"I understand, Ian," Carmelo said, smiling softly. "Say no more. You are a fine diver. I'm glad I was of some help."

He reached out with both hands and grabbed Ian's hand as Manny appeared between the two men, his smile wide and bright.

"Manny! Hey buddy, did ya see it?"

"Eet was an excellent dive, Señor Een," Manny said. "Excepcional. Si, Carmelo?"

"Yes, Manuel, a great dive," Carmelo said.

"Come on up to the restaurant now," Ian said to Manny. "We gotta celebrate. Carmelo, please. Come up and have some lunch and a few rounds of celebration. It would be my pleasure. I'd like to introduce you to my friends."

"Okay, fine. I would like that," Carmelo said. "I will be up in a few minutes."

"You got it." Ian grabbed his shorts and pulled them on. "Come on, amigo," he said to Manny. "Let's party!" He pulled his shirt on as they walked out the locker room door.

"The conqueror returns, victorious! All hail, the master of the mountain, oh wingless one!" Spook was cranked up and bowing as Ian entered the dining room. "Mah man!" he yelled, walking up to meet Ian before he reached the table. "In-freakin-credible!" He put both his hands out and Ian smacked them. "Fantastic man. Glad you're safe."

"Hey, thanks," Ian said.

"Well, shit, man, I am impressed. That's all there is to it. Anyway, quit flapjawin' and let's do some serious partyin'." Spook shoved a beer at Ian.

"All right," Ian growled and took a big swig of the beer and sat down at the table.

"Wow, Ian," Kim said, wide eyed, "I've never seen anything like that before, especially by someone I know. That was amazing."

"Thanks, Kim."

This is starting to feel real good, Ian thought.

"Hey Donna," Ian said teasing, "now look, I'm sure you have a ton of things to say but you know once you start talking you never stop so try to be short and sweet about it. Okay?"

Donna blushed and her white teeth flashed. She managed to speak, her voice very soft.

"It was really fantastic. You must feel great."

"Thank you. You know I was just thinking that, feeling great I mean. I've been so caught up in thinking about the damn thing that I'm just now starting to feel like feeling great." He looked at everybody at the table.

"No shit Sherlock," Spook said sarcastically, then smiled. "More beer!" he yelled. "Cervezas, más cervezas!"

Two waiters turned their heads abruptly, then smiled. Ian could see people at the other tables looking at him and his group, smiling and nodding.

"Well, I'll tell you something," Robyn said, leaning on the table towards Ian, "I was damn impressed, besides being scared out of my wits. Right up until you went I swore you were just nuts. But after it was over I realized how much of an accomplishment it was."

Ian looked at her and realized that he hadn't really looked at her. He liked her some more.

"It was definitely important to me, thank you," he said, quietly.

"Well, you did it for yourself." Robyn was speaking quietly but excitedly only to him, the others grabbing beers and making noise. "That's something special I think. You climbed up that cliff and put yourself on the line. That's a real commitment to what you want and…." She looked up in the air and shook her head. "Listen to me will you. What am I writing a speech? I'm sorry," she said, looking back at him. "I guess I'm still caught up in all the excitement."

"No no. Go on," Ian said, smiling. "I'm starting to feel real special."

"Well, you should."

As soon as Robyn said it Ian realized they were looking eye to eye.

"Like I said," he fixed his eyes on hers, "I'm starting to."

He liked her even more. They looked at each other for a few seconds and then she, fortunately, decided it was time to get back to the party.

"Something must be special," she said, haughtily. "Or maybe I'm just crazy. I don't usually get all this wound up about anything for nothing."

"They say there's something contagious about insanity. MORE BEER!" Ian hollered and grabbed a bottle from the waiter who had just arrived with a full tray. "Manny, did you get something to eat?"

"Yes, Señor Een, thank you. Señor Spook ordered me a cheeseburger."

"Good. I'm getting hungry myself. Did you guys order?"

"No. We were waiting for you," Kim said.

You know what?" Ian said. "I'm craving Mexican food. Go figure right? I feel like eating real Mexican food, with hot stuff, chilies an all. Whaddeeya think?" He looked around the table.

"Sounds good to me," Spook said.

"I love Mexican food," Robyn said.

"I can't eat the hot stuff," Kim said, looking nervous, "but I'll eat the regular stuff."

"All right, Donna," Ian said, looking mischievous, "you're going to have to say something now."

She smiled and said, "Sounds good to me."

"What, you been coaching this girl, Spook? She sounds like you. Hey! Carmelo!"

Ian waved and then stood up. Carmelo crossed the room to their table, acknowledging attention from the restaurant patrons as he walked.

"You are enjoying yourself, I can see," he said, looking at the mass of beer bottles on the table. Ian grabbed one and handed it to him.

"There you go. Join us, please. Let me introduce you."

Ian made the introductions all around.

"How do you do," Carmelo said, and shook everyone's hand.

"This," Ian said to the group, "for those of you who might not have recognized him, is the other crazy guy on top of the cliff today. This is Carmelo, Manny's cousin,...and my lifesaver."

"No, no. You were fine," Carmelo said, looking at every one. "Wasn't he excellent today?"

"Outstanding," Spook answered. "But then so were you," he added. "I can't believe you do that every day."

"Thank you," Carmelo said, modestly. "By the way, I mentioned this to Ian earlier but I want to say to all of you, thank you very much for the way you have treated Manuel here." He nodded at Manny who smiled shyly. "He has expressed to me his appreciation for your personal interest in him. I can't say all of our American visitors take quite the same attitude. I hope you are enjoying yourselves. Aside from your experience last night, this is a wonderful place to spend your holiday."

"Hey, we're havin' a blast, Carmelo," Spook said, "and now that Ian's got the dive under his belt, we're goin' non-stop for the rest of the week. Right, amigos?" He lifted his beer and made a crazed smile.

"Carmelo," Robyn said, "I hope you don't mind me asking but where did you and Manny learn English? You both speak it so well."

Carmelo laughed. "I learned English as a child, just as Manuel has. My family was always involved with tourism here and so English has always been spoken around us. I went to school in California on a scholarship and lost most traces of an accent there. As for Manuel, I constantly correct him on his pronunciations and I suppose it sinks in after a while. Is that not so, Manuel?" he said, winking at the boy.

"I hope you're not offended," Ian said, suddenly sensing his and Spook's informality with the boy was a contrast to Carmelo's guardianship. "He's such a hard worker we call him Manny the Hustler. He's amazing."

"Oh no," Carmelo, chuckled. "He's quite proud of it. He says it's his special American name."

"Yeah?" Spook said. "All right, Man-NEE."

Spook reached his hand across the table and Manny slapped him five.

"So, Carmelo, what did you major in at college?" Robyn asked.

"Surprisingly enough," he said with a grin, "hotel and restaurant management and business. I really enjoy the industry. I've been around it all my life, and in Acapulco I'll always have a job."

"That's for sure," said Kim. "I can't believe all the hotels we've seen coming through town."

"So you probably know the restaurants pretty well," Ian said.

"I'd say I'm fairly well acquainted with most of them," he answered, modestly.

"Well I'm craving some Mexican food, I mean the real thing, the works. We were going to order some here for lunch. What do you think?"

"The food here is very good. You would not be disappointed with most anything you order. But if you truly want a Mexican dining experience, then you must come to my restaurant for dinner. I have two of the finest chefs in Mexico. You will enjoy food like never before."

"You're kidding?" Spook said, amazed. "You have a restaurant? I just assumed you worked here."

"I have over the years," Carmelo answered. "This is where I got my start, from the diving, and then various jobs in the hotel and kitchen. I still help out from time to time in a management capacity, but my restaurant is my full-time commitment." He winked. "If you have time left in your holiday," he glanced around the table, "I would love for you to come as my guests."

Ian looked at Spook.

"Let's go tonight," Spook said, looking ready.

"Ladies," Ian said, "we seem to be a bad influence on you but would you like to continue this helter-skelter relationship this evening at dinner?" He finished his sentence looking right at Robyn. Robyn returned his look and then turned to the others.

"Sounds interesting," Kim said.

"I heard Donna say yes," Spook said, grinning.

"Get outta here. Really?" Ian said, trying to look stunned.

"Well look," Robyn said, "we'd love to go but on one condition; we pay our own way."

"That goes for us too, Carmelo," Ian said. "Please don't be offended in any way, but if your restaurant is as good as you say it is, and I'm sure it is, you deserve to be compensated. Deal?"

"This is the first time I'm forced to accept a deal where I win. What time would you like to eat?"

"Can we make it late?" Robyn asked.

"That sounds good to me," Spook said. "I want to party and spend the afternoon suckin' Margaritas by the pool."

"An excellent itinerary, amigo," Ian said. "How about nine?"

Everyone nodded in approval.

"Excellent," Carmelo said. "The restaurant is called Gran Clavado. A taxi or your hotel will know where it is." He raised the beer bottle up and drained it. "And I must get going. Please enjoy yourselves the rest of the day, I'm certain you will. I look forward to seeing you all tonight. Buenas tardes, Señores a Señoritas." He smiled and stepped away from the table, nodding at Manny, then leaving.

Manny informed Ian and Spook that he would be going back with Carmelo and that they should tell Carmelo this evening if they needed him tomorrow.

"Come on, Manny. What do we owe you so far?" Ian asked.

"Twenty American dollars," Manny said, very businesslike.

"Twenty dollars?" Ian said, not believing.

He and Spook looked at one another.

"Manny, you gotta be kidding," Spook said. "Man, a haircut'll cost ya that much. You're cheatin' yourself...."

"Wait a minute," Ian said, interrupting him. Somewhere in between all the beers he remembered Manny's professional sensibilities. He did not want to offend the young businessman.

"Okay. This man's a professional, Spook, and he's set his price. He gave us excellent service at a stated cost. Twenty dollars it is."

Ian motioned for Spook to pull out his money.

"Here's my twenty dollars." Ian handed a twenty to Manny.

"Here's my twenty dollars," Spook said, stuffing the bill in Manny's shirt pocket. "Thank you sir. I highly recommend your services."

Manny looked at them, genuinely puzzled.

"No, Señores, it ees twenty dollars for every…."

Now, now," Ian interrupted. "Don't go trying to change the price. You stated twenty as your price and that's what we paid you. You trying to haggle for more? No way."

He was trying hard not to smile. He could see in Manny's face that the boy understood what was going on. There was a small battle being waged between his professional ethics and the fact that at this point, technically, he'd been outmaneuvered.

"Manny," Ian said, quietly, "you've done a great job. You've earned what you've been paid. Hey, you don't have any rules about tipping do you?"

The boy reluctantly shook his head.

"Well, then here's your tip. The Acapulco Chamber of Commerce shouldn't have any problem with that." He stuck another ten in the boy's shirt pocket.

Manny's eyes widened, then he smiled.

"Thank you, Señores."

Ian ruffled his dark, satin hair.

"See ya."

Ian got up and walked several steps away from the table to the waiting Carmelo.

"Listen Carmelo, thanks again. This was really big for me today." He shook Carmelo's hand again.

"I do understand, Ian. Enjoy yourself now," his expression turned more serious, "and be careful."

"Okay."

Ian watched him walk away then turned and paused a moment, not sure what the "be careful" was for, then shrugged his shoulders and turned back to the table.

"KICKED ITS ASS!!" he hollered, waving a clenched fist above his head, and the party began.

chapter 19

THE REST OF the afternoon was spent sipping Margaritas and throwing themselves into the pool. The sun was hot and lying poolside was a test of will. By four-thirty Robyn and her friends headed back to their hotel.

Ian was beat. All the adrenaline pumped for the day combined with the hot Mexican sun and celebratory beverages had him wishing for a nice air-conditioned room and a bed with cool sheets. He mentioned the same to Spook who quickly agreed.

Ian was asleep three minutes after he hit the pillow. He slept deeply, going through a series of short dreams that later, when he awoke, he remembered in fragments. None made any sense other than the fact that they were about recent events. First, he saw Manny sitting on a bucket in front of a three-walled hut. His clothes were filthy. The hut was empty; no furniture, no people, not even animals. Ian realized he was driving the school bus he'd ridden from the airport. When he saw Manny he slammed on the brakes and opened the door of the bus. Manny's eyes were glistening with tears, staring right at Ian. Then Manny's voice could be heard but it wasn't coming from Manny. It was coming from the air. "Kkkiiihhhiiillling meh meh meh me," the voice sobbed. "He he he he killhill hill hill meh me." Ian concentrated on the voice and slid away from the scene.

Still driving the bus, he could see the road clearly now. But he couldn't control the bus. A car would come the other way and he'd turn the wheel to avoid it and nothing would happen. The bus would continue in the same direction till the oncoming car would swerve at the last second and bounce off the side, crashing down the side of the mountain. After three cars passed, Ian panicked, feeling out of control. He slammed on the brakes and the pedal went to the floor, the bus barely slowing. Ian could see the end of the road and knew the bus was not going to stop in time. He opened the door and jumped, watching the bus disappear over the edge without a sound. He got up and ran to the spot, staying slightly back from the edge.

Looking down, he saw a body floating face down in the canyon, which was now the canyon at La Quebrada. He kept moving towards the edge of the cliff to get a better view but felt as though someone was behind him, waiting to push him. He finally edged close enough to see the body clearly and when he did, it was the bad man from the parking lot; at least, deep in his dream state, Ian felt it was the man from the parking lot not actually having seen his face. But then the man turned his face towards Ian and grinned. It was the face of the Big Bandito from the Silver Mine. Ian shook his fist at him and hollered, "You should be dead, you bastard." As soon as he yelled he felt an ice cold hand on his neck and one on his back.

"DAMMIT, I KNEW IT," he screamed, digging his heels into the stone. "I KNEW THERE WAS SOMEONE THERE. THEY'RE GOING TO PUSH ME OFF. THEY'RE GOING TO KILL ME. YOU KNEW IT, YOU STUPID SON OF A BITCH. WHY DON'T YOU EVER LISTEN?"

He could hear his voice reverberating through the canyon mixed with Manny's voice from earlier. "Kiihilll hill hill hill ma ma ma me me."

Suddenly, Ian thought of something that might save him and at the same time realized how silly it was. He started laughing and yelling.

"MONEY. HA HA. MONEY. THAT'S IT. I CAN GIVE YOU MONEY. I CAN GIVE YOU ALL MY MONEY AND YOU WON'T KILL ME. RIGHT? THAT'S ALL YOU WANT. HA HA. LET ME GIVE YOU MONEY!"

He felt the hands on his neck and back relax. He was already figuring out how much money was in his bank account, how much he had with him and how much he could sell his car for.

"I'll give you seven thousand dollars," Ian said, over his shoulder.

The hands were still firm against his body, pushing against him enough that Ian had to keep leaning back to hold still.

"That's everything I have in the world. Everything!"

The hands relaxed some more. Ian pictured going to the bank and withdrawing everything, his car being driven away. It made him angry. Why should I have to give up everything I worked for to some creep. I earned it. I put up with all the bullshit to get it. It's mine.

"IT'S MINE, YOU BASTARD! IT'S ALL I HAVE IN THE WORLD!" Ian yelled.

He dropped to his knees, reaching back over his head at the same time, and grabbed hold of the man's head. The force of the man leaning against him carried him forward as Ian pulled on his head. As the man flipped over, Ian looked at his face and screamed.

"NOOOOOOOO!"

It was Spook, his face contorted in disbelief as he sailed out over the edge of the cliff.

"I was just kidding," Ian heard him say, his voice trailing and echoing as it faded into the canyon.

"Ohhh God, not for moneeeeeeeee."

Ian felt the thud against the cliffside, then another one, then a faint splash. He couldn't look. He couldn't go near the edge. He crawled backwards away from the edge and sat down with his back against the rocks.

"This can't be real," he said, quietly. "Something's not right."

He looked out toward the ocean. The moon was bright, lighting up the water and cliff. He heard a buzz and then he saw it, coming straight at him.

ZZZZZAAP!

It hit the stone above him. He heard the buzz again.

ZZZZZAAP!

Another one hit.

"What the...?" He ducked his head into his hands.

ZZZZZAAP!

Now they were coming faster, splatting against the stone all around him, brushing by his face and hair.

ZZZAP! ZZZAP! ZZZAP!

They were hitting him all over his body. He put his arms up to cover his head but he could feel them slapping against his skull. The buzzing was now so loud that he began to panic.

That was what woke him up. As he slipped from sleep to waking he realized the buzz was real and instinctively swatted the air in front of his face. The tone of the buzz thinned and then increased again as something neared his face.

"What the hell?"

This time he felt the movement of air near his face which caused him to sit up and swat at the same time. He saw the creature, relatively small considering the effect it had on his imagination, smack into the wall just below the ceiling. It caromed off the wall and flew wildly back across the room. The thing was nothing more than an overgrown bug, but the feeling of it brushing by his face was not a feeling Ian cared for, like cobwebs in the dark. He reached down and picked up a sneaker and got out of bed, watching the erratic flight of the creature as he moved.

He glanced down at the other bed. Spook was lying flat on his back, coffin style, with his mouth wide open, a continuous mucousy sound coming from the back of his throat. The bug landed on the wall above Spook and Ian moved toward the foot of Spook's bed, in a direct line with the bug, then backed up about three steps.

"All right you piece a prehistoric shit. You're history."

Ian hauled the sneaker straight back over his shoulder then flung it forward, hard, like a tomahawk. It made one revolution and hit with a splat and a crunch, flat on its sole, the bug now completely out of view. The sneaker seemed to hang on the wall for a second as if attached, and then suddenly dropped. It landed flat and motionless with a fleshy smack on Spook's cheek. Ian stood frozen, looking first at the now Rorschach-like smear of the evil Mothra on the wall, then down at the size eleven Nike resting comfortably on its new-found roost.

Spook's snoring stopped, then began a series of nose-contorted short bursts. At their completion Spook waved his arm, knocking the sneaker off his face. He turned his head slightly left and resumed snoring.

"The man's incredible," Ian said, and headed for the shower.

chapter 20

GRAN CLAVADO SAT on the mountainside off the Costera overlooking Acapulco Bay, the most interesting scenery at night being the lights adorning the huge cruise ships anchored out on the water. Ian and Spook met the girls outside, and Carmelo greeted the group warmly when they entered. He was dressed sharply in a tan, linen suit, white shirt and gold tie, looking very much the owner of a successful establishment. He stepped back behind his staff as the group of five were led to a table on a large veranda on the bay side of the restaurant.

"I'm gettin' sick a sittin' next to you when I eat," Spook said, looking at Ian. "Us left handers always get abused by guys with big right elbows. Do you mind, Kim?"

He stepped behind the empty chair next to her and cocked his head.

"I don't mind Spook, as long as you don't go wackin' at me with your left."

"I'm much more considerate than my friend," he said, and sat down.

"Excuse me," Ian said, feigning indignance. "Robyn, would you mind my company?"

"Not at all," she said, smiling.

When they were all seated, Carmelo stepped up to the table.

"If you are interested in eating authentic Mexican food, I would like to do something special for you tonight." He looked around the table. Everyone agreed. "Excellent. I am going to have my chef prepare a sampling of many of our best dishes so that you will have the opportunity to try a little of everything. If you prefer any of these dishes over others, we can prepare more of that dish while you continue. But I assure you," he said, his face lighting up, "you will enjoy everything."

"Outstanding," Spook said. "My kind of thinking."

"Carmelo, are you sure?" Robyn asked. "That sounds like a lot of extra work for your chef."

"It was his idea," Carmelo said, laughing. "I asked him for some suggestions to recommend dishes to you and he immediately insisted on doing this. You must understand something about excellent chefs. Cooking is not work to them, but more of an artistic expression. And they love to show off their works of art."

"Well, in that case," Spook said, "I have an eye for art. Ready when you are."

"Excellent," Carmelo said. "I insist on providing you with some very enjoyable wine on the house. And I won't take no for an answer."

"I think that's a reasonable offer," Spook offered. "Carmelo, you can tell me what to do all night. You won't get any arguments."

"Supply him and he'll follow you anywhere," Ian said, joining in the laughter.

"I will be back," Carmelo said. "Enjoy!"

Two and a half hours later Spook mumbled, "I can't eat any more."

"Thank God," Kim said, shaking her head. "I thought we'd have to sleep here."

"Some fabulous stuff, huh?" Ian said, to no one in particular. "I need to walk this off. Anybody for a nice walk on the beach?"

He'd been thinking about asking Robyn, but he still wasn't sure he wanted to make a move. He was amazed at how comfortable he'd become with her in a short time, but that produced a whole lot of disturbing questions. This would all be over in a few days. Where would that leave him at the end of the trip?

"That sounds like a great idea," Robyn said.

"Walking?" Spook said. "Whatta you kidding? I can't move. Just wheel me into a bar and leave me there."

"How about if we just roll you off the beach into the surf and watch you sink?" Kim said, smartly.

"Oh, do I detect a note of sarcasm, contempt, perhaps?"

"Well, you were supposed to try everything, not try everything four or five times," Kim snapped. "No wonder you can't move."

"Well, I don't like to see food go to waste."

"Oh, you can sleep guilt-free tonight there, Orson."

The rest of the group burst out laughing as Carmelo appeared at the table. Everyone offered their compliments and Ian could see the pride in Carmelo's face.

"You will present us with a bill now, won't you?" Ian said, accenting the word "will".

"You won't change your mind?" Carmelo said.

Everyone at the table immediately protested.

"Oh my goodness," Carmelo said laughing, startled by the unanimous reaction. "I'll get you a bill at once." He turned and waved his hand and then turned back to Ian. "Ian, could I speak to you for a few minutes before you leave?" He was still smiling.

"Sure," Ian said. He turned back to the table. "Figure out the damage everyone and I'll be right back to help pay, I swear."

"Yeah, right," Robyn said. "Didn't you disappear at bill time last night too?"

Ian gave Robyn a touche look then followed Carmelo through the restaurant to a private office. The office was small and dimly lit, most of the light coming from a desk lamp. Despite the coziness of the room, something about the quiet in the office made Ian uncomfortable momentarily and he tried to lighten the air.

"Boy, that was some feast, Carmelo. I'll never eat frozen burritos again."

There was no immediate response from Carmelo and Ian knew something was up. Carmelo closed the door and when he spoke, his tone was serious.

"Ian," he said, "something occurred today that I'm not one hundred percent sure of, but rather than just ignore it, I thought I should let you decide."

Ian was confused.

"What do you mean?"

"I was going to say something right after the dive today but you and your friends were all so excited and enjoying the experience that I didn't want to spoil your party, especially since I'm not certain."

Now Ian was concerned and getting a little annoyed at being dangled like this. He hated when serious things popped up in the middle of a good time.

"Carmelo, please, just tell me what it is. Have I done something wrong?"

"Oh, no, no my friend, nothing like that."

"Well, then spit it out."

Now that Ian knew it wasn't his mistake, he was tired of the suspense. Carmelo was looking at him, seemingly afraid to say what he wanted to say.

"It's just that, I'm not sure that...."

"Car MELo," Ian said, sternly.

Carmelo's eyes came to rest sharply on Ian's.

"Ian, I think someone tried to kill you today."

chapter 21

"WHAT ARE YOU talking about?" Ian said, forcing himself to smile.

Carmelo winced and said, "I told you I'm not sure."

"Okay, well...how about if you just throw it out on the table and we'll see if it makes any sense?"

There was a pause, then Carmelo spoke.

"Today when you made your dive from the cliff, I think someone fired a gun at you and missed." Carmelo looked at Ian for a response and got nothing. "Just as you made your dive," he continued, "something hit the rock beyond you. I didn't see it actually hit, I just felt the force of it and heard the sound of it smacking into the rock."

He looked again at Ian for help. Ian's mind was already whirring through the experience of the dive, but he started with obvious questions first.

"Did you hear a gun being fired anywhere?"

"No."

"Did you see anyone around with a gun?"

"No, but it could have been fired from far away."

Ian was struggling with the conversation. He couldn't begin to make a connection between himself and anyone trying to kill him.

"Look, Carmelo, the first thought that comes to my mind is why in the hell would anyone want to kill me? I mean who? Who am I? I'm not from here. It's not like I'm somebody important, or known. Is this something that happens to tourists? Like, do people come here and get shot for no reason or what?" He started to chuckle nervously. "Is there a backlog of unsolved murder cases involving American tourists shot for no reason?"

"No, no, no," Carmelo said, sensing Ian's irritation. "I am not trying to alarm you unnecessarily in any way, my friend. Rather I'm trying to alert you to a possibility of something. But that is my frustration. I don't know what. I was concentrating on you and your dive at the time, and mentally preparing myself. What I think happened, that is the shot, I more sensed than actually saw. I instinctively pulled back from the cliff and stayed behind the rocks waiting to see or hear something else. But there was nothing else. No other shots, or noises, or whatever. I started to think maybe, if it was a gunshot, maybe I was the target, why, I don't know. I honestly didn't know what to think. I only knew I wanted to get down from there quickly. So I waited a little longer and then stepped quickly and went."

"How come you didn't tell me earlier?" Ian asked.

Carmelo looked apologetic.

"As I said, I was going to when we got into the locker room. But you were so excited about your dive and then Manuel came in. And then you and your friends were all enjoying your success in the restaurant. If I had been one hundred percent certain I would have called you aside and said so but I wasn't. Rather than spoil your afternoon, I thought I'd tell you this evening."

Ian's mind flashed to the cliff-side restaurant and played back the scene from earlier that day, remembering Carmelo's departure and the odd "be careful" at the end. Something about it made him take this whole conversation a little more seriously. He went back to the dive and started sifting through as much of the details he could recall, and somewhere in the last nano-second of the recall the buzzing sensation near his head percolated upward in his mind. It immediately mixed and jumbled with the afternoon's weird dream and the bug in his room.

"Are you okay?" he heard Carmelo say.

He realized he was staring hard at the floor.

"Uh..., yeah..., yeah. I remember something just as I went for the dive,...as I bent to leap forward. Like a buzz and a whoosh, but...."

He was still probing the adrenaline-fired flash of the dive's details, trying to separate and identify them. He heard the splat against the rock.

"I remember thinking afterwards that it was one of those damn bugs you have down here. You know those monster bugs that fly around and bash into things. I killed two in my hotel room already, including the big daddy today."

"Well," Carmelo said with a hint of satisfaction. "Then, at least you have some sense of what I'm talking about."

"But I guess I have to go back to my first point, Carmelo," Ian countered after a pause. "I mean, why me? Who am I? What made you think it had anything to do with me? Whatever it was?"

He looked at Carmelo as if challenging him to justify the whole conversation. Before Carmelo spoke, Ian could tell by his face, he had an answer.

"The incident with Manuel," Carmelo said, quietly. "The man asked about you and about some other man that you were supposed to know. If there is a man looking for you who does not think twice about choking a young boy, then perhaps he has a serious reason for wanting to get to you. It's the only reason I haven't convinced myself to dismiss the whole thing."

Ian felt cold. The night in the parking lot was now running through his head, and the anger and shock that it drew up was rumbling around inside him. Only this time another emotion, one that had not occurred to him that evening, was creeping into the scenario. Fear.

"Ian, please understand," Carmelo continued, "I have brought this to your attention for several reasons. Obviously, I wouldn't want to see anything happen to you or any of your friends. You are very nice people and unless you tell me otherwise, this makes no sense."

Ian picked it up right away; "tell me otherwise." Figures I might be a drug dealer.

"Obviously, my other main concern is Manuel," Carmelo continued. "He has already been an unexpected victim of someone's interest in you."

Ian felt offended and sorry at the same time. He would've choked that guy like Manny was choked if he could have caught him.

All right, Carmelo doesn't know me, doesn't know me at all, except for today. So why did he invite us here tonight? To tell me he thinks I'm bad company and to stay away from Manny? Besides, I don't know him. He's the one who lives here. Maybe he screwed around with the wrong people or he's the local connection here and he's using me.

Before Ian could say anything, Carmelo spoke again.

"The other thing is, now I'm afraid, because I don't know whether this thing is real or not. If it is, have you become involved in my businesss or have I become involved in yours? Either way it is going to take both of us to figure it out. I was hoping you would agree and not dismiss the whole thing as my imagination."

He looked sharply at Ian, and Ian could see the fear on his face.

Way to go ass, Ian thought. You're standing here getting insulted and the guy's scared and looking for help. He doesn't even know if it's his problem but he's willing to stay involved. Sometimes, Connors, you're an idiot.

"Carmelo, I don't think this is your imagination, so don't worry about that. I'm not sure that it's anything more than coincidence, especially since you're not sure about the gun shot. I'll tell you this much, and it's the truth. I don't know anyone in Mexico, and I don't have any connections or dealings with anyone in Mexico, or anywhere else for that matter, of any nature, legal or illegal. I don't even have any enemies. I don't think I have that much effect on people." He managed a smile. "So I have absolutely no idea in the world why anyone would want to shoot me. Why don't we start by proving or disproving the main evidence? Do you dive tomorrow?"

"No," Carmelo said. "I do not dive again until Saturday."

"All right," Ian said, "can we get up the cliff tomorrow evening and have a look at the rock? If there was a shot fired, the bullet or something should still be there. Right?"

"I would think so," said Carmelo.

"No bullet, no mystery. Okay?"

"Okay."

"And in the meantime," Ian said, "I'll keep an eye out for any more coincidences. You too."

Carmelo nodded.

"I'm going to tune in Spook, just so we have another pair of eyes looking. But I won't say anything to the ladies." Ian paused and looked at Carmelo's tight face. "Relax," he said. "I'm sure it's just coincidence. But it's good that you said something."

Carmelo bunched his lips together and nodded.

"And thanks again for that feast tonight."

"You are very welcome, my friend." They shook hands. "Please, for the time being, be extra careful. Keep your radar on as they say."

"I will. I promise. It's usually on anyway. See you tomorrow evening," Ian said, and opened the door.

"Buenos noches, mi amigo," Carmelo said, and sat down heavily.

chapter 22

ON THE WAY back to the hotel Ian related the conversation with Carmelo to Spook, who reacted with as much disbelief as Ian had. But Spook noted that Carmelo's behavior after Ian's dive was noticeably peculiar, raising the possibility of the truth of his story just a step higher. The two agreed to pay more attention for the rest of the trip but to leave any mention of the story out of the conversation with the ladies.

"Speaking of señoritas," Spook said, "are you makin' a move on this one or what?"

They pulled into the underground garage.

"Hey, I'm enjoying the atmosphere here," Ian answered, the question stirring something inside him he couldn't quite identify. "Beautiful scenery, good food, good drink, good company. Que sera sera, or whatever that is in Spanish. Or is that Spanish; I don't know. Anyway, I enjoy her company, all of their company actually. They're a lot of fun."

That's what it was, Ian realized. Fun. It had been a long time since he had associated a relationship with a woman with fun; real, plain, old ordinary fun.

"I'm taking a walk on a moonlit beach with some nice company, Spook," Ian said, trying to chase a memory away. "Take it for what it's worth."

"Well, I'm goin' to the pool bar and watch the moon from there," Spook said, as they got out of the car. "If anyone wants to join me I'll keep a stool open."

"I'll check the car in and meet you there," Ian said.

"How about we BOTH check the car in and we walk up together?" Spook said, smiling.

Ian looked at him then flashed a look around the dimly lit garage.

"Uuuhhh...okay. Good thought. Why don't we?"

The layout at the Casa Grande was not as extravagant as the Royal Prince, but for two guys from the cold north on a tropical night, just as effective. Sitting around the softly lit pool near the colorfully lit bar, fifteen feet above the beach, guests looked out on a commanding view of Acapulco Bay, now changing various shades of black, blue and silver as the surface rippled under the moonlight. The bar was a large rectangle with a thatched roof, surrounded first by stools and then by wood tables and chairs, each table with a small candle burning inside a glass lamp. The atmosphere was cozy despite the fact that it was all outside. The girls had already arrived and were at the bar.

"What, you get lost, Spook?" Kim said.

"Hey! Don't start on me," Spook answered. "I didn't elbow you at dinner. Don't press your luck."

"Oh," she said, turning her nose up, "I guess you don't want that cold beer I just ordered you then."

"Now wait a minute," he said, softening.

Ian looked at Spook and Kim and shook his head.

"I'm walking. I'm just no good with these domestic problems."

"I'm ready," Robyn groaned, hopping down from the stool. "If I don't move now I never will."

No one else moved so Robyn and Ian headed down the stone steps to the beach and kicked off their shoes when they reached the sand.

"I hate walking in shoes on the beach," Robyn said.

"Yeah, me too, although this sand ain't Jersey shore sand. This stuff hurts."

Ian kicked flat-footed at the loose ground.

"It's definitely more coarse than Jersey," Robyn said."

"You've been to the Jersey shore?"

"Of course."

"Why 'of course'?" Ian pretended to be insulted.

"Where else would someone from Pittsburgh go if they wanted a seaside resort without flying?"

Ian thought about it.

"Well, I don't know. Now that you mention it, the only thing I can think of is Maryland but I guess the distances aren't really that much different. Where do you go?"

"Well, we've been to Ocean City and Wildwood, but we've stayed most often in Stone Harbor."

"Right, I should have known," Ian said, raising his eyebrows. "Where the money is." He grinned when he said it.

"What is it with you and money?"

She didn't sound annoyed, but it wasn't all kidding.

"Oh nothing, nothing. Just teasing."

"I don't have any money. I'm just working and paying my way, like you, I guess. My Dad's been successful with his work and I know we've always had what we needed, but I never considered us as having money."

"I guess it's force of habit," Ian said, feeling guilty now that she seemed to be defending herself. "It's funny. By my standards your family has money. Something I assume based on where you live and where you go. We all do it. What kind of car, what clothes label, what brand of beer. It all signals something to somebody about who we are and what we have. Actually, I just hate it. And I hate it more about myself than anybody else. The ridiculous part is none of it's even accurate. We've become so aware of what everything we have says to other people that we want things because they say something, not because they do something. So then we're all running around saying something that's not true about the thing that we think is saying something and...."

He suddenly realized that nervousness was making him babble. He stopped walking and looked at her with his face all bunched up.

"Two questions. Am I making any sense at all, and, are you paying any attention to me anyway?"

Robyn burst out laughing causing him to do the same. In between gasps she managed to get out an answer.

"Yes...and yes."

When she finally stopped laughing they started walking again.

"The scary part is you were making sense," she said.

"You think, maybe? Anyway this is not a good subject for a beautiful moonlight walk on a beach. I've been trying to leave all this junk back home."

She turned her head and smiled at him warmly.

"Sometimes it's places and circumstances like this," she waved her hand, "that give you the different perspective you need." She said it softly.

Ian looked at her, listening to what she was saying, and thinking that, like he'd noticed earlier that day in the restaurant, she was very pretty. Very pretty.

"Well said."

They walked for about five minutes in silence, kicking the water and enjoying the air. But Ian kept watching her whenever he thought he could get away with it. Maybe it was the setting that caught him up, but he knew it was more than that, that she was the kind of person who would be pretty, and intelligent, and appealing, even back home.

"So what else is on your mind?" she finally said.

"What do you mean?"

The question caught him off guard.

"Just like the dive was showing on your face, there's something else there now. And it isn't our money conversation."

Damn, he thought. Either she's good or I need a face lift.

He really didn't want to say anything about Carmelo and the bullet so he went for the obvious. At least, it had become obvious in the last ten minutes.

"Maybe it's you."

He purposely said it coyly. That way it wasn't as risky. If she laughed at him, he could laugh back and act like it didn't really mean anything.

"Well, it's about time," she snapped back.

Hers was coy too, but coy with an edge. She stepped toward him with her hands on her hips.

"I was starting to think I might have to dive off a cliff or something."

They were facing one another now.

"I hope I didn't offend you," he said, quietly. "I guess between the dive and, well…, back home stuff….I've been real cautious." He looked right at her as he said it.

"Vacations are too short for cautious." She reached up and put both hands on his face and kissed him.

Ian started tingling all over. He'd forgotten how nice it felt to be kissed and caressed. The sensation was familiar but everything else was different. The shape of her mouth, the way her lips fit his, the smell that rose from her skin. She pulled away gently, and then he put his arms around her and kissed her. He loved the taste of her mouth.

"Obviously you have thought about this," Robyn said, a big warm smile on her face.

"I picked you off a beach out of hundreds of people, didn't I?" he said, kissing her forehead.

"I wouldn't say hundreds. Besides you were feeling pretty good by then weren't you?"

"Didn't affect my judgment, now did it?"

He kissed her again then pulled back.

"No, look," Ian's voice turned soft, "the other night was just fun and company and a whole lot of things. You guys came by, and it seemed like a vacation kind of thing to do. But when we talked and I had a chance to watch your face, I knew there was somebody real there. If there wasn't we would've had some laughs and said goodbye. The real person in there has been nice getting to know. I'm just movin' slow lately."

"Slow movin' guys are rare these days, Ian. I like it. I just didn't want the whole vacation to slip by without getting a little closer. And if you're carrying something with you from back home, don't worry about it right now. Let's just enjoy the Fantasy

Island set while we can." She looked up at him with her pretty face. "Okay?"

He put his answer on her lips.

chapter 23

BILL GOLDEN SAT down wearily at the cluttered desk of his study and pulled the stack of bills toward him one more time. The cozy den of the stone colonial had become his place of refuge whenever he'd been home. With his legal problems throughout the last year, chatting with the neighbors wasn't an inviting consideration. The Main Line neighborhood of Radnor was a Philadelphia suburb just far enough up the Line to generate a large mortgage and an attitude, but not so far up that meeting the mortgage every month was guaranteed. That was determined by hard work and good business deals. People who lived in the estates in the really wealthy Main Line towns just exercised a stock option when things got thin. Bill Golden had worked hard and kept his attitude in check, but it didn't seem to matter now.

Golden looked hard at the top bill, placed it on the desk, then repeated the process with the next one, his mind making a half-dozen calculations by the time he finished restacking. There was no way to make it work no matter how many times he went through the pile, and at this point he didn't think he had the energy to find one if there was.

"Honey, why don't you come to bed?"

He looked up slowly to see his wife, her face marked by all of the nights she'd come to his door like this since the arrest. She was beautiful once. Somewhere in between all those lines was a soft, peach-colored skin that glowed like a sunny-day hayride on a farm in Bucks County a hundred years ago. Somewhere between those lines was a woman who cared so much and made him so happy that he'd made up his mind to give her everything and set out a plan to make it happen. She was worth it. She made it all worth it.

And now after all she'd been through, all he'd put her through, there she stood, still beckoning him faithfully to the one place of certain peace he'd ever known on this hard planet. He wanted to cry, but she didn't deserve that.

"Not yet, dear, you go on up," Golden answered, trying to sound confident. "Kevin said he would call with some news and I want to wait."

He always wanted to wait now. He couldn't face her at night in the dark, in the place where he could never be untrue to her, and pretend everything was all right. So he waited. And then she would be asleep and he would not have to lie or pretend.

"You need your sleep, Bill, your strength," she reminded him gently as she walked towards him. "Good night."

She stooped and kissed his forehead, placing her hands on his shoulders. He reached up and patted one hand and she turned it outward squeezing his. The ritual complete, she turned and left the room without stopping.

Normally he would walk to the cabinet and withdraw the bottle, the cushion he needed lately to shut it all down at the end of another day of disbelief. But tonight he wanted to stay clear-headed. The call from Kevin had the real possibility of being positive. The last appeal had kept him outside jail for a little while longer, and Kevin had said it was a good sign, a sign that not everyone involved with this case was willing to accept the overwhelming but circumstantial evidence against him.

The phone rang, startling him from his thoughts, his eyes glancing at the brass ship's clock on the wall across from him. Time. He looked at the phone, now on its third ring, and forced himself to hear it stop then ring again before he pulled it from its cradle, pausing in the space between it and his ear.

"Hello," he said, the word coming out in a straight line.

"Bill, it's Kevin."

"Yes, Kevin, how are you?"

The difference between the right response and the wrong one was easily measurable in the millisecond that it took the voice on the other end to begin answering. Bill Golden blinked and Kevin answered.

"I'm sorry, Bill. I couldn't persuade them to bargain with us anymore. They want you once and for all. It's Cook making an example, you know that."

"I understand, Kevin," he said. "I do appreciate all your efforts and I certainly hope you don't feel any responsibility for this. It just isn't working out."

"Bill, I'm still not giving up," the voice said. "I'll continue to make my presence known until someone either sees the light or gets tired of me. I just know it will take time."

"I know you will, Kevin. It's late now and I know we're both tired."

"Bill, we'll change this eventually, okay? Listen," the voice softened and hesitated, "they want you to report to prison in two weeks, on the thirteenth."

A pause.

"Time," Golden said, almost whimsically, the corners of his mouth pulling back slightly from the phone.

"I'll be over to see you tomorrow, Bill," the voice said, backing away. "Get some rest."

"Fine, Kevin. Thank you."

"Good night, Bill."

He set the phone back down quietly and leaned forward, his arms on the desktop. A plan of action was already forming in his head. It was only for him to step through each segment of it to get the result, just like every successful deal he'd put together. He reached for a pen and quickly made some notes on the deskpad, then pulled his portfolio in front of him and wrote in earnest. When he had finished he closed the portfolio, pleased with his sense of organization and confident of the success of the plan. He stood up slowly and walked from the study, turning off the light as he exited, still checking off details in his mind.

Moving up the stairs, he went from bedroom to bedroom quickly, not making a sound. First, the children's rooms; his son, a wildcat thirteen year old. He kissed the boy's sleeping head thinking how Bill, Jr. would not let him do it if he were awake; then Audrey, sweet Audrey, an eleven-year-old going on twenty-one. He touched her long auburn hair, knowing she would be the one all the boys would want. But she'd make them work to get there then break their hearts. He stood at the door of his bedroom watching his wife sleep in the slash of moonlight that cut across her face. He could not go in, knowing that to go to her would stop his plan. He memorized the illuminated face as his lips mouthed the words "I love you," then he moved quickly back down the steps and around to the kitchen door, snatching his keys from the wall hook and slipping quietly out the door.

The light of a full moon bathed the blacktop driveway and the orb itself caught his eye with its brilliance as he moved across the space between the house and garage.

"Time," he said, never stopping, his left eyebrow arching to take in the huge white globe for as long as possible. He stepped around the side of the garage and unlocked the door with his keys.

When Bill Golden closed the door behind him he knew his plan was foolproof. No one, in the short time he'd taken to produce the plan, would have a chance to ruin it or foil it; not the lawyers, the DA, not Kevin, not even his wife and children, whom he loved so dearly, now more than ever.

And he was right. No one heard the twisting, squeaking sound the rope made as it strained to pull itself from itself. And no one saw the visible inward flex of the small garage caused by the weight of Bill Golden's body as it swung from the rafter.

chapter 24

IAN AWOKE THE next day feeling very good. He thought immediately of the dive. The combination of triumph and relief put him in a state of emotional balance. As he reached up to rub his eyes, the fragrance of Robyn, whether perfume or her skin, gently touched his sense of smell and instantly reminded him of kissing her on the beach. Someone new and exciting in his life, for however long, was another pleasant thought.

He checked his mind for dreams and couldn't remember any, which meant he had slept soundly. The meeting with Carmelo pushed its way to the front, but Ian quickly buried it as future business and proclaimed the day a great one.

"Hey, Romeo, about time you stirred."

Spook was looking back over his chair from the balcony.

"Oh man, do I feel good today," Ian hollered as he stretched his arms and body, then started singing. "Woke up this mornin' ain't got dem Statesboro blues."

He stepped to the balcony rail and looked out at the mountains and water. Gorgeous, he thought, just beautiful.

"My apologies to Blind Willie," he said, cheerfully. "So what's on the non-agenda today?"

"Today's Wednesday, buddy," Spook said. "You said to remind you to call your office about something."

"Oh shit!" Ian said, turning around. "I completely forgot!"

"Well, I didn't, and ain't that why you pay me the big bucks?"

"Ed's doing me a favor and I've got to cover him."

Ian wasn't thrilled with having to shift his mind back to the business-world reality of his job, not here in the middle of all this feeling good. But it was a small price to pay for being here.

"What time is it?"

"About ten."

I'll call after we eat."

At eleven o'clock Ian was lying on the bed with the phone to his ear.

"Listen," he said, trying to sound sexy. "I can get anything I want with a bottle of cheap tequila."

The wobbly voice of Betty reverberated back over the connection.

"You're such a slime sometimes, Connors. I'll bet you bought a case of the cheapest stuff you could find."

He could hear the laughter in her voice.

"You're right," Ian said, still playing sexy. "I'm sending a case home. Half for the office girls and half for you."

"You creep. I'll deal with you when you get back. Who do you want? Ed?"

"Yes, please."

The transfer went through and Ed Bernardi's voice wobbled out as well.

"Ed Bernardi."

"Ed, it's Ian." Ian spoke quickly as if nervous. "Look, I've got something I want to send you but I have to send it fast."

"Ian, what the hell are you up to?" Ed was laughing softly, a little unsure of what was going on.

"Ed, you're gonna love her. She's gorgeous and she's dying to settle down with a nice American businessman who's well endowed."

Ed was laughing comfortably now.

"Well, you picked the right guy."

"Yeah, I know, Ed. I told her that. I told her you have lotsa money. She's a dancer and personal entrepreneur. Her name's Carla but her business associates call her 'The Spanish Fly'. Guaranteed to give you a buzz." Ian was laughing now.

"I know her," Ed laughed.

Ian liked that about Ed. You could never catch him off guard. He was always ready with a preposterous addition to whatever preposterous thing you laid on him.

"I met her at the last convention, only she told me she was from NEW Mexico. Maybe she said nude Mexico, who knows. Hey, really, how's the vay-cay?"

"Fabulous, Ed. It's just perfect. Hey, I did it. I made the big leap."

"No shit, really? All right! Congratulations! Was it tough or what?"

"It was pretty scary but in a good way. It felt great." The feeling washed over Ian again as he thought about it. "Really great."

"That's terrific Ian. I'm glad for you."

"Thanks, Ed. So what's up? Company close down while I was away?"

"Just the West Coast. Listen, I went over the folder you left me and the only thing I don't understand is the deal on deliveries."

Ian launched into an explanation while Ed stopped him from time to time to verify certain points. The whole thing took about three minutes.

"Okay," Ed said. "That's what it looked like, but I wanted to be sure. Everything else looks okay. Anything you can think of?"

"No, I don't think so. So anything else new in the world of Cook?"

"No, not really," Ed answered, then paused a few seconds. "Hey, remember that guy from the investment group, Bill Golden?"

Ian's memory went into search. The name sounded familiar but no face was coming to mind.

"It's not ringing a bell," Ian said, a little disappointed.

"Remember the investment plan guy?" Ed prompted. "Doner, Ellis? We went to an employee meeting?"

Ian made a few mental connections and a fuzzy image of a charged-up man at a meeting came into his head. The circumstances surrounding the name were clearer to him than the man's face.

"Wasn't he the guy they nailed for making the money from that fund disappear? A few million wasn't it?"

"That's the guy," Ed said. "They found him swinging from a rope in his garage early this morning."

The thought chilled Ian instantly. It wasn't the guy so much as the thought of someone hanging himself. When Ian heard something like that it always made him try to imagine what level of despair a person had to get to, to actually leap or shoot, or in this case step to their death. How could you know you were going to die, and do it?

"No shit. What happened?"

"Well, seems the guy'd been going through hell the last year or so. When the money disappeared, about ten mill I think it was, they went after him because he was the exec on the account. He swore from the very beginning he didn't take the money and tried every way he could to prove it. But the money was gone and he was at the end of the line, so they prosecuted. They found him guilty, and then he appealed, and then back and forth for over a year. The guy was out on bail and his last appeal was shot down, and they guess he just couldn't take it anymore."

"Oh man, that's sad," Ian said.

"The really sad part is you have to figure the guy was telling the truth all along, right? I mean if he had ten million dollars stashed somewhere that he went through hell to keep, you'd think he'd a hung in there, if you'll excuse the pun, to spend the money someday."

"Yeah, that's right." Ian paused and then wondered out loud. "What a bitch. What people do for money, or because of it, hah?"

The story bothered him a little more now.

"Hey, my friend," Ed said, hearing the distance in Ian's voice, "I didn't mean to ruin your day."

"No no, you didn't. Just makes me appreciate being on vacation a little more, actually."

"That's the spirit," Ed said, perking up again. "Hey, get the hell off the phone and get a drink. It must be after twelve down there by now. Have one for me."

"As we say down here in Meheeco, muchas gracias. Thanks for covering today."

"No problem. As we say back here in the business world, you owe me." Ed was laughing again. "See ya, friend."

Ian let the phone hang from his hand for about a minute, the significance of the conversation sinking in. Yeah, Ed, you're right. In that world we always owe. What little we get we gotta give back somewhere. And that poor devil swinging in his garage. How much did he get? Whatever it was, it sure didn't come close to what he had to give. Not even close.

Ian didn't like the way his thoughts were going. He rolled upright and hung the phone up, then stepped out on the balcony where Acapulco Bay hovered in majestic blue in the late morning sunlight.

Enough reality, he said to himself, staring at the water as the phone call slipped into the waves. I'm in Paradise, and not a snake in sight.

chapter 25

THE DAY HAD been both active and lazy. Ian water-skied on the bay while Spook went for the boatride. Both of them went para-sailing, then finished the day off sipping fruit drinks by the pool. They ate a light meal from the hotel buffet and were back in the room and showering by six-thirty. When Carmelo pulled into the hotel driveway at seven-thirty, Ian decided the trip back to the cliff would be interesting rather than sinister.

"How's it going?" Ian said, as he slid onto the front seat of the Jeep.

"Fine, thank you," Carmelo said. He was smiling but didn't look relaxed. "How was your day today?"

"Mellow," Ian said, beaming. "Appropriately mellow. Did some things and did nothing."

Carmelo looked both ways then shot out onto the Costera.

"That is good. That is what vacations are for. One of these days I might take one myself but it is tough in my business. You go away for a few days and when you come back things are a mess."

"I'll bet," Ian said. "So have you had any other thoughts on this thing with the bullet?"

"No, not really," Carmelo said, a little more seriously. "I'm anxious to go and get this over with and prove myself wrong. How about you?"

"Na, it still doesn't make any sense," Ian said, casually. "I'm pretty sure we'll just find a dead bug stuck to the rocks."

"I hope you're right," Carmelo said, as they sped up into the mountains.

* * *

An hour later Spook sat slumped in a chair in the middle of the outdoor bar area, his skinny legs stretched out across another chair. The legs shot out from a baggy pair of khaki shorts that collided with a shirt in dire need of therapy. The ensemble and Spook's position signaled to other patrons to stay away, and no one had misread the sign. He was surrounded by empty tables.

"Hey, my man, Man NEE. What's happenin?"

Spook had his palms out to slap ten as Manny appeared from across the pool area.

"Hello, Señor Spook. How are you?" Manny said, smiling from Spook's animated greeting.

He put his palms out and collected Spook's ten then gave him ten back.

"Just fine, ma man. Sidown. Hey, how about a soda?" He turned and spoke over his shoulder to the bartender. "Could I get a nice cold Coke for my friend here?"

The bartender put a tall frosted glass on the bar and filled it. Manny stepped to the bar, took the glass and said thank you to the bartender, then returned to Spook's table.

"So what's doin'?" Spook said. "To what do we owe the pleasure?"

"Where is Señor Een?" Manny asked, looking very serious.

"As a matter of fact, Manny," Spook said, "he's with your cousin."

Manny looked confused.

"Weel they return soon?"

"Yep," Spook said. "We're meeting Robyn and her friends here in about an hour to go dancin' so he'll be back by then. What's up, ma man? Somethin' looks like it's worryin' you."

"Did they go to La Quebrada?"

Spook hesitated then answered.

"Yeah, they did. How did you know?"

"When I saw my couzen last night he was concerned about sometheeng that had happened and he told me not to work for you unteel he could be sure about eet."

Manny had his business attitude showing. There was a reason for his being there.

"Well, there was something," Spook said, "but not anything to worry about."

"Señor Spook, there is something I must tell you that I did not before."

Spook stared at the boy, waiting.

"Yesterday at the cleefs, I saw a man. I cannot say for certain because I did not see hees face thee first time, but I know thees man is a bahndeeto. And from the way he looked at me I think maybe he was thee same man who choked me."

Spook's face bunched up and he sat up in his chair.

"Are you sure?" he said.

"As I said, Señor Spook, I cannot be certain because I did not see hees face that night but...." He hesitated and looked down at the ground.

"It's okay. What is it?"

Manny looked back up.

"I remember later that day that I know this man's face from somewhere else."

"Well, that's good," Spook said, calming down a little. "Where?"

Manny's eyes shifted back and forth from the bay to Spook's eyes.

"It ees the same man who was in thee white car that almost caused us to crash."

Spook sat up straight.

"You mean the creep that was sittin' at the bottom of that hill comin' down from the shrine?"

Manny nodded his head.

"What the hell's goin' on?" Spook yelled, and thumped the table with his fist. He stared out across the bay then turned to the boy. "That means the creep was sittin' there waiting for us. He followed us there, waited at the bottom knowin' we had to come back that way, then followed us to the Royal Prince." He paused then spoke to all of Acapulco. "Shit! Then he followed us again to the cliffs yesterday...," Spook slowed, still piecing it together, "...and Carmelo says somebody took a shot during the dive. This is all getting very weird."

"I know I should have told you yesterday," Manny broke in.

Spook put his hand on Manny's shoulder and squeezed.

"Hey, come on. You did the right thing. You weren't sure, and now that you are you came to us. Take it easy."

"But what about Señor Een and Carmelo? They don't know."

Spook snapped his head back and sucked his teeth and smacked the table again.

"Somebody could have followed them out there tonight. Come on," he said, coming up out of his seat and heading around the pool. "I have to get a car." As he passed the bar he yelled to the bartender. "Do me a favor will ya?"

"Si."

"Three attractive women are supposed to meet me here about nine-thirty. Tell them Spook said wait. Spook! We had an emergency. We'll be back, okay?"

The bartender gave him thumbs up.

"Come on, Manny," Spook said, turning and running. "You got to get us to the cliffs the way your cousin would go so if they're on their way back we'll pass them."

The two stopped running at the car rental desk inside the hotel.

"What do you mean, you have no cars?" Spook looked frantic. "You have to have something. It's an emergency."

"What kind of emergency, Señor?"

The desk clerk did not look impressed.

"What's the difference," Spook said, sharply. "If you have a car, then give it to us."

"Well, I really don't."

Spook turned to Manny and shook his head.

"I don't believe this. Manny. Can't you tell this guy something to get us a car. I know he's got one."

Manny stepped up to the desk and said in Spanish, "Señor, I know you don't usually like to give the tourists the better cars this late unless they have drivers, but this is very important. It involves my cousin who is the proprietor of El Gran Clavado restaurant. He will be very grateful if you can accommodate our friends."

Spook watched the expression on the man's face change from indifference to interest.

"You will explain to them the policy for me," the man said, answering Manny in Spanish as well. Then he looked back at Spook with a perfectly straight face and said in English, "Here are the forms, Señor, you must fill out. I will get…."

"I don't have time to fill out all this stuff," Spook interrupted. "Look, I'll sign the form, you run my credit card off on it. We're staying at the hotel and I'll come back to fill out all the forms later, I promise, just let us get out of here quickly."

The man was starting to get the point.

"I'll have someone bring the car around."

"No," Spook said, his patience finally depleted. "Tell us where it is and we'll go get it ourselves."

"If you insist, Señor. It is a silver Chevrolet Caprice. It is the only one so you will find it easily. Here is the key. Take the elevator to the basement and turn right. Your card please, sir?"

Three minutes later Spook wheeled out onto the boulevard, a nervous Manny beside him.

"Let's just hope the creep in the white car had a prior engagement tonight," Spook said.

chapter 26

IAN WAS HALF-WAY up the cliffside, Carmelo just a few feet above him. For some reason, maybe the excitement and anticipation of the dive, Ian didn't remember thinking much about the climbing the other day. Now it seemed like real work.

"You know," Ian puffed, "with all the modern technology available, how come you guys haven't had an escalator or elevator or something installed. I mean just for the non-performance situations. Like right now."

"Yes, that would be interesting, wouldn't it," Carmelo answered. "But I don't think it would sit well with tradition. This climb is part of the ritual. If you are not fit to climb, you are not fit to dive." He said it very matter-of-factly.

More like if I'm dumb enough to go up here and throw myself off, I'm dumb enough to keep climbing, Ian thought. He was going to say it but realized it might be offensive. Two minutes later they were on top.

Ian looked around again, drawing in the view. It was strange how different it seemed now, so calm, so empty. He could hear music floating from the hotel into the canyon. Not only were the sky and water different, the sun down low over the water now, but also his sense of himself on this jagged wall of rock in the middle of the world. There had been a conquest of sorts for him here on this spot, and the meaning of it filled him with a relaxed confidence. The idea of finding a bullet embedded in the cliffside didn't really concern him. There was this sense of power, this knowledge and acceptance of himself, that let him feel it could be dealt with calmly and easily. Standing here now in the setting sun he felt he could easily leap forward and do it again.

"It would have been right about here," he heard Carmelo say.

Ian turned to see Carmelo feeling the rock with his hand.

"Somewhere in this vicinity."

Ian stepped next to him and began searching the rock with his eyes for a blemish of some sort. He looked to the place where Carmelo's hand was and scaled upward, stopping at a whitish splatter in the midst of yellow and gold stone.

"What's that?" Ian said, pointing.

"Where?"

"About two feet above your hand to the left. The rock is whiter than the rest of the stone, like it's been chipped away."

Carmelo stepped onto a piece of rock at his feet and reached his hand up. As he did, Ian squatted down and looked at the loose gravel at the base of the wall.

"There is an indentation," Carmelo said, unsurely, "not like a bullet hole but more like something hit hard and shattered the face of the rock." He stepped back down and looked at Ian beneath him. "A bug did not do that."

Ian looked up and saw the fear sliding into Carmelo's eyes. He stood up.

"All right. Let's do this." Ian stepped to within inches of the cliff edge and faced the canyon. "I was here when whatever I thought it was went by my head." He put his arms out to indicate his position. "Now looking up at that spot where something hit puts a pretty steep angle on where it came from." He stepped back away from the edge and pointed his finger at the spot on the rock. "If I follow that line, assuming it had to cross over me...," he drew his finger down an imaginary line in front of him as he spoke, "...that bullet or whatever, had to be fired from down below, down there somewhere."

His finger stopped at a point on the water beyond the base of the canyon wall. When his eyes settled in on the place he was pointing to, something in him tingled slightly.

He was looking at a boat, bobbing gently on the surface, almost indistinguishable. The strong rays of the setting sun directly behind it blackened its features from the front leaving only a shape-shifting silhouette floating in and out of the dark gullies of the waves. Maybe it was the oddness of it being there, there where he had pointed; maybe it was his heightened instincts standing there sleuthing his way around. Or maybe it was all the bad TV shows and movies he'd seen. Whatever it was something told him to get out of the way. Fast!

"GET BACK!" he screamed.

As he turned left to move Carmelo back with him he heard the whizzzz and saw the shirt on Carmelo's shoulder shred and blood spray behind him. Carmelo's face reacted not with pain but with disbelief. Ian hooked his right arm around Carmelo's waist and yanked him backwards to the ground all in one motion. As he did another whistling scream passed to his right and this time he heard the rock face explode into little fragments.

"Do you believe this shit?" Ian said, through his teeth. "What the hell is going on?"

He was not feeling fear at this moment, but outrage.

Carmelo was looking at him as if waiting for an answer. They were tucked behind a small crop of rock, the same rock Carmelo had ducked behind the day before. From here Ian didn't think they could be reached.

"How are you doing?" Ian said, and looked at his shoulder. "Does it hurt?"

"Actually, it's numb," Carmelo answered softly.

Ian looked closely at the bloody mess and could tell it wasn't a huge hole, more shredded than deep. He wasn't sure whether it was serious but he didn't want to say anything discouraging to Carmelo, who looked very scared.

"I'm no doctor, Carmelo, but I think you lucked out. It tore up the skin but I don't think there's anything in your shoulder or arm." Ian got up on his knees and turned around to face the canyon. "I guess you were right about yesterday, only for the life of me I can't figure out why."

He crawled forward then peeked to see if the boat was still there. The screaming whistle blew by and the rock face to his left exploded again. He dropped his head to the ground.

"Shit! This is nuts!"

He backed up to Carmelo and into a sitting position with his back to the rocks.

"Is there a back staircase or something? We're trapped up here."

"The only way down is back down the face of the cliff, or dive."

"Maybe they'll leave when it's dark," Ian said, and then realized how silly it sounded. "Yeah. We'll holler, 'Are you out there'?'" Ian started chuckling nervously. "Is there anybody home?"

The thought struck him as absurdly funny. Carmelo was not as amused.

"If they are determined to kill us they will wait," Carmelo said.

"But it's getting dark." Ian looked at the sky. "They won't be able to see us to shoot us."

"The moon is already up, Ian," Carmelo said, flicking his eyes to the left, "and it is full."

Ian looked and there it was, full and round and already luminous in the darkening sky. He searched the viewing area for someone to shout to, but it was empty. He looked towards the hotel which showed signs of life and began yelling.

"HEY! CAN ANYONE HEAR ME? IF SOMEONE CAN HEAR ME LOOK TOWARDS THE CLIFF!"

He waited while the words bounced around the now dark canyon. He listened hard but could hear no response. The music seemed louder than when he'd first heard it. He yelled again, and then again, waiting each time for some acknowledgement. But none came.

"Maybe they heard me yelling and decided to split," he said to Carmelo, whose shoulder looked pretty disgusting now.

The blood had seeped all over the left side of his shirt and shoulder and down his arm. Ian knew it looked worse than it was but, nonetheless, he didn't like it.

"How's your shoulder doing?"

Carmelo grimaced as he spoke.

"I can't move it. I've never been shot before so I don't know what it is supposed to feel like, but it feels like someone dropped a large rock on it rather than a bullet."

Flesh wound or no, Ian thought, I don't like the looks of all that blood.

"We just can't sit here all night. You need that looked at. Dammit!" he said in frustration.

He turned and crawled back towards the canyon, then stopped and pulled his shirt off. He threw the shirt lightly into the air. Three screamers blew by, one hitting the shirt and pushing it left as it tore through it. He turned and looked at Carmelo.

"I think they're still here," he said.

The color was leaving Carmelo's face.

After what seemed like an hour of sitting stiffly against the rock, Ian noticed it was as dark as it might get that evening, and he started to squirm. If Carmelo wasn't hurt, Ian thought, I'd sit up here all goddamn night. But I don't know what might happen to him.

A thought that had slipped quietly into his mind, a thought he was trying to keep quiet, was now getting louder and more noticeable.

"What's the tide like now, Carmelo?" he said, seriously.

"I don't think that will cause them any interference," he answered weakly.

"No, I mean down there in the canyon? Is there enough water to dive into?"

Carmelo looked at him through closing eyes, wider now at Ian's question.

"Ian, it is too dark below. You can't see the water. It would be like diving blind."

"Look," Ian said, trying to sound convincing to both of them, "you can't stay up here all night and those folks don't look like they're planning to leave in the near future. They know they have us and since this is probably their second attempt they're not going to leave unsatisfied again. From the way they hit my shirt, the moon's bright enough and they've got their sights trained right here. I can run and dive quickly enough that they won't see me till I'm halfway to the water, I hope. Once I'm in the canyon I'm safe. I can go get help."

"But the dive," Carmelo said, shaking his head. "In the dark? It is too dangerous."

"Hey, you're the one who ought to know that seeing the water is only for the last second. I still have a good sense of how long I have to hold the dive from yesterday. There's nothing to see on the way down. And now the moon's up there on the left, up high. I figure there's a good chance I'll see a reflection on the water before I hit. That's all I need." He looked at Carmelo hoping for some confirmation. "It's not like I really want to do this. But we can't just sit here; you especially. Besides, whatever the reason, it seems you're in this on account of me."

Carmelo looked too weak to argue.

"All right then." Carmelo shifted place. "Help me get as close to the edge as I can. I'll watch the waves outside the canyon and give you as good a chance of a full canyon as possible. I can time it fairly well."

"All right, but stay flat," Ian said, "and after I go don't be moving around. I don't think you're bleeding much but don't go shaking things up."

Ian had climbed barefoot at Carmelo's suggestion and his shirt was already a victim. He took off his white tennis shorts, his briefs offering a lesser target.

Good thing I don't wear boxer shorts, he said, to himself, I'd have to dive naked. They'd find me in one place and my nuts in another after I hit the water.

He turned Carmelo around by his feet keeping him flat on his back, then pushed him from the bottom of his feet, little by little till Carmelo said, "Okay, I can see the ocean. I'll tell you when to go."

"Now listen," Ian said, "when I go there'll be a shot right away. It'll be right in this area because all they'll see is something move. Stay put till that shot goes by, then wiggle back away from the edge. By then they'll be looking elsewhere."

Ian backed up as far as he could to the far side of the diving area. He would have maybe a six foot running start, three behind cover and three out in the open.

"All right," he said, crouching low, "I'm ready."

Right now he wasn't even worrying about the dive. His main concern was getting off the cliff cleanly. Either a lucky shot by the shooter or a misstep in the last three feet of his run would make any speculation about the dive meaningless. If he could get out into the air cleanly, then he could worry about the dive.

"Get ready," he heard Carmelo whisper, faintly.

He felt himself tighten all over. Ten seconds went by, lasting forever.

"Go now," Carmelo said, and a second later Ian flashed by in a dead run, the skin of his feet making a ssskkk, ssskkk, ssskkk against the flat stone.

Instantly a shot whistled overhead and smashed into the rock to Carmelo's right. There was another whizzing sound, and then a distant splash of water as Carmelo's grasp of his surroundings grew fuzzy. Nothing in the sounds indicated the success or failure of Ian's attempt as the eerie white light of the moon gently closed Carmelo's eyes.

chapter 27

"WE SHOULD HAVE passed them by now," Spook said. "They wouldn't still be up on the cliff. It's dark."

"We have not passed them, Señor Spook. I have watched carefully."

Spook checked the rear view mirrors, inside and out, and saw no sign of life in any direction. He pressed the gas pedal slowly and eased the car's speed up.

"Maybe they stopped at that hotel for a drink and forgot what time it was."

Manny did not answer. Four minutes later they saw the lights of the hotel and the large parking lot used by the tourists, empty except for one car, a white one.

"Manny, am I crazy or is that the car from the bottom of the hill?" Spook said, quietly.

"I theenk it is," Manny answered, his voice tight. "There ees someone in it."

"Well, now we're gonna get somewhere," Spook said, in a gravelly voice. "I'm gonna pull the car up into the hotel lot, over there where he won't see us get out. We'll go inside and check for your cousin and Ian. You know anybody works in there?"

"Yes."

"If we don't spot our guys you find someone you know and stay with them. I'm gonna sneak around by the diving area and circle behind this creep and yank him outta the car. And he's gonna tell us what's up or I'm gonna beat the crap out of 'um."

Spook's eyes were fiery now. He pulled the car up to the hotel and parked it on the other side of the building. Going inside they walked the length of the hotel, arriving at the far end of the restaurant which was about half full. Spook scanned the crowd.

"I don't see them," Spook said.

"Nor do I."

"All right then, Manny, find a friend."

Spook walked across the restaurant to the front entrance, then headed down toward the spectator's area, keeping low and hugging the wall along the canyon. When he reached the end of the wall he stopped. He could see the dark silhouette of the man in the car, the head tilted slightly to the left as if napping. Spook squat-walked low to the ground out into the lot, moving perpendicular to the car till he was even with it, then turned and moved the same way towards the back of it. In a few long minutes he was crouched behind the bumper of the car where he stayed breathing deeply for a moment. Moving to the right side of the car he began inching toward the door. A loud click froze him where he crouched.

"Do not move, Señor," a Mexican voice said, firmly. "When I tell you to, stand up."

Spook's body tightened. He looked right to left as far as his eyes could see without moving his head and saw nothing.

"Stand up and turn around," came the voice again.

Rising slowly, Spook twisted to his left and saw the moonlight glint off the barrel of a gun and then a face he'd seen once before.

***

When the first shot flew by, back where he'd been a split second ago, Ian knew the shooter would never catch him, and now the reality of being eighty-five feet in the air in the dark flashed onto the screen in his head.

Nothing about this dive is going to be right, he thought. He could tell he was dropping head-down too fast because of the flat, running start. He couldn't see anything below him and to look harder meant going over even sooner. He knew already he was going to be long on the landing, even if he did see the water. But something about the circumstances, being pinned down on the top of the cliff with Carmelo wounded, told him none of that mattered. He had to do this, and if he didn't come out of it very well, he didn't have much choice.

Ian knew the water had to be there now. His feet were coming even with his head, like someone walking on their hands. He had to chance pulling his head down and putting his hands forward, maybe get his neck and some of his back into the water before he hit hard. If he didn't and the water came up he'd hit face first. It could knock him out, even snap his neck. Or maybe just break his back.

God bless me, Ian thought, and put his head down, just in time to catch a brief flash of light on the surface of the water which was right there. The top of his head exploded first, smacking the water hard and causing the rest of him to go limp. As the rest of his body tumbled over into the water, the lower part of his back hit with a thump and knocked the wind out of his lungs. He was still conscious but the bells and sparks going off in his head made it impossible to orient himself up or down. He was underwater with no air and no idea where the surface was. Instinct had gotten him this far, but now he didn't think his body could help. He felt warm, not panicked. Maybe he would float to the surface, but not before he started swallowing water. Maybe he'd just float out to sea.

Then, down around his thighs, he felt something push his body. His foot scraped something, a rock maybe, then his leg, and then the push again. His head broke the surface of the water and he tilted it back to gulp air, getting half a mouth of water with it. He immediately sensed a chance of survival and started moving his legs and arms, choking on the water at the same time. He opened his eyes to see he was directly in front of a group of rocks, one almost within his reach. Then he felt the push again from behind and grabbed the rock with his hand. As the water level in the canyon swelled raising him up, he pulled himself onto the rock and rolled over on his back. He lay there with his eyes closed, his body and mind somewhere between death and disbelief.

"Señor Een, Señor Een," he heard seconds later, and opened his eyes to see the handsome face of Manny the Savior dripping water on him.

"Why am I always...so...happy...to see your face," Ian said, still gasping for air to fill his lungs. He was so disoriented he thought little of how strange it was that he was looking at Manny, here, in the bottom of the canyon.

"What has happened? Why deed you dive in thees darkness?"

Ian could see enough of Manny's face to tell he was scared.

"I can't...explain now...Manny...get back...the hotel... call the police and and...a doctor...an ambulance."

"But Señor Een what...?"

"Manny, please...do what I tell you...get the doctor...for Carmelo...on the top." Ian pointed weakly to the cliff. "Stay in the dark...just in case. Go, go!"

Manny turned and scrambled across some rocks then dove into the water. Ian could see across the canyon now to the top of the cliff where he'd just come from. The cliff wall was drenched in moonlight. He couldn't believe how clear it was.

It's a wonder the shooter didn't pick me off with all that light, he thought. Almost didn't have to.

Ian went into a physical inventory, slowly moving his arms and legs, hands and feet for any sign of damage. He moved his neck last, feeling more the weight of his head than any pain. His back was sore, the impact of the water still stamped across it, but everything seemed intact. His head was throbbing though. He sat up using his elbows and feet to move himself backward, and put his back against a rock.

Suddenly piercing light struck his eyes from the right causing him to squint hard which in turn caused his head to throb again. The canyon was now bathed in floodlight, Ian completely illuminated on his slimy divan.

God, I hope the shooter's gone, he thought.

Manny was back in the water, swimming towards him and at his side a minute later.

"Are you okay?" Manny said, right away.

"Got a headache, buddy. J'get a doctor and the police?"

"Yes, and an ambulance. They are comeeng."

"Good job. Come on, I want to get on the other side, out of here."

"Are you sure? Wait for thee doctor."

"No, I can do it. The water will feel good on my head."

Ian struggled his way up, feeling the pain in his head roll from one side to the other. Manny grabbed his arm and steadied him. He looked down at the boy, this ever-amazing boy, he thought, and smiled.

"Hey, Manny, thanks for pulling me out."

Manny smiled a smile that momentarily removed all the pain from Ian's head and said, "We protect each other, Señor Een, do we not?"

"That we do my friend," Ian said.

chapter 28

SPOOK'S FACE TOLD the man with the gun he was considering possibilities. Running, attacking, something. Tito Ramirez had seen tough guys all his life and plenty of crazies, but this kid was neither. Which was exactly why Ramirez didn't trust him. He knew what to expect from tough guys and crazies. He liked getting tough guys, bad guys, especially bad guys from other countries. But now he wasn't sure if he had a bad guy.

"Don't shoot anybody, mister," Spook said quietly, as he rose. "I don't even know you."

"Move back over here and sit down," Ramirez said, motioning with his empty hand.

Spook moved around the car to the spot where he pointed.

"Sit down and put your hands on top of your head. That's good."

He said something in Spanish to the man in the front seat of the car, then walked towards Spook as he spoke, circling behind him and checking with his free hand Spook's waist and under his arms and chest.

"Who are you?" Spook said. "What the hell do you want? Where did you come from?"

"It is I who will ask the questions, Señor."

He pulled down Spook's left arm and placed a handcuff tightly on one wrist, then the other.

"What the hell are you doing?" Spook yelled.

Ramirez could hear the panic in his voice. No tough guy.

"We didn't do anything to you, to anybody! What do you want to kill us for?!"

"I'm not interested in killing anyone, hombre," he said calmly. "Let's take a ride and get us both some answers, ay?"

The only way Ramirez was going to figure this kid and his pal out was to get them together and ask some direct questions. The time for watching and waiting was over.

"Ride? Ride where?"

"To see some friends who will help us answer our questions." Ramirez put his gun back inside his hip holster. "Stand up."

Spook got up unsteadily. Ramirez grabbed him by the arms and led him to the back of the car.

"Watch your head, Señor," he said, as he pushed Spook down inside the car.

He was enjoying putting this American fellow on the hot seat, to see him squirm a little. They all thought they could come into his town and do as they damn well pleased, blowing off the poor, dumb Mexicans with their dollars and their attitudes; and their half-assed Spanish. But not Tito Ramirez. This was his turf—Mexican turf. And to hell with anyone who tried to take it.

"We see some friends," he said again.

The man in the front seat of the car had not moved till now. He sat up straight and started the car. As he did strong light shattered the darkness around the hotel and voices could be heard. Ramirez could make out instructions being shouted around the canyon side of the hotel. He spoke sharply to the driver again then ran at a quick pace across the lot to the canyon.

* * *

Ian, still groggy from his landing, was grabbed immediately and put in an ambulance where he tried to answer a thick-accented policeman's questions. It had taken thirty minutes to get Carmelo down. Several divers, working other jobs at the hotel, carried him down, being the most sure-footed and familiar on the trail. Carmelo was still conscious when they found him, although delirious.

By the time Ian, Carmelo and Manny reached the Hospital Privado Magallenes, it was eleven o'clock. All Ian could figure out about the trip from the canyon to the hospital was that there weren't any straight roads between them. His head was still rolling as they wheeled him into what seemed like a modern building. Not very large by American standards, but Ian could sense the place was well run, people moving about efficiently and quietly. A doctor, a quiet man in his mid-forties, took charge of him as soon as he arrived. After a half hour of questions and poking he addressed Ian formally.

"You have a minor concussion, Señor," said the doctor in clear English, looking directly at Ian with eyes so narrow he couldn't tell how the man could see. Ian squinted hard to read the small blue badge on the man's left pocket but could not decipher a name.

"I suggest you rest and keep your head still for a few days and spend tonight here. Drink plenty of fluids, but not a lot of solid food for twenty four hours."

"How's my friend?" Ian asked.

"He will be fine. I've cleaned the wound and there does not seem to be any permanent damage. He needs a good week or two of rest."

"Thank you, doctor. Look, there's not a problem if I spend the night back at my hotel is there?"

"I do not recommend it," he said, walking towards the door, "but if you are determined to do so make sure someone keeps an eye on you for at least twenty four hours."

"Fair enough."

"You were lucky," the doctor said, stopping and looking back at Ian with the eyeless slits again.

Ian raised his eyebrows, not knowing how to respond.

The door closed, then opened immediately. In walked Robyn, Donna, and Kim. Ian felt a rush when he saw the worried look on Robyn's face.

"What the hell is going on?" she said. "Are you all right?"

Ian found her concern very appealing.

"Yeah, I'm okay."

"What happened?"

Ian didn't want to explain it all right then.

"Look, that dive the other day was just too easy. I wanted to try it again, only make it tougher. Carmelo said try it in the dark so...." He smiled at all of them.

"Come on, Ian," Kim snapped. "What's up? We go to the hotel, we get stood up with a message about emergencies, then we wait like idiots and get another message to come here. Where's the other one hiding?"

Ian was confused.

"You mean he's not with you?"

"Of course he's not with us. We haven't seen him yet tonight."

"What are you talking about?"

Ian looked at Robyn hoping for some calm explanation. It was calm but didn't explain enough.

"When we got to your hotel at nine-thirty Spook was gone," Robyn said. "He left a message that said there was an emergency and to wait. We sat there and had a few drinks till about ten-thirty when the bartender said that someone had called to tell his friends to meet him at this hospital. Here we are, and we still haven't seen Spook."

Ian's mind was racing already, trying to make sense of what was happening.

"Is Manny here?"

"We didn't see him when we came in," Kim said. "Is he here?"

"He should be," Ian said.

As he said it the door opened and in walked Manny.

"Manny!" Ian said. "My lifesaver. Is there another hospital around here that Spook could have gone to by mistake?"

Ian did not like the response on Manny's face to the question.

"Señor Een…."

"Manny, what's the matter?"

"Señor Een…," he did not want to say it, "Señor Spook is gone."

The room was deadly quiet. Manny looked ready to burst into tears.

"What, Manny?" Ian said, as calmly as possible but it didn't help.

Manny broke, and in between sniffles he managed to give some details of the evening's events.

"Señor Spook brought me to thee cliffs," he sobbed. "I told heem about thee bahd mahn and he came to protect you and the bahd mahn was at thee cliffs in hees car and before you go to the 'ospital I go look for heem and thee car ees there but the bahd mahn's car ees not and they are gone."

When he finished getting out as much as he thought told the story his face tightened and stayed that way. Kim quickly knelt down in front of him, pulling him to her.

"It's all right, Manny. It's okay. Don't be upset."

"Manny," Ian said, struggling to get down from the gurney, the weight in his head swinging. He knelt down on the floor and waved Manny over to him. "We look out for one another, remember?" Ian put his hands on Manny's shoulders. "Take your time and start from the beginning so I can figure out what to do. Okay?"

Manny nodded his head. "Do you remember thee bandito that grabbed me at they Royal Prince?"

Anger flared up in Ian at the memory but he kept Manny calm and talking.

"Yes, I do."

"Wail, I did not see hees face that night so good, but I think I saw heem again."

"Okay," Ian said. "Where?"

"He was at thee cleefs when you made your dive."

"How did you think you saw him when you didn't know what he looked like?"

He said it gently, wanting to pick up every detail from Manny without upsetting the boy.

"Because when he looked at me, eet was like he knew me and was watching me."

"Okay, go ahead."

"I did not know eet in my mind unteel today that I theenk he was thee mahn in they white car who almost caused us an ahkceedent."

The face of the disinterested driver at the bottom of the hill appeared in Ian's mind and he began to make the connections.

Followed us to the shrine and waited at the bottom of the hill; followed us to the Royal Prince; followed us to the cliffs the next day. Then I get shot at.

"And he was there tonight, at the cliffs?"

Manny nodded his head. "Yes."

And I get shot at again.

"Now you told Spook all this?" Manny nodded again. "And he quick came here in case the bad man was following me again, right?"

"Yes."

"What happened when you got to the cliffs?"

"Thee mahn was in hees car. Señor Spook said to go and find someone I know in the 'otel and stay weeth them. He was going to find out what thee mahn was doing. I waited and then I went out to the cleefs to see eef you and Carmelo were steel there and when I reached thee water I see you coming down. I waited to see eef you were okay but I didn't hear or see you, so I dive een to find you."

Ian stood up slowly and pulled Manny to his side, surrounding the boy's head with his arm. Ian looked at the floor. Inside him was a battle; worry at the thought of his friend possibly having been murdered versus anger at the stupidity of Spook's confronting a potential killer.

"What the hell did he go and mess with that guy for?" He looked at Robyn as if she had an answer.

"Ian, I obviously don't know all of what's going on here," she said, "but don't you think you should be talking to the police?"

"Yeah. They were there at the cliffs. I've been waiting for one of them to come in and start asking me questions."

"Well, how about I go find one and get him in here?" Kim said.

"That's a good idea, Kim," Robyn said. "Take Manny with you in case you need a translator."

"Okay. C'mon, Manny?" Kim put out her hand.

Before they could move, the door opened and a man stepped into the room. Manny took two steps backwards, stopping behind Ian's leg. All eyes in the room focused on the man, now leaning against the closed door.

There stood Manny's bad man.

chapter 29

SOMETHING IN THE man's expression told Ian to pay attention. He looked dangerous. His face was dark, but not just by complexion. There were lines, almost scars, carved deep into his face, so deep they formed overlapping shadows that blotted out any sense of expression. By his rumpled clothing he could have been anyone; a tourist, a store owner or a bum. But that face said he was something far more serious. Ian knew now it was the face in the white car at the bottom of the mountain.

"Are you somebody in charge?" Ian asked. He was confused by everything at this point, his head still wobbly and now this odd stranger's sudden appearance.

"I want some answers," Ramirez said coldly, "and I do not wish to waste a lot of time."

There was a razor-edge to the man's words, and it forced Ian to study him more intently. The face was leathery like Ian imagined the man's insides would be. His hair was blade-like clumps of thick black, pushed back by hand in several directions and ending irregularly around his shoulders and neck. There was nothing about the man's average height and size that was intimidating to Ian, only the darkness of his face, which made him hard to read. But Spook was missing, Manny got roughed up, and he and Carmelo were shot at. Maybe this was the guy behind it all. Dangerous or not, the guy was irritating the hell out of Ian.

"Who the hell are you anyway?" Ian said angrily, his voice rising. "Where is my friend!?"

"Your friend is fine," the man said, yelling back at him. "And I am someone who is going to make your life difficult if you do not cooperate with me."

"Pal, you've ALREADY made my life difficult. Now I'm gonna do the same for you."

As he said it, Ian moved towards the man. He had it worked out. Drive the son of a bitch into the door, hit him in the gut, forearm to the side of the head, down he goes. If he doesn't tell me where Spook is right away, kick him!

Before Ian took two steps the man reached inside his jacket at the hip, and out came a dark gun. Ian heard a collective gasp and one shriek come from the room. He had never seen a gun like this, except on TV. Maybe that's why he didn't think the man would shoot him. He stopped nonetheless.

"Look, creep, your friends took their best shot at me twice and blew it both times." Ian could hear his own words and knew the only thing holding him together was his anger. The man's expression changed, softened slightly, but Ian was hot. "Now I know the police are out there somewhere. So you fire that gun and they'll hear it. But that doesn't matter," his voice and anger surging, "because it doesn't look big enough to knock me down before I get my hands on your throat! And when I do I'M GONNA CHOKE THE LIVIN' SHIT OUTTA YA!"

Ian could feel the insanity, a few seconds away.

"ALL RIGHT! all right, calm down," the man said, and put the gun back into his jacket.

Ian still wanted to choke the guy, but the surprise of seeing him put the gun away interrupted the process. As quickly as he'd entered the room, Ramirez turned and was gone. It took a few seconds for Ian to realize what happened.

"Don't let him get away!" he yelled, moving towards the door. He grabbed the handle and swung the door open, yelling as he did.

"SOMEBODY STOP THAT GUY! POLICE!"

Before he could get through the doorway he crashed chest first into a uniformed policeman.

"Quedese alla. Bajo control," the officer said, pinning both of Ian's arms to his sides and pushing him backwards to the bed. Ian was strong enough to resist but instinctively deferred to the man in uniform.

"That man, he's a killer!" Ian yelled at him. "Stop him! He's getting away! Hablo Inglés? Dammit! Manny tell him!"

Manny ran to the officer's side and yelled in Spanish, "Officer, that man is a bandit! He has tried to kill us! He...."

The officer looked down at Manny and smiled, still moving Ian back to the gurney.

"Entiendo. Dile a tu amigo que se calmara. Se encuentra bajo control."

"Señor Een," Manny said, not looking convinced, "he says to calm down. Eet iss under control."

Ian's face was still full of anger as he looked at Manny then back at the officer, but now frustration was carving out a place in his features. His backside hit the gurney and the officer let go of his arms. Ian looked at everyone as the policeman walked back to the door. The officer opened the door and raised his eyes to meet someone coming in the door. He stepped aside and in walked the dark man again, immediately followed by Spook.

"Oh man, you're all right!" Spook yelled, running up to Ian and hugging him. "Man, you had me worried."

"Me?" Ian said. He was totally confused now, his emotions bouncing around inside him like charged particles as he tried to decide which one to use. "Where the hell have you been?"

"With Officer Ramirez." Spook sounded sheepish, tilting his head in the direction of the dark man.

Ian and everyone else except Spook looked at Officer Ramirez leaning against the door with no expression on his face. The room was dead quiet.

"Officer?" Ian said, not to anyone. "This guy's a cop?" He looked down at the floor. His head felt about three times its weight. "Now I'm really confused."

"No more than I have been, Señor," Officer Ramirez said, his voice slow and emotionless. "Until I was convinced by your friend that you are here on vacation only, I have not had a clue as to what is going on. I feel there are more questions to ask."

Ian could detect a note of condescension in the cop's voice.

"I took a little ride to the police station with the Officer," Spook said. "He seems to think we're involved in something we shouldn't be." Now Spook looked embarrassed. "Since I tried to sneak up on him, he's been pretty hard to convince otherwise." He turned his face toward Ian and away from Ramirez. "I'm not so sure I have yet."

"You found him at El Salto?" Ian asked.

"Yeah," Spook said. "Him and one of his men. Out in the lot."

"Were you sitting there when I was getting shot at?" Ian asked, directing the question to the officer. The thought annoyed him.

"Shot!?"

The word came out into the room from three different people.

"It's possible," Ramirez answered.

"Well, what were you doing there? If you were tailing me, why the hell weren't you there when I was shot at?"

Beyond this immediate confusion there were a whole lot of things Ian didn't like about this. Ramirez showed no reaction, his words coming out cold.

"There are many questions that need to be answered. Mine more than yours for the time being."

Ian saw the man could care less about the confusion or the fact that Ian's head was pounding again. It was time to concede the standoff for now.

"I have no problem with that," Ian said. "But I have a request. Could we possibly do it in the morning? My head is killing me. All I want to do is check on Carmelo and go to bed."

"I think that can be arranged," Ramirez said. "Your rental car is outside. I had it brought here."

"Thank God," Spook said, looking at Ian and rolling his eyes. "That guy at the hotel wasn't too happy as it was."

"I'll have an officer escort you back to the hotel and he will stay there this evening, since you feel your life is in danger. I'll meet you there in the morning, say, ten o'clock."

It was not a request.

"That's fine," Ian said. "Listen, I'm concerned about Manny's safety as well."

"I am going to stay here tonight, Señor Een," Manny said, "weeth Carmelo."

"I'll have an officer posted outside the room," Ramirez said.

Ian looked at him as if to say, you better.

"Are you sure about staying, Manny?"

"Yes."

Ian could tell by his face he was sure. He nodded his head and smiled.

"Okay," he said quietly and ruffled Manny's hair. Then he looked up. "Let's get out of here."

On the way out Ian was able to confirm that Carmelo was cared for and sleeping. He and the group said their goodbyes to Manny at the door and watched him go into the room. Then they all walked out of the hospital.

"Hey, you guys didn't know how to have fun till you met us, ha?" Ian said to the backs of Donna and Kim. Robyn was beside him, her arm around his.

"Yeah, you guys are one adventure after another," Kim said, over her shoulder. "I'll have to call you up whenever I go on vacation."

"Another action packed evening, eh?" he said, to Robyn.

"Oooh yeah," she said with a mock-serious face.

"I didn't know I had such a dull life till I came here," Ian said, half believing it.

"What do you know about what's going on, really?" Robyn asked.

Ian knew nothing would make much sense unless he filled her in, so he quickly told the ladies the story of Carmelo and the bullet and reminded them of the incident with Manny at their hotel, bringing them up to date with the evening's events.

"There's got to be some sort of connection that's just gone by me completely, only I haven't had any reason till now to really search for one. But I'll start in the morning when my head's a little clearer." They came to the cars. "Can I have a raincheck on that dance date?" he asked.

"I don't know," Robyn said, smiling sweetly. "Hanging around with you could be fatal."

"This is true. Can I call you tomorrow? I'm really disappointed we didn't get to do anything tonight, for reasons other than the obvious ones."

"I'm sorry too," she said.

He could feel the closeness behind her words.

"When do you leave for home?" he asked.

"Sunday afternoon."

"Same for us. Good. We still have the weekend,...if you're interested."

She reached up and gently put her hand under his chin.

"I hope this doesn't hurt your head," she said, then kissed him. "Bye," she added, and walked across the lot. Kim was already in the driver's seat of their car with the motor running.

As they pulled by Ian hollered, "Drive safely, ladies." It made his head hurt. He watched them leave, then turned to see Spook's rental car slide to a stop in front of him. "Nice wheels, James."

"Just get in and put your seat belt on," Spook ordered as a small police car pulled up behind them. "Maybe we won't lose you that way."

"You got a lot of nerve," Ian said, smirking as he got in the car. "What's with the I Spy routine, going after banditos and shit?"

"Hey, I was worried about you, and Ramirez, the 'bad man,' was the key to it all. At least we thought he was. You're the one went mountain climbing in the dark without anybody to back you up."

Spook pulled out of the lot and on to the road. The debate continued almost all the way back to the hotel. As they pulled into the garage Ian settled the argument by raising a point they both agreed on.

"I know one thing," he said, "I don't trust that Ramirez as far as I can spit."

chapter 30

"RISE AND SHINE and greet the glorious new day, oh ye thick of skull."

Spook was staring down at Ian, holding a glass, the contents of which Ian couldn't see.

"Whaaat?" Ian said, sleepily, parts of his eyelids still stuck together. "What's up?" The entire inside of his mouth was dry, not a wet spot anywhere to get it going. "Aaaagh. Ya got liquid there?"

"Golden nectar, my friend," Spook said.

Ian slid towards the headboard to prop himself up and immediately felt the soreness.

"Ooo," he said, grabbing the back of his neck. He took the orange juice and swished some around in his mouth before drinking it. "I feel like we were out drinking all night. What time is it?"

"About nine o'clock."

"Is that all?" Ian said, closing his eyes. "Why didn't I sleep till noon?"

"Cause your brain still works," Spook said, laughing.

"I don't know for sure right now."

He could feel the fragility of his head, as if the insides would rattle loose if he shook it quickly.

"What time is the Officer coming?"

He said "Officer" in a sour way, still not convinced the guy wasn't really a thug.

"About ten." Spook snatched the empty juice glass from Ian's hand. "He said he'd call right before he came."

"Good. When he calls, tell him to meet us out by the pool bar. I want to sit out in the air and soak all day."

"Good to me."

"I want to call the hospital and see how Carmelo and Manny are doing."

Ian leaned over in the bed to grab the phone and felt the rattle in his head again, although not as bad this time.

"Why don't you wait?" Spook said, frowning.

Ian put himself back down on the pillow gently, his face bunched in pain.

"I'll wait."

Ian eventually managed to struggle from the bed to the shower where he spent ten minutes letting the water run over his head. By the time he finished and dressed, the call from Officer Ramirez came in. Ian and Spook headed out of the room to meet him, followed by the policeman posted outside their door.

The long, blue pool of the hotel sparkled crisply in the morning sun. Ian was surprised at first to see so many people already lounging, both in and around it, but the lower heat of the early air quickly offered an explanation. Ian settled into a lounge chair with the sun behind him. The heat felt good on his body.

Restorative powers, he thought. Sun and sea air. That'll do it. Got to get it together on this thing here. Figure it out and get rid of it.

It was interesting to him that fear was on the bottom of the list of things he had been feeling since last night. It was the first clue for him that coming to Acapulco and making the dive had accomplished something. He remembered the feeling of calm and power he felt the night before, standing on the cliff for the second time, before the shooting; an invulnerability of some kind. And he had it only because he recognized he could not control the things around him. The cliffs, Manny, the shooter, the beauty of the sunset on the bay; these were things that were here when he came and they would be here when he left. If he just tried to co-exist with them he would be at peace, and strong. He did not need to bend the shape of the world around him.

At ten a.m. sharp, Officer Ramirez stepped along the pool, almost unaware of its existence, his tan linen suit begging for a tailor. The suit was in no way an attempt at business or formality, an open-collar, white shirt acting as backdrop rather than complement. Ian watched him as he walked, the same cold, disinterested look on the detective's face as the night he almost killed them on the downhill curve.

Cold by nature, Ian thought. Doesn't like or dislike what he does, just does it.

It was hard to see this man as their ally. Ramirez had fit the bad guy role too well up till now, and it wasn't going to be easy to see him any other way. If there had been something the least bit likeable about him it might have been easier, but there wasn't.

Ramirez flapped his hand at the uniformed officer as if to shoo him. The man nodded and went to the shade of the bar. Ramirez walked right at the two friends and stopped in front of them.

"So what can you tell me, Señors?" Ramirez said, abruptly.

Ian and Spook looked at one another, their eyebrows touching their hairlines.

"What about good morning, Señors?" Ian said, firmly. "What about, how are you, Señors? How is your head, Señor? Lovely day to be alive, Señor." The man's expression didn't change a bit as Ian spoke. "Would you like a cup of coffee or something to drink?"

A slight adjustment in his face, then stone again.

"No, thank you," Ramirez said.

"Is it at aallll possible," Spook said, "that you still don't trust us? Or do you treat everybody this way?"

You've never been accused of being subtle there, Spook, Ian thought, chuckling to himself.

"That is possible," Ramirez said.

"Which?" Ian said, "that you don't trust us, or that you treat everybody that way?"

"Both."

Sense of humor, Ian thought.

"Okay, that's fair." Ian decided to make the first move. "Look, we really don't know what's going on. You seem to have a lot of questions as well. Why don't you trust us until you find some reason to really distrust us?"

Ian searched the man's face for a clue and got one. The officer's hard stare dropped and he looked at the ground as he spoke.

"Señors, the last several months have been difficult, particularly with this case. I will take your suggestion."

It wasn't an apology so much as a truce. This was a man who could not afford to soften, considering his work. But it did make Officer Ramirez slightly more tolerable than he had been a minute ago.

"Thank you," Ian said, with no trace of victory. "Now what can we tell you that can help you?"

"Why are you here?" Ramirez said.

"I already told you that last night! We're on vacation!" Spook answered, a little too defensively.

"I know what you told me, Señor. I am interested in what your friend has to say."

His tone was still calm. He didn't seem to be offended by Spook's snappy response.

"All right, relax Spook," Ian said. "I understand what the officer is getting at. We're on vacation. We're a couple of guys from Philadelphia on a nice getaway vacation."

"And have you done anything out of the ordinary, for a tourist, that is?" the man said.

"No," Ian answered. "Some sightseeing, some shopping, eating and drinking, like everyone else."

"Well, not exactly," Spook said.

Ian and Ramirez looked at him with surprise but no one said anything.

"Your dive, Ian," Spook said. "I don't think leaping off the cliffs is standard tourist behavior. Most people come to watch."

Ian laughed. "You're right, I didn't even think about that. Okay," he turned his face back to Ramirez, "I took a dive from the cliffs up there at La Quebrada. Actually two."

Ramirez wasn't laughing, but he didn't seem as stone-faced as earlier.

"When did you first suspect there was something wrong, that is, someone might be trying to harm you?"

"Not really until last night," Ian said. "When somebody started shooting at me. It was a real clue."

"Then why were you up there last night?"

"Because of a suspicion someone else had. Carmelo, our friend that was shot, told me on Tuesday night, after my first dive, that he thought someone had fired a shot when I was up there that day. We went to look for a bullet or some indication that it was true, or just his imagination. Obviously," Ian chuckled nervously, "it wasn't his imagination."

"The first time you were shot at, on the cliff," Ramirez said, intently, "your friend Carmelo was on the cliff top with you, no?"

"Yes," Ian answered, not sure of the point of the question.

"And last night when you were shot at again, this friend was on the cliff with you again?"

"Yes, obviously." Ian was stumped now. "You know that. What's the point?"

"Señor, you claim to have no idea why you are being shot at, that you are an innocent tourist on vacation in a foreign country full of strangers."

Ian could feel the tone turning slightly accusatory.

"Did it not occur to you that you are not the target? That the target is your friend, Carmelo Paloma?"

Ian was momentarily lost for words. He knew he had considered that possibility briefly in the beginning but had dismissed it. Ramirez's presentation just now had been so clear and quick, Ian couldn't remember what it was that had let him feel he could dismiss it.

"Yeah, I thought of that but...."

He was still searching his memory for the reasoning, then came upon it. When he did he knew immediately how weak it would sound when he said it.

"Carmelo said there was no reason anyone would want to kill him."

"And you know this man Carmelo well enough to know he would not lie to you? You are sure it has nothing to do with him simply because he said it does not?"

"No, I don't know him well enough, it's just that he...he's a.... Look," Ian decided to put some challenge into both sides of the discussion, "I have pretty good instincts about people. You can accept that or not, but it's true. Now when Carmelo brought this thing to my attention I pressed him about it, and nothing in his answer or in the way he answered gave me the slightest reason not to believe him. And from the short amount of time that I have known him, I sense him to be an honest, straightforward person. Is it possible he could be lying? I guess it is. Is it possible he's involved in something? Hell, he lives here, I suppose it's possible. But what about the other incident, at the Royal Prince?"

"I would like you to tell me about that, Señor," Ramirez said, his interest obviously increasing.

"Some creep...."

"That we thought was you," Spook interrupted.

"Right," Ian said, "grabbed Manny, Manuel, the young boy, out in the parking lot while we were inside eating. The guy was choking him and asking him who we were."

"Is this boy not related to your friend Carmelo?"

Man, this guy's got all the angles covered, Ian thought.

"Yes, he is."

"And is it not possible that the boy was confronted because he may be involved with his cousin in the same business his cousin is being shot at for?"

"No way," Spook said, annoyed at the inference. "That kid is an angel, he's as clean as they come."

"Absolutely," Ian said.

"More instinct?" Ramirez said, delicately.

"Call it whatever you want," Ian said, feeling the jab. He understood probing. But not by going for Manny.

"Let us assume your 'instincts'," Ramirez said it less offensively this time, "are correct about the boy. Is it possible whoever wanted to get to Carmelo Paloma felt an innocent boy might be the way?"

Ian let the thought roll around in his mind for a minute.

"I suppose that's possible. But the man asked Manny what we knew about someone named Wilson. Why would he ask Manny about who we know or don't know if he's trying to get to Carmelo through the boy?"

"I don't know," Ramirez answered with apparent honesty. "Perhaps the man was assuming something I assumed, that your contact with the boy had something to do with his cousin. Mehbe, mehbe not, but for this 'creep' as you call him, it was worth checking while he had the boy. What happened with this man?"

"Well, fortunately I was headed out to give Manny some dinner and spotted the guy in the parking lot, choking him. He took off when I yelled and chased him. He was driving a white car, a lot like the one you were driving that night. By the way, thanks for nearly killing us."

Ramirez looked away, then said, "At the time I was not so interested in your welfare as I was in your activities."

It was not an apology.

"You were following us that night?" Spook said, to confirm the fact for everyone.

"Yes, I was." Ramirez hesitated a moment, unsure whether he cared to offer any more, then added, "I left you at the Royal Prince shortly after you arrived."

"Okay now." Ian sat up in his chair. It was time to go on the offensive. "We've been telling you a lot about what's been going on with us, but the fact is we're the ones operating in the dark. Fill us in on a few things. What were you following us for in the first place? What's your case?"

Ramirez sat down for the first time since he'd arrived, pulling a chair out from another table and plopping heavily into it. He sat back and rubbed his eyes, then his forehead, using the same back and forth motion across his face with his right hand.

"About a year ago," he started, looking as if the story was painful to tell, "large sums of American money, larger than usual, started showing up in several black market currency exchanges in the Acapulco, Ichtapa, and Mecheeco City areas. Mechican currency is the only legally acceptable currency in this country for you to operate with. As you know when you enter this country you must exchange your American money for ours in order to spend it. Now, do not think me foolish. I'm sure you have already seen that bypassed in certain situations. Peddlers on the streets, grass peddlers, whatever. That will always be the case. The American dollar, regardless of its performance in world markets is still a valuable commodity in this country. And so rather than waste a lot of time and money trying to catch petty thieves making a few dollars from the tourists, we monitor the flow of the money. We have enough people operating within the black market system to know on a regular basis how much foreign currency comes and goes. When that amount changes considerably, it is an indication of laundering, that is, someone with large amounts of cash wants to spend it and cannot without drawing attention. To these people it may appear to be easier to come to this country and sell it off through legitimate businesses with illegitimate proprietors, because they think the 'stupid Mechicans' are not so sophisticated in these matters. But we have been successful in following a trail of sorts."

Ian was drinking in everything the officer was saying. He had forgotten about his earlier annoyance and was completely caught up in the underworld story unfolding before him.

"I think I'll have a drink now," Ramirez said, his cool countenance softening just a bit. "An orange juice, perhaps."

Spook got up immediately and stepped to the bar, returning in a minute with a glass of juice. Ramirez waited till Spook handed him the glass. He took a long, deep swallow, emptying half the glass, then set it down on the table in front of him. Before he could continue, Ian jumped in.

"So what is this, big drug deals, international espionage, what?"

Ramirez looked amused.

"No, Señor, nothing that complicated. The amounts of money and the manner of disposal would suggest theft, embezzlement perhaps."

"So where do we fit into all of this?" Ian said, still trying to find a connection. "Why were you following us in the first place? We certainly didn't drop any large amounts of cash anywhere."

"For the same reasons as the way the case has been going," Ramirez answered, his eyes narrowing, "simply by association. Let me ask you a question first. Have you met anyone on your vacation other than Mechican people?"

Ian wrinkled his face in a show of complete confusion at the point of the question.

"Of course we have," Spook said. "Oh, okay. I guess you're going to tell us now that our female friends from Pittsburgh are a bunch of counterfeiters. Man, this is getting bad."

"No, Señor, I am not talking about the young ladies. Who else have you met?"

Ian was a thinking, but not effectively. Robyn had popped into his mind and was breaking his concentration, along with the preposterous idea that she and her friends were criminals.

"I don't know," he said. Who?" He looked at Spook. "Any ideas?"

"Where'd we go?" Spook said.

"Okay," Ian said. "First day, nowhere. Second day, some local stores and we hit another hotel pool."

"Everybody was Mexican," Spook said, "or at least they pretended to be." He laughed, but Ramirez didn't change his expression.

"All right," Ian said, "Monday we went to the cliffs. Picked up Manny on the way. There were other Americans at the cliffs, but we didn't meet any of them. Did you, while I was talking to the diving coach?"

"Na," Spook said. "Just sat in the bar."

"Then we shopped," Ian continued. "Manny took us to a couple of stores."

The film was running in his head. He saw them all get in the car and leave the cliff hotel, turning as Manny instructed. The first stop, the store where he bought the silver cross and Spook's hats. The long dusty tables the glass case the Boss Bandito little bandito. WAIT! WAIT!

"Wait a minute!"

Ian brought his head up. He could have said it right away but he wanted Spook to follow him and remember it at the same time.

"The first store, where you got your hats," he pointed at Spook who nodded in agreement, "the heavy guy I said hello to that I said I thought I knew his face but couldn't place it. Spook, you said to forget it because I probably saw the guy at a ballgame or something. I never figured out who the hell he was either. I forgot about him ten minutes after we left the store and I haven't thought of him since."

"Yeah," Spook said, "I remember, although I didn't really look at the guy, I just noticed that you did."

Ian looked at Ramirez, waiting for some reaction. Ramirez stared back at him and without moving his eyes, reached inside his jacket with his right hand and pulled out a photograph which he turned in his hand to face Ian. Then he leaned forward and dropped it on the table.

"I have to make a call," Ramirez said, rising from his chair. "Take a look at this and tell me if this man is familiar?" He walked slowly to the bar.

Ian saw the face before the photo hit the table and knew without touching it, it was the Fat Man.

chapter 31

KIM RALETTI AND Robyn Baldwin were sitting on the balcony of their room at the Royal Prince enjoying what was left of the morning sun while it was still tolerable.

"So, what's with you and Ian?" Kim asked, good-naturedly.

"What do you mean?"

Robyn looked at her, not avoiding the subject at all. She knew from the first night they had their impromptu dinner with the guys that Kim was not entirely comfortable with the arrangement. Robyn knew it well. It had led to similar situations in the past. Robyn trying new things and Kim getting, at first, nervous, and then annoying, and then downright interfering. At one time or another in their lives it was smoking cigarettes, smoking pot or drinking, even though they were mostly phases Robyn passed through. Almost always it was the men she met. Kim never approved of any of them. In Kim's eyes they were always too fast or too immature or too stupid for Robyn. Kim had a much higher opinion of Robyn then Robyn did of herself, which was why Kim drove her crazy in a very caring sort of way. She knew Kim was looking out for her best interests all the time but she wasn't sure Kim knew what Robyn's best interests were. She wasn't sure Kim knew what her own were.

"Well," Kim said, clearly seizing the opportunity she'd created for herself, "you know these guys are into some deep trouble right about now, I mean people shooting guns, people following people; and poor little Manny getting choked by some freak, I mean this is not a casual acquaintance for a relaxed vacation, you know."

"But he's so cute," Robyn squealed, like a high school girl at a dance.

"Oh, good," Kim said, smirking. "Make like it's a joke now."

"It's not a joke," Robyn said. "I know what you're saying and it's reasonable, but there's nothing that serious for us to be concerned about. I like the guy. He's a nice person, a little troubled, yeah, but, I don't know. Did you ever meet someone who is just who they are, and it shows, right up front to everyone but that person?" Robyn stopped to consider the thought herself, seeing an interesting comparison as she did. "He reminds me of you." She looked smugly at Kim who wasn't expecting the comment.

"What in the hell are you talking about?" Kim shot back. "For a minute I thought your brain was working again but I guess not."

"No, really," Robyn said, realizing it was time to tell Kim something she'd wanted to tell her for a long time. "Ian is one of those people who is his own worst enemy. He demands things of himself, puts standards on himself that no one else does. He's somebody who has a lot to offer in what he does naturally, but that's never good enough for him. He's interested in other people and how they feel, and he's willing to help anyone who asks for it. Outwardly, he's confident because he insists he be that way. But he's shy underneath, not confident at all about the things that mean the most, like other people." Robyn paused to let her observations sink into both of them. "And you're the same damn way," she continued, laughing as she said it. "You don't give yourself enough credit for who you are and what you do. You're unselfish and caring to anyone who needs it, except yourself. You don't give yourself the same understanding and freedom you give others."

Kim was staring at a piece of string on her shorts.

"I mean if these guys were such bad news, why did you even let us get involved with them in the first place? Why didn't you just chase us all back to the room when they invited us to dinner?"

"Well," Kim said, shrugging her shoulders and looking at Robyn, "I thought you really wanted to, like you were getting itchy to do something different after a couple days of hanging around here."

"See," Robyn said, pointing her finger, "because you thought I wanted to. God forbid it was because you thought you wanted to. And how come you let us continue to bother with them after dinner?"

"Oh well, that's different." Kim's tone was a little more confident. "That poor little Manny was upset. That had nothing to do with those guys."

"And that's different," Robyn said, mocking her. "Poor little Manny. No, Kim, it was just you being yourself again. Manny was upset and so was Ian, so you did what comes naturally to you, you got involved because you were needed. At the hospital last night you were running around demanding people tell you what's going on and where is this one and who are you? 'I want some information,' you yelled. You were tough in there because you cared about those guys and Manny." Robyn kept looking at her but now Kim wouldn't pick her head up. She reached over and took Kim's hand. "Look, the point is you don't let yourself have the pleasure of knowing you the way other people know you, the way I know you. You've always looked out for me and I love you for it, even when you were a pest. I think we've been good friends for a long time because we're a good balance. You protect my impulsive side and I prod your cautious side. I see a lot of you in Ian. Maybe that's why he appeals to me."

Robyn squeezed her hand and felt Kim squeeze back, holding it for a few seconds longer.

"I don't think I can change," Kim said quietly.

"I wouldn't ever want you to," Robyn said, brightly. "But listen to me when I tell you things like this and believe me." Kim smiled shyly and nodded. "And get loose on our vacation here! Get crazy! Don't tell me that Spook isn't an interesting creature. Come on now."

"Oh God." Kim shook her head. "Creature's a good description. He's in his own world."

"Yeah, but he's funny. I'm not talking about falling in love or romance, I'm just talking about enjoying people. Those guys are fun, each in their own way. Admit it, outside of this recent development, we've had a lot of laughs with them."

"I know," Kim said, conceding. "It's just that this thing is getting pretty serious from what Ian told us. It's already gotten Manny and his cousin involved. I just don't want to see you getting hurt, physically or emotionally."

Robyn picked up the worry in her voice.

"I don't think there's any concern physically, Kim. Honestly. As for emotionally, don't worry. I'm not a love at first sight person, you know that. Four or five days of vacation are not enough for me to get in deep with someone. And Ian is not pushy in that department. I think he's a little tender right now anyway. Sorting some things out, you know? Me, I'm just enjoying the vacation and enjoying the company, male and female. Okay?"

The phone rang inside the room.

"Okay," Kim agreed. "Did you make any plans for today?"

"No, not really. Ian said he would call, but to tell you the truth...," the phone rang again, "now how's that for eerie timing. Donna will get it, about time for her to wake up anyway. To tell you the truth, I feel like staying around here today. I need a catch-up day to prepare for the weekend."

"That sounds like an excellent idea."

Kim saw Donna shuffling towards the sliding glass door.

"Hey, sleepyhead, what brings you to us?"

"The phone," came the sleepy reply.

Donna Miller was still out of it but trying hard to come around.

"It was that Officer Ramirez from last night. He says he wants to come here and talk to us around noon. I said we'd be here. We are going to be here, aren't we?" Her eyes were still half shut.

"What the hell does he want?" Kim snapped.

"Relax," Robyn said. "See what I mean? He probably just wants to find out who we are. We did show up at the hospital last night."

"Well, he didn't ask," Donna said, "he said he was coming. He gives me the creeps."

"He does take his job seriously, doesn't he?" Kim said, matter of factly. "Let's go have coffee by the pool and then jump in. It's getting hot. The coffee smells good but it will make me sweat."

"Pah-spyah, dahling, pah-spyah," Robyn said, raising her chin and fluttering her eyelids. "Women of ah statcha neva sweat.

❋ ❋ ❋

"That's the guy," Ian said, "sure as hell. You see, I know this guy from somewhere, but I couldn't place him at the time. Something about his expression was like he knew me when we met, in that store near the cliffs."

"The Silver Mine," Ramirez interjected.

"Right, but I'm not sure if it was the same thing for him, you know, if he knew my face but couldn't place me."

"But you do not know who he is?"

"Not right now. I had other things on my mind that day, and it sort of caught me off guard. It wasn't important. But I'll tell you what, I guarantee between today and tomorrow I'll remember. I'll dig it out," he pointed to his head, "cause it's there."

"You feel sure you will remember?" Ramirez pressed.

"Definitely, "Ian said. "What's his connection?"

Ramirez hesitated a minute. Ian figured he was trying to decide how much of his hand he wanted to show. It was clear Ramirez was not giving more than he was getting, and only after he got it first.

"He seems to be the only connection we have to some of the money flowing through certain places."

"How'd you know Ian even met the guy?" Spook said, his tone suspicious again.

The detective looked at each of their faces then looked at the uniformed officer still sitting at the bar. The officer was facing the other way talking to the bartender.

"You keep everything that's discussed here, right here. Understand? You don't discuss this with anyone."

Spook and Ian nodded their assent, their curiosity tweaked. Ramirez spoke quietly, more quietly than he'd been speaking already.

"We have a man on the inside at the Silver Mine. American money has always trickled out of there, but never any more or any less. It is one of our sources for monitoring the flow. Then one day larger amounts start to show up which means a new resource has been developed. Our man was there when you and this man met."

Little Bandito, Ian thought.

"You being an American, acknowledging this man, we suspected there might be a connection. So we watch you."

"Does this guy have a name and would I be way out in space if I guessed it was Wilson?" Ian asked.

Ramirez was unfazed.

"It is the only one we've heard, and it must be false because we cannot find information on him through any of our usual methods. I personally contacted the FBI in your country but they showed nothing. That does not surprise me. I have nothing on the man but a suspicion, and I have no other clues. If he has never been convicted of a crime, no information would be available. But this Andrew Wilson continues to surface from time to time. He is our only lead."

"You don't know where he is now?" Spook said.

Ramirez pursed his lips and shook his head.

"I suspect he's somewhere in the area." He looked coldly at Ian. "You are still alive."

For the first time since he'd known someone was trying to hurt him, Ian felt a real sense of fear. Something gritty and realistic in the demeanor of Officer Ramirez translated the message clearly. This was his world, a cold and emotionless world; a place where people like Ian weren't supposed to go.

"It is very important that you remember this man." Ramirez reached for the photo of Wilson. "You seem certain you will. When you do, you contact me only. I must emphasize that. Do not talk to anyone else about it. You will not know who you are talking to. Call this number and ask for me." He pulled a wrinkled card from his jacket pocket. "If I am not there ask to have the call returned, say nothing else. Do you understand?"

"Yes," Ian said, not thrilled with Ramirez's patronizing manner. There was a brief period of weighty silence as he and Spook considered the ominous instructions. Then Ian's thoughts shifted.

"I need you to do something for me. I want to call the hospital and check on Carmelo and I don't want to run into a lot of red tape. Would you make the call and get me through to him?"

Ian didn't ask in a friendly way, more as a condition of his cooperating with Ramirez.

"That is not a problem."

Ramirez stood up and walked to the bar. Ian turned and watched as the bartender placed a phone on the bar and Ramirez began dialing. He spoke quietly into the phone and after about a minute turned and extended the phone to Ian. Ian looked back at Spook, then jumped up and grabbed the phone. As he spoke he looked back at Ramirez who was trying hard to appear disinterested in the conversation. After a few minutes he turned and spoke to Ramirez.

"Can you get the boy a ride over here and back?"

If Ian was Ramirez's only clue, the cop was going to have to earn it. Ramirez nodded yes, a look of annoyance on his face this time.

"Manny, an officer will pick you up, about one thirty." He looked at Ramirez again, who gave no reaction. "Okay? See ya then." Ian handed the phone back to the bartender and said thank you.

"I do not have a lot of officers to spare, Señor. I will have to send this man to pick up the boy. I suggest you stay here in the hotel, preferably in the company of the other guests, until he returns."

"We'll be fine, thank you," Ian said. He did appreciate what Ramirez was doing, he just didn't like appearing too grateful. Gratitude was surely a weakness in this man's eyes. "I appreciate your helping the boy out. He's a good kid, he works hard."

Ramirez gave instructions to the uniformed man and then walked away from the bar, looking back at Spook and Ian to draw them with him. When they were just beyond the table they'd been sitting at, he turned back and looked at Ian.

"Think, Señor, think hard. You may be saving your own life, and remember," he looked at both of them, "speak to no one but me. Call that number. If I do not answer, just leave your name."

"One more thing," Ian said. "Could I see that picture of Wilson again?"

Ramirez handed him the picture. Ian looked hard at it. In the picture, the Fat Man was sideways with his right hand extended in the act of reaching or pointing. The fingers of the fat hand were so round and full that no space existed between them. The face showed little by way of features, all distinctness swallowed up in the fatness, which was what seemed familiar. What was not familiar, and was probably where Ian's mental block lay, was the vacancy in his eyes, or at least the left one which was clearly visible. But Ian was sure the right one was just as empty. He handed the picture back to Ramirez who took it and walked away without saying another word.

When Ramirez reached the cool of the hotel lobby a stocky man in slacks and open collared shirt moved toward him. Ramirez stopped, looked back at the Americans by the pool, who were paying no attention to him now, and spoke to the man without looking at him. The man nodded silently then walked away, disappearing into the scenery as magically as he had appeared. Ramirez continued through to the far side of the lobby and stopped at a set of phones, grabbing one and dialing immediately.

chapter 32

OFFICER TITO RAMIREZ arrived at the Royal Prince Hotel at eleven-thirty and found a message at the desk informing him that the young women he wished to speak to were at poolside. He trudged resentfully through the hotel and out the other side.

The conversation with the American men had been useful. He had established in his mind that they were probably the innocents they claimed to be, only he knew they could no longer be truly innocent. They had crossed paths with Wilson, and the fact that Ramirez knew so little about Wilson worried him. Anyone, particularly an American, who could come to Ramirez's jurisdiction and keep that low a profile was a threat. But these young men, for some reason not clear to the detective, had flushed Wilson out, however briefly, into the open. Tito Ramirez's detective's instinct told him, stay close to the American diver and his friends.

Kim had seated herself facing the most logical place of arrival for a visitor.

"Isn't that him?" she said.

"Yes, that's him," Donna said. "He's so creepy."

They watched Ramirez scan the poolside chairs until he met their gaze. When he did, none of them knew what to do, except to look away. They didn't exactly want to wave to him. Robyn continued looking long enough to nod and smile weakly, confirming his choice.

"Now let's be polite, ladies," she said. "He's just doing his job."

"Good afternoon." Ramirez offered a hint of politeness. "I must get some information to be complete in handling this case."

Despite the hardness developed from the job and displayed abundantly the night before, Ramirez's cultural upbringing would not let him be quite so rude to the mujeres.

"Just what is your case, Inspector?"

Kim had been preparing for the Inspector all morning. Ramirez' face tightened a little.

"Why don't we start with my questions, Señorita, and then, if I can, I will answer yours."

Kim backed up in her chair.

"When did you first meet the two gentlemen from Philadelphia?"

"We met them here, on…a…Monday, Monday night," Robyn answered.

"How did you meet them?"

"They introduced themselves to us, and we all had dinner together."

"Did anything unusual happen that evening?"

"Like what?" Kim snapped.

"Unusual," he repeated, without changing his tone or expression.

"Oh, you mean Manny?" Robyn said. "Yes, well, the guys had Manny with them and he didn't want to come in, into the hotel. So he waited in the car. Ian wanted to take some dinner out to him and when he did there was a man choking him out in the parking lot."

"Poor kid was all shook up," Kim chimed in.

"Did you see this person that choked him, as you say?"

"No," Kim said. "We were still here waiting for Ian to come back."

"So you do not know what this person looks like?"

"No, we do not," Kim answered, emphatically.

"What do you know about these two men?"

"What's to know?" Kim shot back. "They're a couple of guys on vacation, just like us. One of them likes to jump off cliffs and one of them's a real piece of work. We didn't interview them."

Ramirez was getting irritated. He really didn't think there was much to discover with this group and it was becoming more work than he cared for. He was not sure where these women fit into the activities of the last several days but he had to make sure they did not become a surprise at some point in the future.

"Do you have any reason to suspect that these two men are here in Acapulco for any other reason than a holiday?"

"No!" Kim folded her arms.

"Officer," Robyn felt compelled to soften the effect of Kim's answer, "they are nice guys. We've spent some time with them, not a lot, but enough to know that they're not here doing anything illegal. They seem to have gotten involved in something they honestly don't know anything about. As for us, we know even less. We didn't know anything until last night at the hospital. That was the first time anything was explained to us, and that was by Ian, who, as of last night when I spoke to him at the hospital, still didn't know what was going on himself."

"You're the only one who seems to know anything," Kim said, coming on strong again. "And that doesn't seem to be too much either."

Ramirez reached in his pocket and handed a duplicate of the same wrinkled card he'd given Ian.

"If you think of anything that might be helpful or you hear of anything new, please call me at this number. If I'm not there just leave your name. I will call you back. When are you planning to return to your country?"

"Sunday afternoon," Robyn said.

"If you decide to return sooner, I would like to know."

He looked at each of them, finishing with Donna. He had been curious at first why this woman had offered no answers but now he could smell the intimidation she was feeling from his presence. He stood up and walked away quickly.

"Do you believe that guy?" Kim said. "Job or no job, that was one rude son of a bitch."

"I admit," Robyn said, smiling, "he won't win any charm contests, but who knows? He runs around all day in the hot sun, sitting in cars watching criminals at night. And all around him people are sipping drinks by poolsides. We probably spend more to stay here per day than he makes in a week. I don't see that as a happy job."

"I understand all that," Donna said, quietly, looking at her hands, "but the guy is just so creepy. If he wasn't so creepy I could feel more sorry for him."

"Do you believe that, what you told him?" Kim said, the bite in her tone still sharp.

"Believe what?" Robyn wanted to be offended, feeling Kim's energy pointed at her, but she wasn't sure yet.

"What you said about them not doing anything illegal. You're sure?"

Now Robyn was sure she was offended.

"You really are too much sometimes, Kim! What have they done to even suggest they're here for any other reason? What are they dope smugglers or something? My God!" She got up from her chair and grabbed her beach bag, her anger now visible as she turned back to Kim. "My instincts are usually pretty good and they tell me there's nothing more to those guys than there is to us. Those are the same instincts that have told me most of my life that you're not really the nitwit you act like sometimes."

She spun on her heel and stormed off toward the hotel lobby which she reached quickly.

"Any messages for Room five eighteen?"

The young man behind the counter reached into the honeycomb of polished wood behind him and pulled out a small, pink, slip of paper.

"Thank you," Robyn said, trying to regain her cool by being polite.

The slip was a message that Ian had called fifteen minutes ago. She walked across the lobby to one of the bright, flower print couches with a telephone next to it, and sat down. She picked up the phone, automatically getting the hotel operator.

Robyn's annoyance at Kim and the feeling that she had done an unnecessary but excellent job of defending Ian, made the thought of hearing his voice appealing. That he had called made her feel good as well. She could tell they were both in a strange limbo, caught between really being attracted to one another and not wanting to be that attracted. Vacations were the worst places to get involved with people. The settings and circumstances were so unnatural and misleading. When they were over the real world was always waiting and it never looked anything like the one you came from. Neither did the object of your desires, usually.

"Yes. Poolside bar, please."

"Hello, is this who I think it is?" Ian said, playfully.

"Who do you think it is?"

"Is this the well-built blonde with the topless bathing suit I met on the beach last night?"

Strange as it seemed, the thought of Ian on a beach with someone else tweaked her for a split second and then went away as quickly as it came.

"I was on a beach topless last night but I'm not blonde. Are you one of the male exotic dancers?"

There, that ought to fix him.

"I can dance, but it's not very exotic. All right," he said, his tone changing, "no more fooling around. You don't sound like you're in the mood. Would I be moving too quickly if I said I miss your face?"

"No, I don't think so. In fact, I think that sounds like a very safe and very nice thing to say. You know, not too mushy, not too formal. Safe."

"Are you okay?" he said. "You sound a little annoyed."

"You do read well, even over the phone," she said. "No, it's absolutely not you. I'm not sure what it is, although it ended up all over Kim. Sometimes she says the stupidest things."

"Just a disagreement?" Ian offered.

"Oh, I don't even know if it was that. Actually I think it's just that Officer Ramirez. He makes us all uncomfortable."

"Ramirez? What do you mean?"

"He just left." She could hear the surprise in his voice. "You didn't know he was here?"

"No. He never said anything. What did he want?"

"He wanted to know about you guys, when we had met you, what we knew about what's been going on, you know, all the things that we don't know anything about."

"Geeeeez," Ian said with a hiss. "I guess he asked if you thought we were criminals, like did we ask you to stash money for us or something?"

"Yes, that's about what it came to. Kim wasn't cutting him a break from the very beginning and he didn't appreciate it. I could tell. But I told him he was wrong."

"Well, thank you," Ian said, softly.

She could almost see the warm smile on his face. She gave one back.

"Well, you're welcome."

"So what's the matter with Kim?"

"Oh, I don't know." Robyn was trying to think of a way to explain it to Ian without making her sound cold. "She's just very protective of me. She always has been. I love her for it dearly, but sometimes it clouds her judgment."

"I get that. Best friends, right? Nobody knows me better than Spook and vice versa."

"Exactly," Robyn said, smiling again at the comparison.

"Well, circumstances haven't exactly been ideal for clear-headed thinking on any of our parts. Hey, we're lucky to have friends that care about us, right?"

"You're sweet, you know that?" Robyn said.

"What? Where'd that come from?"

"Just shut up and take it."

"All right, I take it. Thank you."

Robyn could almost hear him blushing.

"So what are your plans for the day?" Ian said.

"Oh, I think we might lie on the beach all day. How about you?"

"Manny's coming over to our hotel to spend the afternoon. He's been at the hospital since last night and I managed to talk him into getting out of there for a while. I lured him in with cheeseburgers and Cokes. Since we have police protection here I figured he'd be safe."

"Oh, that's really nice. How's Carmelo?"

"He's hanging in there. I spoke to him earlier and he was pretty spaced from medication but he seems okay. Any chance I could talk you into coming over to my place?"

Robyn was tempted but knew things had to be resolved with Kim.

"Ian, listen to me. I'm going to pass but not because I wouldn't really like to see your sweet face right now. I'm going to use today to get things back on track around here, if you know what I mean. Do you understand?"

"Yes, I do," he said. "But I'm disappointed. Is that okay?"

"Yes."

"What are you going to do tonight?" Robyn asked.

"I don't know. You know the more I think about it this crap is starting to cramp my vacationing. I feel like I'm not allowed out of the house for being bad or something. Why don't we all go to dinner again? I'm dying to try this place, Carlos and Charlie's up the street."

"You think it's all right?"

"Sure. We'll take our cop with us. Besides, I think whoever the bad guy is will back off now that the police are involved."

"All right. Let me give you a call later in the day, around five say. Okay?"

"Okay. Talk to you later."

***

"Man oh man," Ian said after he hung up the phone.

The bartender looked at him, not sure what to do.

"It's such a weird feeling, you know?" he said to the bartender.

"What ees that Señor?" The bartender took it in stride.

"When someone starts to get inside you. It's scary and exciting and...." Ian realized he was about to start babbling to a bartender. "Give me a pitcher of margaritas, por favor."

The bartender smiled and a minute later slid the pitcher across the bar.

"I have to give this Wilson character some serious thought today," Ian said, setting the pitcher and glasses down on the table in front of Spook.

"You're damn right," Spook said. "The sooner you pin this guy down, the sooner we can get on with our vacation. I told you that memory of yours is a pain in the ass."

"Not if it works."

"Hell, that's probably why this whole mess started. That guy thinks you know him, Ian, and thinks you're going to rat on him for something."

The skin around Ian's eyes bunched up.

"But for what? What did he do that I would know about? I've never seen anyone commit a crime." He sat back in the chair, letting the silence settle his mind and organize his thoughts. "If he did what I did," Ian spoke to the air, "thought he knew my face but didn't really remember me, I doubt he would have been concerned enough to try and kill me," Ian crossed his arms on his chest putting one hand under his mouth, "assuming he's the one trying to do it. But let's assume he is. That means he has to know who I am in some capacity, where I live, where I work, what I do. Now, I know this guy is not someone from where we live. I can tell by how thin my memory of him is. Whenever I know a face this thinly it's usually just a one shot thing. I saw him somewhere or met him somewhere and that's all."

"You would've had to meet him for him to know who you are, wouldn't you?" Spook suggested.

"Right. So he's definitely someone I've met, but probably only once. That means my next logical assumption is he's a business acquaintance."

"At one of your accounts? Or at a convention or something like that?"

"Well, if I'd met him in an account I'd know him. No, it doesn't feel like it."

"How about conventions?"

"Only went to one. Last year. Didn't get to meet hardly anyone, except people from my accounts." Ian shook his head, a little disgusted. "They just brought me along as a gopher. Checking arrangements and crap like that. A few meals with my customers and the big-wigs. Don't think so, but it's possible."

Ian could feel things starting to crowd his mind and knew it was time to back off. Remembering something like this usually happened when he wasn't trying. Associations with other things triggered something, and, POP, it came into his head. He had given it enough thought for now to narrow things down some. It would come. He was certain.

"You know Ramirez went over to the Royal Prince to grill the girls?"

"You're kidding?" Spook said, a look of annoyance on his face. "What the hell did he want with them?"

"Checking our cleanliness through them. Sounds like he got them pretty riled up, especially Kim."

"Well, that don't take much," Spook said. "Did they tell him we were fine upstanding citizens in a case of mistaken identity?"

"I believe they did," Ian said. He decided not to go into the Kim-Robyn tiff. "I invited them for dinner tonight if it's all right with you. We keep talking about that rib place up the street. We should go there tonight, with or without them."

"I've been dying for ribs all week. I'm ready," Spook said.

Ian noticed Spook by-passed the invitation question neatly.

"Maybe we do a little dancin' after that," Ian said.

"How's your head?" Spook offered, an impish grin on his face.

"Feeling better every minute," Ian said, and took a long drink from the margarita in front of him.

chapter 33

A SMALL DOT on sprawling Revolcadero Beach, Robyn baked in the hot sun, the oil on her skin thinning and evaporating faster than she could reapply it. The white towel on the chaise lounge soaked up the perspiration running off her body. She tanned well, but that was in the sun over Pennsylvania and New Jersey, not one this close to the equator. This was a fifteen-minute-intervals sun that would burn her in no time if she wasn't careful.

But it felt good. No, it felt fabulous. If there was a way, Robyn would have bottled it and taken it home with her and opened it up when the cruel, depressing winter of the Allegheny Valley began. She pictured herself heading home, driving from the airport towards town, passing through the mountains to the Fort Pitt Bridge, then hop-scotching her way across the rivers. First, the Monongahela, the Golden Triangle to her left, its point forcing the Ohio River to abandon its personality for the birth of two others; then across the Allegheny. It wasn't the fastest way home but she loved the view from that route. It made the city look like a magic floating island, its metal and glass-skinned skyscrapers glistening with or without the sun, steaming eternally up the Ohio in search of itself.

All Pittsburgh needs, Robyn thought with a laugh, is an ocean with a beach and three or four months each winter like this.

She had been on the beach for about fifteen minutes by herself and sensed movement next to her. She turned her head, shading her eyes. Donna spread a soft bamboo mat on the sand next to her, then a towel. She sat down facing the ocean and began rubbing lotion on her skin.

"You alone?" Robyn asked.

"For now," Donna said. "I think Kim will come eventually."

"Well, what do you think?"

"I think she's just being Kim."

"I know that. What do you think about the guys?"

"Oh, I don't think they're criminals."

"Donna," Robyn said, getting a little frustrated, "don't tell me what you don't think, tell me what you do think."

"I think they're really nice guys who are on vacation just like us. And something weird is happening that's not their fault."

"Thank you," Robyn said, feeling vindicated. "I didn't think I was crazy. What do you think about Ian?"

Robyn watched Donna's face as she asked the question. It softened.

"I think he's very special."

Like pulling teeth, Robyn thought.

"What does that mean? Would you like to hold his hand, would you like to take him home, would you like to bear his children? God, Donna, would you like to screw his brains out?" Robyn was getting rattled.

One of them tells me everything I don't want to hear and the other tells me nothing.

"I'm sorry, Donna. I didn't mean to take it out on you."

"That's okay, I understand."

"Well, I wish someone would explain it to me because I don't," Robyn said, crossing her arms on her chest and sitting back in the chaise.

She sat staring at the water, too frustrated and confused to say anything more. She sat that way for a few minutes and then closed her eyes. As soon as she did, Donna spoke.

"Ian is attractive. He's also strong and full of adventure but he seems to be a good, generous person." Donna was looking at the ocean as she spoke. "Unlike too many men."

"Yes," Robyn said, pleased. "I think so."

"I think Spook is too, in a funnier sort of way," Donna continued.

Robyn smiled.

"Do you think Spook is attractive?" Donna said, without changing her tone of voice.

"Well...," Robyn said, quickly, then realized she wasn't sure. "I think he's a nice guy. He's funny you know. He's one of those guys that has his own distinct way about things and he...."

"Robyn," Donna said, interrupting her, "you're not answering the question." Her soft-spoken tone didn't change.

"Okay. "Spook's not unattractive, he's...."

"There you go," Donna said, "telling me what you don't think instead of what you do."

"Touche`," Robyn said. "All right, make your point."

"The point is Spook is a nice guy and he's not a bad looking guy, but he's different. And he's not quite this and not quite that. The guys you meet are usually like Ian. They're nice guys that are attractive in most anyone's opinion. That's not true for Kim. She doesn't seem to meet guys that are just plain nice and attractive. They're always like Spook, a little of this and a little of that. Maybe that gets frustrating to her sometimes. Maybe just once she'd like to be the one that gets to meet an Ian."

Robyn was stunned; first, because she'd never given quiet Donna that much credit for introspection. She respected Donna's intellect and knew that despite her shyness or quietness, whichever it was, this was a very bright girl. But the quietness had mistakenly led her to believe that Donna's smarts were all cerebral, with little applied to affairs of the heart.

And second, because she, Robyn, who gave great credit to herself for being sensitive in these very matters, had completely missed what Donna had so clearly seen.

"Well, Kim's not as aggressive as I am about the people she wants to meet."

"That's because she always defers to you in things like meeting people. She trusts your judgment better than her own sometimes and when she doesn't, she just wants you to be happy, so she backs off."

Donna paused and the sound of waves filled the silence as Robyn tried to digest the new perspective.

"Don't misunderstand me, Robyn. There's no good person or bad person here. You have to understand how much influence you have on Kim, and she has to understand that much of it is because she wants you to have it. Maybe if she could see that, she could work on her confidence, get her own set of rules that aren't as influenced by you. You would respect them and she'd feel less overshadowed by you."

Robyn was staring at her. Everything Donna said made perfect sense.

"You're absolutely right," Robyn said. "I guess sometimes you get so used to people that you stop paying attention to them."

As Robyn spoke Kim walked out of the jungle towards them, trying to look unaffected. When she almost reached them, Robyn got up from her chair and knelt down in front of Donna.

"Thanks for paying attention to us," Robyn said, and hugged her.

Robyn stood up and took two steps to meet Kim, grabbing her beach bag from her hand and dropping it on the sand next to Donna. Kim stared at her, a look of resistance on her face.

"Come on, girlfriend," Robyn said, grabbing her hand, "let's take a walk on the beach together."

Donna watched her friends disappear up the beach. None of them saw the stocky man with the binoculars sitting on the restaurant porch a hundred yards downbeach, or it would have struck them how equally interested he was in them.

* * *

The waiter put another bottle of juice in front of the thick man, careful not to knock over the expensive binoculars which sat, lenses down, on the table in front of him. Garo put the bottle to his mouth immediately and flipped it up and down without tilting his head. His eyes never moved off the dark-haired woman on the beach, now sitting alone. He was thirsty, and he had waited a long time to quench his thirst. Too long. He was sick of El Gordo, the Fat Man, and his gringo superior attitude, leading him on like a street beggar hoping for a meal. He was sick of Officer Tito Ramirez and his brooding, overbearing attitude about the dirty work that had to be done. It was always him, Garo, who did all the dirty work for both of them. He was just the errand boy, tailing this one and strong-arming that one. He'd done it at first to get ahead. He knew that here in Acapulco he would never get ahead by being a hard-working public servant. You had to be on both sides of the law to get anywhere in this town.

So he was willing and obedient, and smart. Smart enough to have a mind of his own beyond what his two bosses told him because the rewards never came. A little credit here, and a few pesos there, but never in proportion to the dirty work and the second-class attitude from both of them. It was time to make his move. Time to play the ace that neither one knew he held. The best thing right now was that keeping an eye on these women was what he was supposed to be doing. He was getting paid for it. Very soon, he'd be well paid for it. He pushed his shiny black hair back off his forehead, running his hand all the way to the back of his head. He grabbed the bottle, flipped it back up for another sip then traded it for the binoculars. He could still see the other two women clearly, a good five hundred yards up the beach. He stood up, barely increasing the height of his thick body, and walked towards the beach.

chapter 34

MANNY ARRIVED JUST as the temperature hit ninety-three degrees Fahrenheit. He had on what appeared to be a new, white tee-shirt with the word Acapulco slashed across the front. A pair of bright yellow swim shorts and new sandals completed the ensemble. Walking quickly alongside the police officer, he looked like a tourist. Ian knew he'd bought the clothes recently, maybe on the way here. But if that made him comfortable enough to accept Ian's invitation, then terrific. Just a few short days ago, he would have politely refused.

"Hey, amigo," Ian yelled.

Manny spotted him from across the pool and waved, the million dollar smile illuminated by the sun's reflection on the water.

"Yo, MAN-NEE," Spook hollered. A few heads in the pool turned to see who the loud American was. "Whas hapnin'?"

"You didn't eat anything, right?" Ian said, as Manny got to his chaise.

"No, Señor Een."

"Good, because I just put the order in for some cheeeeessse-burgers and ice cold Cokes. Sound good?"

"Oh yes."

"Manny, this is probably a dumb question," Spook said, "but can you swim?"

"Yes, Señor Spook."

"Okay, I just wanted to be sure," Spook leapt from his chaise and grabbed Manny, "before I threw you in the pool." He scooped him up in both arms, shook the boy's sandals off his feet and jumped in the pool still holding him. They both came up laughing and splashing. Ian watched the two of them for the next fifteen minutes, playing like two kids in the water instead of one. Finally, Spook waved and shook his head at Manny, conceding to youth. As Spook made his way back to poolside, Manny headed for the diving board. Ian watched with pleasure as the boy jumped and flipped, one dive after another from the bouncy platform. It was himself he saw, twenty years ago, at the swim club, trying to fly.

"Look at him, Spook."

Spook hung the boy's teeshirt on the back of a chair, then grabbed a towel and turned back towards Manny.

"You could almost forget sometimes that he's just a kid," Ian continued, "what with all that business side of him. But look at him. He's havin' a ball."

Spook kept watching with a big smile on his face. Then he sat down.

"So, Ian, what do you think about all this now? Any new ideas?"

"Yeah, actually," Ian said.

The margaritas, the sun, and a quick nap in the chair had allowed him to awake with his mind less aggressive and more able to process things.

"Both times an attempt was made to shoot me, I was on the mountain. I don't think between the cops and the way this Wilson operates that anyone's going to come looking for us at a restaurant. We're definitely getting out tonight. I'm not blowing a paid-for vacation hiding in this hotel. We're doing whatever we would normally do, except with our eyes and ears open a little more."

A smile spread across Spook's face.

"Glad to hear it, man. I'm not suicidal but I am claustrophobic. I'm ready to get out. Are the ladies coming?"

"I really don't know," Ian said, wondering as soon as Spook asked the question. "Why? You have an interest?"

"No! Well, yeah but…."

"Lost for words are ya, lad?"

It was fun to see Spook speechless for a minute. Ian sat back in the chaise and let out an extended sigh. It all felt great right then and there.

"The sun feels good. Sometimes I swear living in a climate like this has got to extend your life by five or ten years. You realize if we weren't here right now, where we'd be? Racing around in the damn car fighting traffic." He pictured the office as he narrated; a very dull pulse of light in his mind. "Seems like my life revolves around turning in expense reports. You need the money to function but it's like documenting your life day to day. Where was I Tuesday? What did I spend for lunch Wednesday? How much gas? Where's the receipt? It never ends. The accounting department knows my whole boring life, day by day." Ian saw the offices again. Something skittered across the front of his mind. "Between writing it down every day and calling in to tell them where I am at the moment, it's nuts."

It skittered again. He wasn't trying to catch it. He wasn't sure what it was. It was like watching TV in the living room and sensing something, a mouse or stray light, move quickly across the kitchen floor. Maybe you'd see it again, maybe you wouldn't. But the subject; work, accounting, the office, something there. He kept talking to keep the channel open.

"I swear the first couple days we were here, the first thing I wanted to do when I woke up was call in to the office. Like I was programmed."

The office, something about the office. Don't try to find it, just keep the same images rolling around. The office, calling in, Betty out front, Ed in his office. What else? Expense checks, the mail, reports, accounting, upstairs.

It flashed across his mind quickly and he knew it was something. He waited and let it run by again, this time looking at it. Upstairs offices; Frank Gellig's office. Two years ago, a meeting; a presentation with other employees and Ed Bernardi; two guys; the guy Ed was talking about on the phone, the guy who just hung himself! The investment firm, Doner Ellis something. Bill Golden swinging from a rope.

And the other guy, a plain nondescript, doughy-handed man who left no impression except his size and calmness, calmness in his eyes. Not the same eyes he'd seen recently; angry eyes, that's what threw him off. Take the size and the doughy hands and make the eyes angry.

THE FAT MAN! THE PICTURE! WILSON!

"DAMN!" Ian came up out of his chair and into the air. "Damn, I knew it would come, I knew it. Son of a bitch."

"What?" Spook said, startled by Ian's movement.

"I got it! I got him! Wilson, The Fat Man!" Ian's blood was racing. "I have to call the office!"

He took off running, headed for the lobby where a bank of phones stood.

Spook stood there, a twisted grin on his face, watching the back of his friend disappear.

chapter 35

"BETTY, THIS IS Ian!" Puff, puff. "How the hell are you?" Puff.

"Whoa, take it easy kid. You're all out of breath. You got a lot of nerve calling me now. You could've waited ten minutes. I'd slap you if I were her."

Ian's mind raced and the sooner Cook International's receptionist caught on to his state of mind the faster he'd get an answer.

"Betty, Betty, I need your help, your memory. This is important. I'll explain later."

Despite the thousands of miles of telephone cable Ian knew Betty had gotten his vibe. Her voice was more serious now.

"All right, take it easy. What is it?"

"I'm going back two years now, okay? The investment firm that the company uses...."

"Doner, Elson, and Simons."

"Right, okay. The guy that Ed Bernardi just told me the other day hung himself...."

"Bill Golden."

"Riiight! Okay. Two years ago Ed and I had a meeting with Frank Gellig and other managers when they first were talking about an employee investment plan or something."

"That's where the money came from that Golden was accused of taking."

"Okay. There were two guys that day we met with. The other guy was a large guy, heavy. Real calm, real pleasant but real heavy...."

Ian didn't want to tell Betty the name. He wanted her to confirm his memory. There were other ways to check the guy out, but Betty didn't miss much.

"His name was Warren Ebbetts."

"YES!"

"Yo kid, my ear! What's going on?"

"This Warren Ebbetts, has he been around to see anyone? Have you seen him in the office?"

"You mean recently?"

"Yeah."

"That'd be pretty hard to do, kiddo."

"Why? Does he come in the back door or something?" Ian was a little annoyed.

"Nooo, I've seen some stiffs walking around the office that work here but I never saw one walk in the door. He's dead."

Ian felt his chest tighten.

"Dead!? What are you talking about?"

"I'm talking about dead. I don't remember the details, I just know the guy died. I remember because that was one of the things that screwed Bill Golden, that is if Golden was telling the truth."

"Talk to me, Betty, please." This was not sitting well. A few seconds ago Ian was on his way to some understanding. Now, he was confused again.

"All right," Betty said, calmly. "When Golden was trying to convince everyone he didn't take the money, the only person that could have possibly backed him up, or nailed him down for that matter, was Ebbetts. They worked together on the program. Golden was the big manager responsible for it but Ebbetts worked on it too. How much Ebbetts knew about what Golden did or didn't do with the money is in the ground with him."

"Oh my God, I don't believe this," Ian said. Spook was standing in front of him now. Ian looked at him and said, "She just said the guy I thought it was is dead."

Spook's expression wrinkled slightly.

"Betty, look, I'm the last guy in the world to challenge your memory but this is too important. I need a big favor."

"Come on."

"I need you to get the facts on this Ebbetts. See if you can find an obituary. Call Doner Elson, anything. I need to know for sure about this. It's really important. And I need it today." He said the last sentence timidly.

"All right. You have me worried now. Call me back in about an hour, okay?"

"Okay. Betty, I appreciate this."

"Don't worry, you'll pay."

More than you know Bet, Ian thought, as he hung up the phone.

"Do you believe this?" Ian could feel the tension building inside him. He quick-stepped back to the chairs at poolside and poured a watery Margarita. "I finally come up with the guy, the name, and the guy's dead."

"What're you talkin' about, man?" Spook said.

Ian explained the short phone call in detail. "I thought I had him," Ian finished, still feeling inside him that he did.

He let the thought stew in him a little more but was surprised that along with the instinct to let it start worming its way into his gut, something else was saying, so what? If he's dead, he's dead. It's out of your control. If it's not the guy, it's not the guy. You'll think of something else or other information will come up, so back off.

"Let's wait and see," Ian said, more to himself than Spook. He took a deep breath and physically shook himself to purge the tension. "Let's see what Betty can find out. If there's something more there, she'll find it. I've been wrong before."

"How's the water, Manny?" Ian yelled to the boy.

Manny was still splashing around about ten feet from the side of the pool and hadn't picked up on the commotion.

"Eet ees beauteeful, Señor Een."

"Then I should check it out," Ian said, with a devilish smile and went from his chair to the air above the water in three steps, leaping high and looking down at Manny with the same smile as he dropped. When he hit the water he pushed both arms forward engulfing the boy in a wave of churning froth.

"You want to make the big dive, buddy?" Ian said, coming up from the water. "In here?"

"Okay," Manny said.

Ian picked him up out of the water with both hands and in one motion placed him on his shoulders. The boy was light for his size.

"Give me your hands now," Ian said, letting go of Manny's sides and grabbing his arms. "You know how to dive out, right? Not down."

"Yes, Señor Een."

"Okay, good. Ready, set, dive!"

The boy let go of his hands and Ian dropped his arms, feeling the push of the boy's feet against his shoulders. Manny flew forward, horizontal above Ian's head, and hit the water about three feet away, head in first, never going more than two feet below the surface. He came up as smoothly as he went in and turned to laugh at Ian, rubbing water from his eyes as he did.

"I think that whack on the head last night has finally taken effect," Spook said to no one in particular.

chapter 36

THE FAT MAN threw his keys and Panama hat on the table of his modest condo. He reached in his pocket for a handkerchief with his other hand and wiped the sweat from his face and neck, digging deep between the fatty folds of skin. Despite the cool air of the condo, heat surrounded him like an aura. His thin red hair lay plastered to his head, revealing large patches of scalp between the strands. Custom-made linen pants bunched and stuck to him underneath the awning formed by the guayabera covering his stomach. He pulled at the pants, first behind him and then at the crotch, puffing from the effort it took to circumvent his own bulk.

He was not happy. He hadn't been happy for the last several days, ever since he'd seen that shit from Cook International. He knew the minute he'd seen him in the Silver Mine where he was from and why he was there. To make Warren Ebbetts' life, the new one he'd made for himself, hell.

Maybe he's on vacation and maybe he isn't, Ebbetts had thought, but either way he'll go running back blabbing about who he saw in Mexico. And with all the noise about Bill Golden's suicide some cop or lawyer or insurance son-of-a-bitch will decide to follow up on it.

They'd never find him of course. Ebbetts had made preparations for that a while ago. He'd just disappear from the area. Mexico was a big country. And it was connected to other countries: Guatemala, Belize, beautiful little countries that he could set up shop in. The Yucatan Peninsula was nice.

No, being found wasn't his concern. What concerned him was the inconvenience it would cause him. He had established a nice network of laundries in the area. Ixtapa and here in Acapulco—wonderful towns, full of tourists and greedy Mexican dealers. He had a fat, steady paycheck.

In the beginning it was rough. After he had made the deposits in the accounts his partner had designated, it was only a matter of time before the money showed up as missing. He had cut it a little closer than expected. Fortunately, he had already planned his death for the weekend, just before Golden had discovered something wrong with the account. He hadn't anticipated him being as sensitive about the Cook account as he was. If Golden hadn't been checking on it regularly, he might not have noticed the money missing for at least another few weeks. And all the likely fuss over his, Ebbetts', own unfortunate demise would have probably distracted Golden for another week. There would have been less chance for someone to tie the two together. But as it turned out, he died before anyone but Golden really got involved, so no one ever did tie anything together, at least as far as the Fat Man knew.

It was a shame about Bill Golden, too, Ebbetts thought to himself, a shame Bill wasn't as smart as Bill thought he was. Warren knew that day in Bill's office, when Bill first discovered the money was missing, that the too-tightly-wound man wasn't going to handle it well. He had hoped at worst they'd wash Golden out and force him to start a new career somewhere else. He hadn't expected Golden to be indicted, and certainly not convicted. And now this week, the suicide. More than Bill could bear, but that was Bill, always overreacting to tense situations.

It was sad to Warren Ebbetts. But his sadness had nothing to do with remorse or compassion. It was sad that someone like Bill hadn't found a way, a way to get beyond that pathetic world. Bill wasn't a "fat cat". He didn't have money, he earned it doing the same crap Warren did. Begging. That's what it felt like to Warren Ebbetts. It wasn't like selling a product. It was like selling a dream, the dream that one day all these pathetic, penny pinchers would be able to live like the "fat cats" they worked for.

Please give me your money. Ebbetts heard the spineless, disgusted voice of his former middle-class self. The hard-earned pay you get for doing the mindless things you do day in and day out. What kind of dream would you like? The "retirement" dream, the one that lets you think you'll have a nice home in Florida on the water and plenty of room for the grandchildren? How about the dream that lets you think you'll be able to afford college for your children? Or for you more aggressive people, the "second home for vacations" dream. Poconos, Stone Harbor, Avalon?

Warren Ebbetts opened the front door of the condo and, without looking, spit, then slammed the door shut and walked to the living room phone.

Bill Golden was a sad piece of history. He overestimated himself and paid the price. Now Warren had another partner to deal with, another one who thought he was smart enough, but not smarter than Warren Ebbetts. Warren had already managed in the almost two years he'd been in Mexico to exchange over a million and a half dollars of the ten. And the opportunity he saw in the dirty work that his partner wanted no part of, was in skimming off the exchanges.

Every six months, when his partner came to Mexico, Warren Ebbetts presented him with a complete accounting of the transactions he'd conducted. It was always an excellent display of bookkeeping and his partner was always pleased. And Warren always left smirking to himself, already tasting the fine champagne he would drink in his partner's honor, grateful for the opportunity; the opportunity to stick it to the "fat cat," his partner, who was like all the others he'd worked for all those years. They never got dirty and they never had enough.

No, it had all been worth it to Warren Ebbetts. He was living like the "fat cats." He'd ditched that miserable wretch of a wife who took up space and money in the same house as him, and he answered to no one, except his partner. And that could always be fixed. There was always someone willing to take care of things like that. But for now his partner was necessary. Now all that bothered him was this pain in the ass from Cook who could make things messy for him. His partner was due in tomorrow and he had expected the problem to be gone by now. He wanted it finished.

Ebbetts picked up the phone and punched the numbers sharply, wiping his neck again with the handkerchief. When he heard the voice he wanted on the other end his face bunched.

"Now look," he said, menacingly into the phone, "no more shooting at cliffs. No more BULLSHIT! I want you to take care of this. Run the son-of-a-bitch off a cliff, I don't care! Just get it done. I have an important meeting at two o'clock tomorrow and I want this guy and his friend to be a meaningless tragedy by then.

Do you understand!? If I have to explain this to my partner, you get your plug pulled. No more cash flow! You savvy!?"

Ebbetts heard the false bravado in the voice on the other end and knew he would have to make his position clear to this fool. He spoke very quietly, his tone sinister.

"You have other, more personal areas of vulnerability. I don't think you want me to involve them, do you?"

He paused, letting the threat have its full effect. Now he could hear resignation in the poor soul.

"I didn't think so. Then we understand each other."

The Fat Man set the receiver down sharply and reached across the table for his handkerchief to wipe the fresh layer of sweat from his face, replacing it with a thick sneer.

"Bastard."

chapter 37

IAN WAS ANXIOUS to hear something. He'd splashed around in the pool and chewed the ice in two margaritas before he'd been unable to stop himself from going to the phone. He looked at his watch realizing it had been just about an hour, give or take a day, then squinted down at the phone and his finger, trying not to misdial.

"Betty? It's Ian. Whatta ya got?"

"Okay. Boy, do you owe me for this one," Betty answered with a puff. "I called Doner, Elson and talked to the receptionist there."

God, they've got an underground society, Ian thought.

"She wasn't with the company back then but she got hold of Bill Golden's old secretary. This woman went to the memorial service for Ebbetts."

Ian's ears perked up. Why not the funeral?

"Memorial service? What, why, what?"

"Now wait," Betty said. "Be patient and let me give it to you one thing at a time. It will make more sense that way. Besides, I've got Cindy on the board covering right now and I can't keep her there long."

Somehow Ian knew it wouldn't be cut and dried.

"All right, all right. Go ahead."

"I sent Jerry, the courier, you know, to the library and told him to look for an Inquirer for that date and get a copy of the obituary. He not only found that but he found a small article about Ebbetts. So thank Jerry when you get back."

Ian was trying hard not to lose it. He wanted information on Ebbetts not a tour of Betty's research process. But he also knew she'd gone to a lot of trouble and he'd be an ungrateful slob if he wasn't patient.

"Okay, I will," he said quickly.

"All right, I'll read you the obituary first. 'Ebbetts, Warren P. June 2, 1977, of Elkins Park, Pennsylvania, age forty-four. Beloved husband of Sophia, neè Ditelli.' Looks like no kids. Memorial service at St. James Church. No funeral home, no funeral."

"Why no funeral?" Ian asked, the few strands of self-control now seconds from snapping.

"That's what the article's about. Let me read it!"

"Betty, at the risk of sounding ungrateful, don't read it. Just tell me quickly what it says." The tension in his voice shot through the line again.

"Okay. He fell overboard and drowned while sailing on Chesapeake Bay. The body was never recovered. According to the article he was on a weekend sailing trip with a client. They hit some rough weather, a squall or something it says, and Ebbets and another guy went overboard. The other guy,…what happened to the other guy? Oh, okay, the other guy was a mate, like a boathand you hire for the day. He wasn't a client. The client, the survivor, thinks the mate hit his head when they went over. He said he heard a loud thud. He managed to stay in the boat, on a line or something and held on till the storm ended. Then it gives some more information about who he worked for and stuff about the boat."

Ian's head was spinning. If he hadn't been so sure about his recognition of the Fat Man, he might not have been as skeptical. But he was.

"Betty, we're talking right out of a movie-of-the-week plot here."

"What do you mean?" she said.

He realized she didn't have any of his details or skepticism.

"It's a long story," he said. "I'll explain one of these days, I hope. Does it say who the client was?"

"Uh huh, it's a....where is it now, aaaaa here! Carl Alvarez."

The name meant nothing to Ian.

"How about the mate?"

"Uh...his...name...was...aaaaa Richard Spencer. Says he was a college student, University of Maryland, grew up sailing and worked as a hand on weekends. Young kid, what a shame."

"Betty, is Ed Bernardi in?"

"Yes, he is."

"Listen, I really do appreciate this and if I get the chance to I will definitely make it up to you. I need you to do one more thing and then I'll leave you alone. Take everything you have there and give it to Ed, and transfer me in. I don't want to go into it with you now but this vacation is starting to get hazardous to my health, and I need to find some more things out."

"Okay," Betty said, hesitancy in her voice. "Listen, Ian, if you really have a problem down there why don't you just come home?"

"I thought about that, Betty, but I don't think I can just yet. I can't explain it but...."

"Well look, you be careful kiddo, and if you need any more help you know I'll do anything for you. I just like to tease, you know that."

Ian could hear concern and guilt creeping into her voice and it made him uncomfortable.

"Betty, I know that." He lightened his tone and chuckled. "You can bet on it. You'll be sorry you offered."

"Oh you brat!" she said, more like Betty.

The line went through its series of clicks, tones, and rings and then Connie answered.

Shit! Ian said to himself.

"Sales. Connie speaking."

"Hi Connie, this is Ian."

"Oh hi," she said. "How's the vacation?"

Ian grasped for self-control again.

"Just fine, Connie. I need Ed right away. I'm kinda hung up here."

"Sure, here you go."

She didn't sound insulted, thank God. More clicks and rings.

"Ed, it's Ian."

"Hey pal, what're you getting lonely without me or what? You don't call me this much when you're working."

"Ed, did Betty get there yet?"

"Is she supposed to be here? Oh wait, I see her headed this way. What's up?"

"She's going to give you some stuff and then I'll explain."

"Okay, this sounds like fun. But it better not be your damn expense report." He could hear Ed's voice move away from the receiver, then back again. "Ian what the hell's going on? You got that woman acting spooky."

Ed's voice had caught the seriousness from Betty's.

"Ed, I need your help. It has nothing to do with work. I'm in some serious shit down here and I need help on your side of the border."

Like a good salesman, Ed knew when it was time to lose the bull and get to business.

"Wait, Ian. Let me shut the door. Connie," Ed said as he stood up, "take a message on any other calls till I'm done."

He pushed the door shut and spun back.

"Okay," he said, sliding into the chair behind the desk. "What the hell's up?"

"Get comfortable," Ian said, and for the next five minutes told him all that had happened up to his first call to Betty today. "Now I finally pull this guy out of my head, and guess who I come up with?"

"Warren Ebbetts," Ed answered. He had looked at the obituary in front of him while Ian was telling the story.

"Right. Do you remember who he is?"

"I wouldn't have up until a few days ago when the Bill Golden thing happened. I read an account in the paper covering what happened two years ago, and then the suicide and they mentioned Ebbetts in the article."

"Well you remember our meeting with them two years ago in Frank Gellig's office then, right?"

"Yep."

"Ed, there's always a chance I'm wrong. And maybe I'm feeling a little pressure here because someone wants to end my vacation sooner than expected, but I'm not convinced my Fat Man isn't Doner Elson's Fat Man. And everything in that story you have in front of you has me writing Alfred Hitchcock movies. This guy drowns, right before the shit hits the fan on his buddy. No funeral, no body. Didn't you tell me they never found any of the money that Golden was supposed to have taken?"

"That's what the story said," Ed answered. "Ten million dollars."

"And I told you it didn't make any sense for a guy who had embezzled ten million dollars and hid it away somewhere, to kill himself. Two of them in on the deal. Both of them dead. One body found swinging in his garage, the other nowhere to be found. Then I run into somebody I think is this Ebbetts, who according to the police here is tied to currency laundering under another name, and I'm getting shot at. Am I out in left field or what?"

"It does sound like a movie," Ed said.

"Can you help me?"

"You know I will. But I have a question first."

"Why don't I just leave?" Ian said, cutting him off.

"Well, yeah. Let the police handle it."

"It's a fair question to ask, Ed, so don't think me arrogant or stupid. I guess there are a lot of reasons, some of which are just coming to me."

Ian had been thinking about them ever since Officer Ramirez showed him the photograph of the Fat Man. The reasons seemed to have a lot more to do with other people. Ian's arrival in Mexico so short a time ago, had set into motion a lot of wheels, turning every which way the lives of the people around him. People he cared about or had come to care about; Spook, Manny, Carmelo, Robyn and her girlfriends; all of these people had been affected. Maybe they could all go home and everything would be fine, but maybe not.

He saw Carmelo and Manny in the most jeopardy. They weren't going anywhere. Carmelo wasn't even able to go about his everyday business because of Ian. And that had Manny staying nearby, interrupting his own work.

No, he owed something to these people. He owed them their normal lives back again. He owed it to Spook to finish out their vacation and not run home looking over their shoulders. Besides, if the Fat Man and his cohorts were serious enough they might try to stop them from leaving. Who knew?

But most of all he owed it to himself to deal with this thing. It had become personal. He resented being put in this position without knowing why. And he was damned if he was going to run home with his tail between his legs because some Fat Man thought he was a problem!

"Let's just say there are some things in my control and some that aren't. I have to stay for the ones that are."

"That's good enough for me. What can I do to help?"

"Thanks, Ed. Okay, I need you to get all the information on this whole boating accident that you can. See if you can find out anything about the other two guys on the boat, especially the one who survived, Alvarez I think his name is. If this thing was phony, he had to be in on it. See if you can find out if Ebbetts' wife is alive and if she's around or if she recently left the country or something, you know? Go on the assumption that there is something phony going on and anything that comes up looking the least bit funny, let me know. I don't know how you're going to find all this out, old buddy, but you've always been a pretty resourceful guy."

"Oh, I got some ideas already. I never told you I always wanted to be a detective?"

"Nope," Ian said, chuckling.

"I always wanted to be a detective."

"Well now's your chance." Ian was still chuckling. "Oh, listen, see if you can get a picture of Ebbetts."

"Seriously, Ian, do you have the police involved down there?"

"Well, yeah, but I'm not so sure that's a plus. The guy I'm dealing with is a strange bird. I don't trust him. I can't tell whether he doesn't know shit and wants me to figure it out for him or he knows a lot more than he's telling me. Either way he's not doing me any good. I plan to tell him that I think the guy is Warren Ebbetts then let him find out what he can and see what he tells me back. If he tells me nothing, then I know he's holding out on me. I'd rather be a step ahead of him than behind, especially since it's my behind."

"I'll make some calls. You call me if anything else happens."

Ian grabbed a piece of hotel stationery and gave Ed the phone number.

"Got it. Look Ian, just be real careful, okay? I just ordered new business cards for you and they're not cheap."

"Get off the phone."

Ian hung up the phone and took a deep slow breath. He could feel his internal motor running hard. He thought once again about why he was staying to figure this thing out and realized there wasn't a whole lot of sense to it. He remembered another situation, a hundred years ago it seemed. Back in his teaching days. He had to walk away then. He couldn't now.

"Really not much crazier than jumping off cliffs," he said to the phone and blew the air out of his lungs.

chapter 38

ED BERNARDI HUNG up the phone and reached behind him to a shelf full of telephone books, grabbed the Yellow Pages, and flipped quickly to the section listing lawyers. Kevin McGarvey's name had been mentioned in the Philadelphia Inquirer article he'd read two days ago about Bill Golden's suicide. His finger slid down the page stopping at McGarvey, Miller, and Peevey. He tapped the number into the phone with his finger.

Ed was taking Ian's request very seriously. He and Ian had become good friends over the years, bridging the difference in their ages, almost fifteen years, with common ideas and opinions about things. They had brought a lot to each other's worlds. Ian never ceased to amaze Ed, his character and strong headedness always emerging in difficult situations. Ed admired that because it was something he always had, at least until the last five or six years when the pecking order in the company had started shifting. Ed was a talented and productive manager, always looking out for the company's interests. It was just recently that he'd started to question whether the company was returning the favor.

Ian had brought him some new light, some fresh views of what working was all about. At first Ed had considered it to be the optimism of youth, but as he got to know Ian better he realized it had more to do with Ian's interpretations of things. Ian had unknowingly taught him a lot about value and meaning on a personal level. It was a big adjustment for Ed Bernardi and not one that came easily in the Cook environment. But he had started to go to sleep at night feeling good about what he had done all day rather than bad about what someone else thought he had done.

What Ed gave to Ian was support, encouragement, and the experience of having been around a little longer. On the job he was someone with whom Ian traveled and shared personal time. Out there in the hills of Upstate New York or Western Pennsylvania, home was a Holiday Inn. When Ian or Ed made the sales trips by themselves, it was always depressing. At five or five-thirty everyone went home to their houses or apartments, their families or their friends. Salespeople went home to a room with a TV, or more often than not, the hotel bar.

But not when he and Ian traveled together. They had fun. They both loved food, they both loved bars and they both loved to flirt. Ed was much better at it than Ian. Ed would start with the girl at the car rental desk in the airport, right through to the woman at the hotel reservations desk. If there were no cars available at the rental desk, Ed could get one. If there were only a few, Ed could get a Cadillac. If the hotel was full of conventioneers, Ed still got a good room. He taught Ian how to treat people like they were important, because they were.

"They're your home away from home," he'd say to Ian, "and when you get to their town treat them right. They'll take care of you."

Ed always knew where the free buffet and happy hour was.

"Save the expense account for the customers, or a rainy day," he would say.

Then when the freebies were gone they'd go to a little tavern somewhere off the beaten path with a pool table and a shuffleboard. They'd drink cheap beers and eat chicken wings and have some laughs like they were in their own neighborhood.

And they'd talk. They'd talk about where they'd been, where they were, where they thought they were going. Travelling together they'd traded a lot of their lives with each other over the years. Now, with the sense that Ian might be in trouble, Ed was holding nothing back to help his friend.

"McGarvey, Morgan, Peevey. Can I help you?" said a crisp voice.

"Yes, may I speak to Mr. McGarvey please? Ed Bernardi from Cook International."

The company name might help draw interest, he thought.

"Kevin McGarvey."

"Hello, Mr. McGarvey. My name is Ed Bernardi."

"Yes, Ed," the voice said, amicably, "what can I do for you?"

"Well, it's a little complicated," Ed said. "I don't know if I can explain it over the phone, but I think if we got together you could be of great help to me. Would you have time now by any chance?"

Never sell your product over the phone, Ed said to himself.

"Well,...actually...."

Ed couldn't tell if he was stalling to look at his schedule, or just taken off guard.

"Could you give me some idea what this is about, Mr. Bernardi?"

Stalling, Ed decided. Have to go for the clincher.

"It's about your recent client, Bill Golden. Actually, you and I may be able to help each other."

The phone went quiet for five seconds then the lawyer said, "What about Mr. Golden?"

Ed Bernardi answered more firmly.

"As I said, Mr. McGarvey, we may be able to help each other."

Ed waited, then heard the coin drop.

"How far away are you?"

A half minute later Ed hung up the phone and scooped up all the clippings in front of him.

"Connie," Ed moved out of the office, "I'm heading out. I have to meet a customer downtown. Not important if no one asks, a guy from Acme Markets if someone does. I'll call in. Okay?"

Fifteen minutes later he was on I-95 headed south to downtown Philadelphia.

* * *

"Departamento de Policia."

"Officer Ramirez, please," Ian said.

The phone was now sweaty hot in his hand from the conversations with Bernardi and Betty. The pool water on his body was already dry and replaced by perspiration.

"Hees no heehr," the voice said.

"Would you ask him to call Ian Connors please? He has the number."

"Si, Señor. Spell please."

"I-A-N C-O-N-N-O-R-S."

"Theng you, Señor."

Ian hung up the phone and looked at his watch. He picked up the phone again.

"Operator, the Royal Prince Hotel, please. Thank you."

Ian tapped the table in front of him. He was picturing Robyn's face again, and the thought pleased him.

"Room five eighteen, please."

"Hello."

It was Kim.

"Kim, is that you? It's Ian."

"Oh, hello, Ian."

She didn't sound thrilled but she sounded civil.

"Do you always answer the phone with a sexy voice or just when you're in Acapulco?"

There was silence. Probably trying to decide whether to hang up or blush, Ian thought.

"Just when I'm in Acapulco," she said, not unfriendly.

Definitely calmed down. If I ask for Robyn she'll feel like I dismissed her.

"You ready to let us make up for standing you up last night?"

"I don't know," she said. "What do you have in mind?"

"How about Carlos' and Charlie's? Then we'll walk it off for awhile, get our second wind and hit one of the clubs for dancing?"

"I don't know," she said.

Ian could tell she was warming.

"Don't toy with me, Kim, I'm only a man, and a weak one at that."

"Don't you want to talk to Robyn about this?"

She wasn't being sarcastic but still feeling him out.

"I'll talk to her eventually, but I figure you're the brains of that operation, so if you're interested you'll get the others to go. I've seen you handle Spook and that's no easy trick. I'd like to take you on some sales calls with me. With your savvy and your looks we could make a killing."

Ian hoped he wasn't overdoing it because he did like Kim. Whatever the problem was between her and Robyn he didn't want it to be his fault.

"I don't know, Ian," she said. "You sound to me like you don't need much help in the sales department. But I'll think about it."

She added the last part as a truce, Ian thought, smiling, because she wasn't buying his line, but appreciated his trying. Either way, she wasn't unhappy.

"I'll give you to Robyn. If it's all right with her and Donna, it's fine with me."

"I'm glad."

Ian heard her say something to the room and then Robyn's hello.

"Well," Ian said, "she sounds happy, or not unhappy."

"Yes,. . .well. . . ."

"Can't talk, huh?"

"That's right."

"Things smooth?"

"Yes, definitely."

"All right, so how about it tonight? Kim's already in. Carlos' and Charlie's and then a little later, boogie."

"Sounds good to me. Anything new on the case?"

"Maybe. I'll tell you later. So you want to meet us at the restaurant about nine?"

"Okay."

"It'll be nice to see you," Ian said, softly.

"It'll be nice to see you."

"It'll be nice to be seen. Get off the phone, and don't be late. I hate people who say they'll meet you and then don't show up." He started laughing.

"Yeah, I know a few people like that. Goodbye."

Ian hung up the phone and walked towards the pool, his stomach tingling. All the information about Ebbetts and talking to Robyn had his adrenaline pumping like rocket fuel. A minute later he was poolside with Manny and Spook.

"What the hell have you been talking about all this time?" Spook said.

"Oh, this and that," Ian said.

"So what did you find out?" Spook was getting agitated.

Before Ian could answer, the police officer came to the table.

"Señors, I am due to feenish my sheef. Ees the boy going weeth me?"

"Yes," Manny said, jumping up. "I want to get back to Carmelo." He grabbed his shirt and sandals and quickly put them on. "Señors, thank you very much for today. I had very much fun."

"Hey, we're glad to see ya," Spook said, rubbing Manny's head.

"Comeere, buddy," Ian said, and put his arm out towards Manny. "Did you get enough to eat? Want a Coke for the ride?"

He put his large hand on the back of Manny's neck.

"Yes, plenty, Señor Een. No, thank you."

"Okay. You tell Carmelo we'll be out to see him tomorrow."

Manny nodded his head. Ian squeezed his neck affectionately.

"Thank you, officer," Ian said.

"Adiós," Spook said. He turned back towards Ian. "I like saying 'adiós', you know. It's so Mexican-American. Now spit it out, Ian. What's the scoop?"

Ian sat back and folded his hands on his lap, trying to organize his thoughts for his own benefit, and ultimately Spook's.

"All right," he said, after a minute of silence. "Whatever else we do or don't know, at least now I've found some reason for me to be in the picture. Here's how it goes. The guy I recognized as Warren Ebbetts is supposedly dead. He supposedly died about two years ago in a boating accident on Chesapeake Bay. I keep saying supposedly because I'm not convinced he's dead, and nothing I've heard so far has changed my mind. He was on a boat with two other guys; one a client and the other a boathand. Neither of their names mean anything to me. Alvarez and Spencer."

Ian had thought that the client's name was a Mexican name, but whether that meant anything other than the fact that Ian was in Mexico right now, he wasn't sure.

"Supposedly a storm came up and rocked the boat. Ebbetts went overboard and sunk like a rock. The boathand, a local young kid, hit his head and went in as well. All this according to the only survivor, the client, Alvarez." Ian indicated his skepticism with a frown.

"So?" Spook's eyes were wide open.

"Well," Ian stretched his hands out in front of him giving himself another few seconds to roll his suspicions around in his head, "first of all, it's all based on me feeling really sure that this Wilson and Ebbetts are the same character. I might be leading myself where I want to go but I really believe they are. Soooo then a lot of things make sense. First, ten million dollars disappears from an investment account, an account that both Ebbetts and another guy named Bill Golden worked on. My company's account, by the way. Next, and I don't know the exact dates and times yet, Ed Bernardi, my boss, is digging all that up for me right now. Anyway, next, Ebbetts drowns. No body recovered. Then Bill Golden gets arrested for stealing the money, something he swears he never did from day one, right up till he hangs himself this week. The only guy who might have been able to clear him from the beginning conveniently disappears into the Chesapeake."

"What about the others on the boat?" Spook said.

"I don't know yet. Hopefully, Ed's going to get me some more info on that. In my little scenario the logical explanation is Alvarez isn't really a client. He's in the deal as an alibi, a witness."

"And the kid, the boathand?" Spook said, quietly, seeming to know the answer.

Ian looked at him nervously then stated the obvious.

"An unfortunate alibi."

"You're sayin' they just killed him?"

"It would make sense," Ian said. "It certainly pads the story, makes the client look a lot more sincere. You know, 'the poor man, he's lucky to have survived' and all that crap."

"So what's the tie-in with you?"

"I ran into the guy, into Ebbetts, three days ago. A dead man!"

Spook still looked unsure.

"I met Ebbetts at Cook, at my company two years ago, at a short meeting, maybe an hour long. The account he ripped off. He makes himself die and he runs into me two years later in Acapulco. I don't recognize him but I look like I recognize him. He looks like he recognizes me. Maybe he recognizes me right away. A guy he met at the company whose account he ripped off.

Who knows what he thinks? I'm gonna run back and tell my company, the police? He's got to assume I know who he is and that I know he's supposed to be dead. Even though I didn't know any of that till now."

"So he's got to shut you up right away," Spook said, getting the idea and getting excited.

"Right," Ian snapped. "So the next day they're shooting at me on the cliff." The more he explained it the more sense it made to him.

"It all makes perfect sense, Ian," Spook said, interrupting Ian's thought, "and I'll be surprised if you're wrong."

Ian made a face that said, thanks. I don't think I'm crazy, I'm glad you don't.

"But he didn't try to do anything till the next day," Spook continued. "And then he tried again the day after that. How does he know for sure that you haven't turned him in already? That you didn't see him in the store and leave and go right to a phone booth and call the police or your company?"

Ian hadn't thought about that, and now that Spook had brought it up, he was at a loss.

"I don't know, Spook. I guess there's no way he could know for sure."

There was a silence and then just as quickly Spook continued.

"I know how," Spook said, with an unpleasant look on his face. In fact, it was downright ugly.

"We don't trust this guy Ramirez at all, right?" Spook said, looking Ian in the eyes.

As soon as Spook said the name Ian felt a twinge.

"Not as far as I can spit."

"When did we pick up our first shadow in this town?" Spook said.

Ian looked at him, not sure what he meant. He could tell Spook had his head into the whole picture now and like an actor preparing for a role, was immersing himself in the part, lingo and all.

"Shadow?"

"A tail, a shadow," Spook explained, trying to enhance the explanation with his arms and hands to no avail. "Ramirez said they tied us to Ebbetts when you met in the store, you know, his 'inside' man. Later that day, Ramirez is sittin' at the bottom of the hill while we're out sightseein' and headed for the Royal Prince. We were probably watched at some point after we left the store where you met Ebbetts. And Ramirez has been followin' us ever since. At the cliffs when you made your dive, Manny saw him. The next night you go up to look for a bullet, we run into him in the parking lot. We probably didn't know it but he's been behind us all week." Spook's face said, I rest my case.

"With only one exception," Ian added. "He's conveniently nowhere to be found when Manny's out in the parking lot getting choked." Ian's face was starting to redden, and not from the sun. "And now he's over here today showing me a picture of Ebbetts, trying to see whether I recognize him or not, the son of a bitch!"

"That's why he insisted we only talk to him." Spook pressed on. "He's working with Ebbetts, probably getting a cut of the money as it gets laundered. It makes sense. He pretends to be investigating Ebbetts, or his version, Wilson, and instead covers his ass. Ramirez can mix with good guys and bad guys and no one can ever question why."

Another thought hit the front of Ian's brain and exploded. He crossed his arms and looked out across the water.

"So maybe the only reason we're still alive is because Ramirez and Ebbetts still think we don't know who he is."

The fiery Mexican sun was beginning its descent on beautiful Acapulco Bay.

chapter 39

Ed Bernardi fought his way up Callowhill Street to Tenth and turned left, then crawled south toward Market Street looking hard for a parking lot. He saw one and hooked a right onto the lot, pulled up to the rickety wood outhouse that was the attendant booth and stopped.

"Two hours, tops," he shot to the slow man coming out of the booth, grabbed the ticket and quick-stepped his way to Market Street and across.

Good old Billy needs a bath, he thought, looking west to City Hall. William Penn stood calmly atop the building looking for help, his skin and clothing a blue-green-brown combination of tarnished metal.

Bernardi sprinted two more blocks to the PSFS Building and went in, just in time to catch an elevator spilling a load of passengers into the lobby. He fought his way to the doors, stepped quickly inside, punched sixteen and then rapidly hit the "CLOSE DOOR" button six times not wanting to hold the car for anyone. When the doors closed and the elevator moved, he realized he had broken a sweat and that he hadn't covered that much ground in that short a time in almost ten years. Something during his conversation with Ian had told him to move quickly.

Ian's an optimist. Thinks everything will work out if he puts his mind to it. But dead people and shooting-that's something else.

When the doors popped open at sixteen, Ed was halfway thru them before he realized there was a wall of people in front of him.

"Excuse me," he said, putting his head down and giving a clear signal he wasn't stopping. He spotted the brown oak doors at the end of the hall with the name McGarvey, Miller, & Peevey painted in gold.

"Mr. Bernardi to see Mr. McGarvey, please," he told the receptionist as soon as he got through the doors. "He's expecting me."

Ed glanced around the office taking in the old style look of the place; lots of oak trim, dimpled glass and a hanging light fixture with nineteen thirties written all over its brass and frosted bowl. The chairs were cordovan leather wingbacks with brass studs, and as Ed followed the matching couch to its end a short, trim man in his late thirties with a prematurely thin head of hair walked toward him. He was dressed like,...a lawyer, Ed thought. White shirt, red pin-dot tie, navy-blue suit pants.

"Mr. Bernardi, I'm Kevin McGarvey, nice to meet you."

Ed thought the smooth, boyish face peering through gold-rimmed glasses said something less friendly and more suspicious.

"Would you come in my office, please?"

Ed followed him to a small comfortable office.

"You seem young to have your own law firm," Ed said, trying to feel the man out as he sat down.

"I don't actually," the lawyer said. "My father is the McGarvey on the door. Brian McGarvey. He still maintains a limited practice." He smiled carefully. "What is it you need to see me about?"

Ed reached into his suitcoat pocket and pulled out the obituary and the article on Warren Ebbetts' boating accident and held them in his hands on his lap. He watched McGarvey's eyes follow them.

"According to an article I read a few days ago you represented a man named Bill Golden who was accused of embezzling about ten million dollars of investment money he'd generated through my company."

Ed watched the lawyer's face the way he watched customers' faces. Must be a good lawyer, he thought. He hasn't moved an eyelid.

"Unfortunately, the article was written as a result of his suicide," Ed continued and saw the man's eye's momentarily look away when he said suicide. "How did you feel about the case and what happened to Golden?"

The lawyer's forehead wrinkled and he narrowed his eyes. Ed had obviously struck a nerve.

"Mr. Bernardi, how I feel about Mr. Golden and his case is not really a matter for your concern. You said on the phone there might be some benefit in our meeting. I have yet to discover any. Would you please get to the point?"

A lawyer all right, Ed thought. He leaned forward and placed the paper clippings on the desk facing McGarvey.

"The name in that obituary should be somewhat familiar to you. He was Bill Golden's partner. I don't know what you did or didn't do back when you first studied the facts in the case against Golden but if you've ever had the feeling something wasn't right all along, that's where you should start looking."

McGarvey looked at the clippings as Ed spoke.

"What makes you think there was something not right all along?" McGarvey said, still maintaining his cool.

"Why would a guy that stole ten million dollars that was never recovered, hang himself? Not much of payoff that way."

Ed was working him.

"I'm still not sure what it is you want from me," McGarvey said.

He put the clippings down and sat back in his chair. Ed leaned forward in his seat.

"All right then, I'll get to the point. I have a friend who may be in serious danger. I need to find some things out as quickly as possible, even sooner. I think you can help me find those things out quickly."

"And why would I want to help you or your friend?"

Got 'um, Ed thought.

"Because I think you know your man Golden got a raw deal," he said quietly, letting sympathy dictate tone. "I think you were frustrated by a case that didn't quite make sense in your gut and in the end, I think that Bill Golden's suicide bothers you a lot more than just losing a case. I think we can help my friend and clear Bill Golden's name all at the same time."

McGarvey had his head down now, his cool gone. He sat that way for a minute. Ed kept quiet, giving him the time to sort things out. Then the lawyer spoke in a voice devoid of emotion.

"I've never been surer in my life, Mr. Bernardi," McGarvey said, quietly to the desktop, "of a client's innocence than I was of Bill Golden's." He picked his head up and looked toward the window. "I watched that man be stripped down to nothing, a piece of skin at a time. I've seen clients wear down from the process of jail and courts, but usually it's the arrogance they feel for having been caught. With Bill it was seeing his life destroyed, everything he'd worked for taken away, for something he didn't do. His family. God, his kids." Emotion came back into Kevin McGarvey's voice. "Good kids. His wife. She never gave up on him." He let the sentence hang in the air. "And now they have next to nothing." His voice sounded matter-of-fact now, almost business-like. "No father, no husband. Doner, Elson, Simons refused to pay any pension money, his life insurance policies bailed on account of the suicide. Thank God he had investments. Not much left though after the last two years, but at least his family still has a house."

He went silent but continued to stare at the window as if the entire two years were being played on a screen just outside. Then he turned in his chair back towards Ed, putting both forearms on the desk.

"You're a pretty good reader of people, Mr. Bernardi, if you managed to see in the last ten minutes that this case has had an effect on me. If you're telling me you think between us we can prove Bill Golden's innocence, I'll do anything I can to help you and your friend. And I'll cover whatever it might cost. When was the last time you heard a lawyer say that?" He smiled weakly.

"I'm glad you feel that way," Bernardi answered. "Thank you."

"Where do we start?"

"How does this sound?" Ed said. "My friend says," he jabbed his finger towards the picture of Warren Ebbetts on McGarvey's desk, "that man is not dead. He's alive and well and laundering the money in Mexico."

McGarvey's face went wide.

"How did your friend discover this?"

"Purely by accident. He thinks he ran into him in Acapulco about three days ago. My friend is still there and so far has had two attempts on his life as a result. Look, let's go about it this way. Do you have any pressing commitments for this evening?"

"Just a racquetball date around eight."

"Good, maybe you'll make it. Ask your secretary to bring you everything on the Golden case, especially any investigative reports on where the money went before it disappeared, who saw it last, etc. And anything at all on this Ebbetts guy. While she's getting that I'll explain my friend's situation and his theory on what happened. Then I'm going to need your resources or contacts, whatever, to get as much information as possible on the death of Warren Ebbetts. Okay?"

McGarvey picked up his phone and began giving instructions to his secretary. When he finished he said, "She's getting it now."

"Can I use your phone?" Ed wanted to check if Ian had called back.

"Sure. Go ahead." McGarvey got up from his chair and headed out the door towards his secretary.

As the lawyer rounded the door frame Ed said, "You got any coffee around here?"

chapter 40

AT EIGHT-FIFTEEN, THE officer for the next shift knocked on Ian's hotel room door. Spook peered cautiously through the peephole and saw the uniform.

"Buenos noches," the officer said when Spook opened the door. "I'm here to attend you." He did not smile. It was obvious to Spook he was not happy with his assignment.

"Okay, great," Spook said, the poker face eliminating any interest in conversation. "Are you supposed to go with us when we go out?"

"Yes, Señor, wherever you go, I go." He said it with the stony expression of a threat.

"All right. We'll be heading out in about thirty minutes. Would you like to come in?"

"No thank you, Señor. My position is here."

"Okay," Spook said, and closed the door. "Our new custodian has arrived," he yelled, walking back to the balcony.

He and Ian had been sitting on the balcony sipping vodka and tonic and enjoying the view.

"Seems like a friendly chap," Spook said, eyebrows raised. "Not at all underworld-like."

"Ramirez has a perfect cover now for having us watched twenty-four hours a day," Ian said, irritation clear in his voice. "He can tell anyone who asks it's for our own protection. And he's probably one of those guys that nobody has the balls to question in the police department." He paused, and then his face softened. "That's okay. As long as we've got a cop watching us, Ramirez can't really do anything. When he takes our guard away, we'll have to worry."

"So did he act funny when he returned your call?" Spook said.

"Yeah," Ian said, with a look of concern. "He seemed edgy, almost like he knew I didn't call him just to tell him we're going out tonight."

Ian had heard clearly in the tone of Ramirez's voice that the detective sensed there was more to the call than what Ian had decided to tell him at the last minute. And he was sure the officer who took Manny back to the hospital had been grilled when he returned to the station, reporting that Ian had spent time on the phone. After considering that Ramirez was probably one of the bad guys, the thought struck Ian that this was all now a deadly game of strategy. Before, he had been blown by the wind, unsure and unaware of all that had been going on around him. He had had no control of events, no knowledge of their significance, and little-to-no control of the outcome. But not now. Now he knew things. Now he understood that he was dealing with serious people with the ability to kill, if the boathand on the sailboat was any indication. Now he had to either pack his bags and go, right away, or stay and play the game, delicately and cautiously. To misread or misinterpret anything that occurred, or had occurred for that matter, could prove fatal. It struck him immediately that Spook had to understand the same thing.

"Listen," Ian turned in his chair to face his friend, leaning forward with his forearms on his thighs, "this is really important. We've probably both thought of this individually but let's acknowledge it. We say the wrong thing to the wrong person at the wrong time and we've got serious shit on our hands."

He looked at Spook's face and realized his friend had, but hadn't really, considered it.

"Before we were just dumb, being dragged along for the ride. Now we know a few things, or at least we're assuming a few things. If we run into Ramirez, and you can bet your ass we will, we gotta be cool. Nobody offers anything. We're dumb tourists, just like last night and this morning, and none of this makes sense and we're pissed off by it all. If it comes up, I was on the phone today to my office just to check in with my boss. He's a pain in my ass and I had to call him while I was away."

"You think he knows you talked to someone today?" Spook said.

"I'm sure he picked the officer's brain that was here. And if he's any kind of decent detective, he checked to see who I called. That's why I'm not lying about who I called, just why."

"We should watch what we say around this guy too," Spook said, motioning with his thumb towards the door.

"Absolutely. Look, tonight we're having fun. We don't have to talk about any of this crap. We keep our eyes and ears open, but we're still on vacation."

As soon as Ian said it the thought was so absurd he burst out laughing. He flopped back in the chair and held his stomach, his voice going up two octaves in pitch as he screeched.

"We're on vacation! This is a friggin' vacation!"

Spook was infected by the high-pitched laughter, his own slow chuckle beginning to grow.

"ONLY ME," Ian shrieked, tears now running down his cheeks, "ONLY I COULD GO ON A VACATION TO GET AWAY FROM IT ALL,..." he was waving his hands now and his voice was so high pitched it was barely audible. "...and this is what I get. Oh, geez."

His stomach hurt now and he let the laughter work its way out till his stomach loosened. He wiped his eyes as sobs of laughter erupted at random. Spook was caught by the absurdity as well, his laugh full on now. He spit his words out quickly.

"And to think you never thanked me for talkin' you into comin', you bastard!"

The word "bastard" came out as a wheeze and both of them rolled to one side of their chairs and fell out. They were on vacation again.

chapter 41

CARLOS AND CHARLIE'S was a long restaurant on the beach facing Acapulco Bay. Ian and Spook took a taxi and got there before the women, setting themselves up at a table closest to the water. They had just gotten a round of beers when Robyn and the others walked in.

At least that's the way Ian saw it; ROBYN and the others. Robyn had ignored his comment about "nothing fancy" this time. He felt like a high school kid watching his date walk down the stairs. She wore an electric-blue mini-skirt that started, or ended, about mid-thigh, a thigh that he could see was Hollywood tan and tight. He couldn't tell if it was the length of the skirt that made it appear that way but her legs looked long, from the low-heeled sandal which made her calves tighten, to the place where they disappeared into the bottom of the dress. Her thighs weren't touching at that point and Ian shivered at the thought. He followed the shimmery blue to a black and blue colored sash tied loosely around her waist, just tight enough to pull the top of the dress snugly across her breasts which peeked playfully above the neckline, two dark arcs forming just below her collar bone. Her tan and the lighting in the restaurant were playing shadow games all over the exposed skin above the dress. Ian flashed back to the beach at the Royal Prince the first night they met and recalled the sunlit silhouette in the bikini. It amazed him now that because his mind was so preoccupied that night with other things, he'd paid little attention to her sexuality. Maybe that was good. It had given him time to feel about her from the inside first, with his emotions instead of his hormones. He was glad now, because looking at her at this moment his hormones were completely out of control.

The finish to his fabulous consumption of her as she walked across the restaurant was her face. Her hair was pulled back, its shiny brownness streaked with lightly sun-bleached pieces that fell randomly across her forehead. Her eyes, big and brown, were light around the sockets, accenting the tan on the rest of her face.

When Ian looked at her she was smiling, smiling at him. If he had asked her why, she would have told him it was because she had seen him devour her as she walked into the restaurant. Robyn saw in his face exactly what she'd hoped to see when she dressed herself earlier. Everything she put on, how she put it on, what she didn't put on, was all decided by how she wanted him to react. Kim and Donna had told her she looked great before they left and she saw the double takes in the hotel lobby as they left the Royal Prince. She never even saw the neck injuries she caused right there in Carlos and Charlie's as she walked through the room. But it didn't matter. What mattered was how one person and one person only was looking at her tonight. And he was looking at her in a way that made her know she'd hit every note in the song.

Ian realized he'd lost it by letting his mouth hang open. He snapped it shut and tried to look in control.

"Good timing, ladies."

He stood up, reaching his arm out towards them. He gained control of his senses long enough to notice that Donna and Kim also looked sexy. Kim had on a tight, vested pants-suit with a halter top underneath that did service to her snug figure. Donna wore a short red dress, the fabric not being as eye-catching as Robyn's. But it wasn't necessary. It was now clear to Ian whose silhouette had caught his eye on the beach that night at the Prince. Donna's figure was sculpted. It needed no garment to proclaim its existence.

Spook also stood up and the process of getting seated began. Robyn went unabashedly to Ian and said, "Hi," in a quiet voice that made him shiver again. Then she pecked him on the lips.

"Why did you do this to me?" Ian said, whispering in her ear.

"Do what?" She looked at him quickly, a slight show of fear on her face.

"You're going to make me sit here looking at you through an entire meal before I can grab a hold of you and kiss that sexy mouth of yours?"

The fear disappeared immediately from her face and she blushed. Ian couldn't believe it. He could actually see it through the tan.

"I'm sorry," she said, with just the right amount of playfulness.

Everyone was sitting down now and getting comfortable. Ian turned to Kim and Donna and said, "Don't you all look fabulous tonight. My, my. Who needs a drink? I'll get them. I'm headed that way. Be right back. Robyn," he had her hand now, "come here. I want to show you something before we eat."

Ian pulled her along behind him before anyone could say anything. He kept moving briskly across the restaurant to the other side of the bar where a short hallway dead-ended, forcing patrons to turn right for the rest rooms. To the left was another short hallway with a door at the end that looked like an office or storeroom. Ian went left and stopped halfway down the hallway.

"Where are you going?" Robyn said, amused.

"Right here," he said, and put his arms around her, looked at her eyes hard for a split second and then kissed her, savoring every sensation his body and lips were giving and getting. He couldn't remember the last time he'd felt like this, if ever. He pressed her tightly to him, his muscular arms feeling the power to crush her if he wanted to. He held her that way for about fifteen seconds then released his tight grip, sliding his arms down to her waist and letting her wobble in the space between them and his body.

"Wow," she said.

She put her hands up to his chest. He could feel her tracing the outline of the muscles with the flat of her hands.

"That's exactly what shot through my head when you walked in the restaurant," Ian answered. "I hope you're not mad I ran you away, but there was no way I could sit there for long without getting this close first."

"Mad? I would've skipped dinner altogether for this."

"You look fabulous."

"Thank you. I was hoping you'd feel that way."

"Well you got me. I'm putty in your hands."

"I'll keep that in mind."

"Come on," Ian said, acting disappointed, "we have to go back and pretend we're interested in food and friends." He kissed her again, grabbed her hand and headed back up the hallway.

"What were the drinks again?" he said, feigning confusion.

"Margarita and two beers," she said, laughing at him.

"Oh, yeah, right." He pulled her arm forward forcing her to walk in front of him. "Walk ahead of me," he said. "I want to see if that dress looks as incredible from the back as it does from the front."

"You're bad," she said teasingly, and stepped proudly ahead of him.

Ian slowed to put some distance between them.

Oh my God! he said to himself, it does.

"So where are we dancing this evening, handsome?" Robyn said, running the side of her finger along his cheek as everyone finished their food.

Ian twitched.

"We'll be dancin' in the dark if you keep that up," he said. "I thought I'd leave that to your group. Women always seem to have very clear ideas about things like dancing, among other things."

"I'm glad you added that." Robyn gave him a scolding look. "I thought you were going to add shopping and appliances."

"Now you ought to know me better than that by now," he said, looking hurt. "I'm a man and I can cry." He looked at her seriously for a second to confuse her and then started laughing.

"Girls?" Robyn turned to the table. "Where do we dance tonight?"

"Le Dooommme!" Kim howled. "Baila, baila! Ole!"

"This woman is ready to fly," Spook said.

"A guy at our hotel told us it's the best place to dance, all night if you want," Donna said.

Even Donna's loose, Ian thought. She's speaking in public.

"But it's too early," Kim said. "You don't go there until around eleven thirty."

"So what do we do till then?" Robyn asked, looking at everyone.

"How about we take a ride to the cliffs?" Ian said, holding back the burst of laughter that had already formed from this absurd thought.

"OOOOO."

"Baaaaaa."

"Get the hell outta here."

Napkins and pieces of ice flew at him from all directions.

"Geez, can't you take a joke?" Ian said.

Everyone was laughing, the nastiness of the last few days behind them. Ian felt the vibe from the group. Maybe it was a false sense of security on all their parts, but it didn't matter. This was the vacation they'd all come for, and the fact that two friends had become a fun group of five friends made it great.

"How about a moonlight cruise?" Spook offered.

"Ooo, that sounds nice," Kim said. "How'd you think of it?"

"One of the brochures in the room, you know, things to do," Spook explained. "We could take a one hour cruise, see Acapulco from the water, sip a few cocktails and be back to dance by midnight."

Ian loved it when Spook used the word "cocktails." It was his formal word for anything he drank; beer, wine, it didn't matter. They were all "cocktails."

"Oh, how eleegahnt," Ian said, with a snooty British accent. "Sharles, bring thee yacht around, we shan't be needing the cah. Weeuh having COCK-tails on the wauhtah. Veddy veddy good, Edwahd."

"Edward?" Kim shrieked.

Everyone picked up glasses, extending their pinkies.

"Yes yes. Pip pip."

"Jolly good show, Edwahd."

The Royal party departed for their waiting yacht in fabulous spirits.

chapter 42

"IT'S THE LOOOOOOVE boat," Spook was singing in the taxi. "It's the loooooove boaaaaaaat."

"Oh man, Spook," Kim said. "Sounds like a Bill Murray imitation."

They were all jammed into one small taxi headed down the Strip, Ian and Robyn in the front with the driver and the others smashed into the back seat. The cocktails had brought their party to the next level.

"Your singing aside, Spook, the cruise was nice," Ian said. "Acapulco looks gorgeous from the water doesn't it? The lights all over the mountains."

"Very romantic," Robyn purred.

"You think so?" Ian said, teasingly. "I guess so."

"You creep." Robyn tapped him on the head.

"Where we headed now?" Spook said.

"Le Dome," Kim answered.

"Is our escort still with us?"

Ian twisted his head around and looked out the rear window, spotting the little police car behind them.

"Yes, he is."

The taxi pulled up to the night club, a giant metal bubble decorated in pulsating lights rising from the palm trees. People were standing around the outside, dressed in flashy outfits; men in baggy pants and open-neck shirts, girls in hot colored mini-skirts and spiked heels. Ian could hear and feel the internal pulsations of music bulging at the outside of the building's skin. It was rhythm that made a body start to move instinctively.

"All right!" Kim yelled, scrambling to extract herself from the back seat.

Robyn's shoulders were moving around in rhythm, her right one bouncing off Ian's chest as she paid the cab driver.

"Let's go, my fine Latin-Irish stud, to the dance of love."

"Latin-Irish stud?" he said, laughing hysterically.

Inside the club was a huge circular room with tiers of tables and chairs completely surrounding a polished-steel dance floor. Swirling colored lights overhead bounced off it, creating disorienting effects in the room. A sophisticated speaker system was distributed around the room and the effect was both numbing and exhilarating. Without actually making the decision, all of them were on the dance floor, caught in the hypnotic mixture of the music they could feel and the crowd they could see. Colors and reflections flashed in their eyes and bathed their bodies.

Ian was slowly opening and closing his eyes. When he closed them he was in space, moving rhythmically through the inside of his head. He felt fluid-like. Nothing in his body felt solid or fixed in place. He let the sound control his movement as it ran the length of his body and arms, then to his center again. When he opened his eyes he saw a psychedelic sexual fantasy gyrating before him in the form of Robyn. Her electric blue dress was now completely charged by the shimmering and changing shapes and colors. Ian watched the exquisite outline of her breasts, the soft round impressions of her ass, the "ss" hissing in his brain as he said the word to himself, her long legs, bent at the knees, spreading apart and coming together, again and again.

And her face, a face of love and lust and abandon, floating sensually along with the electric blue body. It wove in and out of the reality around them, like an early waking dream. Deep inside him he knew the best part was it wasn't a dream. He could reach out at any moment and touch the fantasy that floated before him and draw it to him and consume it. And he knew before the night ended he had to.

He reached over, pulled her to him and walked her off the dance floor towards the bar area.

"What?" she said, playfully.

"I need a drink and I need to be closer to you, soon."

She responded by putting her arm around his waist.

"Is this place fantastic or what?"

"It's really something," Ian said, realizing more and more how much he wanted to get out of the place.

It was a place for wild partiers or cruisers, for people alone looking for other people alone. A week ago it would have been perfect for Ian. But tonight he had what all these people were looking for and he didn't need this place.

"Can we leave?" he whispered in Robyn's ear.

She looked at him and to his relief she didn't look surprised or bothered.

"Yes."

Ian quickly moved back to the dance floor and spoke in Spook's ear. Spook nodded, never stopping his movements. He was smiling at Donna and Kim as they danced.

"Be careful," he yelled, flashing a look at Ian and then turning back to the party.

Ian was already on his way back to Robyn with his mind even further ahead. He didn't see the short pug-faced man until he crashed into him, three feet from Robyn.

"Uuh, whoa! Sorry, man. Didn't see you."

Ian kept moving, catching the man's hard little face out of the corner of his eye. The guy didn't say anything, acting almost as if Ian had not run into him. The only afterthought Ian had as he grabbed Robyn's hand and headed for the door was that the little fireplug had hardly budged when Ian bumped him. Ian was out the door too quickly to notice the scan the man gave Spook and Kim on the dance floor or the hard eye-to-eye he gave Donna Miller.

Robyn and Ian slipped past the officer now dozing in his car, caught a taxi and were at Ian's hotel in ten minutes, holding one another tightly the whole time. Ian unlocked the door and cautioned Robyn before she walked in.

"I know everybody says this but it's true. Pay no attention to the mess."

"Can't be any worse than my place," she giggled.

Ian stepped in ahead of her quickly and flipped the wall switch down, killing the lamp they had left on. Not just to hide the mess, but something about the light in the room threatened to transfer his feeling of excitement and romance into sadness; a messy, empty hotel room he'd seen on the road too many times before. In the dark, magic still existed. The lights from the mountains came on, filling the balcony doors with constellations. He stepped across the room and slid the door open and a warm, humid breeze immediately filled the room, pushing the open curtains into the air.

"How about a vodka and tonic?" he asked, nervously. "Fresh lime."

"No thanks." Her voice was sweet.

"Check out our view. It's pretty nice."

He stepped out onto the balcony. He could tell she was watching him. For all Ian's aggressive confidence, he was not that way with women, especially one he was this taken with. He had asked Robyn to leave with him because he had been overwhelmed by the need to be with her, alone. She stepped behind him and put her arms around his waist.

"I'm glad you wanted to leave," she said. "As much as I love dancing and clubs I wanted to be alone with you."

"That's exactly how I felt," he said, feeling reassured.

He turned around and looked at her and saw two faces at the same time. One was the face of a stranger, of someone he'd just met and really didn't know. The other was the face of someone he had always wanted to know. He kissed her as he had kissed her on the beach, exploring every aspect of her lips and mouth. He could feel her breasts and nipples pressing thru the thin dress and his shirt. He moved his right arm lower till his hand felt the smooth curve where her back became two soft cheeks and pressed it gently, moving the flat of her abdomen against his groin. Her leg moved to one side of his allowing them to press harder against each other.

Ian felt powerful. He moved his hands down to just below her hips and pulled her hard to him. Their mouths were still exploring each other, their movement speeding up and slowing down in response to the contact below. Ian's brain was buzzing.

At that moment Robyn slid her hands down to his and held them, walking sideways into the room without letting him go. She walked him to the bed, now bathed in moonlight, and unbuttoned his shirt, gently sliding it down his arms behind him, the large veins and hard muscles of his arms accented in the shadows and light. She unbuttoned his pants and slid the zipper down smoothly, then pushed them down at the waist, bending slowly till she reached his calves where she grabbed the whole pant leg with one hand as he lifted one foot, then the other. Then she stood up half way and kissed the skin above his briefs, his groin muscles tightening reflexively. Sliding her fingers inside the waistband of his briefs till she felt the hardness of his buttocks, she stretched out her fingers and gently pulled down, allowing enough room for him to escape without discomfort. When she released him he closed his eyes and felt the blood rushing in surges throughout his entire body. He had never been treated so tenderly.

She kissed him on his chest as she stepped out of her sandals. Ian reached down and undid the sash around her waist. Then, reaching up to her bare shoulders, he slid the blue dress down her arms and turned her towards the bed. He sat down on the bed and slid the dress the rest of the way, taking the opportunity to feel her skin all the way to her feet. Underneath she was wearing a white lace bra that sat under her breasts, holding them up for admiration. Her bikini panties were also white lace, their whiteness now glowing in the moonlight against her tan thighs. Ian gasped audibly. For a moment, and only a moment, he thought it all wasn't real. But the heat generated in the space between their skins told him otherwise.

She reached behind her in a way that only women can and undid the bra. Ian wanted to look at her as she was, just a little longer, but the sight of her naked breasts changed his mind. They were perfect to him, milky white, outlined by the bathing suit she had worn while tanning. Ian pulled her to him and kissed her stomach and breasts and then stood to feel them pressed against his own skin.

As they lay down together, Ian was never so sure, so confident about what he wanted. What he wanted was to make her happy, to make her feel good, to make her know how much he wanted to do these things for her. He used his lips to touch every part of her body. He couldn't remember ever having the sensation of actually tasting another person's skin, but with Robyn he found himself wanting to bite deeply into her flesh as though it were soft flavorful food, the origin of which he had no idea.

As he entered her she gasped and clutched at his back, and another bolt of electricity shot through his body. Their pace was naturally quickening and Ian slowed, not wanting it to be gone so soon. Robyn felt his slowing and responded by concentrating on other areas; his chest, his buttocks, his arms.

Now they were exchanging power, tuning one another in, calling and answering, their bodies locked into one another's nerve endings. No one was in control and they were both in control. As their pace quickened again they both charged ahead knowing they would explode at the same time. And they did.

Robyn came up off the bed and slammed into Ian's chest just as he rocked backward, arching his back and letting his head fly as far as his neck would allow. He pulled his head forward, reaching for her with both hands and took one last look at her face, she looking clearly back at him, her eyes betraying the fear of how vulnerable and powerful they had both become at that moment, and then his mind let go.

Images smashed against the dark backdrop of his brain, powerful waves, light bursts and finally him, Ian, hurtling from a cliff at the top of the world hundreds of miles above the surface, of what he didn't know. He was still pushing hard against Robyn as he let out a guttural scream that came in tandem with the final rush from his body into hers.

He wanted to fall forward to the bed, his body utterly limp, but he would have crushed Robyn who was still contracting her body around him. He caught himself on either side of her with his arms, knowing they would only hold him for a minute. He bent his head down and kissed her tenderly, then fell to the side of her, their arms and legs still intertwined. She turned her body and head to face him, sliding her arm around his neck.

He took a last look at the face he knew he would see in his mind for a long time, pulled Robyn tightly to his chest and closed his eyes.

chapter 43

ROBYN FELT THE cool, dark air of the morning rush through the taxi as it sped toward the Royal Prince. Her body was still flush with the sensations of the evening and her mind was feeling Hollywood smug. Here she was, she thought, at four o'clock in the morning, heading to her million dollar hotel in Acapulco after an evening of moonlight cruises, dining and dancing, fabulously topped off by incredible lovemaking with a handsome and sexy, but extremely sensitive, hunk. Eat your heart out Jackie O.

Robyn knew that she and Ian had reached a level that would have her considering future possibilities, but right now that was icing on the cake. She was too busy enjoying the overall excitement of being a woman of the world. The thought made her giggle as the lights of the hotel appeared through the windshield.

As they got closer Robyn realized the lights were not aligned but scattered, some brighter than others, and shining in all directions. Halfway up the driveway the taxi halted as a uniformed policeman stepped forward and raised his hand. Robyn could see now that the front of the hotel was a tangle of cars, white and blue lights dotting their tops, the light bouncing off the large leaves of the palms and shifting the shadows with each rotation. Set squarely in the center of the windshield view was an ambulance, its significance suddenly taking on a terrifying meaning as she squinted into the glare, the long, white form appearing and disappearing like a throbbing ghost.

She felt her chest contract, thinking that it was absurd for her to assume that anything in the scene ahead had a relation to her and her companions, and at the same time that Ian's mysterious encounters of the week had finally resulted in some form of evil success. She was conscious of putting money in the hand of the taxi driver as she slid out of the back seat, never taking her eyes from the ambulance which now had two men inserting a red and white shrouded stretcher into it. Somehow she was moving undaunted at increased speed to, then into, the hotel. She went directly to the steps knowing her only hope of getting to the room was to continue to see and feel movement, something the elevator would deny her. She looked at each step as she climbed quickly, focusing on not falling to distract other thoughts, as the glaring light bounced off the concrete walls. When she reached the fifth floor landing and groped for the door she would not allow herself debate at the possibility of whom or what she might find when she got to the room.

Robyn turned left and heard her heartbeat pounding off the walls of the hallway, the scene near the end of the hall now telescoping toward and away from her. Officer Tito Ramirez was pulling the door closed on her room.

"Oh God! Kim! Donna!" Her own voice was not recognizable.

Ramirez looked up at the eerie sound, a strange look on his face.

"Señorita," he said firmly.

"Oh God!" she repeated. She could feel her head starting to break apart, her body still moving toward the door. "KIM! DONNA!" she yelled into the cavernous hallway.

Ramirez sensed the force of her movement and moved to the side.

"Señorita!" he said again, this time more sharply to get her attention. It made no difference. She was now three steps from the room.

Robyn felt the words in her head begin to gnarl and distort and knew when they came out they would form a shriek. Before it happened the door opened and the startled face of Donna appeared. She seemed to comprehend almost immediately what was happening and caught Robyn in mid-flight.

"DONNA!"

"Sh sh sh sh sh sh sh," Donna breathed, and put her arms around her. "It's okay. It's okay."

"Oh God," Robyn blurted. "KIM!"

"Oh hell, now what?"

The disembodied voice of Kim floated from the open door. Seconds later she appeared scratching her head.

"What are you yelling about?"

When she saw the look on Robyn's face her tone changed.

"Robyn! What's wrong?"

Robyn reached out and hugged her, realizing how stupid she looked and feeling too relieved to care.

"I saw the ambulance," she said, straightening herself up a little at a time, "I thought…."

"I know," Kim said, giving her a firm look. Robyn saw her eyes look past her to Ramirez then back. "It's been a long night. Let's get some sleep."

"Señorita," Ramirez said, coldly. He was not about to give the other women a chance to dilute a powerful opportunity. "There has been a murder here tonight. One of my men. Where have you been all evening?"

Robyn was still facing her friends and saw the look of annoyance on Kim's face. Kim raised her eyebrows as if to say, just tell him the truth. We did.

Robyn took a minute to find an answer in her now unfamiliar mind then said, "I was with everyone else till about midnight and then I was with Ian Connors at his hotel till around three thirty."

"Just you and him? Someone else saw you there, maybe?"

Robyn could hear the wheels turning in the Officer's head.

"Yes, we were alone. No, no one saw us there unless someone saw us walk through the lobby." She said it firmly, bringing the challenge to the surface.

"It is late and I am certain you are tired." It came out dryly as if to indicate he was not suggesting anything, and in doing so did. "We might talk again later today. Buenas noches."

Ramirez turned and walked away not waiting for confirmation.

Inside the room Robyn quickly threw off her dress, donned a long teeshirt, and fell into bed before any explanations could be made. Kim and Donna followed and then Kim explained.

"Some cop got killed on the beach just beyond the restaurant. Ramirez made sure to tell us the guy's throat was cut."

"What did he do, come running here the minute he found a body in the neighborhood?" Robyn was annoyed.

"Well, that's what I thought when he knocked on the door," Kim said with a hint of uncharacteristic apology.

"And she told him so," Donna said, a faint smile on her face. They all smiled.

"I'll bet you did," Robyn said.

"Turns out the guy was assigned to watch us," Kim said, and the room got very quiet for a minute. "But I don't know what that means," she continued, her tone of apology gone now. "Was he watching us to protect us, from what I don't know, or was he watching us, like we're criminals? Anyway, Ramirez came right up. And he loved the fact that you weren't here."

"I'll bet. How long have you been here? I left Ian's at three thirty and Spook wasn't back yet?"

"We left the club about one thirty and got back here before two," Donna said. "We were tired. We were asleep when Ramirez came."

"Spook rode with us here and kept the taxi," Kim said. "We don't know where he went after that. He was actually talking about being hungry. Do you believe it?" She shook her head.

Robyn figured he purposely stayed away from the room for a while for her and Ian's sake. Nice guy.

"Well, did the cop follow you when you left?" Robyn asked, trying to make sense of the night.

"Who?" Kim looked puzzled.

"The policeman?" Robyn said, surprised at the question.

Kim and Donna looked at one another then back at Robyn. Then Kim's expression changed.

"Oh, not the guy that was with us all night. This was a different one, named Gado or Garo, one we supposedly never saw before. Which is why I question what his purpose was," Kim added smartly. "I almost get the feeling this one's been following us around for a while. Look, enough excitement for tonight," she said, getting up off the bed. "This is getting to be a regular thing. We'll never be able to go back to our dull existence in Pittsburgh. Are you all right?" she said warmly to Robyn.

"I really don't know," Robyn answered, a flash of the ambulance being fed creeping into her mind. "Sleep will probably help."

chapter 44

IAN SLEPT THE sleep of angels, waking to the sound of water running in the shower. Robyn's face immediately appeared in his mind. He kept his eyes closed so as not to disturb the image as he brought himself around. Then he heard the sound of a man coughing and his eyes flew open. He sat up in the bed and looked across the room. In the other bed was a rumpled heap of covers.

Spook in the shower, Ian thought. Where's Robyn?

Ian got out of bed quickly. He couldn't believe she left without him knowing. At the same time he knew he had slept more soundly then he could ever remember. He rapped on the bathroom door.

"Spook? That you?"

"Yo!" came from the running water. "Almost done."

Damn, Ian thought. When did she leave? Why didn't she tell me she was leaving?

A rush of thoughts came into his mind, mostly insecure ones. But he knew he couldn't have misread her face or her actions last night that badly. No, maybe Spook came back and surprised her or something. He calmed himself down enough to wait for some help. Long minutes later the bathroom door popped open.

"Hey," Spook said, with a big smile. "Beautiful day in Acapulco."

"Did you see Robyn?"

"No," he said, calmly. "You were zonked when I got back. That was about four. Why? Something happen?"

"No," Ian said quickly, then smiling added, "well, yeah. But's it's boring. You wouldn't want to hear about it."

"That's okay. I can see it all over your face."

Ian relaxed a little. It was an acknowledgement, an acceptance that made the thought of him and Robyn feel more right.

"I better call her," Ian said. "I have to call Carmelo today too. We should go see him." As he walked around the bed to the phone, it rang.

"Hello? Carmelo! Wow, that's weird. I was just getting ready to call you. We wanted to come up and see you today."

Ian listened to the weak voice on the other end then responded.

"Absolutely. Sure, that'll work out great. I'm really glad you called us. About an hour or so? We'll be there." He hung up. "How's that for ESP?" Ian pulled pillows up to the headboard and sat on the bed. "Carmelo was calling to see if we'd come help him escape from the hospital. He said he's going nuts in there and he could be home doing some work instead. But he needs some help getting set up there, plus he can't drive. I told him we'd take care of him. Okay with you?"

"Sure," Spook yelled into the sink, rinsing his face. "Glad we can help him out."

"Yeah, me too."

Ian turned back to the phone and called Robyn's hotel. She answered the phone.

"Robyn? It's Ian."

"Good morning," she said, in the sweetest voice he'd ever heard. He knew immediately there was nothing wrong, nothing to be insecure about. Last night's emotions were all packed inside those two words.

"Where did you go?" Ian said, gently. "I was worried."

"You were sleeping like a baby. I didn't want to scare Spook whenever he walked in and I didn't want to get anyone here nervous so I slipped out about three-thirty and took a taxi back. I would've loved to stay otherwise," she added. "I wish I had."

There was a definite change of tone in the last sentence. Ian picked up the phone and walked to the balcony.

"What?" he prompted.

She told him the events of early morning, her voice betraying the concern she felt for her companions.

"Have you heard from Officer Ramirez yet, by any chance?" she said.

"No, but I guess I will. Are you okay?"

Ian wanted to hold her tight and chase all the bad things away. He felt a little resentful that the fabulous mood he'd awakened to had been disturbed, probably for Robyn as well.

"How about if we book another week and you and I just stay here and forget about the rest of the world?" He knew he couldn't but he wanted her to know how he felt.

"Wouldn't that be nice," she said, dreamily. "But neither one of us can do it. Hey, Philadelphia and Pittsburgh aren't that far apart."

"They just got a lot closer. You know you've started something that may not end for a long time." He wanted to say may not end at all.

"I'm glad you feel that way."

Her voice was milky. Ian felt good, and safe. For today, and maybe a lot more todays, he had someone very special in his life, and he felt like he was special in hers.

"All right," Robyn said, shaking some of the dreaminess out of the conversation, "what are you guys doing today?"

"We're running up to the hospital. Carmelo called and asked us to help him out. He's getting clausy in the hospital so we're taking him home. We should be back here by about noon. Why don't you come over here around then and we'll do something for the day?"

"I might be alone."

"That's what I was hoping," Ian said.

"All right, should I wait at the pool bar?"

"No," Ian said. "I'll leave word at the desk to give you the room key. In fact, I'm hoping my boss calls back with some information for me. If he does, write it all down and tell him I'll call him as soon as I get back. It's too early there to call him. Okay?"

"Okay."

"I miss you already," Ian said.

"I know how you feel. Bye," she said and hung up.

"Shit!" Ian yelled and came back into the room.

"What's the matter?" Spook said, stepping out of the bathroom.

Ian retold Robyn's story.

"Let's get out of here before Ramirez shows up and ruins the day."

"What do you think about the murder?"

"If Ramirez is finding reasons to kill his own men, or letting Ebbetts get away with it, then we're really in deep shit," Ian said coldly. "I'm thinking it's just coincidence. Let's move."

Ian knew they both didn't believe that. But now wasn't the time.

chapter 45

THREE HOURS BEFORE Ian and Spook jumped into the rented Thing to drive to the hospital, Ed Bernardi and Kevin McGarvey were surrounded by Maryland farmland, headed south on Route Fifty. They had spent most of the previous evening combing through trial transcripts and pre-trial investigative reports trying to find a clue in the mass of documentation that was the final two years of Bill Golden's life.

Ed Bernardi didn't think there would be much of significance there because it was all aimed at what Bill Golden had or hadn't done. Warren Ebbetts was dead by the time Golden went on trial, so his name only came up in preliminary investigations and trial hearings as a matter of record. But Ed wanted to be sure.

Even the paper trail inside Doner, Elson and Simons was clean. The money had been siphoned off early in the process. With Cook International's investment records showing one set of numbers before and Doner, Elson's showing another afterward, the only place the money could disappear was in the middle, right in the hands of Bill Golden. And since no one had any reason or desire, unfortunately, to look anywhere else, no one was going to find anything else. Bill Golden, if he had truly been set up, had been set up nicely. He was put in the position of having to argue a negative. He couldn't prove that he didn't take the money and, with Ebbetts dead, there were no other suspects.

Ed knew his only chance of shedding new light on the case was in discovering who Warren Ebbetts had been, or might still be. He had called Ebbett's wife from McGarvey's office to see if she was still in the area. She had answered the phone in what Ed had read as a jovial mood. She was reasonably cooperative with him after he explained he was trying to return some money he had borrowed from her husband.

"I borrowed a few bucks from him about three years ago and I wanted to thank him for not chasing me for it. Things have been tough for a few years but they're finally coming around."

"Better than you think, Mr. Bernard," she said, smartly. He didn't correct her. "My husband died about two years ago so it looks like you saved yourself some money."

"Oh, my goodness," Ed said, trying to act surprised. "I'm very sorry."

"Don't be."

"Well, Warren was a good man and very helpful to me," Ed said, sounding sincere. "What happened, if it's all right to ask? Was he sick?"

"No, he had an accident," she said, not sounding like she wanted to be bothered talking about it. "He drowned."

"Oh, that's tragic," he said.

"Well look, Mr. Bern..., whatever, it wasn't tragic, it was God's will."

She said it flippantly. Ed was beginning to understand now from her voice. Mrs. Ebbetts had had a few drinks and this was not her favorite topic for discussion.

"Warren's gone but he left me the best part of him, his insurance policies and some investments. Now we're both resting in peace. You keep your money and spend it on somebody who'll appreciate it. Okay?"

"That's very nice of you, Mrs. Ebbetts, thank you."

So Warren Ebbetts was not a hit at home. And Mrs. Ebbetts offered little by way of new information. The last bit of potential information was in a police investigation report in Easton, Maryland where he and McGarvey were headed, the place where the fateful sailing voyage had begun.

Easton was a quaint town full of English and Southern influences, the two blending comfortably enough to produce colonial architecture of the brick and shutters variety, along with a laid-back earthy vibe born of farmers and fishermen. Ed Bernardi had been here once before, but only for the pleasure of a company-bought meal at the Tidewater Inn, a local landmark. Easton was on the verge of being "discovered." It had been for most of its existence a backwater crabbing town. But the Maryland and Washington, D. C. money crowd, having enjoyed its maritime advantages for many years, began seeing it in a new light. There was snob appeal to be cultivated here, especially in St. Michael's, Easton's extension into the Chesapeake. As he turned down South Harrison Street and pulled up in front of the small, brick building that served as the police station, Ed Bernardi could smell "progress" and soaring property values all around him.

McGarvey's involvement in the Bill Golden case was enough to convince a Detective John Glancey with a phone call to open the file for them. As they shook hands in an office inside the station, Ed Bernardi thought the tall, sandy haired man in his late thirties had more the air of a salesman than a detective.

He wore a big smile and greeted the two of them with a friendly handshake.

"How was the ride down from Philadelphia?" he said, no trace of Eastern Shore accent.

"Pretty smooth once we got past the Twin Bridges," Ed said. "We hit rush hour."

"It's always slow through there, even when it's not rush hour," he said. "I'm originally from the Philadelphia area. Still have family up there, so I run up every once in a while. In fact that's one of the things that caught my eye when I investigated this case. This Ebbetts fellow was from Elkins Park. That's where I'm from. I know the house he lives in, or lived in."

"What we were hoping," Ed said, wanting to move along, "was to get some more information about the other two passengers. Ebbetts drowned and his body was not recovered, correct?"

"Yes," Glancey said.

"The young fellow, Spencer, his body was recovered?"

The detective had the file open now and was pulling sheets of paper out of it.

"That's also correct. But not for over a week. He washed up a good ways away from where they were sailing. Body was in pretty bad shape." His tone was getting slightly more official now.

"And this third man, Alvarez. Did you talk to him?"

"Yes I did. Obviously he was very shook up, in shock almost. He couldn't believe it happened. And he couldn't believe he was the only one to survive."

"Was he hurt, you know, bruised, cuts?" Ed asked.

"There's a copy of the medical examination in the folder. Off the top of my head I know he was cut and had a good size egg up here, on his forehead. I remember seeing that myself because it was a beauty." Glancey stood up. "Why don't I let the two of you look at the file and see what answers you can get? Then if you have any other questions I'll see if I can answer them for you."

McGarvey was already looking at file papers. He nodded his head.

"Would you gentlemen like some coffee?" Glancey said.

"Love some," Ed said, eagerly. "Black."

"Two, please," McGarvey said.

When the detective left Ed turned to McGarvey.

"Anything?"

McGarvey started reading bits and pieces out loud as he picked through the file.

"Boat launched from Easton Point Marina, thirty four footer..., three passengers. Here's a picture of Alvarez." He held it up, looked at it and handed it to Ed. "Good looking guy, definitely looks Mexican, or Hispanic anyway."

Ed looked at the picture of a handsome man in shorts, without a shirt. He was very tall with a lean, muscular build. Don't trust his face though, Ed thought.

"Does this guy look sneaky to you or am I just overly suspicious?"

McGarvey ignored the question, his attention focused on the file.

"What company did he work for?" Ed said, tossing the picture back on the desk.

"It says....Las Mesas Incorporated."

Ed pulled a notepad out of his suitcoat and wrote it down.

"Did he own the boat?"

"Doesn't say."

"Any verification on the storm that hit them?"

"You're tough," McGarvey said, chuckling. "Wait a minute..., here's a....yeah. Weather service verified existence of sporadic storm weather on the water. Nothing one hundred percent guaranteed, but who's going to argue?"

"What about that medical exam, the bump on the head?"

"Yes, it's here," McGarvey said. "What do you want to know?"

"What does the report say about injuries?"

"Severe contusion to the blah, blah, blah. Translated from the medical it says he had a big egg on his forehead above the right eye. Laceration..., had a nasty cut on his left arm. Bleeding had been controlled and the wound bandaged by the time he arrived at the hospital."

"When did they do the examination?"

"Here," McGarvey said, handing him the report. "Tear into it, Dick Tracy."

Ed scanned the sheet noting particular entries, then dropped it back in front of McGarvey. He stood up and looked around the office, nothing in the neat, tan room catching his eye except a Seth Thomas clock swinging its pendulum like a hypnotist.

"When did this accident take place?" Ed asked, starting to pace the room. "What time of day was it?"

"Ehhh, approximately one thirty in the afternoon," McGarvey answered. "Alvarez was towed in about three hours later, Marine police picked up his SOS about two hours after the accident."

Ed's ears perked up.

"They didn't bring him in till about four-thirty, huh. Seems like a lot of time before he sent the SOS, doesn't it?" He looked at McGarvey who shrugged his shoulders.

Glancey came back in the room carrying two coffees.

"Here you go, gentlemen. Find anything that helps you?"

"Thanks," Ed said, grabbing the coffee and sipping it quickly. "Yeah, couple of things. Can you find out for us who the boat was registered to? I didn't see it in the report."

"I'm sure I can get that for you."

"Oh," Ed said. "Another thing, Detective, you said this Alvarez had a big egg on his forehead."

"Yes he did. It was in the medical report wasn't it?"

"Yes it was. I'm curious. How soon after Mr. Alvarez was rescued did you first see him?"

"Well, they towed him in around four-thirty. I walked down to the pier after I got the call so…, maybe four-forty-five."

"The doctor's report says he examined the patient at five twenty five. That was more than four hours after the incident occurred."

McGarvey was looking at Ed now, not sure of what he was after.

"I guess that's correct," the detective said.

"One more thing. Where can I find this Doctor Lawson from the report?"

"When you walk out the door of this building, make a right and go six doors down. You'll see his shingle." Glancey smiled, satisfied he'd given at least one firm answer this morning.

"So what do you think?" McGarvey asked Bernardi as they headed up the house-lined street.

"I think I keep looking for reasons to buy the story and I can't find any," Ed answered. "Everything seems flimsy to me."

"Well, we can take your perspective into consideration," McGarvey said.

"Hell, I have no argument with that. But maybe it's my perspective that's letting me see how flimsy all this is. You see, back then no one had a gripe, no one had a reason to question any of this. Ebbetts' widow sounded like it was the answer to her prayers and, according to that report, that kid Spencer had no family to make a fuss, just a girlfriend who claimed him. Even that seems convenient to me. They probably hand-picked the kid."

Dr. Edgar Lawson's shingle waved gently to the two men as they stepped single file through the office door. After his receptionist explained to him that his visitors were not patients Dr. Lawson appeared in the waiting room and invited them into a quaint sitting room just off his offices. He was an old fashioned gentleman in his late sixties who walked as slowly as he spoke.

"Hah can I be of hailp?" he asked, his Southern Virginia roots entwined in his speech.

Ed Bernardi refreshed the doctor's memory about the boating accident and indicated that some details were still being cleared up.

"You examined Mr. Alvarez, the only survivor, when he arrived at the hospital and you indicated in your report a large lump on the head, above the right eye. Do you remember that, Doctor?"

"Yes, ah do. Vary lahge, vary tenda."

"I don't know much about medicine, Doctor, but would a bang on the head received almost five hours before you examined it still be that big five hours later? I'm just wondering?"

Ed didn't want to offend him, just stir some thought.

"Contoosions of that sawt varay," he answered without hesitation. "It depends on the ahrea bruised as well as the purson broosed."

Ed was afraid of that. Too specific.

"Is it possible that a large lump like Mr. Alvarez had could go down some in four or five hours?"

"Of cawse, my dear man. Ahds ah it would. But nothin' you could swaih by."

"How about the cut on his left arm?"

"Now thaihs somethin' to considah."

Ed's scalp shifted and he sat up in his chair. "In what way?" he said, quicker than he wanted to.

"The cut was bandaged befaw ah eggxamined it. Awful blooday. Seemed lahke maw blood than necessary fawra fahve houwa old wound. Especialay since he'd rinsed it in the wawta. But ah just figahed the medic made maw a mess of it than necessayry."

"You mean like the wound shouldn't have been as bloody as it was by the time you saw it?" Ed wanted to be clear.

"He'd a bled that much for fahve houwas he woulda dahd. But as ah said, it wasn't impawtant at the tahm."

They thanked the doctor for his time and moved quickly back to the car. A visit to the DNR office before they left gave them nothing more than the boat's registration through Las Mesas Incorporated. Ed knew there was nothing solid he could hang his hat on. The doctor had been both encouraging and frustrating. One more reason to think the whole story was bad and one less way to prove it. Just like everything else about the incident. As sure as Ed was that nothing he'd learned could prove it false, he was equally sure the whole thing stank, and Ian was messing with some real sharp, deadly people. The whole scheme, which is what he was sure it was now, had been planned and executed perfectly.

"I want to know who this Las Mesas Incorporated is," he said, in the car as they headed north. "They owned the boat as well as Alvarez and they have a Mexico City address. That's a little too close to Acapulco for me."

"I called my office with that before we left," McGarvey said. "Maybe by the time we get back we'll have something on it."

Ed rolled the information around in his head all the way back to Philadelphia. When they walked into McGarvey's offices he practically leaped at the secretary.

"Did you get any information on the Las Mesas company?"

"Yes, I did," she said, warily, then looked at McGarvey. "I put it on your desk."

Ed was already in McGarvey's office looking at the paper on his desk. What he saw made the hair on the back of his neck stand up.

"Oh, Jesus," he said, and fumbled in his pocket for the number Ian had given him.

chapter 46

THE THING CREPT up to the Hospital Privado Magallanes, a two story building in gleaming white stucco that tested the merger of modern and Spanish architecture. Hard right angles and sheets of glass fought furiously with arches and tile accents leaving Ian more disturbed about the building's mission than the architect's. He hadn't seen much of it in the dark the night he was there. Considering his state of mind that night, he was glad he hadn't.

After checking in at the nurse's station, he and Spook made their way down the hall to Carmelo's room. Ian still carried guilt over Carmelo's unfortunate involvement in the problem with Ebbetts. Being able to do something for him and the fact that Carmelo thought enough of their friendship to ask, helped Ian deal with it.

"Buenos dias, Señor Carmelo," Ian said, with a big smile as soon as he opened the door.

Carmelo smiled weakly. He was sitting in a chair next to the bed, dressed in casual clothes with a small travel bag at his feet. His arm was in a sling.

He looks pretty worn out, Ian thought. No, he looks downright bad.

"Hello, Ian, hello, Spook." His voice was as weak as his smile. "Thank you for coming. I'm not back to full strength but enough to know I have to get out of this place. I worry too much here about the restaurant and what is going on in the world." He waved his hand and managed a smile again.

Looking at Carmelo, Ian wasn't sure it was a good idea for him to leave the hospital. The more he stared the more he saw a man in pain.

"Are you sure you're giving yourself enough time?" Ian said.

"No, but I know what I have to do. I can lie around at home as well as I lie around here. Let us go."

Carmelo slid forward in the seat to stand up and his face tightened. Spook moved towards him and reached to help him up while Ian quickly grabbed his good arm.

"Ooo," Carmelo said, grimacing. "I'm very stiff." Then he looked at Ian and forced the smile again. "But I will loosen up."

"You better take it easy," Ian shook his head. "Where's Manny? Does he know you're leaving the hospital?"

"Yes," Carmelo said. "He does not approve either. I sent him to the house to do some things for me there. He said he had a wonderful time yesterday at your hotel. That was very nice of you."

Ian shrugged his shoulders. "No big deal."

As they stepped toward the door it opened and a nurse pushed a wheel chair in ahead of her. She spoke to Carmelo in Spanish.

"Si usted esta decidido a ir por este camino es la regla."

Ian looked at Carmelo.

"She says the rules are I have to leave in that."

"Well, that's not a bad rule." Ian smiled at the nurse. "Ask her if we can keep the chair when we leave. You could use it."

"You worry about me too much," Carmelo said, easing into the chair. "Stop at the desk. I think I have to sign some papers."

In five minutes they were in front of the hospital settling Carmelo into the front seat of the Thing.

"They are still renting these to the tourists, eh?" he said, chuckling uncomfortably.

"Best deal in the fleet," Spook said. "Just a little weak on these mountain roads."

"They are weak all over," Carmelo said. "That is why they rent them to the tourists. You can't go fast enough to hurt yourself."

They headed out of the hospital lot and then, as Spook would have described it, up. Aside from the few turns Carmelo pointed out, the one thing consistent about their direction was that it pointed the front end of the Thing upward, the vehicle straining against the grade and the weight of its three passengers.

"Obviously you live in the mountains," Spook eventually yelled.

"Yes. It is a very peaceful place, away from the busy noise of the city."

"And the tourists," Ian added, with a smirk.

"Yes, that too." Carmelo nodded his head.

They had been driving about fifteen minutes when all signs of civilization began gradually falling away, with the exception of attractive mountainside homes appearing from time to time out of nowhere. Ian could feel his ears popping from the increased altitude. As they followed a curve between two rock formations jutting thirty feet above them the road leveled off. In the distance to Ian's left sat shimmering, crystal-blue ocean.

"Oh! look at that," he said, pointing.

"Man, what a view," Spook said, reverently.

"It is beautiful, isn't it?" Carmelo stared at the water as he spoke. "This road runs along the coast for the next twenty miles. I have this view from my house. Now you know why I wanted to leave the hospital. I will heal much more quickly seeing the water and sky."

Ian looked at him as he finished the sentence. He could see in Carmelo's face and hear in his voice the weight of his thoughts, having known that weight himself as recently as a week ago when he'd packed his bag for this trip. Ian had come to appreciate in this short week the value of changing the environment around him. Acapulco had given him new surroundings, and hand in hand had come a new perspective. Robyn had much to do with that today, but he would have never gotten to know Robyn or someone like her had he not changed the world around him and let the world around him change him in turn.

The Dive had been the first step and it had made all the difference in the world. He had stripped himself down to his skin and exposed it to the sun and the rock and the water. He had stepped to the edge and placed himself in a position of uncertainty. And now he knew that when he did, it was because there was nothing back there in his life that he was really sure of. Back there were all the things he'd used to build scenery around him like backdrops on a stage. Office buildings, suits and ties, cars and people, painted onto large canvasses moving by him while he stood still going nowhere. He had always sensed the inertia, but found it easier to do nothing about it.

But here, he'd begun to understand what Carmelo knew. The beauty of the simplicity, the simplicity of the cycle that Carmelo made himself available to every day: the earth beneath his feet, the sky above and the water below. To be willing to forsake one for the other, to step from that place of comfort, of security, and leap, arms outstretched, to taste momentary freedom in the sky; and then, having reached for it, accept the inevitable fall with as much grace as possible and make peace with the earth again.

Ian knew now there would be more dives in the years to come but not from the flatlands of Cook International.

The road weaved its way left and right for another two miles when a low, one story house, attached somehow to the side of the mountain, appeared on the right.

"Turn in there," Carmelo said, pointing.

Spook pulled into the driveway alongside Carmelo's Jeep. Spook and Ian hopped out quickly and helped Carmelo out of the front seat. Then they all stopped to take in the view.

"Boy, this is gorgeous," Ian said to the vista.

"I told you," Carmelo said, looking out at the water as if to confirm that all was as he had left it. "It is all the medicine I need."

They helped him up the steps which led to a side door in the house. There a deck began that ran to the front of the house and around the other side. The front of the house was almost all glass. Inside was bright but cool, the living room decorated simply. There was nothing elegant or pretentious, just a neat and comfortable space that gave the impression that it was Carmelo's home, not just his house. And the view was as incredible as it was from the deck and the driveway.

Carmelo walked slowly to the refrigerator and opened it. There was little inside, which Ian noticed.

"Do you need something, Carmelo?"

"Actually," Carmelo answered with a weak smile, "that is one of the things I need your help with. I need to get some food into the house. I haven't had a chance to put some things in and now, I don't know how much I could handle. Would you mind getting some things for me?"

"That's why we're here, man," Spook said. "Tell us what you need and where to get it and it's done. Hell, I'll whip you up some meals and put them in the freezer or somethin'. You name it."

"Let me make a list of some things," Carmelo said, taking a notepad from a drawer. "Make sure you get some beer. Whatever you like. I'll write the English and Mexican names for some of these items in case you're not sure, but you shouldn't have any problem." He finished writing and handed the list to Spook. "There. When you pull out continue on this road. The store is down the mountain a little way. You will be able to get everything on the list there. Tell the woman it is for me and she will make up a bill that I will pay later. Otherwise she will charge you like a tourist," another weak smile appeared "so don't let her see your money." He picked up keys from the kitchen counter and handed them to Spook. "Here, take my Jeep. The store is downhill on the way out but uphill on the way back. You will find it much easier than your rental car."

"I'll stay or go," Ian said to Spook. "What do you want to do?"

"I'll do either," Spook said, raising his hands.

"I will be fine," Carmelo said, interrupting them. "Why don't you both go and enjoy the ride. It's very lovely. I'm going to take a shower. It will give me time to get settled."

Ian looked at Spook, sensing Carmelo wanted some time alone.

"Okay, if you're sure."

"I'm sure," Carmelo said, sounding tired.

"All right then," Ian said. "Turn right out of here?"

"Correct," Carmelo said. "Remember it is a downhill mountain road with many curves. Wear your seatbelts."

"Always do," Spook said, and headed for the door.

Ian looked at Carmelo again as Spook left the house.

"Are you sure you're okay by yourself? You look pretty wiped out."

He studied Carmelo's face again and what he saw troubled him. There was pain in his face but it was not only the pain of injury. Something else weighed heavily on his new friend, and Ian hoped it was not concern for them.

"You're not still worrying about us are you?"

Carmelo looked back at him, and Ian saw the same face that had told him a few nights ago that someone had tried to kill him. Ian could hear the sadness in his voice as he answered.

"I fear for all of us, my friend."

Ian paused to let the words sink in. "Well don't," he said, not really believing it. He turned slowly and walked out the door trying to understand the uneasiness that had just come over him.

chapter 47

ROBYN WAS SITTING on the balcony at the Casa Grande Hotel sipping her third iced tea when the phone rang. She had been there over an hour waiting for Ian and the others to return. She wasn't angry or upset, just impatient to see him again, to touch him and reassure herself that he was real. And a little apprehensive, considering the way things were going this week. She half expected him to be late returning. In the short time she'd known him he hadn't been on time for any of their arranged meetings. Ian seemed to give people the time he expected to be there, which was always optimistic, but rarely realistic.

She answered the phone on the second ring expecting to hear his voice stammering out some perfectly reasonable excuse.

"Hello," she said, trying to sound sexy, and succeeding.

"Hello," Ed Bernardi said. "I'm sorry, is this Ian Connors room?"

"Yes, it is," she said, quickly changing the sound of her voice while she blushed for the empty room.

"I'm trying to get a hold of Ian Connors. Is he there?"

Robyn could hear the agitation in his voice.

"He's not here right now. Is this his boss, Ed?"

"Yes, it is," Ed said, sounding encouraged. "Did he leave a message?"

"Well, he told me you might call. My name is Robyn. I'm a friend of his." Already she wanted to tell this stranger that she was more than just a friend. "Ian went to help someone get home from the hospital. He should have been back by now, but it probably took longer than he expected. He said to take down any information you might have and he'd call you back as soon as he could."

"Shit!" Ed said, away from the phone but not far enough away that Robyn didn't hear it.

"Is there some problem?"

There was a momentary silence.

"Look, Robyn, is it?"

"Yes."

"I'm going to give you some information that is very important. I'm assuming Ian trusts you if he told you to speak to me so I'll have to trust you as well. You have to get a hold of Ian as soon as possible and tell him to call me but tell him this first. The company that the client, Alvarez, worked for, as well as who the boat was registered to, was called Las Mesas Incorporated. The company doesn't exist. It's a paper company that exists only as a bank account."

Robyn was scratching notes on the hotel writing paper as fast as she could, writing the names in big, bold letters.

"The only name on the account," Ed continued, "that we could trace so far is an Andrew Wilson. That's a name Ian's heard before. There are some other things I want to tell him but it would be hard to explain them to you. When was he supposed to be back?"

"About noon. It's one-thirty now." Robyn was feeling uneasy. Ed Bernardi's worry was finding its way through the phone lines to her. "Should I do something?"

"Try and get hold of him. Does that person he's helping have a number you can call?"

Robyn's mind started hopping through a list of possibilities; Carmelo; last name; the hospital; the restaurant.

"I might be able to get it."

"All right, try. Tell him to call me right away. In the meantime I'll try to find out more about that phony company. Here's my number."

Ed gave her McGarvey's number and said goodbye. Robyn hung up the phone and sat on the bed for a minute trying to decide the best course of action. Obviously there was more going on than Ian had told her since the night they spoke at the hospital. She knew nothing about this Wilson or his phony company. She only knew that Ed Bernardi gave a clear signal that things were getting worse. And Ian was not back yet. She picked up the phone and dialed the hotel operator.

"Hello Operator, would you connect me with the police department? Thank you. Officer Ramirez, please."

"Ramirez."

Robyn pictured the creepy policeman as he had looked yesterday at the hotel pool and shivered. But she knew if Ian was in danger this was the only person who could react quickly enough to help him.

"Ramirez," he said again, almost with ignorance.

"Officer Ramirez, this is Robyn Baldwin, Ian Connors' friend."

"Yes, Miss Baldwin," he said, his tone changing, "what is it?"

"I'm not sure how to explain this but I'm concerned about Ian. You see, he was supposed to meet me at his hotel almost two hours ago and he hasn't arrived yet. His boss called from the United States with some information for him and he seemed very concerned that he wasn't here."

"What kind of information was it, Miss Baldwin?" Ramirez asked, quickly.

"Something about a man named Wilson and his phony company."

"Wilson? Is that correct?"

Robyn didn't like the sound of Ramirez's voice now either. This information seemed to mean something to everyone but her and it made her uncomfortable. But finding Ian was more important.

"Yes. Look, Officer, I don't know what all this is about but for now can't you just find Ian? Don't you have someone with him, one of your officers?"

"Señor Connors decided last night that he was not in need of my protection when he left the club. I did not send an officer today."

The sarcasm was clear in Ramirez's voice. Robyn felt like a bad schoolgirl but decided, whether Ramirez liked it or not, she was not going to be intimidated and he was going to do his job.

"Look," she said firmly, "the fact is I haven't heard from him in too long. He went to help Carmelo go home from the hospital over four hours ago and he really should have been back by now. I don't know where he lives or his phone number or I would have called him myself."

"That is not necessary, Miss Baldwin," Ramirez said, sharply. "I will go there myself. When I see him I will have him contact you immediately so as not to worry you further."

"I'd appreciate that very much, Officer. Thank you."

Robyn heard the phone click before she finished her sentence.

* * *

"We need to find out more about this Las Mesas outfit, Kevin." Ed Bernardi paced the lawyer's office.

"The colleague of mine who got us this specializes in banking and business contract law," Kevin said. "He might be able to help us track the paper trail, find a connection to Ebbetts maybe."

"All right," Ed said, grabbing the phone. "I've got to call in to my office and pretend like I give a shit what's going on there. While I'm on I'll check in with our resident money man. Maybe he can suggest something."

When Ed called there was only one message, a meeting in the office tomorrow.

"Keep covering for me, Connie," he told the secretary. "You have the number here if you really need me. I'll keep checking in. Can you transfer me to Frank Gellig's office?"

"Mr. Gellig's office," a woman's voice said.

"Sarah?"

"Yes?"

"Sarah, this is Ed Bernardi, is Frank in by any chance?"

"No, I'm sorry, Ed. He's on vacation for the week. Can one of the other fellows help you?"

"Uhh, who covers for him?" Ed was trying to find a polite way to ask an impolite question, but Sarah would understand. "I mean who else knows as much as Frank about money things, Sarah?" Ed couldn't see her smiling into the phone.

"Let me give you to Ted Haggerty, Ed. Hold on."

"Ted Haggerty here."

"Ted, Ed Bernardi."

"Hey, how the hell are ya, you old skirt chaser?"

"So far so good," Ed said, playing along with the tease. "Ted, this might sound like a strange question but how much do you know about setting up phony companies?"

"What do you need?" Haggerty laughed.

Ed liked Ted but he wasn't in the mood for fun now.

"Ted, this is important. I need to find some things out quickly."

"Oh," Haggerty said, getting the hint. "Tell you the truth, I don't know that much about it. Never had much reason to."

"That's okay," Ed said. "Thanks anyway."

Ed was about to hang up when a thought crossed his mind.

"Ted!" he yelled sharply.

"Yeah, Ed?"

"You ever hear of a company called Las Mesas Incorporated?"

"Las Mesas Incorporated," Haggerty repeated. "As a matter of fact I have. Heard of them, that is. Not much else. Funny you mention it. About, I don't know, two years ago maybe, that name showed up on a printout for our employee investment program. I had never seen it before so it stuck out like a sore thumb. I took it in and showed it to Frank, and he said he'd never heard of it either and it must be a mistake."

"What happened?" Ed said. Haggerty recognizing the name had stunned him, but why, he wasn't sure.

"Frank said he'd get a hold of the guys at Doner Elson and have them straighten it out. I guess they did. I never saw it again. You thinking of investing in it? Hot tip, ole buddy?"

"No, not me," Ed said, preoccupied, his mind still searching for some significance in the chance discovery. He was still searching as he hung up the phone and grabbed his coffee.

chapter 48

"Go ahead, Spook, let her rip." Ian threw the keys at Spook and walked around to the other side of the roofless Jeep. "You're the man I trust most on mountain roads," he said, smiling.

Spook took the compliment without comment and jumped into the driver's seat. Ian climbed into the passenger seat, pushing the seat back on its track.

"Don't know whether a convertible is a good or a bad thing in Mexico," Ian said, feeling the hot sun on his neck.

"Better view of the scenery," Spook answered, and pulled out onto the road. "I never drove one of these babies before. It shifts pretty smooth. Nice tight clutch."

"You need it on these roads," Ian said, already feeling gravity pull them forward. "That 'Thing' would never get us back."

Ian said nothing more for another two minutes, looking around them as they rode, avoiding the nagging thought in his mind, then gave in.

"Carmelo looks like hell," he said, turning halfway around to see Spook's face.

"Yeah, I know," Spook said, softly.

"I don't think he should have left the hospital," Ian continued, "but I don't know him well enough to argue with him. He does have a point though. That house and view definitely have some therapeutic value. Maybe it 'll do him good."

"Yeah, that's some place," Spook said, distractedly.

They were moving quickly down the mountainside now, the curves sharpening with their increased speed. Ian saw the look of concern on Spook's face.

"What's the matter?"

As he said it Ian saw Spook's right foot pumping the brake pedal, softly at first and then harder.

"The brakes, man."

As soon as Spook said it Ian leaned forward, noting the speedometer at about forty miles an hour. They were still headed down at a fairly steep degree. The rushing air around the open-top Jeep was starting to eat the sound of their voices.

"You losing the brakes?" Ian hollered.

Suddenly the road veered dangerously to the ocean side of the mountain. Spook swung the Jeep tightly with the curve, forcing Ian to brace himself with his left hand to stay in his seat. He hadn't put his seat belt on.

"The brakes were kinda mushy the first time I tried them!" Spook yelled. "Now they're disappearing!"

It wasn't the volume in Spook's voice that told Ian there was something seriously wrong, it was the fear. Ian held onto the side and the dashboard of the Jeep to keep from banging around as the curves appeared, each one becoming more treacherous than the last because of the speed, and one other newly arrived condition. There was nothing to the ocean side of the road any more. It was cliffside now. To the right were sheer, flat walls of rock with occasional outcroppings jutting nastily close to the road.

Ian began calculating the possibilities outside of the brakes miraculously returning. To pull to the right almost guaranteed they'd bounce off the flat wall of rock and end up out of control, or smashed into one of the outcroppings if they chose to try it at the wrong time. The road ahead was not visible for more than fifty feet at a time. He flicked his eyes back at the speedometer and saw the needle bouncing around in the space between fifty and sixty.

Spook pumped furiously on the brake pedal, his right foot hitting the floor flatly each time. He pulled up on the emergency brake and there was a slight slowing of little significance. The smell of the brake burning caught Ian's nose.

Suddenly a car appeared from a blind curve just ahead of them. Spook was holding the vehicle to the middle of the road the best he could to allow room to set up for each turn. He saw the car and swung the Jeep sharply, a little too sharply to the right. Ian slammed up against the side of the Jeep and his neck snapped to the right. As he did he felt the Jeep start to tip the same way. He looked down and saw the road ahead cocked at an angle and headed towards him. He put his feet against the inside wall of the jeep and flung his weight across the seat pushing towards Spook as he did. The vehicle came down hard on its left tires slamming Ian's face against Spook's shoulder. At the same time he heard the blaring horn of the other car as it passed by no more than inches away. He sat up immediately.

"Spook!" he yelled, "you got any brakes at all?"

When he sat up and the air hit him again Ian knew the answer. They were flying down the mountain with Spook barely, if at all, in control.

"No!" Spook yelled, jerking the Jeep back to the right then left again trying to find a balance.

"Time to get out!" Ian yelled back. "Move us to the right a little and then jump!"

He saw Spook look over at him, his face frozen.

"Come on! Just roll with it when you hit the ground! We got no choice. Move it, Spook!"

Ian knew Spook's was the tougher exit. He would have to get away from the steering wheel. Ian put his own feet under him on the seat. He could already feel the scraping and burning that would come when his body hit the hard, hot roadway. But he knew they had to do it. The alternative was one more leap into the sky with no graceful, earthly reconciliation, just death.

The Jeep was now doing fifty miles an hour, the only reason it was still on the road being Spook's amazing anticipation of the curves and his arrogant refusal to give up control. But now he was holding on by luck rather than skill. It was time to bail out. Spook had the Jeep in third gear, trying to downshift. Ian could hear the gearbox whining as it sought to break free.

"I'm gonna line it up!" Spook yelled. "I'm gonna try and downshift once before we jump! Hold on a second after I do to see if we slow down any! If we slow or not, that's when we jump! Ready?!"

Ian nodded at Spook, then watched as Spook turned the engine off and grabbed the stick. Ian scraped for a last drop of moisture in his throat but couldn't find one.

***

When the two Americans left, Carmelo shuffled slowly to the other side of the living room and picked up a pair of binoculars. He put the strap awkwardly around his neck with his good arm and walked to one of the sliding glass doors opening onto the front deck, pulling weakly till it opened. He stepped onto the deck and walked to the railing, his eyes fixed on the ocean. He put his arm on the railing to steady himself, the strength in his legs waning while his eyes swept back and forth across the vista, the shimmer on the water disappearing as the sun moved higher in the sky.

Then he heard it.

Echoing off the mountain walls and through the small canyons, the sound came in soft delays carried to him by the wind. It was diffused and without any real power as it pricked at his ears, but his knees buckled and he fell to the deck still gripping the rail. He hung there for a few moments, listening for the final sounds of the meaningless tragedy. When he heard no more he pulled himself to his feet and walked to the side of the deck. Raising the binoculars to his eyes, he scanned the cliffside miles down the road. His eyes caught a small flash and he held the glasses still, focusing with one finger.

There, just below a bend in the road in the small stretch of ground between the base of the cliff and the ocean, lay the burning vehicle, nothing more than a small torch attached to a long, thin line of black smoke.

Carmelo pulled the binoculars over his head and walked back into the house, made his way to the couch and sat down. He reached weakly and clumsily for the phone on the table next to him, dropped the binoculars on the floor and dialed a number.

"Yes," he said, into the phone, his voice weak and tired and angry. "It's done. Now you stay away from the boy, do you understand?"

He paused a moment for a confirmation, then hung up the phone.

chapter 49

WHEN THE ENGINE had been turned off it created an eerie silence on the mountain road, not unlike the sound Ian heard in the air at La Quebrada. The wind whooshed past his ears, almost drowning out the sounds of the Jeep's gearbox and the tires on the hot road. Spook hit the clutch and pulled the stick down hard at the same time. A gut-ripping sound came from underneath their feet, the sound of metal chewing metal. Spook pumped the clutch several times and the stick dropped down, the eye-watering squeal ceasing at the same time. The Jeep and both of its passengers lurched forward at the same time. Ian had to push against the dashboard to keep from losing his position. The jeep slowed noticeably, enough for the two friends to know it was time to go.

Just as Ian came up off his seat he saw Spook open his door and roll out. Ian knew when they jumped they had to get flat as soon as possible to distribute the shock across as much of their bodies as possible. If they stayed vertical, they'd roll head over feet with no protection.

Ian hit the ground in a bunched position, his right knee shredding on impact. Everything after that was a blur. He knew he was rolling and sliding, various spots on his body signaling their contact with the hard surface of the road. No one spot stayed in contact with the ground long enough for Ian to register pain there. He wasn't sure whether he wanted to stop rolling, knowing the pain from all those combined bruises would hit him at once when he did. Somewhere in the tilt-a-whirl ride he had become he heard an explosion. He could tell it wasn't near him but the sound seemed appropriate as small charges inside his head detonated with each roll. He was still conscious and right now that was the most important thing. He didn't want to go out. He could deal with anything that might happen to him but going out meant he wouldn't know if he was going to die.

He slowed, his body making one last revolution which he went with willingly. When he finally stopped he didn't move, waiting for the inside of his head to catch up with his body. The heat of the road beneath began burning into his side while the sun above him cooked his face.

Heat. Good heat, he said to himself, happy to know the sensation.

He checked his ears next, listening for any sound at all, then significant sounds. First, he heard the wind again, the steady but now noticeably subdued version fluttering across the top of his body. He could feel the hair on one side of his head and on his right arm standing up as the air pushed against it. Then he heard the sound of someone's voice, not one he recognized. It was still some distance away but moving towards him.

Time to open the eyes, he thought. He pulled hard with his eyelids and saw a smear of light that forced him to shut his eyes quickly, turning the image into a negative inside his head. Then he opened them slowly, letting the light bleed in till he saw the blue sky sitting at the end of a short, flat plain of asphalt. To the left of the sky he saw a man dressed in tan pants and a white shirt running towards him, shouting in Spanish.

Ian knew he could sit up but he wasn't sure he wanted to. Now that he sensed he had survived, his thoughts went to his friend. Had Spook been as lucky? Images of a twisted, bloody body on the roadside challenged his courage. Then he heard, "Ian?"

The sound pierced his skull like a needle. It was Spook's voice, the same fear of not getting an answer packed into both syllables.

"Ian?"

Ian wanted to answer immediately but wasn't sure his voice would work. "Spook?"

It came out very quietly, but it came out. He tried again, pushing harder.

"Spook?"

"Yeah."

Ian almost laughed. Spook sounded like, So who else would it be, dummy?

"Can you move?" Ian still couldn't bring himself to look around. Staying still was safe.

"Ohhh,...if you wanna call it that," came the answer.

Ian had to move now. He tightened his arm below him and pushed up slowly on his forearm. It hurt everywhere. But he was moving and it didn't matter now. He kept going, ignoring the pain, knowing if he stopped he wouldn't get going again. Skin burns were now making themselves known to his nerve endings. He got to a sitting position and looked around. Spook was sitting up, about twelve feet to his right, just inside the center of the road.

"Puedo hacer algo, Señor? Pensè que estaba manejando loco."

The man in the white shirt was next to him now and rattling off a non-stop flow of Spanish which, under the circumstances, Ian wouldn't have understood even if he spoke the language. Except for the driving crazy part.

The man was helping him get to his feet.

"It's okay," Ian said, trying to slow the man down.

Ian kept trying to think of a word that meant "fine" or "okay" and all he could think of was "grande". The thought of telling this man he was feeling grande didn't seem appropriate. He limped his way with the man's help to Spook who was sitting on his backside as if in meditation, doing his own physical inventory. Ian bent to touch him and his right knee buckled. He just let himself fall to the road, again not having the energy to stop himself. He rolled onto his back to absorb the fall and then sat back up.

"Ah, shit, Spook." Ian looked Spook in the face now, trying to read his condition. "Anything messed up?"

"Just my arm," Spook answered, rubbing his right arm as he spoke. "I ended up on it and it's like numb and tingly."

"Give it a minute to see if the blood was cut off. Anything else?"

"Everything," Spook said, a little less painfully.

"Yeah, I know the feeling."

Something about the two of them sitting there talking filled Ian with a sense of strength. They had survived, apparently without serious injury. A broken arm might be the worst, which, considering the situation would be a minor inconvenience. Somewhere in the back of his head, anger was brewing. He stood up, this time without help, as Spook shook his arm and flexed his hand, shifting his weight to try and get up as well.

"Pins and needles," Spook said. "The feeling's coming back." He raised his head and looked at Ian's face. "How come you seem to know when there's gonna be a problem and you give me the keys?"

Ian smiled.

"We lucked out. Where did the Jeep land?"

Spook twisted his head in the direction of the ocean.

They walked slowly to the other side of the road and peered down at the dying flame that marked the final resting place of Carmelo's Jeep.

"We could've been there," Spook said.

"That was the plan," Ian said, the anger now moving forward.

"What?" Spook looked at him.

"We were supposed to be in there." Ian looked back at Spook. "You didn't think it was an accident, did you?"

"I didn't think about it at all yet."

"Those brakes were gone, weren't they?"

"Well, they did seem kinda mushy from the start. I guess it fits into everything else that's been going on this week. Poor old Carmelo. First him, now his Jeep."

Ian just stared back at Spook, the anger now showing in his face.

"What? What? What's the look for?" Spook said. "They didn't want Carmelo? Why use his Jeep if...?" Spook stopped talking and his face tightened. "Not Carmelo," he said, looking at Ian incredulously. "Are you serious?"

Ian paused a minute to consider the challenge, knowing at the same time there was nothing to consider. Things were coming together, events, circumstances, certainly not reasons, but he'd know them soon enough provided he stayed alive.

"I'd like to be wrong, Spook. But who asked us to come take him home today? Who asked us to get groceries and insisted we take his Jeep? Who was the only person that knew we'd be in his Jeep on a downhill mountain road!?"

Ian wasn't sure if the anger was coming from this latest attempt on his life or the betrayal he felt. There was still a possibility that Carmelo was an innocent pawn, but this accident was just too damn real and too damn close to successful.

"Can you give us a ride?" Ian said, to the Mexican man who had been standing with them watching their conversation. Ian motioned with his hands to make the point.

"Si," the man said, appearing grateful to help.

"There's no point in standing here," Ian said. "I haven't seen another car since we crashed. I want to see Carmelo's face right now. Then I'll know for sure."

The two Americans walked painfully up the hill to the Mexican man's car. Ian's mind raced as they headed back to Carmelo's house, sorting through details and trying to make sense of it all.

"Wasn't Manny supposed to be at the house?" he asked.

"Carmelo said he'd sent him to the house to do some things," Spook answered, confirming Ian's doubts.

"So where was Manny when we got there?"

No one answered the question.

It was quiet in the car now, both of them feeling the pain of their bruises. And Ian knew the closer they got to Carmelo's house, the closer they were to some understanding of what was going on. Ian saw the house from a distance and pointed to it as he spoke to the driver.

"Amigo's casa," he said, feeling foolish. "Telephone. Gracias."

The driver nodded and began speaking in Spanish again. He pulled into the driveway and Ian and Spook got out, thanking the man in English and Spanish as best they could. He looked at them, understanding their thanks but looking confused. He drove off shaking his head, talking in Spanish.

Ian looked at the house, looking for any sign of Carmelo. He wanted to surprise him as best he could to get an honest reaction from him. If Carmelo had been a good actor all along, he might be a better one now. Then again he might be tired of the role-playing and decide to shoot him and Spook on the spot.

They stepped quietly to the side door and Ian tried the door knob. It was open. He turned the knob and stepped inside slowly. As he moved across the kitchen to the living room he could see Carmelo sitting on the couch facing the ocean, completely still. The two scraped and ragged tourists moved into the living room and stood looking at the figure staring out at the ocean. He turned his head slowly and looked at them, almost as if he did not recognize them. Ian saw something flash in Carmelo's face, maybe surprise, maybe fear, then just as quickly, deadness. Ian knew for sure.

"Why?" Ian said, calmly, his anger temporarily diffused by the look on Carmelo's face.

"What shall I offer you?" Carmelo said, his voice hollow. "A reason? An excuse? There is none." He turned his gaze back to the ocean.

Ian felt anger again. He might find pity for this man if given some explanation, but he wanted facts.

"Carmelo, I'm not interested in your self-pity right now. I want some answers. I want the whole goddam thing explained to me, now. Where's Manny?"

The mention of his name made Carmelo's eyes move toward the floor.

"He is fine. He is with my aunt."

"Does he know anything about this?"

"No. I have tried hard to protect him from it. But like many other things, I have not been a good father."

Ian looked at Spook, then back at Carmelo.

"You're Manny's father?"

"Yes." Carmelo now stared at his legs. "Another mistake I made many years ago, when I was much too young." He breathed deep and was silent.

"I'm listening," Ian said, firmly. He stared hard at Carmelo as if to force the story out of him with his gaze. After a minute, Carmelo spoke.

"For his sake I gave him to my aunt. His mother was a whore who was glad to get rid of him so she could go to America with some wealthy criminal. Manuel was just a baby. It was better for him to have some kind of mother, so my aunt agreed to take him if I stayed close to him. The only time I wasn't was when I went away to school. But that was when he stopped being a baby and started being a boy."

Ian realized his legs were beginning to shake and sat down on a chair. Spook sat down on the other end of the couch. The vacuous figure of Carmelo had disarmed them. They had nothing to fear from this man anymore.

"But I took that scholarship because it was the only way. I knew he would never have a decent life if I didn't make one for him. So I went to the American University and I learned everything I could. Mostly about how money is what makes everything happen in this world. I was a spic, wetback waiter and busboy in America, not a young man working his way through college. When I came back home, everything was the same. I was just a busboy and a waiter and a baggage man with a college degree. I worked at the hotels and the restaurants but I still had no money. And I am Mexican. So I stayed an employee of the American investors who owned the hotels and restaurants."

"How'd you get your restaurant?" Spook said.

"I saved a little money and I opened a small cantina, a pathetic place." His voice was still slow and emotionless. "I catered to the Americans who liked the atmosphere of the real Mexico but didn't want to be near the common people. I chased my own people away so that the tourists didn't get offended. I am barely staying in business, and one day two years ago, a man comes in and asks me a lot of questions about how I'm doing and what I want in life. I have met this kind of man many times in California but he is never talking to me, always to others." Carmelo's voice tightened slightly from the thought.

"Warren Ebbetts," Ian said.

Carmelo looked at him, confused.

"Warren Ebbetts?" Ian repeated. "The man you met?"

"I do not know that name," Carmelo said.

"Andrew Wilson?" Spook offered.

"Yes. Wilson." A look of disgust came over Carmelo's face. "He offers me an opportunity to expand my business and to increase its flow of cash. In return I do some things for him."

"Like launder some American currency?" Ian could see the trail now.

Carmelo nodded his head.

"So you end up with one of the busiest restaurants in Acapulco but you're forever in debt to this jerk, Wilson," Ian said, shaking his head.

"It was not so bad at first. Look at this house." Carmelo waved his hand slowly in a broad stroke. "I have lived well. Most importantly, I have been able to take good care of Manuel. And I have put away enough to take good care of him in the future, to get him a good education." Carmelo's face softened, his mouth displaying a light smile. "He is such an intelligent child." The thought lingered on his face for a moment then traded places with one of anger. "With an education from the right school, he can make the contacts to do anything he wants. He will not have to spend his life bowing down to tourists."

"So when did it all get dirty, Carmelo?" Ian said.

Carmelo's body and face sank back into the couch.

"When you arrived. Up until then I did nothing but handle money. When Wilson met you, it made him very angry and very ugly. He said he wanted to scare you away, back to the United States. He said you were someone he knew who could cause us both problems. I told him you were planning to dive the cliffs and he said that would be perfect. When he had someone shoot at you I thought it was to scare you, but the shot was very close and I did not think you even knew what happened. I told him that and he said I should tell you that I thought someone had shot at you and see how you reacted. When you suggested we go up to the cliff and look around, he said it was a perfect opportunity to shoot at you again and make it convincing."

"By getting yourself shot?" Spook said.

"That was an accident. I think," he added. "You moved out of the way just in time and I was there. But that is when I started to think that Wilson was trying to do more than scare you."

"So how did we get from you going along with his plans to scare us to you putting us in a Jeep with no brakes to kill us?" Ian said, his anger showing now.

Carmelo leaned forward and put his head in his good hand. He sat that way for a minute, obviously trying to comprehend his own answer.

"Wilson threatened me about the money at the restaurant, but I would have given that up. Then he threatened me with Manuel. He reminded me how he had his man choke Manuel the night you rescued him and how he could easily have his man complete that task another night." Carmelo looked up at them, his face twisted and defiant. "I am not a murderer, Señors. I could not shoot a gun at you or stab you with a knife. And, as if it were not hard enough to betray you, you have shown my son great kindness since your arrival here. There is no excuse for what I have done today. But I was put in a position that threatened the safety of my son. It was not something I needed to understand. It was only something I had to do." He paused, then spoke more softly. "As I look at you here now, I am truly glad that you are alive. And yet in my heart I know that means my son's life is in danger the minute Wilson finds out."

Ian could feel the division within his own heart. He wanted to hate this man who had deceived him and his friend and twice almost led him, Ian, to his death. And yet the image of his son, Manuel, million dollar Manny, poked deeply at a place in Ian. In the same situation Ian would do anything to protect his child. The difference was he wouldn't put himself in a position like this in the first place and that was something Carmelo had to face.

"Carmelo," Ian said, standing up, "you know I can't hate you for protecting your son, but you must see that it was you who put him at risk." Ian felt pain all over his body as he stood but he was more angry than sensitive at this point. "Whether you thought you were doing something for his future benefit or not, you let a man with no concern for people's lives, hell, a murderer, take control of your life, and that's what brought you here. When you put yourself at risk, you put Manny at risk. And now us. You can't walk away from that. You have to deal with it. There is something I need to know," Ian continued, his voice changing slightly. "Have you ever heard the name Alvarez?"

Ian watched for a reaction but there was none.

"It is not an uncommon name, but as far as all this is concerned I don't know anyone by that name."

"So you had nothing to do with a boating accident in Maryland?" Spook said.

"I don't know anything about it. Look, I have no reason to lie or mislead you any further. I have never dealt with anyone except Wilson. I've never even seen any of his associates although I know they exist, like the one who choked Manny and maybe shot me. Wilson has always come alone to see me, or called me. I don't even know where he lives."

"We still don't know about Ramirez then," Spook said to Ian. "If we knew for sure we could call him in."

Ian turned back to Carmelo.

"Carmelo, understand something, the only way Manuel will ever be safe is if Wilson is put out of business. Let me tell you something about your associate. If he's who we think he is he stole a lot of money from the United States, killing at least one person to cover his tracks. He wants us killed now, so what makes you think Manny will ever be safe?"

Carmelo didn't answer, the pain in his face twisting it harder.

"You have to come up with some way for us to get a hold of this guy. I don't know if we can trust your local policeman, Ramirez, either." Ian walked toward Carmelo, thinking as he walked.

"I want to meet this son of a bitch, Wilson, face to face and drag him into the police station myself!" Ian was glaring down at Carmelo.

Spook looked at him, caught off guard by the quick rise of anger.

"What are you thinking?" Spook said.

"I don't know yet," Ian answered sharply, "but I'll think of something."

"You sure you want to go after this guy?" Spook didn't sound put off by the idea.

"I'm sure I'm tired of people trying to kill me for no reason. I'm just bruised and abused enough to take that bastard and choke the livin' shit out of 'im with my bare hands!" He turned to Carmelo again without taking a breath. "Now help me out, Carmelo, and maybe Manny will get to enjoy that future you saved up for!"

Ian could have taken two steps and cracked Carmelo on the side of the head. He wanted to knock some sense into him instead of watching him withdraw. He felt the lid on the rage box inside him flutter but this time he had control of it. He was saving blowing the lid off for when he met up with Ebbetts.

Finally, Carmelo said, "Wilson is meeting with his partner today. I know where that is."

"What partner?" Spook said, sharply. "I thought you didn't know about anyone else?"

"This is his American associate. He comes here every six months and they meet for the afternoon. I was never told but I assume they go over money matters. Wilson came to settle some cash with me once and asked me to drive him there and pick him up. He had a briefcase with him with ledger books and papers in it. I dropped him off and picked him up about two hours later. When I did, he was smiling and very pleased with himself." Carmelo looked away as he said this, his face tightening at the mention of the smug Wilson.

"And this guy is here today?" Ian said.

"Yes. That is why he wanted you dealt with. He didn't want to have to discuss any problems with his partner. He is meeting with him at two."

Ian looked at his watch and realized that the crystal was shattered.

"It's twelve-twenty," Spook said, seeing Ian's problem.

"You're going to take us there," Ian ordered. "How far is it?"

"About fifty minutes."

Carmelo looked unsure about Ian's demand. Ian saw the look.

"Carmelo, I'm not asking you, I'm telling you. Now get some spine, man, and let's go."

"Git back, Jack," Spook muttered as the trio moved toward the door.

chapter 50

WARREN EBBETTS FORCED himself into the space between the steering wheel and seat of the air-conditioned Chevrolet Caprice. He pulled the car out of the parking area of his condominium and headed toward the entrance to Las Brisas, just off the Strip. That was where his associate, a local low-level crook, had told him he would find Manuel today. The same nasty man who had choked Manny in the parking lot at the Royal Prince had kept tabs on the boy for the last two days, and had detailed his whereabouts to the man he knew as Andrew Wilson. Wilson had told him to call at noon with the location of the boy along with orders to keep him in sight till Wilson arrived.

Wilson had heard from that spineless Carmelo just before leaving the condo and felt good about the elimination, finally, of the pest from Cook International. But Carmelo Paloma's state of mind was questionable. Wilson could detect that clearly over the phone. He knew about those kinds of problems. Alvarez had gotten a case of the guilties about two months after returning from Maryland. Alvarez thought the plan to kill Wilson was very clever, brilliant for that matter. But he hadn't planned on the mate. Wilson had sprung that on him the day they set sail from Easton Point.

It was an insurance policy. Making Alvarez an accomplice in the murder guaranteed his silence. But it had upset Alvarez much more than Wilson expected, so much so that Wilson had to get rough with him just before they parted company, bouncing his head off the side of the boat.

Despite the message, the young man's death had continued to haunt Alvarez, even back home in Mexico. It bothered him to a point where Wilson knew he would have to deal with this security risk. Fortunately, someone, not Wilson, did. That was the beauty of Mexico, Wilson thought, as he drove down the Strip taking in the scenery. There was always a mountain, a cliff. And people were always falling off them. About six months ago police had found Alvarez near La Quebrada, in a canyon, his throat slit cleanly. Alvarez never did keep good company Wilson thought, chuckling to himself.

But Carmelo was a different situation. He was valuable as an outlet and Wilson had invested a reasonable amount of money in the restaurant to create that outlet. To kill Carmelo would be to kill a resource, and that was not good business. Better to control the resource. Wilson knew the boy was all the control he would need. He would keep the boy with him for the day, till he had time to verify the unfortunate death of a pair of young Americans vacationing in Acapulco. It would also send a clear signal that the boy was accessible to him at any time should Carmelo's sense of guilt become overwhelming.

The Fat Man pulled the Caprice into a gas station where his thug stood beside a pay phone. The tall man looked like he'd slept in his car for the last two days. His hair was sticking up in the back and a thick lawn of stubble covered his face. Wilson drove alongside him and handed him fifty dollars in American currency, getting a whiff of the man's odor in the process.

"I won't need you again until tonight. Call me at nine o'clock."

"Si," the man said.

"And get yourself cleaned up for Christ's sake."

Dirty peasant bastards, he said to himself as he pulled back out onto the highway.

A mile up the road Ebbetts spotted the boy where the thug had staked him, sitting on a wall at the entrance to Las Brisas, the trademark pinks and whites of the houses peeking out from the side of the mountain. It was one of several spots from where the boy had been working his tour guide business according to Wilson's crusty accomplice. And Wilson knew it presented him with a non-threatening way of procuring the boy. He pulled his car up close to the wall, honked the horn and pushed the button to slide the window down.

Manny hopped down from the wall, his smile already shining.

"Hello, Señor. How can I be of help to you?"

The Fat Man put on his own easy smile and soft eyes.

"I need to do some traveling around today, my young friend, and I was informed by your cousin, a Mr. Arroyo, that you are the finest guide in the region. Is he correct?"

"Oh yes, Señor," Manny said, feeling quite proud. "You weell have no problems weeth my services, and I am quite reasonable."

"Well then, it looks like my lucky day, young fellow," Wilson said, puffing up his fat face. "Climb in and we'll be on our way."

Manny pulled the big door of the car open with both hands and climbed inside feeling the cold air from the vents against his skin.

"Where to, Señor?" Manny said, with his finest business smile.

The big car roared up the Strip.

***

"Do we have a plan?" Spook said, looking over from the passenger seat.

"Yes and no."

Ian spoke to the windshield as he watched the road, his mind whirling as he drove. He found from years of driving for his job that he did some of his best thinking behind the wheel. That was one of the problems with that job: he spent too much time on the road doing too much thinking.

The ocean had disappeared shortly after they left Carmelo's house, giving way to mountains and short patches of flatlands peppered with bushes. The "Thing" stubbornly grunted its way at a respectable thirty-five miles per hour as the sun cooked the tops of their heads.

"I want to see what the layout is at this place," Ian said after a pause. He didn't know what he was going to do exactly but he knew it wouldn't come to him if he didn't keep moving toward the Fat Man. "The basic plan is it's time to confront this Ebbetts jerk face to face. Maybe bluff him and tell him I've already notified the FBI or something like that. I don't know; anything to back him off. If he thinks the roof's coming down on him, he'll think more about running then trying to kill us, or Manny or anybody else."

"What about other people?" Spook said. "One of his shooters or something?"

"I'm hoping there won't be anyone else there. I don't know." Ian looked in the rear view mirror, catching Carmelo's face and yelled over his shoulder. "You said he was alone the time you drove him, right Carmelo?"

"Yes," Carmelo said, from the back seat.

"I don't see any reason for him to have anyone else there," Ian continued. "It's just a business meeting with a lot of paper. The last thing Ebbetts should be expecting is company, particularly us. He thinks we're dead. Right, Carmelo?" he yelled.

"Yes," Carmelo answered, meekly.

"What about Ramirez?" Spook said.

"What about him?" Ian was puzzled by the question.

"I don't know, I guess it seems like we should have somebody backin' us up."

"I know what you mean, Spook," Ian said, the thought still gnawing at him, "but suppose we call him? What do you think's the first thing he tells us? Don't go near Ebbetts, right? And what does that tell us? Nothing. We still won't know whether he's protecting us or protecting him." The thought annoyed Ian and it came out in his tone. "If this guy's a good cop he should have found a way to hit on Ebbetts by now. He hasn't! Which means either he's protecting him like we figured or he's a lousy cop. If he's a lousy cop I don't want my life in his hands. He hasn't done much for us so far."

"Yeah, that's for sure. You're probably right."

"Believe me, Spook, the more right I am with this thing, the less I wish I was. Speaking of which," Ian cocked his head sideways without taking his eyes off the road, "Carmelo, anybody you know we can trust?"

"I know who this Ramirez is," he answered. "He's been to the restaurant, snooping around. But I avoid him for obvious reasons. And I have not kept friendships with any other members of the law."

"Too bad," Spook said. "We could use one now."

"You never mentioned you knew who Ramirez is," Ian said, a little tweaked.

"You never asked me about him," Carmelo replied, respectfully.

"Do you know who this partner is, Carmelo?" Spook turned around to look at him.

"No. The closest I've ever been to him is in front of this house we are going to. I have never seen him. I have never cared to. My involvement has always been financial and with Wilson only. That is the way he likes it and that has been fine with me. Until now."

In the mirror Ian saw Carmelo's face tighten and look hard out the side of the car.

"Hey, Carmelo, it's okay. Look, we're all in this together now. We all have something at stake here. Let's concentrate our energy on taking Ebbetts out of the game and things will start to improve for all of us real fast. Okay?"

He saw Carmelo's head turn towards the front.

"Yes, you are right. Time to 'clean house,' correct?"

"There you go," Spook said, smiling.

Ian saw a weak smile appear on Carmelo's face.

They rode in silence, anticipating some indication from Carmelo that they were near. After ten more minutes of driving, Carmelo tapped Ian on the back, pointing to a dirt road on the left.

"There. Turn off here. It leads to the villa.

"What time is it?" Ian asked.

"One-thirty," Spook said.

After the turn, Ian drove slowly, searching the road ahead for cover as the "Thing" threw a cloud of dust up behind them. Low trees, not more than ten feet high, grew in random bunches along both sides. He could still see patches of the paved road but they were moving away from it at a slow rate.

About four hundred yards up the road Carmelo said, "If you go much further you will see the house. It is maybe another two hundred yards beyond us."

Ian slammed on the brakes, the dust catching up with them as they came to a stop. Ian turned the car to his left spotting several high, rocky areas surrounded by a thick cluster of trees. He couldn't see anything beyond that. The "Thing" and everyone in it bounced along as he swung left, then right, slowly picking a trail through the trees. The dust was thick now, burning his eyes and coating his tongue as it swirled around the inside of the open car. Ian couldn't wait to stop just so the dirt would settle. He squeezed the car past a wall of rock to his right and trees on his left and knew he had reached the other side of the thick grove he'd seen from the road. He turned right again and pulled the car up alongside the rocks.

"End of the line," he said flatly, and turned the engine off. He got out of the car and walked to three different locations near the rear of the automobile trying to see the road. "I can't see the road from anywhere back here so I don't think anyone will see the car. You say the house would be that way from here?" Ian spun around to see Carmelo as he pointed.

"Yes, not too far. Maybe a little more left."

"Okay, let's get a good view."

They headed away from the car, staying to the protected side of the rocks and trees. Ian and Spook moved steadily despite the pain they were feeling all over their bodies. Like being bruised during athletic competition, Ian knew he wouldn't feel the real pain kick in until this was all over. Carmelo moved more slowly.

They had gone about three hundred yards when Ian glimpsed the red tile roof of the house, heat bending the air above it. The house was white stucco, true in design to its Mexican surroundings and quite large, much like what Ian always pictured villas looked like. As they moved closer, staying low to the rocks and trees, more of the house appeared. It sat at an angle, the rear being more visible from their vantage point. A pool, surrounded on three sides by a patio, spread out from the middle of the building, the water shimmering like a Hollywood oasis. A white pergola, heavily interwoven with green vines and pink flowers, provided delicate shade over the patio.

"Looks like something out of Architectural Digest," Ian said, to no one in particular. "Guess his partner's doing all right."

"I don't see any cars," Spook said. "But I can't see the front of the house."

Ian watched the patio where he thought he'd seen movement. As they got closer he could see someone sitting in a lounge chair under the pergola. With a touch of panic, he realized if he could see them, they might see him.

"Whoa!" he said hoarsely and ducked down.

Everyone did a double take towards him and then instinctively followed his action.

"What?" Spook said, his dark eyes now wide with alarm.

"There's someone sitting on the patio facing the other way," Ian said. "It's too far to tell who it is, but I don't want him to see us."

He looked around their location. They were still protected from view on the road side but could see where the road turned towards the front of the house. From here they would be able see Ebbetts coming up toward the house.

"This is close enough for now," he said. "Time to wait."

Ian propped himself up against a rock, positioned so that he could see the patio and its occupant if he raised his head up a few inches. He looked at his watch, forgetting again about the crystal.

"Spook," he pointed to his watch, "time."

"Ten of."

Now that he was settled in and waiting, Ian suddenly realized where he was. He was sitting in the middle of a foreign country about to do something, he wasn't sure what, that might possibly cause him serious harm. The thought began to confound him, the almost surreal reality of it challenging him. Back home people were in their everyday lives. At two o'clock in the afternoon he'd probably be driving up the Schuylkill Expressway or the Turnpike headed from one account to another. A few miles from here people were lying by pools ordering refreshing drinks and food. I came here to be one of them, he thought. How the hell did I get here?

Then he reached for the thought that he knew would excuse him.

So what if I was back home driving that car for the thousandth time over those same roads? Where would I be going? South; east? Would it matter? There's so much going on in the world, and I'm trapped in a company car that never goes anywhere but to the next account. I can't even say the hell with it and try something else because it's their car. It's their car, their money in my pocket, their accounts.

The irony and answer was clear.

I'm here because that ain't enough. And I like to jump off cliffs.

He looked around, breathing in the arid air and studying the dirty faces of the two men with him; one with his clothing ripped and soiled, the other ripped and soiled in his own way. Ian shook his head in disbelief.

Here are your possibilities, he said to himself, almost laughing. Make the most of it.

"A car!" Spook said almost shouting, then catching himself.

Ian shot up from his squat and caught the dust of a car moving towards the front of the house.

"Could you see who it was?"

"No," Spook said. "The car's in front of the house now. I can't see anything."

"All right," Ian said. "Keep your eyes on the person out back."

Ian moved himself to face forward, training his eyes on the figure in the lounge chair and flicking them every now and then toward the glass doors at the back of the house.

"Come on, Fat Man," he said. "Be there."

chapter 51

DETECTIVE RAMIREZ WAS on his way to Carmelo Arroyo's house when his radio crackled with the information he'd been waiting for. The officer watching Andrew Wilson had followed the man from his condo and witnessed his meeting with a local bandito at a gas station and his subsequent stop at Las Brisas to pick up a small boy.

Ramirez had been aware of the possibility of a meeting of some significance for the last three weeks. Through his usual collection of legal and slightly tarnished means he had gathered enough information to know someone important to Mr. Wilson was coming to town. That was why he was watching the American pair closely. At first he was sure they were the connection, the American connection to this flow of money. And he had pounced on them, watching their every move. Now, well, he wasn't sure. They had been pretty convincing that night at the hospital and the next day by the pool, but never totally convincing. They didn't seem hard enough, tough enough. But maybe they were just good con artists? A dead officer at the Señorita's hotel early this morning and the American diver unaccounted for. And now, today, Wilson on the move and where are these

Americans? Meeting up with another suspect. Arroyo. Missing a rendezvous with the Señorita. Disappearing for the day altogether.

No one had answered the phone at Arroyo's house. The Señorita had told him of the call from another man in America, an associate perhaps, telling her about phony companies.

No, Detective Ramirez just wasn't sure. Too much and too little. But it was time to come out in the open, time to confront Wilson and anyone associated with him. Put him on the spot and see where the cards fell.

Ramirez headed into the mountains to catch up with his officer. As he drove he checked in regularly on the radio to keep headed in the right direction. At five minutes till two he was informed that Wilson's car had turned off the highway onto a small, dirt side road that led to a villa. Ramirez was five minutes away and stepped on the gas.

* * *

Warren Ebbetts got out of the car slowly, swinging his legs out first and then pushing with both arms to extract himself from the seat.

"This is a good friend of mine, Manuel," he said, pleasantly, motioning to the house with his head. "I need to talk with him about some business we have together and you in the meantime will have some lunch. How's that?"

"That ees fine, Señor Andrew," Manny said, his business manners on display. "I can wait here in thee car. Eet ees no problem."

"Nonsense," Ebbetts said. "It's much too hot to sit out here and besides, we have much to do this afternoon and a good lunch will keep you alert. Come."

Ebbetts put his hand on the boy's shoulder and walked to the front door of the house and rang the doorbell. A middle-age Mexican woman in a light blue cotton dress answered the door and opened it wide for them to step in.

"Señor ees on the pahteeo," the woman said.

"Thank you," Ebbetts said. "Would you be so kind as to provide my friend here with some lunch?"

"Si, Señor," the woman said, and took Manny by the hand. She led him out of the foyer, talking to him in Spanish as they disappeared around a corner.

Ebbetts turned left and walked toward the glass doors at the back of the house, noting the addition of some new artwork and furniture to the already museum-class home.

This is how he stays clean, I suppose, Ebbetts thought. Well, I've your dirty work for you.

He wiggled the briefcase in his hand and smiled, then slid the glass door open and stepped outside.

* * *

"That's him," Ian said, watching the large figure step through the glass door. He watched the big man walk up to the seated figure and shake his hand.

"I think so too," Spook said. "That's a very large person. How we gonna get near the house?"

"Well...," Ian was still working the plan out in his head, "let's see if they stay outside. If they go in, we can walk right up to the house. If they stay outside we might have to double back and come up to the front." Ian stared at the two figures for a minute. "Looks like Ebbetts has a briefcase or something."

"The ledger books, probably," Carmelo said. "That must be his partner in the chair."

"Another car's coming!" Spook's voice was a loud whisper.

"Shit!" Ian clenched his fists.

They all looked towards the road, the dirt and dust again obscuring their view enough to make an identification impossible as the car disappeared around the front of the house. Everyone trained their eyes back on the glass doors again. Three minutes passed before the glass door moved again. A woman in a light blue dress came through first, obviously trying to impede the movement of a tall man who was moving close behind her. Ian looked back at the two men on the patio watching for a reaction. From the way Ebbetts was moving, stepping back and freezing his head in the direction of the visitor, he was not happy with the arrival.

"That's Ramirez!" Spook said. "Son of a bitch!"

"You're kidding?" Ian quickly looked back at the tall man and focused his eyes tightly. "Son of a bitch, you're right!" he said. "I told you he was dirty."

Ian looked back at Ebbetts and the seated man.

"The guy in the chair hasn't moved," Spook said. "They look like they're arguing. They're pointing fingers at one another like they're pissed."

"Ramirez probably decided to crash the party and demand a raise in front of the partner," Ian said. "Damn, I wish we were closer and could hear. See, Spook, it's a good thing we didn't call that crooked bastard."

"Looks like Ramirez is leaving," Spook said, continuing his surveillance. "The woman went back in and now he's standing outside the door."

Ramirez was at the glass door poised to step through but looking back and still engaged in conversation. Then he stepped inside and two minutes later the dust appeared around the car headed back down the road to the highway.

"I'd love to know what that was all about. Shit!" Ian said.

"They're going inside," Spook said. "Let's sneak up there now." He looked at Ian who was sitting on the ground with his head in both hands. "What'sa matter?"

"What are we going to do once we get to the house?" Ian said, without looking at him. "You asked me that earlier, before I knew for sure that Ramirez was dirty. I kept thinking I just might trust him if we grabbed this fat creep. But now we know he's in with Ebbetts, so who do we call?"

Ian could see the disappointment in Spook's face. Spook was ready for the attack, and Ian had just pulled the plug on everything.

"I don't know, who cares?" Spook said, frustrated. "The Mexican government, the FBI, what's the difference?"

Ian felt torn. He had been hoping all along that things would fall into place, or at least not out of place which is what the visit by Ramirez was. But in his head it was just not a sensible thing to go charging into that house.

"I don't know, Spook," Ian looked at the ground, "I just don't think it's the smart thing to do now."

"Someone's coming out again," Carmelo said. He had not stopped watching the house.

Ian didn't even look up this time, disgusted with the whole turn of events. Spook poked his head back around to look.

"Ian," Spook said, his tone changing from reporting to cold, "shit. I think that's Manny."

Ian looked instinctively at Carmelo and saw his bronze face go white.

"It's Manny, I'm sure," Spook confirmed.

"It is," Carmelo said, with desperation in his voice. "O dios mio."

Ian felt anger and fear bite hard simultaneously into his stomach. He spun up and around to retake his position at the rocks already calculating the distance between him and the house. That night in the parking lot he had gotten to Manny in time. This was different. He wasn't sure about this set-up at all.

"He doesn't seem to be concerned," Spook continued to report, keeping a constant watch. "He's just hanging around out there."

They watched the small figure walk to the pool and squat down.

"Does Manny know who Wilson is? Has he ever met him?" Ian looked quickly at Carmelo.

"No, never," Carmelo answered, his face now so strained that a vein rose at the side of his temple, snaking its way to a pulsating dimple on the side of his jaw.

"So maybe Wilson just picked him up as a guide for the day," Spook said.

"Not by chance," Carmelo said, not taking the suggestion.

Ian knew what to do now.

"That settles it," he said, looking at Spook. "We're going over there and get him. And when we do we're going to give Fat Boy a clear message."

Carmelo and Spook looked at Ian. Something about the way Ian sounded seemed to be enough. They were ready for a plan.

"All right, here's the way we do it," Ian said. "Spook, you go back and get the car and drive right up the road to the front of the house. While you're doing that, Carmelo and I will start for the house on foot. We have to move quick and quiet," he said, grasping Carmelo's good arm. "Can you do that with your bad arm?"

Carmelo nodded, not even considering the question.

"We'll get Manny," Ian turned back to Spook, "and meet you in front of the house and put Manny in the car. If Ebbetts doesn't come out to see what's going on I'll knock on the door and tell him what's going on. Let's go." Ian tapped Carmelo and broke for the rocks.

Spook turned and quick-stepped into a limping run, disappearing into the trees.

Ian was out in front of the rocks in seconds. He could feel the stiffness and some pain in his right knee but it disappeared as he stretched into a steady run. Carmelo was right beside him. Ian could sense their vulnerability as soon as they stepped out from behind the rocks. He knew if Ebbetts or his partner were sitting anywhere near a back window or the glass doors, they'd be spotted immediately. The trees here were sparse and Ian tried to run on a line behind one whenever possible but he was visible more than not. He had covered about half the distance when Carmelo did something that didn't surprise Ian but made him tighten up just the same.

"MANUEL! MANUEL! OVER HERE! COME HERE!"

Ian looked back over his shoulder to see Carmelo waving his arm and yelling as they ran. Ian had hoped that Manny would see them as they got closer and come to them naturally. But Carmelo was panicking, and Manuel hadn't seen them yet.

Ian's heart was pounding. The distance between him and the house seemed to be growing, his shredded right knee starting to whine with pain. His feet and legs rose and fell not at all in proportion to the distance he was covering. It was like dreams where he ran in slow motion, pushing off his feet and striding three and four feet at a time but never getting anywhere. He was losing his sense of real sound now as well; his heart pounding in his head as well as his chest; Carmelo's voice behind him yelling for Manny; the sound of the car on the dirt road. All separate soundtracks mixing together to form one unearthly level of noise that had nothing to do with the real scene around him. Ian figured to be grabbing ahold of Manny by now and moving around the front of the house, but Manny still hadn't seen them.

Suddenly, Manny looked up and spotted them. Ian couldn't tell at first if Manny recognized them, but the boy froze in place. As he did Ian saw the large body of Warren Ebbetts framed in the glass doors. He felt the adrenaline release into his system and kicked like a runner on the home stretch, surprising himself at how much more speed he had. The glass door slid open with a thwack! from the force of the Fat Man's anger. He moved the six steps between himself and the boy, more quickly than Ian would have thought possible, and grabbed Manny, whose expression of recognition was now visible to Ian, and pulled him backwards into the house. The door thwacked again and Ian heard the lock turn as he circled the pool and stepped onto the patio. Out of the corner of his eye Ian could see the dust cloud that was Spook moving on his right to the front of the house. He kept running right up to the glass door. He stopped, pulled at the locked door and pounded his fist against the glass.

"COME ON, WILSON!" he yelled, sucking air. "NO MORE BULLSHIT!" Deep gulp. "LET THE BOY GO!" Another gulp. "IT'S US YOU WANT NOT HIM!"

Ian banged some more on the glass then cupped his hands around his face and peered inside. He couldn't see anyone, just a small sitting room with a fireplace to the right and a hallway straight ahead. As he looked down it he saw movement. He pounded the glass and hollered again.

"COME ON, WILSON. LEAVE THE BOY ALONE! THEN WE'LL TALK! you fat son of a bitchin' bastard!"

Ian turned around and started looking for something to throw through the glass door, sweeping his gaze across the patio. Then he saw Carmelo's face, frozen like a starving man before a table of food, knowing he wasn't allowed to eat. Ian ignored him and spotted a small clay pot of flowers next to the pool. He stepped to it, scooping it up and feeling satisfied that the weight would serve his purpose. When he turned back toward the house he almost dropped the pot on his foot.

Ebbetts was standing in the doorway, his left hand firmly around the arm of Manny, who stood in front of him. Ebbetts right hand held a small, black gun, the pudgy fingers barely exposing the metal and none of the butt. The gun and hand rested almost casually on the right shoulder of the boy.

The Fat Man smiled cordially through the glass as if to say, So you wish to talk, do you? He reached over to the door handle with the gun hand and slid it open.

"Gentlemen," he said calmly, "if you wish to speak with me I suggest you go around the house, collect your friend and present yourselves civilly at the front door."

chapter 52

IAN WANTED TO scream. He could feel it inside him, clawing its way from his groin to his throat. He knew what Warren Ebbetts was capable of and the look in his eyes was pure arrogance. Ian, Spook, Carmelo, and the boy in front of him were all just annoyances in this man's life, annoyances that had been around for too long. This man would not worry about the details and clues and the trail he might leave behind. He didn't care. The good guys would not win. No, he would kill all of them and disappear and never lose a night's sleep.

"I'll get my friend," Ian said, as calmly as he could. "Don't do anything."

"Don't hurt the boy," Carmelo said. "Please, Andrew." His voice was steady, almost business-like.

"You are a disappointment," Wilson sneered. "An unfortunate disappointment."

He slid the glass door shut again and locked it. Ian watched him walk away from the door before starting for the front of the house.

"Come on, Carmelo," Ian said, grabbing him by the arm. "Why the hell did you...?" Ian caught himself. "Look, let's just play along. We don't have much choice. Maybe something will come up. Just pay attention."

Ian had no idea what would come up. In the back of his mind this was exactly why he had decided not to go to the house at the last minute, before they saw Manny. He had no edge here. He was empty-handed with only his anger and good intentions to carry him through. If there was a way out of this he would find it with his instincts, with his radar, but right now the screen was dark.

They moved around the side of the house, not sure whether to hurry or go slowly. As they turned the corner Spook, who was sitting in the car, popped out quickly, his face coated in frustration.

"Did you see him?" Ian asked.

"He came to the front door with Manny and a gun and told me to stay in the car." Spook looked flabbergasted. "He was smilin', real smooth like. Ian, this guy's a kook."

"Look," Ian said, trying not to lose his nerve, "we're going in there and watch for something. An opportunity, an opening, I don't know." He looked hard at Spook's uncertain face. "Hey, I'm not trying to come off like some tough guy here, I just don't know what else we can do except jump in the car and run out of here. That means leaving Manny behind. I don't want to go in there and get shot," Ian bunched his face up, "but I couldn't leave Manny here in a million years."

"You don't have to sell me, man," Spook said, his face now less uncertain. "I'm still pissed at this guy."

Good old Spook, Ian thought. If he made up his mind about something, common sense wasn't going to get in the way.

Ian knew there really weren't any alternatives for any of them. Somehow, knowing they had no choice made him stronger. He forced himself to step out of the emotion of the scene for a split second. His mind was clear and working, his radar up. That was his best defense. Maybe, a way out.

"Carmelo," Ian reached over and grabbed his arm again, "you have to stay cool. Just go along with everything till we see what Wilson's got in mind. Maybe he just wants us and he'll let you and Manuel go. If you get a chance to get your boy out of there, you do it. Don't wait for us, do you understand?"

Carmelo still looked uncertain.

"Come on, man!" Ian said, raising his voice. "We're here because of Manny. If you can get him out, go! Do you understand?"

"Yes," Carmelo said.

"Good." Ian took a deep breath. "Here we go."

They filed up the walkway to the front door. Spook rang the bell and the door opened almost immediately. The maid was holding the door, her face strained and nervous. Ian stepped into the foyer quickly surveying an empty room. The others stepped in behind him.

"Thees way," the maid said, leading them down a long hallway. Ian saw to his left the glass door where Ebbetts had appeared, and figured he was now parallel to the back of the house. When they had gone about two-thirds the length of the house, she pointed to a door, also on the left.

"Thayre," she said and hurried away.

Ian opened the door and walked into a large outdoor courtyard. It was surrounded on three sides by the walls of the house with the roof overhanging, shading a small, red-tile walkway. In the center were flowers and large-leaf plants, all exposed to the sky above, which looked like a painting as Ian looked up, the blue and white colors framed by the red clay tiles of the roof. The fourth wall along the back of the house was an elaborate set of black wrought-iron gates. There, along the gates, was a table and chairs, one chair overflowing with the bulk of Warren Ebbetts. Ian realized from the location of the gates that Ebbetts had probably seen them coming as soon as they left the rocks. Manny was nowhere in sight.

"Well, gentlemen, you certainly have created serious problems for me."

They moved toward the Fat Man, walking down two steps to the courtyard level, then following the tile walk around the garden to the other side. Standing ten feet from Ebbetts, Ian looked hard at the putty face, seemingly colorless despite the ever present sun of Mexico. It was the same deceptive face he'd seen the first time at Cook, smiling and full of mirth. But now Ian knew the killer that danced behind it.

"WHERE'S MANNY?" Ian hollered and stepped forward, the rage in his voice surprising even him.

He saw Ebbetts' right hand, which was resting on the table, move slightly. Ian took three steps and stopped. The black gun was flat on the table beneath the hand and as Ian moved the hand closed around it and raised it from the table.

"Now, now," Ebbetts said, in a cold tone, the smiling face disappearing immediately. "Let's handle ourselves in a proper manner."

"Where is Manuel?" Carmelo said.

"He's in the house, in safekeeping," Ebbetts answered, ignoring Carmelo and looking at Spook and Ian. "He is the least of your problems."

"Just what are our problems?" Spook said.

Ian was surprised at how assertive Spook sounded.

"The fact that you have made trouble for me here in Acapulco is first on the list," the Fat Man said. "But today is much worse."

"Why is that?" Ian said, sarcastically. "Ramirez want a bigger percentage?"

Ebbetts looked confused.

"I'm not sure I know what that means so I'll ignore it. No, the problem here today is with my partner. You have brought all this discord to his villa of refuge," Ebbetts waved his left hand towards the house, "and made him quite uncomfortable. He doesn't like to get his hands dirty, you see, and now he feels he has."

"Why the hell didn't you leave well enough alone in the beginning?" Ian felt disgust. "I didn't know who you were. If you had left us alone we would have forgotten about you the next day. In fact we did."

"If I had known that for sure, I would have. But I cannot afford to leave things like that to chance, Mr. Connors. Besides, none of that matters now, does it?"

"Please don't hurt Manuel," Carmelo said. "He has nothing to do with this. Please."

Ian could hear panic creeping into Carmelo's voice.

"I don't intend to harm the boy," Wilson said sharply, displaying his obvious distaste for Carmelo. "Unless you force me to. I will deal with you separately when I'm finished with these others."

"You know, I don't like the way you talk about us," Spook said.

Spook's tone caught Ian by surprise even more this time. It doesn't sound at all like Spook, Ian thought, sensing something. He turned and looked at him.

"You keep talking like we're not here," Spook continued, "like we're some piece of garbage you have to get rid of."

"That is a reasonable comparison," Ebbetts said, slightly amused.

"Well I don't like it, and I'm leaving. I don't have to take this shit. Are you guys coming?"

Spook looked at Ian and Carmelo, a deadly serious look on his face.

What's he up to? Ian thought.

"Do you think that's wise, young man?" Ebbetts said. Even he seemed a little confused by Spook's attitude.

"What the hell do I want to stay here for? I don't even know who you are, except somebody who's ruinin' my vacation. I'm only here 'cause Ian asked me to drive. I don't give a shit about you, his kid,...or this guy." He pointed to Carmelo and made a disgusted face. "Hell, he tried to kill us today."

Ian was trying to piece it together. Spook was trying to create enough confusion here that Ebbetts might do something wrong. Ian had to be ready to make a move on him. But what could Spook do, except offer himself as a target to distract Ebbetts. Ian didn't like the plan.

"Spook," Ian said, turning his face completely away from Ebbetts, "maybe you should reconsider. Maybe we can work something out."

As he spoke, Ian made an exaggerated gesture with his hands to disguise his positioning himself between Ebbetts and Spook. He knotted his brow to show his concern. If Spook saw it, he didn't acknowledge it.

"Bullshit!" Spook swung his hand downward dismissively. "I have nothin' this guy wants, and he doesn't have anything I want. And I'm sick of the way he thinks he can push all of us around. If you got something to work out with this guy, work it out, but I'm going back to the hotel and enjoy what's left of this vacation. Carmelo," Spook looked around Ian, "good luck with your miserable life, man. Big Man, hope things work out for you."

Spook turned to walk away and Ian felt his spine tingle. Ian had his back to Ebbetts now, who he figured was about four feet from him. Ian was directly between Ebbetts and Spook. If Ian tried to turn and grab the gun he'd probably get shot first, then Spook.

Give me a clue, Spook, Ian thought.

Spook's next move was the tell Ian needed. Instead of following the tile pathway back around the garden, Spook headed straight into it, walking slowly as he pushed the big leaves out of the way.

The garden, Ian's mind flashed, that's the cover.

"Then I'll have to kill you now, instead of later," Ebbetts said, and started to raise his bulk from the chair.

Ian felt his body tense, ready to spring. He turned his head just slightly to his right, enough to get a sense of where Ebbetts was without letting Ebbetts see the anticipation in his eyes. He saw the gun come up.

"DOWN!" Ian yelled as he jumped straight up in the air. As he rose he twisted his body towards Ebbetts and kicked both feet at the same time, like punching out of a pike position dive. There was nothing pretty about it, just an awkward attempt to make contact as hard as he could in the hope it would knock the Fat Man's aim off. His feet flew forward as he waited for them to hit some part of Ebbetts, feeling the whole scene happening in slow motion. He could see Ebbetts' eyes flash madly as they went from Spook's back to the odd movement in the air that was Ian.

His left foot hit first against Ebbetts' shoulder sooner than Ian expected, the contact feeling ineffective and powerless. But the right foot landed solidly on the blubbery cheek of the Fat Man's face and Ian snapped his leg out hard feeling the fleshy skin bunch up and move under his thin canvas shoe. Simultaneously he saw the small flash and heard the crack from below his body as the gun fired.

Ian came down hard on the tile. He extended his left arm forward to keep it from breaking under his weight and took the brunt of the impact on his left shoulder, the impact knocking out half of his wind. He scrambled to get up quickly, gulping air, and looked quickly to see where Ebbetts was. The Fat Man was sprawled on the floor, a chair on its side next to him. Carmelo had moved passed him and was picking up the gun which lay about ten feet from Ebbetts' hand. Ian looked quickly back to the garden to spot Spook and saw nothing.

"SPOOK!" Ian yelled, and moved toward the garden. He knew the gun had been fired. He pictured Spook face down in the garden, a small red hole in his back, when he heard a weak, "Yo," as Spook emerged from the large leaves.

"Are you all right?" Ian said.

"Now I know why you dive into water, man," Spook said, breathing hard. "The ground don't give way. How's Fat Boy?"

They turned to see Carmelo holding the gun in Warren Ebbetts face.

"Where is my son? Tell me now or I will shoot you in the face."

Ian could tell by the look on his face that Carmelo was losing control.

"Carmelo!" he said, sharply. "Get over here with that!"

"He's going to tell me where Manuel is or I am going to shoot him. NOW!" he yelled, and shook the gun at Ebbetts.

The Fat Man had his hand up and his face turned away as if doing so would protect him. His eyes squinted in pathetic fear.

"He's in the room at the end of the hall. On the left," Wilson said through tightened lips.

"Who's with him?" Ian said.

"I am," a voice at the hallway door said, and in walked Manuel, held closely by Warren Ebbetts' partner.

chapter 53

IAN FELT HIS brain lock. It froze with the picture in front of him and nothing he could do could move it forward or backwards to have it make sense. Mike Mahon, the Vice President of Corporate Sales for Cook International, his boss, was standing with his hand tightly around the back of Manny's neck. The other hand nervously and awkwardly held a gun.

"I don't believe this."

"Well, Ian, I can't say I'm pleased to see you here today either," Mahon said, in a dry, business-like tone. "In fact, I'm sorry."

Ian's mind stayed stuck. It was too incredulous to take in. All of this insanity around him for the last week, all the sordid details of the past two years, murders, fake deaths, all this the result of a man Ian thought was solid; the one man who had kept his soul in the midst of a soulless corporation. It defied understanding. Mahon standing there with the gun in his hand made Ian's head hurt. It was like his father or Ed Bernardi was standing there. It was all wrong.

"But I'm not all that surprised," Mahon continued. "It explains why there's suddenly a lot of interest by Ed Bernardi in stock."

"Ian," Spook said, "what the hell is this all about? Who is this guy?"

Ian only half-heard Spook. He was still trying to handle his own thoughts. Words rushed to his mind and came out of his mouth.

"What the hell is going on?" Ian said, his voice cold and thin. Mahon said nothing and in the silence Ian's bewilderment began trading places with anger. "What the hell is going on? Who the hell are you, Mike? How are you standing there like that? With a young boy and a gun in your hand? Did you lose it, Mike? Did something snap? Please, tell me that's what happened." The anger rose in his voice. "Tell me your wife and children were murdered or taken hostage or your house burned down and you got fired." Ian felt the disgust and confusion in his throat. He wasn't asking questions anymore. "Come on, Mike. Tell me something that makes sense! WHAT?!"

Ian almost forgot where he was. It all hit him at once and he knew he was going to lose it. Everyone was a greedy, cutthroat, stealing bastard. Everyone was a piece of shit. Warren Ebbetts was not just in Mexico, he was everywhere.

"You're not really interested, are you?" Mahon said, dryly.

"I'm DAMN interested, MIKE!"

The words came out through Ian's teeth along with spittle.

"It's not that complicated, Ian." Mahon still sounded calm. "Money. Money and freedom."

"You made good money, Mike. A guy with your position in the company?" Ian was starting to focus his thoughts better now. He looked at Spook. "Just to fill you in, this is Mike

Mahon, the Vice President of Cook International. My boss! A respected professional in his field. Right hand man to the Old Man. Top of the pile!"

Ian's sarcasm honed an edge with each title. He saw Mahon's eyes narrow when he made the last statement.

"Top of the pile?" Mahon said, almost whimsically, "not hardly. At Cook the only pile is underneath the Old Man. I saw an opportunity for the independence I deserve and I took it."

"Along with a few lives that might've gotten in the way?" Ian asked.

"I don't know about that," Mahon said as if to dismiss the thought.

"WHAT DO YOU MEAN you don't know?!" Ian hollered. "You didn't know about the young guy in Maryland that your friend here murdered to make his death look good?! Huh? There was another guy on the boat with him too. I wonder if anyone's heard from him lately! And how about Bill Golden? You get credit for that one too. Oh, but don't worry yourself about us," Ian said, with exaggeration. "We're just minor details, I guess. Your partner tried to murder me three times, my friend once, and now you use this innocent boy here as your weight?"

As soon as Ian said the words "innocent boy" the lid rattled dangerously on the box inside him. He saw Manny's face looking at him and it became a collage of frightened faces that made his stomach knot. Then the bile and anger took over and Ian strode forward directly through the garden, not even pushing the plants aside with his arms. He saw only one thing and that was Mike Mahon's throat. He knew all he wanted was to lock his big hands around it and squeeze, squeeze till the warm thing in his hands stopped wriggling and turned cold. Mahon saw the look on Ian's face as it flashed from behind large green leaves and it seemed to freeze him temporarily.

"YOU WON'T HURT THAT BOY, Mike!" Ian bellowed. "YOU WON'T HURT THAT BOY! YOU WON'T SHOOT HIM, YOU WON'T HARM HIM! YOU'LL LET HIM GO! NOW!"

Warren Ebbetts had gotten up off the floor and was watching Carmelo and his gun very carefully. Carmelo was dividing his attention between Ebbetts and Mahon, who now held his son. When Ian started walking towards Mahon, shouting, Carmelo turned, realizing the immediate threat to Manuel.

Ebbetts was waiting for it. He reached out and completely engulfed Carmelo's hand on the gun butt with his own ham-like hand, squeezing as he did. As he crushed Carmelo's hand into the metal of the gun, he swung his other arm at the top of the sling on Carmelo's shoulder and the combination of both moves caused Carmelo to shriek in pain, his knees buckling underneath him. Ebbetts slid his hand forward on the gun releasing it from Carmelo's hand which was now a mangled claw. The Fat Man turned immediately toward the other end of the room, switching the gun to his right hand as he did. He could see Ian moving through the garden only ten feet away from Mahon. He could also see the look on Mahon's face floating above the plants, which told him the man had no stomach and was completely intimidated by Ian's bold move.

"IT SEEMS I CAN'T COUNT ON YOU TO DO ANYTHING THE LEAST BIT MESSY!" the Fat Man yelled. "You must get a backbone one of these days," he said to no one in particular, and raised the gun.

Ian was five steps from Mahon, his senses all focused on one thing, Mahon's throat. He heard Ebbetts' voice but only as background. It had no effect on him. But he heard the gun shot. Somewhere in his mind he surmised what was going on behind him; that Ebbetts was yelling towards him, that Ebbetts had the gun back, and that he had just fired a shot. He flinched at the sound but had no instinct to duck or hide. He anticipated the hot flash he would feel somewhere in the back of his body as the bullet struck. He was sure it would hurt but not stop him, his mind locked on the throat. It was all secondary action taking place only in a small, remote part of his head, as if it were in another room. There was nothing in here but Manny, and Mike Mahon's throat.

Suddenly Mahon's face spread wide in alarm, looking beyond Ian, now only a step away. He shoved Manny into Ian and turned and ran through the door into the house. Ian caught Manny as he cleared the two steps in one move then stopped, covering the boy with his body. It had not surprised him that Mahon ran. It was as if he had willed him away with the sheer force of his anger. Ian turned to see what was behind him, still protecting Manny. What he saw was not at all what he expected, but it didn't faze him.

Warren Ebbetts lay face down on the tile, part of his body obscured by the garden. Carmelo was leaning against the ironwork, his face knotted with pain. Spook was still in the middle of the garden, frozen in place by his helplessness in the events going on around him.

Outside the gates stood Officer Ramirez, his long frame and light clothing creating an interesting backdrop as they pressed against the scrolled iron, the gun at the end of his left arm still inside the room.

chapter 54

IAN KNEW THAT Manny was safe. Now it was not about Manny anymore. It was about guilty and innocent. Manny was innocent. Mahon was guilty, and there would be no safe place for him. He pushed Manny gently in Spook's direction then ran through the doorway.

Ian ran straight to the open front door and as he stepped outside he saw Mahon turn the corner on the far side of the house. Ian turned quickly, skidding on the sand and pebble surface and continued after him. As Ian turned the corner Mahon was halfway inside the front seat of a gold Mercedes parked in a carport next to the house. Ian got to the car as Mahon closed the door but the frantic man took a second too long to get the keys in the ignition. Ian ripped the door open, reached in front of Mahon with both his hands and pulled Mahon's arms away, pulling him out of the car at the same time. Mahon struggled wildly to push Ian away but it was pointless. He was flailing at an angry force that had only one objective. As he got him clear of the car and upright Ian finally felt his hands lock tightly around Mike Mahon's throat.

It was just as Ian imagined it. His big hands almost completely encircled the man's throat, his right palm flat against his Adam's apple as he stared at the side of his boss's head. The warm thing that he held thrashed and wriggled. It wasn't even anger anymore that empowered him but more of a robot-like function that needed to be performed. Ian's mind was blank.

Mahon kept struggling, reaching for Ian's hands to pry them loose. When he did the iron lock on his neck tightened. Ramirez came flying around the corner of the house as Spook came out the front door directly into Ian's line of vision. Mahon could see them too.

"He's...trying to......kill...me," Mahon gasped, his voice almost whisper-thin.

"Okay, Señor Connors," Ramirez said, calmly, "you can let him go."

Ian heard the voice, but it had little effect on him. He sensed it was a means of escape for Mahon and there would be no more escaping. He had Mahon, the Fat Man, and his own maddening life in his hands now and it was time to settle up. He tightened his whole body sending an awesome surge of power through his hands and into Mahon whose eyes winced shut. He was now holding the man in the air by his neck, the tips of Mahon's shoes searching desperately for solid ground.

"IAN!" Spook yelled. "IT'S ME, SPOOK! COME ON!"

Ian heard Spook's voice, and it got through.

"I'm gonna choke this piece of shit," Ian said, through his teeth.

"That's probably a good thing to do right about now," Spook said, in a normal voice. "Only problem is if you kill him we're gonna have a lot of trouble hangin' Ebbetts. This guy's the mastermind behind the whole scheme and without him talkin',

Ebbetts will just clam up. Then we won't resolve anything. Let's take him back home and drag him through the mud."

Ian was listening, his thick coat of anger penetrated by Spook's words.

"He's a leech, a worm, Spook," Ian said, talking as if Mahon weren't dangling in his hands. "He'll figure a way out and screw somebody else's life up."

"Come on, man. This ain't you." Spook's voice was almost dismissive. "Manny's safe. The Fat Man's down. And Robyn's probably havin' a heart attack by now wondering where the hell you are. Let's go get a cocktail."

When he heard the name "Manny" it hit somewhere inside him and Ian loosened a bit, but the mention of Robyn struck deeper and immediately his whole body softened. Mahon's feet touched the ground. Ian turned his captive towards him.

"My friend's right. This is better than you deserve." The anger in his voice dissipated. "You're going to answer to Bill Golden's wife and children."

Ian turned him around and shoved him forward at Ramirez who had started walking toward them. Then Ian stood still, feeling the weight of all that had happened in the last several hours wash over him. It actually made his legs wobble and he walked away from the house without choosing a direction. He wandered fifty feet before his body gave out and he dropped to the ground, rolling himself into a sitting position. It wasn't until he sat there a minute that he realized he was looking at the ocean, which sat brilliant in the afternoon sun out beyond the edge of the mountain they were on.

"Y'all right, man?" Spook sat down next to him.

"I feel shaky all of a sudden," Ian said. "Like the whole week just landed all at once."

"Well, it has in a way."

They sat quietly for a minute, Ian sorting through the emotions that flashed one more time before evaporating into dull memory. Spook watched the ocean.

"I feel kind of ugly right now," Ian said, his stomach suddenly hollow.

"Why?"

"I don't know. Just seeing this. Ebbetts, geez, what produces someone like that? And Mahon. I'm still blown away by Mahon. That one's just a mind boggler."

Spook said nothing.

"And then there's me," Ian continued. "I'm exposed to people like that for a couple of hours and next thing you know I'm freaking out." He turned and looked at Spook, the fear evident in his face. "I almost choked that son of a bitch to death!"

Spook looked at him then back towards the ocean.

"You weren't gonna kill anybody, Ian. Who you kiddin'? Whatever you felt, it was just you workin' out a little more of yourself." Spook stood up and then squatted down again with obvious pain. "Oo, shit," he winced, then continued. "Knowin' you, you'll analyze it to death and figure it all out one of these nights when I'm trying to party, and I'll have to hear the whole thing in dissected pieces."

Ian saw one corner of Spook's mouth pull sideways, a smile in disguise.

"In the meantime," Spook added, slowly standing up again, "this show's over and I wasn't kiddin' about that cocktail. Let's get the hell outta here and get back to the hotel."

Ian got up slowly and looked at Spook. Who would've figured him for the voice of reason? What Ian had been feeling for this day was scary and unfamiliar, a severe rattling of his perception of the world, like waking up on the day of a funeral; no routines or safe paths to follow, a day that could not be grasped, only stumbled through in the hope that it would end and tomorrow would be normal again. Looking at Spook, Ian was seeing the good things again, the clean places that existed in most of the people Ian knew. Those places had been far away in the last several hours.

They walked back toward the house watching Ramirez put Mahon in the back of his car. Another police car, lights flashing, was emerging from a cloud of dust on the road. Ian felt the world he knew sliding back to him and the one of Mahon and Ebbetts moving away. He knew he was headed back to something familiar; but he also knew he wouldn't forget what happened, and ultimately, tomorrow, like him, would have to change.

chapter 55

"IAN! GOD, I'M going crazy! Where are you?"

The concern in Robyn's voice sprayed from the phone receiver in his hand and instantly raised Ian's spirits.

"It's a long story. I'll tell you when I get to the hotel, but I think it's finally all over. Will you wait?"

"What the hell do you think I've been doing all day besides having a heart attack? I'm not going anywhere till I see your face."

"Thanks. Got some company?" He could hear other voices in the background.

"Ian, I was going out of my mind. I called Donna and Kim and told them something was wrong, I mean your boss calling and you gone. They came right over to help me worry."

"Yeah, Ramirez said something about Ed Bernardi and your call. Look, we'll be there in a half hour."

"Hurry," she said.

They were all at El Casa Grande at six o'clock. Ed Bernardi had called again just after Ian and Spook had gotten to the room and Ian talked to him while Spook showered. Robyn sat close to Ian on the bed, her hand holding and squeezing his.

"I'm just glad you're all right," Ed Bernardi said, after hearing the details of the day.

"Thanks, it got pretty hairy," Ian said. "I just couldn't believe Mike Mahon, Ed," the shock apparent in his voice again.

"Imagine me on this end," Ed said. "I finally trace this Las Mesas outfit down and Mike's fingerprints are all over it. He figured no one would ever be looking for a connection. I'm no financial wizard but the way it was explained to me was Ebbetts was taking the Cook investment money and releasing it to paper companies that Mike had set up. Kevin, our lawyer friend here, figures Ebbetts knew Golden would suspect something sooner or later so he had the disappearing act all set to go. When it was all over, there was no reason to connect Mike to it at all. If it wasn't for Ted Haggerty in Financial remembering the Las Mesas name from a printout, I might not have made the connection myself. Then I start calling everybody and their mother and I find out Mike's on vacation and one of his stops is Mexico." He paused. "Then, I can't get a hold of you!"

"Tell me about it," Ian said, appreciating the irony.

"By the way," Ed added, "you best stay close to that sweetie you met. That girl's not only sharp, she likes the hell out of you."

Ian looked over at Robyn, making a face at her.

"Yeah, well, can you blame her?"

Robyn look at him confused and mouthed the word, "What?"

"No, I meant there aren't too many sharp women out there that are going to be interested in you," Ed said, laughing as he spoke.

"Every time I think you're all right, Bernardi, you disappoint me," Ian said. "I'm getting off the phone to make up for a few days of interruptions."

"And you will, pal. Am I going to see you on Tuesday?"

The question caught Ian off guard. At first he wondered why Ed would even ask. But he also realized he'd paused long enough to know the answer wasn't cut and dried.

"Well," the pause was now obvious, "yeah. But we might have to talk about some things one of these days."

"No doubt," Ed said, his voice encouraging.

"Thanks for being there, my friend," Ian said.

The party of five regrouped under the thatched roof of the pool bar. The showers had been a painful experience for Ian and Spook. Each of them had several patches of skin burns from their unwelcome introduction to the mountain road, and enough adrenaline had subsided in their systems to let the pain get through. Sitting slumped in their chairs, they were like football players on Monday morning with every tackle and block from Sunday claiming its due. While constantly lubricating their pain, the two of them managed to tell the whole tale of Warren Ebbetts, from Cook International to the "shootout at ho kay corral" as Spook called it.

"MORE MARGARITAS!" Ian hollered.

"Easy there, Don Diego" Robyn said, laughing. "We're going to need a raft to get you back to land."

"SPOOK! YOU WANT MORE MARGARITAS?"

"Yeah man," Spook said, draining the glass in his hand.

"And what would you like, my dear?" Ian said. "I must make it up to you for leaving you sitting in my hotel room completely confused."

"Confused is not the word. I was terrified. Your boss kept calling and every time he did the news got worse. I couldn't get hold of Ramirez anymore. I couldn't do anything. I'm looking forward to my dull life back in Pittsburgh."

"Life will never be dull again, my dear," Ian said mischievously.

"Oh, God." Robyn shook her head and cupped her hand under Ian's face, then changed the topic. "So what happens to Carmelo?"

"Well, he's cooperating with Ramirez with as much information about how Ebbetts operated as he can give," Ian said. "That will probably count for a lot. Ramirez doesn't have a hard case on him, not any more than he has on a dozen other businesses that Ebbetts laundered through. And besides, Ramirez let those businesses continue to operate in order to catch Ebbetts. So he doesn't want to come down hard on that point or one of his superiors might not approve of his methods. Carmelo probably won't serve any time, just probation. Anyway, Ramirez is working a lot of things out with the American authorities to see who can do the most damage to Ebbetts and Mahon. They've got them tied to at least two murders, embezzlement, fraud, I mean they can hang them good."

"Did you apologize to Ramirez for misjudging him so terribly?" Robyn said, a facetious smile on her face.

"Oh yeah, the guilt was too much," Ian said, following her attitude. "What can I say? I read him wrong, not that he gave us much help. He's not an easy guy to read. Fortunately, he read us wrong. That was the only reason he was there to save our asses in the end. He still thought we were in on the deal." Ian paused, an annoying thought worming around in his head. "I'm still not sure who he is, to tell you the truth. I mean, I think he's one of the good guys. I think he's committed to getting the bad guys. I guess it's hard to tell the difference sometimes."

"Maybe," Spook interjected, "his job puts him in the position of havin' to decide that long before some judge does. Just ain't nobody he can trust."

"You may have it there," Ian said, nodding his approval.

"What about Carmelo trying to kill you?" Kim said, almost reluctantly.

"Sssshhh," Ian said, his finger to his mouth. "There was no reason for us to bring that up. Ramirez doesn't know anything about it. It was an accident. Two gringo tourists on an unfamiliar mountain road. We screwed up."

Ian shrugged his shoulders and looked at Spook for agreement. Spook nodded.

"How did Carmelo rig the jeep?" Kim pressed. "He was still in the hospital."

"Ebbetts told Carmelo to get us to the house," Ian answered, "then he would do the rest. So it was really Ebbetts who set it up."

Robyn gave him a smile that looked like admiration.

"Look, it's really not anything noble," he continued. "Carmelo didn't know in the beginning, at the cliffs, that Ebbetts was doing anything but scaring me. The Jeep thing, well..., he was forced into it by Ebbetts to protect his son. I believe that and so does Spook. Ebbetts was a vicious manipulator." He put his head down. "If we're being fooled by Carmelo then we're being fooled, but I don't think so. I don't have a child but somehow I understand that Carmelo acted out of a sense of protection for his son, and I believe that can make someone do something totally against their nature. Besides, in the end, if Carmelo's life is ruined, Manny suffers. This way Manny has a family, a father. I dunno, a chance." Ian could feel his head swimming a little.

"Considering the last couple of days, I think Carmelo's going to make major improvements in his parenting skills."

"Well, you might not consider your attitude noble," Robyn said, sliding closer to him, "but I think it's quite admirable. I also think you're going to make a hell of a father some day."

"Oh yeah?" he said. "Maybe you should stick around and find out."

"You never know," she said, coyly.

"MORE MARGARITAS," Spook bleated.

"Easy Spookster. What about Ebbetts?" Kim asked. "Is the slime gonna live?"

"Yeah," Spook answered. "They took him to the hospital to do some work on him. He'll be ready for jail in a few days. His fat ass'll slim down in prison."

"Look," Robyn said, a sense of conclusion in her voice, "you boys have had it. I say you call it a night. Eat a little something and go to bed early, and let's have late lunch or early dinner somewhere tomorrow." She looked at everyone. "There's a good chance we can have a nice, normal, get-together for a change. Right?"

"God, wouldn't that be nice," Kim said, rolling her eyes.

Ian's head was fuzzier now, and despite the fact that he wanted Robyn near him, her suggestion was appealing. He made a thin attempt to disagree with her but she waved him off.

"Call me when your head is clear," she said, and kissed him sweetly.

Ian vaguely remembered her instructions and the subsequent journey to his room as his head sank into the cool, white mush of his pillow.

chapter 56

WARREN EBBETTS LAY uncomfortably in the hospital bed, his mind slipping in and out of various levels of consciousness and sleep. He felt he was in a small room. A blind-covered window to his left, unseen but sensed through his closed eyes, filled in details like daylight and nearby traffic. The right side of his back near the shoulder ached and stung alternately, and the desire to roll over was almost enough to keep him conscious, but not quite. He knew he had been shot. He remembered the final scene, the pleasure of crushing Carmelo's hand, pointing the gun at that shitpest from Cook, the horrible hot impact from behind. He wasn't sure which hurt him more, the bullet, or being caught unaware by a stupid peasant. Dirty, stupid beggars like the beggars of America. Cops were pathetic in the United States, but Mexican cops were worse. The thought burned deeper alongside the wound.

Sleep was, at first, more appealing. Each time he dropped off he felt warmth. Different parts of his body felt caressed by gentle hands or soft fabrics. Syrupy liquids slid over his legs and chest sending jagged lines of sensation to his groin. Then, an early image of his wife floated across his mind, a well-built woman in her twenties. "Like a brick shithouse," he heard himself say in the dream, and then he grabbed his crotch. He used to grab his crotch when he watched her, from that first time he'd seen her in the nightclub waiting tables to when she would play in the hotel rooms on his business trips. He'd watch her play, touching and exposing herself, her face showing glee at the strain her antics produced in him, his hand squeezing harder and harder as he forced himself to wait, just a little longer.

Now she was smiling at him from across an unfamiliar room, taunting and teasing him, playing peek-a-boo with her breasts by pulling back her low-cut dress, first one side, then the other. He could feel himself getting hard, his hand squeezing and bunching himself up to ease the pressure. He wanted her bad and he was going to grab her and put it to her the way he always did. And right before he did, she would let him play with her breasts for a few minutes and then she'd step back and make him watch a little longer.

She set her legs apart as far as the tight skirt would allow then started hiking it up, a little at a time, inching it up along her shapely legs, her thighs testing the limits of the fabric. Just when she had it past the point of decency, she turned around, peeking back over her shoulder, and pulled it up another inch, exposing the smooth, pink, lower arcs of two moons, the shadowy dash between them flexing in shape as she rocked to one side, then the other. Now she was bending forward, her hands on the mirror in front of her, as she waved her fully exposed ass at him. He charged forward releasing himself from his pants, pushing his extended flesh under and upward with his right hand as he encircled her waist with his left, grunting and spitting as her breasts swung free of the dress.

Then he saw his face of passion in the mirror above hers, and she saw him look. As he watched, her breasts, minutes ago full and ripe, shriveled and sagged, her lascivious face now a disgusting snarl.

"YOU PIG! YOU SLOB! DON'T TOUCH ME!"

He felt a blast of ice cold air rush between her legs, then his, and his once mad erection shrank like him at the horror of the beast before him. She turned, striking him across the face with the back of her hand as she covered her now wrinkled flesh. He closed his eyes to the pain and walked away, holding the front of his pants together with both hands.

As the hospital room came back to him he clenched his fists weakly, only to discover they were shackled to the bed at the wrists. Between the dream and his current plight he almost felt sorry for himself; almost. He quickly recovered, noting that at least one of the stupid peasants was smart enough to have anticipated his thoughts. He was going to escape, somehow, someway, at the first possible chance. He didn't think he could pull himself up off the bed right now but without the handcuffs, he'd grab the first neck that came into the room and give it one hell of a try.

He felt the light in the room change and then sensed movement near him. He tried to open his eyes but couldn't, the gummy seal of sleep and hospital air having overpowered what little control he had. Probably a nurse, he thought. Doctors always talk to you. Ask you stupid questions like how do you feel? Nurses just do their job, like chambermaids in a hotel. Doesn't matter if you're naked or dying, they go on about their business.

He saw the light dim through his eyelids, as if someone was leaning over him, looking at him. He tried to open his eyes again, this time managing to pry a few eyelashes loose, but it took all his energy and concentration and they closed again. He caught a glimpse of a white cotton garment just as he felt a gentle hand raise his head and remove a pillow, then settle his head back on the remaining pillow.

The hand moved to the side of his head and stayed there like a caress. For a moment the hand felt special to him, the closest thing to intimacy he could remember for a long part of his life. He felt the warmth of sweet breath as if a mouth moved to kiss his lips gently and brush the skin of their faces together. And then he thought he heard a whispery voice say, "For Richard."

He was so mesmerized by the delicate scenario inside his head that he did not notice at first, the pencil-like line being drawn across his neck. When the slight pulling sensation finally made contact with his brain there was a feeling of cool, almost mentholated air hovering over the space above the line, immediately followed by a slow stinging.

A second, more forceful line was traced from one side to the other, this one registering immediate shock in the mind of Warren Ebbetts with the realization that his throat was now functioning in an entirely different manner than he had ever experienced. By the time he understood why, blood had already exited his body in sufficient amounts to guarantee his death.

chapter 57

"Do you feel as bad as I do?"

It was a not a question Ian felt compelled to answer. It was obvious from the slow-motion scene taking place in their room that a yes was superfluous and that morning had arrived painfully.

Seeing the look on Ian's face in response to his question, Spook uttered an embarrassed, "Oh."

"Well, we can still try and enjoy today," Ian said, trying to convince himself. He looked at the alarm clock to see how much was left of the day, and it told him less than half. "We're outta here tomorrow."

"Without in anyway suggesting that I'm sorry I came," Spook pronounced, "cause I'm not, that idea appeals to me."

Ian propped himself at the head of the bed and picked up the phone.

"There's only one way to improve this day."

He dialed the phone and then slumped down on the pillows. Robyn answered on one ring.

"It's a good thing you're in such great shape," she said, "or you'd really be hurting."

"Oh, God," Ian said, "even sarcasm is painful today. What are we doing?"

"We want to treat you guys to dinner because we feel sorry for you." She was teasing him again. "So Donna had a great idea. El Salto at the cliffs. We'll get a nice veranda table and catch the 3 o'clock divers and then have early dinner. She figured you never got to really relax and enjoy the whole experience. And you didn't. You were either worrying about your dive or getting shot at. That's not a nice memory to take back home."

Ian was impressed. The thought of playing a true tourist appealed to him now.

"That sounds like a great idea. I mean, really. Tell Donna she's a genius."

At two-fifteen a big Chevy taxi pulled up to their hotel to collect the last two of the five friends and take them to what Ian saw as a final, melancholy reunion with the cliffs at La Quebrada. Fifteen minutes later a second car pulled up to the hotel, this one containing the knotted, sweating face of Officer Tito Ramirez who slammed the door and stormed quickly to the registration desk. If there had been any capacity for tolerance left in the man's body it was depleted instantly when he was told the Americans were gone.

Ian and the others were fortunate to get a table on the veranda, due entirely to the fact that he was recognized by the diving coach in the lobby. The weekend junkets and weekly arrivals had flooded the area with fresh tourists, hungry to see the famous cliff divers and dying to spend their inflated dollars on Mexican souvenirs. Ian was amazed at how many more people there were today than the three times he'd been there during the week. He looked out across the mass of people, who seemed to swarm over the landscape, moving up, down and across in waves while the cacophony of voices and languages mixed with the roar of tourist bus engines. Standing unaffected above all this was La Quebrada, and below, the ever-present wash of the water in the canyon.

Ian stared at the canyon trying to imagine all that had happened there in the past week. But he couldn't. It was all like the boyhood dream, something composed of hundreds of sensual details, stored not in reality but inside him. Today there was very little resemblance between the cliffs of the past week or the cliffs of his youth.

"Are you okay?" Robyn said, gently touching his arm.

Her question drew him from his reverie. Knowing she would wait for the answer, he folded his thoughts softly, then turned to her.

"Yes."

"Okay," she said quietly, knowing more by the one word.

The announcer's voice crackled over the loudspeaker alerting the crowd to the Clavadistas as they entered the water. Ian knew the voice had been there earlier in the week but like everything else it was not familiar. The crowd instinctively turned and faced the cliffs, then began drawing itself to the wall. The divers were already scaling the cliffside and taking their positions.

"Ready to go again there, Tarzan?" Spook backhanded Ian on his bicep.

"Ooo," Ian winced, exaggerating a little and grabbing his arm. "Are you kidding? Even that hurt."

"Oh, you poor baby," Kim said.

Ian stared again at the view but still couldn't find the excitement of the past in the spectacle before him. Maybe it had just been too long a week. He watched each of the divers, some of whom he recognized, set themselves, build the excitement then make their dive. As the announcer worked the crowd diver by diver, Ian realized the top diver was the cocky young buck from his first visit. Suddenly he felt a tinge of excitement.

He slid up in his seat and put his arms on the veranda wall. Something about this kid told Ian this was his first top dive. That was why he was so cocky earlier in the week. He was working himself up for it, trying to prove to the others and himself, that he was ready. But now that he was there, now that the moment had arrived, the boy could not leave all of his uncertainty below him. Even at a distance Ian could see the question in his body. The boy was taking a long time, watching the water, turning his head slightly, stepping.

Here it is, kid, Ian said silently to the boy. No, decide, before you step to the edge. That's it. Don't step unless you're going.

The boy moved to the edge, hesitated, then leaned forward. Ian came up out of his seat realizing immediately that the kid had pulled back just enough to lose his balance. He was now caught between getting back off the edge or falling off the cliff top. Ian felt his stomach tighten one more time.

* * *

By now Officer Ramirez had personally picked and assigned the guards for Mike Mahon despite the fact that Mahon was in a jail cell. He had also assigned plainclothes policemen to both El Casa Grande and the Royal Prince Hotel in the hope that the young Americans would show up soon. In the meantime, he was checking information provided by Ed Bernardi who had called him from Philadelphia around two o'clock. When the officer at the hospital had called earlier and told Ramirez that Ebbetts was dead, Ramirez never asked a question. He hung up the phone and drove straight to the hospital knowing if there was anything to discover, he would have to do it himself. He immediately suspended the officer on duty when he arrived and then started questioning anyone and everyone including the suspended officer.

But there was nothing to discover. The nurse on her rounds had nodded to the guard and walked into the room. The first thing she noticed was the smell of blood, although it did not alarm her. It was a smell she was familiar with. What caught her attention, as she moved across the room to open the blinds on the window, was the deep, burgundy-black puddle on the bed. She immediately pushed the alarm button next to the bed and took the patient's pulse. That was when she noticed, under the handcuffs, the shredded skin and still-damp blood where two fat wrists had struggled. According to the officer on guard, some other medical personnel had entered the room earlier in the day, but he wasn't too specific knowing he couldn't be. He had gotten a little sleepy and could easily have missed someone. At that point Ramirez was more frustrated at the ineffectiveness of his own officer than he was at the loss of Warren Ebbetts. It was no great loss to him.

When he shot Ebbetts yesterday he hadn't made a conscious decision not to kill him, it just worked out that way. Ramirez had left the villa after confronting Ebbetts and his partner and had caught a glimpse of Spook and Ian's car, visible on the way out but not coming in. It made perfect sense to him, confirming what he had suspected all along. He had gone back down to the main road and parked, then traveled on foot to watch for the Americans. When the skinny one returned to the car and went flying up the road to the house, Ramirez moved back in behind him.

All the Americans were in the house by the time Ramirez arrived and so he had worked his way around the outside of the house looking for an entrance. Voices floated from somewhere down the long wall and he had moved closer, spotting the iron grillwork and positioning himself to listen, and then move. He'd heard enough to know he'd been wrong about the Americans. When he heard the raised voices and scuffling he had drawn his gun and stepped to the iron gate. Seeing the raised arm of Ebbetts he put his arm through the space in the iron work and fired immediately, unable to adjust his sight much. The bullet struck Ebbetts high on the right side of his back. It could just have easily killed him.

No, Ebbetts was not his concern now, but his death had presented a new one, one less certain. With all his people keeping an eye out for the Americans, Ramirez held onto the new information from the American boss in Philadelphia and went about the work he was paid to do; investigate. And think. He had two slit throats on his hands in three days. Both cuts looked similar. What other connections were there between the two, he wondered? The first one, his officer, Garo, was assigned to the three American Señoritas who were associated with the two American men; who were associated with the second victim, Warren Ebbetts.

Ramirez knew of Ebbetts and his past now. A slit throat? It was not uncommon that a man like that could easily suffer such a fate, if not by justice, then at least by association. What he didn't know was much about his Officer Garo's life other than what he saw on the job. If there was a connection, it would have to come from Garo's world.

Ramirez got up quickly, stopped by the file room for Garo's folder, and headed to his car, noting the home address in the folder. The address was an apartment in the Mexican part of the downtown mercado, away from the tourist area. The old woman in the bodega downstairs climbed the iron steps and opened the door to let Ramirez in after he identified himself. She cocked her head in curious distrust as he brushed by her and into the apartment.

Ramirez saw nothing odd at first as he stepped into a hallway that served as a foyer, his eyes looking for things out of place. But everything seemed perfectly in place; to his left a sitting room, the stereo neatly distributed across a set of shelves surrounding a new looking television; to his right, a kitchen, the appliances displayed nicely on the table and counters; the refrigerator, silent but cold, and full of beer and packaged food. He walked the apartment from one end to the other seeing nothing unusual before it hit him.

This is not the apartment of a low ranking Acapulco police officer. Not with all of this, Ramirez thought. Any one or two, maybe three of the things he saw showcased around the room might be possible, but not all of this. The appliance array was definitely the result of additional income, not entirely uncommon for police in a tourist town.

Ramirez quickly rifled the kitchen cabinets and drawers and found nothing but the appropriate items, then moved to the bedroom, looking in the obvious places first—under the mattress, inside shoes, inside the pockets of several expensive sportcoats and slacks. He didn't know what he was looking for but knew something was there. He finished his search, leaving the closet door and drawers open, and swept quickly through the bathroom, again finding nothing curious. When he exited the bathroom and turned towards the living room he saw a cardboard box across the room in the corner. It was sitting there in plain sight, lidless, its contents neatly ordered. He walked to it, then squatted down to inspect it.

It was mostly paper. Whatever else Garo was, Ramirez thought, he was definitely organized. The papers were a neat collection of his possessions; insurance policy, police citations and awards, birth and baptismal certificates, guarantees and warranties for his appliances, blank checks, envelopes of cancelled checks, and a checkbook. Ramirez flipped through the ledger looking for anything and found one consistent deposit each month for exactly two hundred dollars, no great amount, but definitely an addition to the dead officer's weekly salary which appeared as a deposit as well, although inconsistently. Ramirez pulled two completed check ledgers from an envelope and found the same two hundred dollar deposit month after month, going back almost a year and a half. There were two more ledgers but he ignored them, suspecting they too would contain the same information. What he needed now was some explanation for the deposits.

He dug further through the papers and found a small manila envelope tucked between two large sheets, the bulge from the contents forming a neat rectangle on the outside. Ramirez squeezed the metal clasps together and puckered the envelope open. The first thing he saw when he drew out the contents was the name and return address on the first small, white envelope. He felt his scalp shift. At the same time he felt air move in the room.

In the second that his body tensed Ramirez knew someone was behind him. And he knew he had given whoever it was that same second to do their damage. Even as he turned to look, he was surprised it had not yet come. He had made peace with his Jesus when his eyes settled on the old woman from downstairs, staring at him from the half-open door. He turned back to the papers, momentarily unsure why he was alive, and scooped up the box. He did not look the old woman in the face when he passed her on his way to the car.

chapter 58

As THE BOY teetered on the edge, Ian screamed, "PUSH!," not because he thought the boy would hear him. It was the scream in his head coming out.

The boy must have heard the same instinctive scream in his own head. He drew as much of a push as he could manage out of his uncertain position and propelled himself off into the air, clearing the rocks and hitting the water with all joints akimbo. Two of the other Clavadistas were in the water immediately, bringing him to the surface. The boy looked limp but conscious. Ian heard the announcer talking about courage and youth and the sound of the crowd growing into loud applause, but his attention was still on the young diver as they carried him from the water and out of sight. He looked back at the chattering, laughing crowd which began to disperse only minutes later, and realized it had been exciting entertainment for most of them, like watching the tightrope walker in the circus who never, ever really falls.

"He almost blew it, didn't he?" Spook was looking at Ian with the education of the week's events etched on his face.

"Yes, he did," Ian said, sitting down and releasing the air trapped in his lungs. "You can't be sure you're gonna make it," he added, almost under his breath, "you just have to be sure you're gonna go." He shook his head.

"You just can't get away from the excitement of this place, can you?" Robyn said. "Well, are we going to dine and relax?"

She looked at everyone. It was almost a challenge. Ian struggled to take Robyn's suggestion. When the idea to come to the cliffs today had been presented it sounded great to him. Now, he wasn't sure. The only feeling he had at this moment was an unsettling one, uncertainty skipping around inside him. He could feel the atmosphere around him changing, like the shift in mood from Sunday morning to Sunday night. Maybe it was just the end of the vacation, but he didn't really believe that. Despite the outcome of this week's adventures and what he had learnrd about himself as a result, Ian was no more sure about where he was going than the young buck on the cliff. He pushed his own malaise aside long enough to notice that the atmosphere at the table was not any better. He assumed it was his fault and attempted to make amends.

"You know, aside from all the craziness, we've had a lot of fun together this week." His voice was calm. "I'm really glad we connected."

"I'll second that," Spook said, and raised his glass.

Everyone picked up a glass and bumped it into a tight pack above the table.

"I'll never want for excitement again," Kim said, a grin on her face.

"I never knew what real excitement was till this week," Robyn said, and made an exaggerated grab at Ian's thigh under the table.

Everyone laughed and groaned and sat back in their seats.

After a few seconds of silence Spook said, "I guess it's my turn, huh? Well, yeah, me too. Good people, good time, good margaritas."

"Oh, God," Kim said, only half kidding, "what eloquence."

Everyone except Spook and Kim laughed this time. Ian peeked at Donna to see if the discomfort of knowing she had to say something next had bothered her yet. She looked quite calm.

"I'm very happy that my good friends decided to come to Mexico with me." Donna said quietly, and extended her arms in either direction, grasping first Kim's and then Robyn's hand. "It meant a lot to me." She squeezed their hands tightly.

Robyn seemed touched by the gesture. Kim shrugged and said, "Hey, it was a good idea."

"And I'm grateful to have met you," Donna continued, "Ian…, Spook. You are good people."

She looked at them individually, smiling as she said their names, then sat back, looking content.

A few quiet seconds passed and Robyn said, "Now that was eloquent."

Ian watched Donna's face for the blush, but it never came. It was interesting the enchanting way she had spoken to all of them, especially to him and Spook. She had looked, really looked at him when she had said his name. He had seen her eyes clearly, eyes that he'd barely seen all week. The whole thing seemed almost out of character for Donna. But then again, it was so sincere. He felt his mood change and looked at Robyn, who was watching him.

"Yes?" she said.

"Nothing," he answered with a weak smile.

"To the ladies room," Kim said. "Give them the wine back."

The three women disappeared into the restaurant. Ian was still rolling thoughts around in his head when he noticed a lanky, Mexican man with stringy hair, who seemed to have appeared from nowhere, watching the women closely as they moved out of sight. The man watched nervously as if uncertain whether to follow, then glanced quickly back towards Ian and Spook, cross-ing gazes with Ian. He turned away quickly and stepped around the corner of the building where he had been standing. Ian spoke quietly without taking his eyes off the place where the man had stood.

"I hate to say here we go again, but here we go again. I just saw a guy watching the ladies as they went into the restaurant. When he saw me notice him he went around the corner."

Spook's face went blank. "What the hell are you talking about?"

"I don't know, but this time let's just go up and ask nicely," Ian said, and rose from his seat. Spook got up with him and they walked calmly around the corner of the building. People moved in and out of the building in front of them, but the stringy-haired man was gone.

"What's he look like?" Spook said.

"Tall, skinny, stringy hair. Mexican," Ian answered, still looking over and around people as they passed by.

"Like that guy?" Spook said, and pointed at the man as he walked past cars parked in front of the hotel.

"Yeah!" Ian yelled, and stepped quickly in the direction of the man. He could sense that the man was heading for a car, pick-ing his way through the parked cars quickly, moving to his right all the time. Ian quickened his pace, determined not to repeat the night at the Royal Prince. The man turned and looked back and saw the two Americans converging on him, then stopped walking. The move at first confused Ian enough to slow down his pace, but he continued, walking warily towards the Mexican who now stood squarely facing him.

"What is it, Señors," the stringy-haired man said, calmly. "There is something you need?"

His accent was very clean but his voice came from his Adam's apple.

"We need to know why you're watching us," Ian said, with little congeniality. "It seems to be a problem we're having this week and we're tired of it."

"What makes you think I am watching you, Señor?"

"All right, that's it!" Ian said, annoyed, and started walking to the man. "No more bullshit!"

Spook moved with him, shifting over one car to the side of the man to cut off a potential escape route. The man, seeing the approach, reached calmly into his jacket. Just as he did Ian heard a car roar into the lot behind him, the sound getting closer to his back until his instincts told him it was headed towards him. In Ian's mind, the car behind him was an accomplice backing his cornered buddy up. Now it seemed like Ian and Spook were trapped. The car tires chirped to a stop and Ian looked quickly back to catch some glimpse of what he was dealing with, only to see the knotted face of a stressed Officer Ramirez.

"PARAR, AHORA!" he bellowed across the lot.

Ian looked back to see the man quickly pull his hand from his jacket and walk towards him. Ramirez gritted his teeth at the man as he walked by.

"You are all right, Señor?" Ramirez said unsympathetically to Ian. "I told him to watch you, nothing else."

"What in the hell is going on now?" Ian accented each word with a puff of exasperation and an exaggerated gesture.

"Where are your friends?" Ramirez asked quickly, ignoring Ian's antics.

Ian stood up straight and looked at him, coldly. "You don't quit, do you."

"Where are your friends?" he repeated.

Ian could tell the man was not to be deterred.

"Still in the restaurant, I hope."

Ramirez gestured toward the restaurant to the stringy-haired man then said "Come," to Ian and the others. As they walked quickly to the hotel he spoke to the space in front of them.

"We have a problem, Señors. It appears this case is not complete. Señor Wilson, Ebbetts, was murdered today in the hospital. His throat cut like my officer on the beach. I spoke with your boss from Philadelphia today. He was able to offer me some valuable information."

They were at the end of the building and turning the corner. Ian tried to absorb what he was hearing. Ebbetts murdered. And what did Ed Bernardi have to tell Ramirez about Mahon or Ebbetts that he hadn't known before? He could see Robyn and Kim walking towards the table, watching them draw near now. Robyn looked confused and fearful. Kim looked annoyed.

"Where is your companion?" Ramirez said sharply to the two women, not offering any explanation.

Ian felt the detective's sense of urgency. "Robyn, where is she? Where's Donna?"

"Ah, ah...," the effect of Ian and Ramirez combined froze her, "she's...she's still in the ladies room. Ian, what?"

Ramirez turned and walked towards the building, waving another man who appeared from the parking lot, also towards the building.

"What's going on?" Kim demanded.

"The Fat Man's been murdered and the killer must be loose," Spook answered. "Ramirez had someone watching us again. I guess he thinks we're in danger."

Ramirez appeared at the patio doors of the veranda, his face unchanged from the stern mask in the parking lot.

"She's not there."

"Oh God. Donna!" Robyn muffled her own outburst of fear with her hands.

"Take it easy," Ian said, trying to calm her. He put his arms around her. "She's around, come on now. She's probably buying a postcard in the lobby or something. Did they check the whole place or just the bathroom?" he said, looking at Ramirez.

"My men are doing that now."

Ian could feel the air thicken as people at the other tables buzzed at the small commotion in their midst. He could see heads turning back and forth and people getting out of their chairs and walking to the wall. As the buzz grew louder an officer appeared behind Ramirez and stopped, looking beyond him. The movement drew Ian's attention as well as his ear, and he realized that much of the buzz was now coming from the area below the veranda.

Wanting to turn toward the sound but not wanting to even more, Ian instead looked purposely at the faces of the people in front of him. Somewhere in his mind he felt if he didn't look at those cliffs then nothing could happen. That was his protection, his rabbit's foot. Just don't look at the cliffs, he told himself repeatedly. Look and you turn to stone.

But as he watched the people before him he knew it didn't matter. It was there, in their faces. In their eyes. First, the squinting strain to see what, at first look, they couldn't see. Then the slow rounding, as the ever-focusing lenses locked on to something distant. And then finally, the widening, as their brains received the completed image. He saw the faces as they rose, multiplied in front of him, accompanied by pointing fingers and bursts of sound. The sound that reached him most clearly was the scream from the woman he was holding.

chapter 59

THE SOUND WAS too much. Ian turned to face the cliffs and what he saw rattled him. Donna was halfway up the side of the cliff, her climb awkward but steady in the brilliant, late afternoon sun.

"What is it?" Ian said to Robyn, shaking her to get her attention. "What is she doing?"

"I….I don't know," she stammered, terror in her words and eyes.

Ian looked immediately at Ramirez. "What is it? What's going on? What did Ed Bernardi tell you?"

Ramirez looked back at him, his face finally showing Ian some emotion. It was a face not of the moment but rather a montage of all the sad, unexplainable grief the detective had witnessed in his long career. He turned momentarily to one of his officers and issued commands, then turned back to Ian. He spoke with just a hint of compassion.

"My instincts tell me this unfortunate Señorita wishes to take her own life."

"Why?"

Ian struggled to understand. He looked back at the cliff and saw two men entering the water at the back of the canyon.

"WHY?!"

Ramirez said simply, without changing expression, "She may be responsible for the death of Wilson, and my officer."

"IAN! STOP HER!" Robyn shrieked. "PLEASE! STOP HER!"

Ian looked at Robyn's tearful, confused face again. He let go of her and said to Ramirez, "I'm going up to get her. Tell your guys to get out of the way."

Ramirez looked slightly startled.

"Do you know what you are doing?"

"No," Ian answered sharply. "Do you?"

He didn't wait for the answer. He was through the restaurant and down to the water in minutes, dropping shoes and shirt and hitting the water on the run. As he swam he looked up to check Donna's progress and was surprised to see her close to the top. He could hear noise and indistinct chatter bouncing around the canyon. The crowd hadn't determined yet if this was a crisis or just more entertainment.

He reached the cliff base only to be confronted by one of the policemen. Ian pointed to the veranda and started to climb, not waiting to see Ramirez wave the officer off. The other officer was only about fifteen feet up, the look on his face indicating his lack of appreciation for the assignment as he looked down at Ian. Ian waved and yelled for him to move then climbed as quickly as he could. As he passed the man he looked up in time to see Donna's legs disappear over the top of the cliff.

"DONNA! DONNA WAIT! IT'S ME, IAN! CAN YOU WAIT FOR ME?!"

He was at a treacherous part of the cliffside, making it difficult to yell and climb at the same time. But he wasn't sure which was better; to try and get to her faster, or keep talking to her to distract her. He climbed a little higher then yelled again.

"DONNA! PLEASE WAIT FOR ME! EVERYONE'S WORRIED ABOUT YOU! ROBYN AND KIM WANT TO HELP! WILL YOU WAIT FOR ME?!"

Ian's felt his heart hit his chest as Donna's face, then shoulders, then toes appeared over the edge of the cliff. She stood there looking out toward the water, her face calm.

"I'm fine, Ian, thank you. Please tell everyone thank you, but I'm fine."

Her voice sounded dreamy, quietly floating down and landing on Ian like snow crystals melting in his hair. He was still a good thirty feet from the top but knew now he would have to talk more and climb less to accomplish anything.

"Why can't you tell them yourself? I know you're fine because I'm with you, but they can't tell."

"It really is beautiful, Ian. I can see now why you wanted to come here."

Ian was climbing again, sacrificing safety for speed. He lost his grip and flattened himself to the cliffside trying desperately to catch hold with any part of his body. His right foot caught an edge and he stopped. He could feel his heart banging through his chest. He pressed his face into the stone in front of him and closed his eyes waiting for his system to settle down. He could still hear Donna making an occasional comment about the canyon and cliff. He was fifteen feet from the top now, to the right of Donna. He looked up at her again and saw the dreamy voice reflected in her face.

"Ian, please be careful."

"Donna, I'm worried about you, not me. Why don't you step back and I'll climb all the way up and we'll talk."

"Oh, no," she said simply. "I'm here because I want to be."

"Why do you want to be?" Ian was trying to keep his voice as calm as hers, but he was finding it difficult. "You're not a diver are you?"

"Oh, no," she said again. "I'm not diving. I'm leaving."

The tone of her voice was so simple Ian thought they could be having the conversation on a train. He felt his insides shift at the word *leaving* as he squirmed his way up a few more feet. The footholds were a little wider and he could rest more comfortably. Plus, he felt with a few steps he could make a quick move over the top and get his hands on her at the same time. But he wasn't ready for that yet.

"Why are you leaving?"

"Because I'm finished here now. Everything is settled, and Richard is at peace."

Richard, Ian thought, sensing the start of some understanding.

"Who is Richard, Donna? Have I ever met him?"

"Oh, no. He died about two years ago, murdered actually. Which is why he hasn't been at peace. Those people, Ian, those horrible people that tried to hurt you. They would have done the same thing again. And then Robyn would have had to worry about you. But they're gone now."

"Ebbetts murdered your friend Richard?"

"Oh, he's my fiancé, Ian. We're engaged, three years now."

Something about the way Donna spoke assured Ian that in a better set of circumstances all of this would make sense. For now it was not as important as keeping her talking.

"Did you take care of Ebbetts, Donna?"

"Oh, yes."

"Who else?"

"Officer Garo. I thought he was trying to help me, but in the end he was like the others. He was cruel and selfish."

"Anyone else?"

"That rude Mr. Alvarez. He told me what Mr. Ebbetts did and then thought that meant he shouldn't be punished."

The mention of Alvarez brought things into focus for Ian. "Was Richard on the boat with Ebbetts and Alvarez?"

"He worked so hard on those boats, Ian. You should have seen him. He loved the water so much he was willing to work just about any time at all. I used to tease him about loving sailing more than me, but I know that wasn't true."

Ian moved up a few feet and put himself in position to move quickly to the top. If he could grab hold with his right hand on the top of the cliff, with his feet planted squarely on two footings, he could grab her arm or leg with his left hand and pull her back away from the edge. But if she fought him she could pull him off with her.

"Donna, I still don't understand why you're here. If everything is settled and Richard is at peace, why not go home?"

"My home is with Richard." There was something very final in her tone now. "I have always wanted to be with him, but I needed to settle things here for him. Now that I have, I'm ready."

The change in her voice washed over Ian. He felt helpless and sad despite the resolution in her words.

"Donna, there's nothing here but an ending."

"Ian, I was quite inspired by you this week. Not only did you help me settle things for Richard, but you brought me to this place, a place of beauty and serenity."

She moved slightly on the edge. Ian felt the panic increase.

"Donna! Please be careful. You're too near the edge."

Her voice came back to him gently, the words making a place inside him forever.

"You said only go to the edge when you're sure you can go, Ian. I'm sure."

"Donna, please don't. DONNA!"

The scream arced invisibly out from him and met with the lovely body of Donna Miller as it fell forward from its perch. For a split second Ian could not help but notice how smoothly she left the cliff top, the long lines of her legs and torso extended nicely, no tension or stress of any kind. Her face was the same calm face of the girl who, a heartbeat ago, stood on the cliff top, drawing in one last breath of earth's beauty. Serenity, falling. There was complete, absolute silence, as if God held the world's breath that it might stop to see this child at play.

The eerily beautiful flow of that second was followed immediately by the sickening sound of the stubborn cliffside removing the life of Donna Miller from its vessel. Ian felt the warm coarseness of the rock against his own body and tightly squeezed his eyes closed, not to shut out the tragedy of the life gone by him, but to hold in the precious droplets of reason his soul would need for lives to come.

chapter 60

THE HOTEL, IN a gesture of understanding as well as expediency, made a suite available to Officer Ramirez and his unfortunate American group. Kim and Robyn sat on a bed holding one another, their eyes red from crying. They looked like every victim of tragedy Ian had ever seen, huddled and withdrawn in defense of what little of their sensibilities were still intact.

By the time Ian had climbed down from the cliff they had taken Donna's body away. He had waited, clinging to the cliff, unsure of his next move. He only knew he could not cross paths with Donna Miller once more. He had not looked down, turning his head enough to look out toward the ocean, fixing his eyes on the ever-tightening horizon. Time passed, and he heard someone holler to him to see if he was all right. Ian yelled to the voice to verify that they had taken Donna away, then climbed down shakily, slowly picking his way on the unforgiving rocks.

When he returned to the others he was surprised to see that Robyn had not broken down. Instead of a sobbing, hysterical woman he did not know, he saw the heartbreaking face of sadness and incomprehension that follows a meaningless death. What he may have meant to Robyn in the last several days was not enough to draw her from that dark place of confusion. He could only be supportive, and, hopefully, meaningful to her some day in the future.

Spook and Ian sat at the other end of the suite. Spook half-filled a love seat while Ian, covered with towels to keep from wetting the soft chair, settled in across the coffee table from him. Ramirez was in another chair, hunched forward over a box of papers on the table. His voice was dry, his own weariness with the case visible.

"When your boss telephoned me, he had discovered something that gave him concern. An intuition, he suggested. He has good instinct. He discovered a life insurance policy that had not been paid on the young man killed on the sailboat, Richard Spencer, because his death was ruled an accident at sea, which was not covered. The beneficiary was his fiancé, a Donna Miller. When your boss saw the name he was not sure if it was coincidence."

Ian was following the story, one part of his brain still searching the air for a foothold as he matched Ramirez's information to the conversation on the cliff top. The other part reflected with no surprise that Ed Bernardi had taken a personal interest in settling matters back in Philadelphia.

"I never mentioned Donna's name to him though, my boss," Ian said.

"She spoke to him on the phone," a crackly voice said fondly.

It was Robyn. She and Kim had heard the conversation and were drawn to the group, like strangers to a campfire. They moved to another love seat facing Ramirez and sat down, completing the circle. Robyn reached over the cushioned arm and held Ian's hand.

"When Ed was calling your hotel," she said, looking at his hand instead of his face, "she answered one of the times. I think he was tired of talking to me," she smiled weakly, "so Donna was a nice change. I heard her introduce herself."

"When he called the number he was given to contact her about the policy," Ramirez continued, "he was informed that Donna Miller was on vacation in Meheeco. Then he was sure it was her. At first he thought she would like to know, but then thought it strange that you," he gestured to Ian, "had not mentioned this to him."

"I guess he missed us at the hotel and was worried enough to bother tracking you down," Ian said, shaking his head. "That sounds like Ed."

"I had my men out looking for all of you to ask the Señorita for some explanation."

Ian felt Robyn's hand flex slightly at the reference.

"Then I looked for something to connect." Ramirez's voice indicated a new chapter.

Despite the sense of tragedy that hovered heavily in the room, Ian felt a touch of relief, comfort possibly, that was circulating within the group. Something about the telling of the tale, the revealing of what chance events had led them all to this place of question, was in a way therapeutic, and at least, distracting.

"And you found out about Donna and Garo?" Kim said, catching everyone off guard.

Ramirez squinted suspiciously at her and said, "You knew about this?"

"Not till now," she answered with anguish, cutting off Ramirez's suspicion immediately. She reached down to her handbag and drew out a folded paper. "Before we left the restaurant the bartender handed this to me. He said Donna asked him to give it to us after dinner. She wrote us a letter."

Ian felt Robyn's hand squeeze his tightly without looking at him, signaling that she had already read it.

"Perhaps you can provide me with some more information then, Señorita."

Ramirez said it with respect. Kim took a deep breath and began.

"Donna was crushed when her fiancé, Richard, was killed. We didn't really know her then or maybe we would have seen something coming...," Kim started to drift but quickly pulled back, "...but anyway, she was certain Richard's death wasn't the accident it was claimed to be because he was too good a sailor. If anyone would have survived what supposedly happened out on the water that day, she was sure Richard would have. She must have felt his loss deeply enough because she tracked this guy Alvarez here two years ago...and...," her head dropped.

And killed him, Ian finished in his head.

"...and settled things with him. Before she did, he told her that Ebbetts had planned everything and killed Richard, and that he was alive in Acapulco somewhere. Alvarez also led her to this Garo," she raised her head and looked at Ramirez, "who was doing a little more than police work it seems. She convinced Garo to track down Ebbetts for her."

He probably thought she was crazy, Ian thought, realizing the sad truth in the statement.

"For two hundred dollars a month," Ramirez said, reaching into the box in front of him. "She sent him the money with a short letter each month. Garo kept them all." He held the pack of letters just above the rim of the box.

Kim reset herself and continued. "She came back here twice over the last two years because Garo had spotted Ebbetts. But each time she came she was unable to find him. She came this time on Garo's say-so as well. We'd all gotten to be good friends in the last year or so, and she suggested the trip to us without saying anything else. I mean, what did we know?"

"You couldn't have," Spook said.

Kim just shrugged.

"What happened to Garo?" Ramirez pressed.

"He betrayed her," Kim said, almost defensively. "He had been doing some work for Ebbetts and knew where he was all along. He was just collecting a check. But Garo knew you," she looked up at Ramirez, then quickly away, "were getting too close to Ebbetts and that would end his monthly check. So when Donna got here this trip, he threatened her for a lot of money, telling her if she didn't pay up, he would tell Ebbetts about her, and Ebbetts would have her killed."

Ian couldn't help rehashing in his mind the thought he'd had at Mahon's villa the day before. How many lives had this animal, Ebbetts, infected and ruined? Donna hadn't even been on the list that day, and now that she was, the list had extended to others in this room. Even dead, the Fat Man could still bring anger bubbling to the surface in Ian.

"It just happens that I had assigned him to protect you. And she settled matters with him, also," Ramirez concluded for them all.

"Yes," Kim answered quietly.

"And she settled with Ebbetts himself, finally, at the hospital," Ian said, wanting to say it with satisfaction, but deferring to the group's tender state.

"She told us she was going to visit some churches she had been to before," Robyn offered, looking down at the floor, "and she wanted to go early in the morning by herself. She seemed so calm and relaxed all day."

"She mentions you guys," Kim said, looking at Spook and Ian. "She wanted you to know how grateful she was for your help in finally settling with Ebbetts. And Ian, she says a lot about you, how it somehow was fate that you introduced yourself to us that night at our hotel, and how you treated Manny and Carmelo, and how brave you were to dive the cliff. She said you were an inspiration, and that it was only fitting that you were Ebbetts' 'downfall in the end' as she put it. 'Goodness should always defeat evil,' she wrote. But that you shouldn't feel responsible for what she had to do."

Ian recalled Donna's oddly personal comment at the dinner toast, his mind wrestling with how much responsibility he was going to take.

"She loved Richard so much," Robyn said, beginning to fill up, "she saw no peace for him or her unless his murderers were punished." The tears overwhelmed the tissue she pressed pointlessly to her face and the room went silent for a while.

Waiting for a car outside El Salto, Robyn curled herself tightly inside the arms and chest of Ian's hug, clinging to his shirt with the same fear of falling that had pressed Ian to the cliffside.

"Oh, Ian," she said with a shiver, "I'm afraid."

"Of what?" His voice was soft.

"I don't know," she said, frustration in her voice. "I don't know. Of all this. Of those men. Of Donna and what she did. I'm afraid to spend my life not understanding what all this was. And I'm afraid to understand because it might make sense."

Ian looked over her head, staring out across the slowly fading canyon. It looked back, unmoved by his stare, much the way it had the first day he'd faced it. He couldn't answer Robyn. He couldn't explain what had brought Donna there, to the top of that hardened eruption high above the world, any more than he could explain what had brought him. But deep in his soul he sensed that for him it had more to do with choosing to rise than choosing to fall.

chapter 61

SPOOK PULLED THEIR bags from the back of the van, waving off offers of help from the local boys.

"I appreciate you getting us to the airport," Ian said to Carmelo, who was leaning against the van.

"It is the least I can do," Carmelo said. "Are your lady friends all right?"

"They're hanging in there," Ian said, sounding optimistic. "They're very solid people. We're all going to Maryland in a week for Donna's funeral. Seems when her fiancé was killed Donna handled the arrangements because he didn't have anyone and she bought two cemetery plots. She asked Robyn and Kim in her letter to make sure that was where she was buried."

The thought hung in Ian's mind as he envisioned a lonely plot of ground in a nameless cemetery, with the four survivors gathered one more time. They had all seen their lives severely shaken in the last week and there would be much sorting out to do in the near future. But he and Robyn had talked, and they wanted very much to sort it together. Right now, that was a rare sense of warmth Ian could find in the empty coldness that had passed through him in the last two days.

"Manuel wanted very much to see you off as well," Carmelo said.

Ian looked over to where Manny was grabbing one of the bags.

"He's a great kid. Really something," Ian said, melancholy in his voice. "You'll do fine if you stay close to him," he added, looking back at Carmelo.

"I have you and Spook to thank for that," Carmelo hung his head. "What you have done is more than...."

Ian cut him off. "Look, Carmelo, without sounding too philosophical, the whole world is give and take. I came down here for a few reasons, some I knew and some I didn't. The dive was very important to me. Getting up that cliffside and down was as life and death to me as anything else that occurred this week. You helped me do that and I'll never forget it. And your son made the rest of the trip more than worthwhile. So maybe my friend and I have given you something and you and your son have given us something in return. I'd say that's a pretty good deal any day on this planet."

They shook hands. Ian turned to see Spook patting Manny's back and rubbing his head. "We ready?"

"Yeah man," Spook answered and walked over to Carmelo and shook his hand.

Manny was standing alone now, looking at Ian. Spook walked back towards Ian, grabbed the tickets from the pocket of his bag and headed toward the sliding doors of the terminal.

"I'm gonna confirm these, man. Catch ya at the bar."

Ian walked over to Manny as Carmelo got back into the van. He could feel a lump developing in his throat. He squatted down in front of Manny, setting his bag down.

"Well, I guess it's time to head home, hey partner?"

"Yes, Señor Een."

Manny was stone-faced, trying to maintain his business appearance.

"I've had a great time, thanks mostly to you," Ian said. "I'd probably still be driving back and forth thru that intersection if it weren't for you."

A reluctant smile spread over Manny's face. As it did a tear squeezed out over the rim of his right eye and traced a shiny path down the dark brown of his cheek. Ian felt his throat close up.

"I weel mees you, Señor Een," Manny said, still holding on to his emotions.

"Not as much as I'll miss you," Ian said and reached out with both his arms to hug him.

The feel of the boy's arms tight around his neck filled Ian's eyes. He squeezed them shut to cut off the flow, then grabbed Manny's shoulder and stood up.

"You have my address and I have yours," Ian said. "You better write to me and tell me how things are going. Especially when you get back to school," he added sternly, then tousled Manny's hair.

"I weel, I promeese. And you weel write to me?"

"Absolutely. I think it's neat having a buddy in Mexico. You know I'll be back to see you. And I told Carmelo that anytime you want, I'd love to have you guys visit us in Philadelphia."

"That would be fahntahstick," Manny said, the big smile coming out now.

There was an awkward silence for a moment, then Ian said, "Well, I better be going. It was a great time, buddy."

Ian picked up his bag.

"Señor Een?"

The sound in Manny's voice drew Ian's heart to him.

"Thank you for mi padre, my father."

Ian looked at him, first with surprise and then with compassion. "He told you?" he said, gently.

"Yes."

Ian looked beyond Manny to where Carmelo sat in the front of the van and saw the look of hope in his face, as if he knew what they were saying.

"He loves you very much, Manny, you know that, don't you?" Ian said, returning his gaze to the boy's face.

"Yes."

"Good. Stay close to him. He needs your help as much as you need his."

The young boy nodded with the wisdom of the ancients.

"Adiós, Señor Ian."

"Adiós, Señor Manuel," Ian said.

Ian turned and walked to the terminal, looking back to wave as he went through the doors. As he passed through, Ian knew the only thing that identified him as the same person who had entered Mexico eight days ago was his passport. Walking through the bustle of the concourse, the smiling face of Manny the Hustler sat pleasantly in his heart and mind.

Other books by Tom O'Grady, Jr.

A Gift is Waiting (November 2010)
Dancing in Donaghadee (November 2012)

TOMOGRADYJR

@GMAIL.COM

23671241R00254

Made in the USA
Charleston, SC
29 October 2013